summer
snow

summer Snow

nicole baart

Tyndale House Publishers, Inc., Carol Stream, Illinois

Visit Tyndale's exciting Web site at www.tyndale.com

Visit Nicole Baart's Web site at www.nicolebaart.com

TYNDALE and Tyndale's quill logo are registered trademarks of Tyndale House Publishers, Inc.

Summer Snow

Library of Congress Cataloging-in-Publication Data

Baart, Nicole.
  Summer snow / Nicole Baart.
    p. cm.
  ISBN-13: 978-1-4143-1623-9 (pbk.)
  ISBN-10: 1-4143-1623-2 (pbk.)
  1. Mothers and daughters—Fiction. I. Title.
  PS3602.A22S86 2008
  813'.6—dc22   2007042729

Printed in the United States of America

14 13 12 11 10 09 08
 7   6   5   4   3   2

For Mom

Because Janice is entirely a work of fiction.
You are everything she is not and more.

Many heartfelt thanks . . .

To Todd Diakow for reasons too numerous to list. Again, this book exists only because of your hand in it.

To Andrew and Amber Van Der Vliet, uncle and auntie extraordinaire. You are so giving, so gracious and loving and patient with our crazy family. We don't deserve you.

To my Bible Study Girls: Gina, Heidi, Jaymi, Melissa, and Sherri. You are my mentors, coconspirators, and friends. I love you dearly.

To the guys at Butler's Café and Coffee. Thanks for letting me take up space on your couch for hours on end while I nailed down this book.

To James Calvin Schaap, for being an excellent professor more years ago than I care to admit, and for your support and encouragement these past months.

To Lana, because you lugged a three-hundred-page manuscript to Grand Rapids and read every word.

To all my family and friends for being understanding when my mind was elsewhere, consumed with Julia and Janice.

To everyone at Tyndale. This entire experience has been the stuff of dreams, and you have all been so encouraging, so supportive and kind. Thank you.

To Mom and Dad. We would be lost without you. A simple thank-you doesn't seem adequate.

As always, to my boys. Aaron, you are my better half. I adore you to the moon and back. Isaac, your stories are far better than mine; I could listen to them forever. Judah, you are quite possibly the sweetest, happiest baby ever born. You all fill my life with joy.

Lord, I am Yours. Make me an offering.

Part 1

humility

IT'S NOT THAT I ever had delusions of grandeur, or even that I think I am better than anyone else, but there is something about donning a tag that says, "Please be patient; I'm a trainee" and asking, "Would you like paper or plastic?" that is uniquely, even brutally, humbling. Paired with a blue canvas apron cinched tight across my expanding waist, the plastic name tag screamed from my chest and made me frighteningly conspicuous at a time in my life when I longed for anonymity like parched earth wants for rain.

Cover me, I thought the first time I dressed in the awful ensemble. Standing alone in my room in front of a mirror too honest to disguise the profound hideousness of it, I felt more exposed than if I had been wearing a skirt that barely covered my floral-print panties. "Oh, God, if You love me at all," I breathed, "cover me."

He didn't answer. But I thought that maybe He was listening—Grandma promised me He was—and I held on to that hope, fledgling though it was. I couldn't claim to understand Him, but I felt a deep and growing need to try, even if He deigned to ignore my current plea for rescue.

"You look cute," Grandma commented diplomatically when I sulked into the kitchen moments later. But by the glint of a smile in her eye I knew that *cute* was a euphemism for *ridiculous*. "Just don't tuck your shirt in, Julia. It won't . . . you know . . . look too . . ." She fluffed her fingers around her midsection, and flour poofed from her hands in small clouds like smoke from somewhere up a magician's sleeve. She cautiously, encouragingly, raised an eyebrow at me.

I looked down to see the petite crescent curve of my belly pressing against the knotted apron strings. Startled by what I saw, I sucked in impulsively. It disappeared—the growing evidence of *her* disappeared, a flat shadow beneath a fold of cerulean. "That's the best I can do," I said dolefully. "We have to tuck our shirts in. It's part of the dress code. And—" I reached into the front pocket of the apron and produced a thin, mustard yellow tie—"we have to wear this."

Grandma almost burst out laughing but only allowed herself a restrained little chuckle. "You know, I see those kids in Value Foods every week, but I never really noticed the uniform. Is that a clip-on?"

I nodded bleakly and snapped the clip at her, alligator-style, before affixing it to my starched collar.

"It's crooked, honey." She wiped her fingertips on a towel and left the bread dough that she had been kneading to circle around the worn oak table and face me. She tugged at the obscene bit of fabric, pulling it this way and that before tucking it under the top of my apron and stepping back. "There." The word sounded almost portentous to me—definitive.

"I'm going to be late," I croaked, clearing my throat self-consciously. "Don't wait up for me. I'm helping out with a restock tonight. They're going to train me how to record inventory. . . ."

Grandma pursed her lips and spread her arms in understanding. I walked heavily into her embrace. "I'm proud of you," she murmured into my hair. "It's really not that bad, is it?"

I didn't want to be melodramatic, but I couldn't drown the sick feeling that was rising past my chest and into my throat, where it sat threateningly at the back of my tongue. *They'll see me*, I thought. *They'll judge me.* But I said, "You're right; it's not so bad. It's just that all the high school kids work there. I'll be the oldest person besides the manager. . . ."

"You only graduated last year," Grandma reminded, trying to cheer me up. "You'll probably even know some of the employees!"

Great, I thought.

But she was doing her best to be helpful, and I managed a wry smile because at the very least she hadn't said, "You'll have so much in common with them!" The disappearing smoothness beneath the straight line of my apron guaranteed that I would have *nothing* in common with my coworkers.

"Well," I said, pressing my palms together and trying to force a little enthusiasm into my voice, "I'd better go or I'll be late."

"Wouldn't want that your first day on the job!" Grandma followed me into the mudroom and gave my back a little pat when my coat was zipped up and my hand was on the door. "It's going to be just fine."

"I know," I replied without blinking.

She watched from the door as I drove away, but the sun was already a memory on the horizon—a thin ribbon of purple, little more than a bruise left by the imprint of orange—and I'm sure all she saw of my departure was taillights. It was better that way. I hated the thought of her seeing how I strangled the steering wheel.

Value Foods was far from the worst place in town to work. There was the packing plant, the egg plant, the paint factory, and a wide assortment of hog farms, cattle farms, dairy farms, and goat farms where my skin could absorb a variety of rancid smells that would stay with me even after multiple showers with lye soap and industrial-strength hand cleaners. The grocery store was tame compared to the rest of the job market in Mason, and in truth, I was lucky to get the job. I needed something full-time, with benefits, and as much as I hated to admit it, I was thankful that Mr. Durst, the manager, lived just over the South Dakota border and wouldn't mind that my pregnancy would progress before the entire town like a neatly drawn life cycle in a full-color science textbook. What was my personal scandal to him? In fact, when I warily mentioned in my job interview that I was three months pregnant, Mr. Durst had looked at me as if to say, *So what?* He did ask, "Will it interfere with your ability to perform your job?"

I assured him I would be able to scan boxes of cereal and bag oranges well into my third trimester if not up to the day I delivered.

He grunted and handed me a uniform from out of a stack on the desk behind him.

"Do you want to know my size?" I wondered out loud, holding the standard-issue pants, shirt, and apron gingerly.

"Small, medium, large, extra large" was his only comment, and indeed, when I located the tag inside the shirt, it read *medium*. For a while at least.

"Start with that," Mr. Durst instructed. "We'll get you more later."

Training was an evening job since, for most people in our conservative little town, the hours after suppertime were reserved for baths and play and television, not grocery shopping. When I drove into the parking lot at seven o'clock, it boasted only a dozen cars or so, and though I was tempted to pull close to the door and save myself the trek through below-freezing temperatures, I dutifully drove way to the back of the lot, where the employees were supposed to park. I yanked my hood over my head and stuffed my hands into my pockets, running the whole way across the empty parking lot with my apron flapping against my knees.

The store was overly bright, and someone had turned the elevator music a tad too loud. A little grocery cart corral at the front of the first aisle was stacked with carts, and only one checkout lane was open. The cashier, someone I didn't recognize, was sitting on the counter right beside the red-eyed scanner and blowing a fluorescent green bubble so big I was afraid it would pop and get stuck in her eyebrows. She sucked it in when she saw me and gave a bored wave, beckoning me over with a flick of her wrist.

"You're Julie, right?" she asked.

Though there was no hint of unfriendliness in her voice, I cringed when she called me Julie.

"Julia," I corrected, trying to sound upbeat.

She just stared. "Okay, whatever. You're late, by the way."

I twisted my watch on my arm and consulted the face again though I had already checked it twice since driving up. "It's a minute to seven," I argued.

"Clark—he's the assistant manager—insists that we be at least ten minutes early for every shift. Better if it's fifteen minutes; he'll forgive you if it's five. But you're late."

"Nobody told me that," I said and regretted how whiny it came out.

She shrugged. "He's waiting for you in the back room."

"Thank you." I started off past the registers.

It was a small thing, the thank-you, but it must have endeared me to her the tiniest bit, because as I was walking away, she offered, "Never sit on the counter." She drummed her fingers on the laminate surface beside her thighs as if to illustrate her point. "But if you're going to, make sure that Clark is in the back room. He'll kill you if he catches you."

I smiled and made a mental note of the name on her tag. "Alicia." And below that: "2 years of faithful service."

The back room of Value Foods was little more than an extended storeroom. The walls were cold, concrete blocks and the shelving was stark and unattractive, the ugly sister of the sleeker, more appealing units that graced the aisles of the store and made things like Ho Hos look appetizing. There was a dingy bathroom near the loading dock and a sprawling metal table that served as a break room at the far end of the elongated hall. Both locations were barely illuminated by naked lightbulbs that fought valiantly to dispel the dismal shadows but lost miserably. When I'd used the bathroom after my interview, I considered telling someone about the one burned-out bulb above the sink. But standing over the corroded fixtures and browning drain, I acquiesced. Crummy lighting actually improved the overall impression of the entire back room.

Thankfully, I knew I wouldn't find Clark amid the boxes and gloom. Opposite the break area at the far end of the passage was a duo of glass-fronted offices. The one on the left—the office with two actual windows to the outside world—was Mr. Durst's. I had been told the other office belonged to the assistant manager, Clark Henstock.

The light was on in his office, and he was looking at me through the glass.

I walked briskly toward him, trying to hold a capable expression that was both professional and eager yet not at all forced. Though no reflective surface played back my features and told me so, my face felt like it was locked in a grimace. I licked my lips, tried again, and finally abandoned the feeble attempt at confidence. The door to Clark's office was open, and I stepped up to the threshold, stopping in the doorframe to say, "I'm Julia DeSmit. You must be—"

"Clark Henstock," he said, clipping off each separate syllable with militaristic accuracy.

I almost said, "I know," but I managed to hold my tongue and was grateful for it when he tossed a pen at me. It came out of nowhere, and my hand shot up almost of its own accord. Against all odds, and for only the second or third time in my life, I made the perfect catch. The Bic thumped satisfyingly in my palm, and a grin unpredictably, and embarrassingly, sprang to my lips. "Caught it," I laughed and immediately felt like an idiot. Wagging the pen lamely, I shrugged one shoulder as if to shake it off and dropped my arm to my side.

Clark assessed me for a moment before stating coolly, "I need you to sign a few papers." He turned to the table against the glass wall overlooking the storeroom and arranged three documents in a perfectly straight row. "Here, here, and here," he said, pointing, when I stepped up to the table.

I signed my name three times. Each signature looked different from the last because I had to lean closer into Clark to reach the far papers and my body couldn't help avoiding his as if we were repelled magnetically. Although I half expected him to comment on it, he merely swept up the documents when I was finished and sank into his cushy chair. Swiveling toward a paper-laden desk, he shoved my papers into an open file and dropped it in a box by his feet. Then he looked at his watch and said without turning to me, "It's 7:04. You're late for work. Next time make sure you arrive on time."

It was impossible not to cringe, but I forced myself to bite my tongue and stay put, awaiting further commands. Clark remained with his back to me, and I determined to be as quiet and enduring as the sweetest of saints. Clasping my hands in front of me, I studied the back of his head while I practiced patience.

His hair was dark brown and noticeably thinning. On a man with a deeper skin tone, Clark's hair loss might not have been so pronounced. But Clark was white in a way that prevented any speculation of diversity in his family tree, and the chalkiness of his scalp peeking through sad little patches of scraggly hair was unnecessarily unattractive. Not that Clark was ugly. He was just trying a little too hard to maintain the coif of his youth when he was obviously pushing forty.

Shave it off, I thought. *Embrace your age.*

Almost as if I had spoken aloud, he whipped around to face me. "What are you still doing here?"

I managed to mumble, "Waiting for instructions."

Clark's sigh was a barely concealed groan. "Take a little initiative, Miss DeSmit. Be a problem solver. I'm not here to babysit." And he spun back to his computer.

I melted out of the office and wandered to the break area, where I shed my coat and hung it over a folding metal chair. It was suddenly very cold without my winter parka, and I wrapped my arms around myself, hurrying out of the storeroom lest Clark turn to see me dawdling and fire me on the spot. Deciding my best course of action would be to find Alicia and ask her what to do, I cut through the aisles and nearly collided with a boy who was almost a full head shorter than me.

"Oops!" He laughed a little too heartily. His yellow tie was crooked at his throat, and his stiff apron was stained with what looked like darkening blood from the meat counter. The thought nauseated me. "Sorry!" the boy exclaimed, wiping his hands on his apron and extending one to me. "I'm Graham. You must be the new girl."

"Julia," I muttered, taking his hand though it was almost painful to do so. His fingers were warm and soft.

"Nice to meet you, Julia. You'll like it here. It's a good job!"

While he looked too young to be working anywhere and his

enthusiasm was overkill, it was hard not to smile back when he was grinning in my face. "Glad to hear it," I commented vaguely, hoping that a response wouldn't encourage him too much.

"Alicia is the shift manager," Graham explained as if he intended to take me under his wing.

I rolled my eyes at the thought of yet another person on the ladder of managerial staff at Value Foods.

"No, no, she's nice," he hurried to clarify, misunderstanding my expression. I started to explain myself but he went on. "Denise can be a bear, but Alicia lets us leave early for our breaks sometimes."

I gave him a little nod and took a small step back to disengage myself from his unsolicited conversation. "I'll keep that in mind," I said, slowly backing away.

But Graham followed. "Hey, I'll walk you to the front. It's almost my break time anyway, and I can introduce you to people as we go."

"Graham, I—"

"Oh, it's okay, really. I don't mind at all." And though he could just barely peek over my shoulder, he took my elbow and steered me down the aisle as if he were some elderly benefactor and I a little girl.

I tried not to sigh as I allowed myself to be led through the store. Though Graham would release me long enough to let me shake the outstretched hands of my coworkers, as we continued to the checkouts he would manage to take up his paternal position again. There was nothing malicious or inappropriate in his gesture, and because he elicited genuine warmth in everyone we met, I did everything I could to be friendly and fine with whatever social particulars made him comfortable. I couldn't escape the feeling that much of my life from now on would be molding myself to fit snugly against other people's ideas and ideals. It was safer there where I could blend in, where I could be smooth and seamless and hidden—predictably contrite for my situation and newly flawless in my efforts at virtue. It made my head ache with inadequacy.

Value Foods wasn't an enormous store, but by the time we passed nine aisles and started through the produce section to the front, I had met half a dozen employees. All of them teenagers. None of them particularly enthused to see me. I was just the new girl—and an old one at that.

I peeked at my watch when we got to the front and waited patiently while Alicia finished with a customer. An older man wearing what looked to be a brand-new overcoat paid for his bottle of wine with a crisp twenty-dollar bill while Alicia grinned at him as if he were the single most interesting person she had ever met. She waved and watched him walk away, and he was halfway through the first automatic door when she finally turned to focus her attention on Graham and me. The easy turn of her lips sunk immediately, and she clicked her tongue as if to chastise us. "It's quarter after seven."

"I know." I didn't offer any more because I was already becoming well aware of how things were done at Value Foods. Arrive on time, do your job, and stay out of Clark's way. I was about to add Alicia's name beside Clark's when the sternness left her face and she shrugged.

"Whatever." She pointed to a mop bucket waiting in the sectioned-off lane beside hers. "We mop the store every few days on a rotating schedule. You're new, so you get the honors tonight. Produce section and freezer aisle. Just remember to put up the Wet Floor signs. We don't want a lawsuit." Alicia craned her neck for a moment and scanned the store. Seeing that the coast was clear, she hopped back onto the counter and squeezed a little dab of hand sanitizer into her palm, working it in as if it were a luxurious cream. "And, Graham," she added, looking up, "you only have ten minutes left on your break."

"Yup," he said cheerfully and waved exuberantly at us as he started away. "Have a good time, Julia! It was nice to meet you!"

I gave him a halfhearted flick of my fingers and unhooked the plastic chain to grab the mop bucket. "Is he always that happy?" I asked Alicia.

"Twenty-four seven," she confirmed. "He's fourteen, you know. I don't remember being that cheerful when I was fourteen. But hey, Graham is fun to work with even if he's a bit . . . um—" she rolled her eyes as she fumbled for the right word—"*enthusiastic.*"

Although I felt silly the moment the question was out of my mouth, I couldn't stop myself from asking, "Do you like it here?"

Alicia snorted. "Of course not. I'd way rather win the lottery or grow a money tree in my backyard. But it's a job." She sucked in her gum and it made a loud pop. "And working with Michael is better than a hole in the head."

"Michael?"

"You'll see." Alicia smiled.

It occurred to me that I should banter, keep up this little conversation and make a friend. But the apron strings were cutting into my waist and my head was already beginning to throb from the fluorescent lights and the music that must have been standard-issue in the eighties for every doctor's office, elevator, and store in the country. Maybe an instrumental version of Michael Bolton or, heaven help us, Chicago. All I could think was *I have to listen to this for four hours?*

"Start at the back and work your way up to the front," Alicia instructed. She watched me push the mop bucket out into the aisle. "You know how to work that thing, don't you?" Her hand pulled an imaginary lever. "Just put the mop head in that slot and pull—"

"Yes, thank you." I quickly nodded, though I had never used a mop before in my life.

"Okay. Have fun." Alicia returned to rubbing her fingers.

I began to back slowly down the aisle past the fruits and vegetables and bins of nuts. The bucket was heavier than it looked, and I was so focused on maneuvering it that when the mister started over the lettuces, I jumped out of my skin and knocked a grapefruit from a mountain of Ruby Reds. It plopped right into my bucket and splashed dingy water on my shoes. Had I a foul mouth, the moment was ripe for a string of curses that may have been deemed warranted by most people. But I bit my lip instead and rolled up my sleeve to fish the grapefruit out. It was slick with brown water and probably bruised, and because I didn't want anyone to buy it, I stuck it in my apron pocket intending to pay for it later. I almost laughed in surrender when I saw the caricature of pregnant round-ness protruding from my belly.

Mopping wasn't as bad as I first imagined it would be, and the monotonous motion actually felt more like a workout than a menial task. Sweep to the left, sweep to the right, swish in the bucket,

squeeze. I wouldn't go so far as to say I enjoyed it, but the solitariness of such drudgery was a definite bonus. None of the other
employees approached me even once. With my hand on the grip
of an oversize mop and the smell of dusty water at my feet, I had
a few stolen moments to ponder the what-ifs of my life. What if
Dad were still alive? What if things were different between Thomas
and me? What if I had stayed in college? What if I had never met
Parker and gotten pregnant? The list could go on forever—past
recent mistakes and on to long-ago losses—and though I wanted
to indulge in a little self-pity, I didn't because Grandma expected
more of me these days. I pushed those thoughts out of my mind
and, with a self-deprecating smile, mopped with all the heart of a
born grocery store employee.

The store itself was dead, and the occasional customers who did
brave the abandoned aisles walked quickly and clutched bulging
coats around them as if this was the last place they wanted to be.
Often they carried just a single item—a loaf of bread, a gallon of
milk. At least two people besides the man in the overcoat stopped
to peruse the wine section.

When she walked past me, I only looked up because her footsteps
were so heavy. Her back was toward me, and she was wearing a jean
coat with faux fur at the wrists and collar. Long, dirty blonde hair
hung in a ponytail, and though I couldn't see her face, there was
something about her that seemed too old for such youthful hair.
She glanced over her shoulder and I dropped my head, not wanting
it to seem like I had been staring at her. I heard her leave then, and
because the sad slant of her back tugged at something deep inside
me, I watched her walk toward Alicia.

I had made it almost to the end of the aisle, and I could see and hear everything that went on between the two of them. The woman laid a half gallon of milk, a bag of pretzels, and two carefully chosen Braeburn apples on the counter. Alicia barely looked at her and didn't even bother to smile, much less flatter her the way she had wooed the man with the wine. For her part, the woman kept her head down and her hands in her pockets as if she was almost apologetic about her presence in the store.

"Four dollars and three cents," Alicia said when the last item had been scanned. She turned to put the groceries in a plastic bag while the woman dug in her pockets.

She produced four crinkled one-dollar bills and spread them out self-consciously in front of her. Passing them to Alicia, her hands returned to her pockets to find the change. She probed and poked, and though I was supposed to be looking at the floor, I could see her fingers thrusting at the fabric and coming up empty.

"Do you have a take-a-penny jar?" the woman asked quietly.

Alicia stared at her. "No."

My hands went to my own pockets, but the pants were brand-new and the only thing I found was lint.

"How much was it again?" Her voice was so soft I could barely make out the words.

"Four dollars and three cents," Alicia repeated matter-of-factly.

The woman dug a bit more, and I wanted to yell at Alicia, "Just let her have it. I'll pay you later!" But instead I put my hand on the mop and looked down. I didn't want the weary woman to think that anyone was witnessing her shame.

I didn't realize I was holding my breath until I heard the woman say, "I guess I'll have to leave one of the apples." When I exhaled, I felt them both look up. Fortunately I was half turned away from them, and the splat of my mop on the floor disguised the tail end of my wheeze.

"Whatever," Alicia intoned.

Buttons were pushed and cash register tape whirred and within moments the woman was gone.

"Sheesh," Alicia said, catching my eye. "Seriously, it was like three cents. Can you believe some people?"

"No, I can't," I said, but she didn't catch the arrows in my look.

I finished the floor with an almost vicious energy, but by the time the front doors were locked and we were ready to start restocking shelves, I had all but forgotten about the woman. Though she nibbled at the corners of my mind, it was easier not to focus on her. And even downright soothing to allow myself the thought that at least one person had it far worse than me.

different

Because I loved Thomas Walker and he did not love me back, it was very awkward at first to maintain a relationship with the Walker family. Though Thomas and I had managed to patch things up with all the inelegant grace of junior high dance partners, I continued to have a bit of a problem looking him in the eye or even being in the same room as him without feeling every ounce of the rejection he so thoughtlessly threw at my feet. But since our friendship spanned years and heartaches that hardened like cement between the inconsistencies of our lives, maintain is exactly what I did.

Of course, everyone knew that something catastrophic had happened, though I hoped that only Mrs. Walker was perceptive enough to string together the details. Thankfully, the deflation of my friendship with Thomas took a backseat to the news that I was expecting a baby, and the rest of the family more likely than not buried any indication of turmoil between Thomas and me beneath this much weightier, more significant discovery.

When Mr. Walker saw me for the first time after learning the news, I could see the tightrope his conscience and emotions had to walk and how difficult he was finding it to balance the two. There was disappointment, and I understood that completely because I felt it acutely myself. But there was also a defensiveness behind his eyes, a fatherly need to shore me up against the onslaught of what was to come, to pull me in and protect me from the world and the consequences of my actions.

I watched the two sides battle across his face, and then unexpectedly he softened and drew me into his arms with all the aching tenderness of someone who loved me far more deeply than I had ever realized. When my head was buried on his broad shoulder and I was lost for words, he confirmed it by saying, "We love ya, Julia." And though he had shaved off the edges by using *we* instead of *I* and *ya* instead of *you*, I knew exactly what he meant. For a moment I wanted to ask him to say it again the proper way, so I could close my eyes and pretend he was my father.

If anything, the disquiet surrounding my mortifying fallout with Thomas and the subsequent news of my pregnancy drew me closer to the Walkers. Thomas was busy with his college courses and avoided home whenever his mother tactfully warned him that I would be around. I was free to luxuriate in the normalcy of laughter in the kitchen and easy conversations that rambled on about nothing more important than whether or not brown sugar was actually healthier for you than white. It was a quiet time for me, a time to sit and slowly unravel the boundaries of our expanding relationship, a skein of delicate yarn that I slipped between my fingers and held fast in my palm—a softness, an unexpected treasure.

At least once a week the Walker women invited me over for some distinctly feminine rite: crafting homemade cards, painting our toenails bubble-gum pink, or baking endless goodies that we slowly devoured one row at a time, cutting little bites and nibbling until the pan was nearly gone. It was rather out of the ordinary for me, the pure girliness of it, but I loved it all the same and found myself observing Mrs. Walker and her daughters as if they were curious creatures on Animal Planet: beautiful, extraordinary, spellbinding, but *curious* creatures. I did not understand them even as I longed to be a part of them.

Our girls' nights in usually happened later in the week, but after my less than wonderful experience at work on Monday night, Mrs. Walker called me to see if I would be up for making cookies on Tuesday evening. I worked during the day on Tuesday, and although the thought of putting my feet up and indulging in a little mindless television was enticing, I couldn't bring myself to say no. Even Grandma, who usually declined Mrs. Walker's invitations so I could have a little room to breathe, conceded to come along.

Most of the engulfing snow that fell throughout the holidays had melted in a warm snap around Valentine's Day. There was a week of winter flooding, the kind of warmth and wet that turns everything to a gooey slush and hinders any attempt at cleanliness or even free movement outside the confines of any building. Customers picked their way through the Value Foods parking lot, stepping high like prized Lipizzaner stallions so as not to soil the cuffs of their jeans with gray snowy sludge. An utter waste of time. It was a wild world for a few days while the sun shone exuberantly, and though it wasn't quite fifty degrees, people braved the outdoors minus a coat or the hat, scarf, and glove paraphernalia that they wouldn't have been caught dead without only days before.

When temperatures suddenly dipped back to zero and then beyond, everything froze solid. It was as if a witch had cast a spell over Mason, unleashing a frost so severe it almost frighteningly arrested any springlike movement of the earth below. The hope of a warming world was so carefully preserved it seemed like a cruel snub. Brown grasses that had been slick with melt were now stiff and bent, lifeless fingers pointing heavenward in blame. Mr. Walker's deep footprints in the grove were perfect impressions cast in silvery granite. Tire tracks along every road became indestructible wells that made driving a treacherous experience. It was an eerily snowless but nonetheless bitterly icy world. It felt wrong.

Grandma and I bundled up as if we were about to summit Everest and headed through the darkness to the Walkers' baking night. I walked behind Grandma, reaching slightly around her to train a flashlight beam on the path before us. It was slippery and uneven, hard to maneuver, and I wished more than once that I had pressed Grandma more earnestly to take the car.

She had been insistent: the Walkers lived next door—only a four-minute walk through the grove—and it wasn't worth the gas it would take to drive there when we had perfectly sound and capable legs. Though at first it had been a matter of preference, as we walked I began to question the validity of her words—particularly when her foot slid in a deep rut and I had to thrust out an arm to catch her. She was light against my embrace, and we stayed there for a moment, the flashlight, forgotten in my grasping hand, illuminating the hostile tree branches above our heads. Grandma breathed heavily once or twice, leaned into me, and then laughed to let me know it was nothing. But as I watched her continue on in front of my own wavering pace, the slight hunch of her shoulders, the slow shuffle of her feet, reminded me: seventy-seven. She was seventy-seven years old. The perspective made me shiver.

I talked then, to scare off the ghosts that cackled in the frigid grove, and when we mounted the steps of the Walkers' front porch, Grandma's cheeks were flushed with gratefulness and maybe even a little pain. She favored her left ankle the tiniest bit. I was about to ask her if she was okay when the front door flung open.

"You *walked*?" Mrs. Walker asked. If I didn't know her I would have mistaken her concern for anger. "It's awful out there! Why on earth did you walk? I could have sent Jonathan to get you!" She rambled on without waiting for a reply and ushered us in with all the doting concern of a mother hen. I even heard her cluck once when she saw Grandma limp a little as she went to sit on the bench beneath the coat hook. "Tell me you didn't hurt yourself!" She sucked in quickly, studying Grandma's face for the truth.

"Not at all, not at all," Grandma hurried to clarify. "A little twist; that's all."

I turned my face to my shoes, concentrating on untying the laces and hiding a smile when Mrs. Walker tsked and bent to pull off Grandma's boots.

"We'll get you some ice. Or heat." She whipped around to regard me. "Which one do you do first? I can never remember."

"Beats me." I shrugged.

"Come on!" Mrs. Walker challenged. "You're the smart one!"

I laughed a little too self-consciously and carefully moved past them into the kitchen. Maggie, the youngest Walker, was already setting out mixing bowls on the counter, and when she saw me, she gave a delighted squeal and mimed a long-distance hug. "Hey, Maggie," I called, saluting her handiwork. "Got peas in your freezer?"

"Maybe California mixed veggies," she offered. "Simon hates peas so much he says they can't be in the same freezer as his peanut butter cup ice cream."

I slid open the deep drawer beneath the fridge, and sure enough, there was a king-size bag of frostbitten vegetables—and they were only half gone. By the time Mrs. Walker and Grandma ambled into the kitchen, two stools were pulled up to the counter—one for sitting, one for the injured leg—and the lumpy bag was wrapped in a yellow gingham tea towel. I noted with some alarm that Grandma was indeed limping visibly.

"We're going to start with cold," I announced, pointing to the stools and looking away from her uneven hobble before I got too uneasy.

"What happened?" Maggie cooed. Her voice mimicked her mother's concern so perfectly that I caught myself glancing furtively between the two. Mirror images. The younger was the shadow of her mother in the years before time had drawn pains-taking lines through the skin around her mouth and eyes. It was a pretty sight.

"Nothing," Grandma insisted firmly to Maggie's softhearted question.

"She hurt her ankle," Mrs. Walker corrected. She situated Grandma with my proffered bundle and pressed the angled cold-ness against her exposed skin.

"Cookies will make you feel better," Maggie comforted. "We're doing cutouts: snowflakes and the letter *M*." She held up the cookie cutters as if just seeing them would prove to be restorative.

Grandma smiled at the ponytailed girl. "Snowflakes to encourage God and an *M* because . . . ?"

A voice called out from the entryway, "Because Maggie has an admirer who calls her M&M. You know, Maggie Marie." Mr. Walker entered the kitchen to the fanfare of steel-toed boots on black slate tiles.

"Jonathan!" Mrs. Walker scolded.

At the exact same time Maggie yelled, "Dad!"

"What?" he asked incredulously.

"You told her secret," I clarified and, pointing down, added, "Boots."

Mr. Walker looked from Maggie's red face to the muddy work boots leaving drips of murky thaw on the floor. "Oh. Well, don't let me interrupt you ladies." He backed out of the kitchen with his tail between his legs.

We all giggled, remembering how in the early days of our get-togethers, Mr. Walker, Jacob, and Simon had wanted to be a part of the festivities. They had rapidly discarded that notion, resorting to the occasional whimper for leftover cookie crumbs or overdone cake corners.

When he was gone and we were alone in our familiarity, it was impossible not to say, "You have a boyfriend?" I didn't mean to tease, but Maggie's eyes hardened enough to let me know it was a touchy subject. I put my finger through the metal *M* lying in front of me and sent it spinning to her on the slick countertop. She purposefully stepped away from it and let it clang to the floor. "Come on," I urged, unable to hide the glimmer in my eye at the thought of eight-year-old Maggie—old beyond her years and innocently oblivious—with a little tween boyfriend. "I bet he calls you M&M because you're so sweet." Wrong thing to say.

Maggie groaned and shot me the sort of chilling look that is made all the more icy because it is delivered with the pure and uncorrupted guile of a child. "Julia, you're worse than Jacob and Simon. I expected more of you."

I winced, though Grandma and Mrs. Walker laughed as if Maggie were only teasing. I could tell she planned to hold a grudge. A young grudge. The kind that is swift in duration but tough in spirit. She refused to look at me as she continued to pull ingredients out of the fridge.

"You can't be mad at me," I cajoled, taking a block of cream cheese from the small stack of refrigerator goods in her slender arms. "You're supposed to tell me all about your boyfriends. Besides, we're the young ones—me, you, and Emily." I lowered my voice to a stage whisper, keeping it just loud enough for the older women to hear. "We gotta stick together."

"Emily's not here tonight," Maggie said frostily. "And you are not a young one. You're almost a *mom*."

I couldn't be angry with a third grader, but her harsh reminder was a fist to the stomach.

"Maggie!" Mrs. Walker warned.

"What?" she threw back.

I shook my head at Mrs. Walker when Maggie wasn't looking to let her know that I took no offense. Maggie and I were close—we had always been so—but my pregnancy had offended her sense of order, and though she still longed to love me, there was a roadblock set against me in the very fiber of her moral little being. She knew right from wrong, and I was an aberration in her ordered world. A *beloved* aberration. And I only made it worse by continuing to be nothing more offensive than myself. A growing self, but myself all the same. I threatened the illusion of black and white, right and wrong, maybe even good and evil. Maggie was having a bit of a time reconciling her world with me.

To make it up to her, and because it was all I knew to do, I did the jobs she hated. I softened the cream cheese in the microwave for fifteen seconds and then stirred the lumps to perfect smoothness with elbow grease and a fork. I cut parchment for the baking pans, measuring the edges dutifully so as not to waste a single inch of the gauzy paper. I put things away as we used them: vanilla and baking soda in the pantry, cream and butter in the refrigerator. I let Maggie crack the eggs and test little morsels of dough to see if we had added enough salt. Most of all, I did everything in my power to ignore the tingle in my back from a day of being on my feet. Though I longed to press the heels of my hands to the soft spot above my hips, I refused to do anything that would draw attention to the one thing that was beginning to drive a wedge between myself and the girl who was nothing less than a sister to me.

My efforts paid off, and Maggie had warmed up a bit by the time the first batch of cookies was cooling on wire racks. I was tinting the glossy frosting an icy blue for snowflake accents when she handed me the broken leg of a still-warm *M* and said, "You know, the *M* is for March. It's almost March."

"I know," I affirmed, trying to keep my gaze blank.

She studied me, inspecting my expression for any trace of condescension. Though I didn't mean to patronize her, I also didn't believe her little alibi, and I quickly stuffed the bit of cookie in my mouth, grinning at her with my lips pressed tight together.

"You're a terrible liar," Maggie complained, punching me on the arm. But at least the earlier malice in her tone had been replaced with annoyance.

"Forgiven?" I whispered when she came to take the bowl of frosting from me.

Shooting me a sharp look to let me know I didn't deserve it, she slowly conceded, "Yes, I suppose so. But stop changing."

I stood rooted to the floor, utterly flummoxed, as she walked away. "Changing?" I repeated, watching her place the bowl in front of Grandma. "I'm not changing."

Apparently there was more than a touch of suspicion in my voice because Mrs. Walker and Grandma exchanged looks. Maggie gave me a curt nod.

"What?" I demanded, starting to feel left out.

Maggie shrugged. Mrs. Walker looked at Grandma.

Grandma said, "Change is not a bad thing, Julia."

I tried not to be hurt, but suddenly I felt like a conversation had taken place that I was not privy to. It was a deserted feeling. Sure, I was gaining a touch of weight, and morning sickness even now managed to make me a little cranky, but I was still the same old Julia that I had always been. There had been no fundamental shift, no transformation that I was even remotely aware of.

The whole thing smacked of an encounter I had in ninth grade with a boy who rode bus number eleven with me. Though we spoke seldom to never, he always took the seat in front of me and apparently listened to private conversations between me and the irregular friends who shared my bench. One day after school, right before his stop, he leaned over the back of his seat and said, "You are the most multifaceted person I have ever met." His voice was even, unemotional, and when the bus driver slid the door open and called his name, the boy smiled at me, not unkindly, and left. I watched his backpack bounce off the edge of each seat as he made his way to the front.

According to Dad, it was a beautiful thing to be multifaceted. When I carefully asked him that night what the word meant, he assured me that it alluded to unexplored qualities and a never-ending array of possibilities. "In fact," he continued, his eyes glassy from chemotherapy but beginning to shine, "the very root of a diamond's beauty lies in the number of cuts—of facets—that are painstakingly etched into the surface."

Dad was reflective and maybe even a little romantic, but though I wanted to find solace in his definition, I simply felt misunderstood. I didn't like the idea of some bus boy reading things inside me that

I could not see inside myself. Who could possibly know me better than me? I was indignant.

And now to be told that I was changing? "I haven't changed a bit," I muttered more to myself than anyone else.

"Well," Mrs. Walker began definitively, "teasing Maggie about her little boyfriend—"

"Mom!"

"—is hardly an indicator of deep, personal change, Julia. But—" she caught my eye—"you are different these days."

I tried not to be hypersensitive as I weighed her words for a moment. Finally I asked, "Good different or bad different?"

"Different different," Maggie clarified.

I tossed up my hands in defeat.

Grandma and Mrs. Walker laughed and looked up from piping icing in dainty designs around the edges of our snowflakes.

"Don't be defensive; there's no reason to be," Grandma chided me gently. "Your life has changed a lot in the past . . ." She paused, thinking. "Well, your life has been full of changes for a long time now, hasn't it? Of course you are going to grow—"

"And *change*," Mrs. Walker quickly added.

"And *change*—hopefully every day of your life."

I couldn't help snorting at such platitudes as I studied them all skeptically. But there was no harm intended in their words, and though I didn't understand and didn't particularly like being some sort of social experiment for their personal dissection and group discussion, I decided to let it go. "Whatever," I said noncommittally and almost kicked myself because it sounded so stupid. Two days at Value Foods and already I had been reduced to conversational assassination. Such a lifeless, quenching word. I had effectively axed any potential of continuing on in this particular vein. And I had actually hoped to gain a little clarity.

But though I never got the answers I hoped for, everyone made a point of keeping the mood light for the rest of the evening. We quizzed Maggie on her vocabulary words and lamented the fact that Emily had chosen to go to a friend's house instead of joining us for the night. Granted, she was studying for a major test in world history, but we missed her nonetheless.

Mr. Walker's help was enlisted to drive Grandma and me home, partly so that we didn't have to make our way in the dark again and partly because Grandma's ankle was a fetching shade of plum. The ice hadn't helped much.

"I'll keep it elevated," Grandma promised Mrs. Walker as she helped us into the already warmed up Ford F-150.

"Call a doctor tomorrow, okay?" Mrs. Walker grabbed my arm as I walked past. "Make sure your grandmother calls a doctor tomorrow. Better yet, you call for her."

I raised my hand in pledge. "I promise. I'll be the very first call into the clinic."

"It's not broken!" Grandma chimed in from the cab of Mr. Walker's truck. "It's just a twist!"

Mrs. Walker nodded gravely at Grandma, then gave me a quick hug and whispered, "Take care of her. I think we take her for granted sometimes. She's not as young as she used to be."

A fact I was well aware of.

I thought of stability as we drove slowly home. Constancy, reliability, a firm foundation that could not be shaken by death or new life or a twisted ankle. A modest, ordinary, day-to-day existence with problems of no greater significance than what to make for supper. *God*, I prayed, *if You're listening to this pregnant checkout girl, if my still, small voice can be heard above Mr. Walker's booming laugh and the roar of his oversize engine, grant me a little stability in my life.*

Change is overrated.

small world

HEARTBURN WAS JUST one of the many small assaults my body was forced to combat and catalog like little red flags of what was to come as my pregnancy progressed. Who knew something as innocent as tomato sauce on a pizza or the few random chocolate chips in one of Grandma's oatmeal cookies could set off a gastrointestinal crusade of nearly epic proportions? I felt like an old woman as my body rebelled, and though I tried to fight off each battle with copious amounts of chalk-flavored Tums, once or twice a week the fire slowly climbing my throat forced me out of bed and into an upright position, where my chances of choking on the insidious sulfur were at least minimally reduced.

Grandma was long in bed late one night while I flipped through television stations with an uncharacteristically robotic intensity: *flip, flip, flip, flip*—the even tone of a metronome. And while the rhythmic flashes and incessant drone tried on more than one occasion to lull me back to sleep, the dip of my head if I drifted off even a little was enough to remind me of why my warm, rumpled bed was an immediate and loathed enemy. I stayed rooted in my chair as the QVC, ESPN, and countless reruns of *Friends* made quick, colorful appearances across the screen of Grandma's aging Magnavox. But somewhere amid the color and clutter, my seemingly dozing consciousness finally picked out a disquietingly familiar scene. My fingers stopped.

Commanding most of the screen was a white-haired man in predictable khaki-colored safari wear. He sported more pockets and zippers than I could count, and the betraying flatness of each confirmed that any need he had in this morbidly exotic African wasteland would be met by the substantial crew he had toted along. I doubted he even carried his own ChapStick. Not that I judged him. He was more than earnest in his pleas for help, desperate even, and it was at once beautiful and unsettling to observe how keenly his heart broke for the people gathered around him. But who could pay attention to him? *She* was there, standing a little behind and beside her khaki-clad savior.

Her eyes were deep and lovely and sad—they looked at once unexpectedly warm and disquietingly fathomless. But the almond-eyed beauty stopped at her sweeping lashes. The rest of her face was worn and beaten, tracked with lines and carved by hollows that proclaimed a life of hardship I could scarcely begin to grasp. Torn clothes draped her fragile frame like an ill-fitting costume on some child playing dress-up. A shoulder peeked out here. A wrist there. I could see the delicate bones of her collar and the beginning of brittle ribs curving in to her achingly straight spine.

She stood tall—erect and unexpected among the many children gathered around—maybe even a little proud, as if to proclaim in the face of her scars: *I am a survivor*. But I didn't believe her. Splayed wide in protective defense, her fingers pressing the tattered fabric as if white knuckles alone could shield and save, her hand both sheltered and exposed the arc of her pregnant belly. The baby would be born soon if the desperate lay of her hand was any indication.

And while the paternal benefactor assured me that I could change her life for a mere dollar a day—enough to feed, clothe, and even educate her—I wasn't moved to reach for my checkbook. She didn't want a handout, and I didn't want a long-distance balm for my battered conscience. Money was not enough. Nor was a new dress, a goat to provide milk, or even a clean hospital in which to have her baby.

Sitting in the rectangle of dim light cast by the television, warmed by hot dry air from the groaning furnace and satisfied with a meal that would surely be nothing less than a feast for her wasted frame, I just wanted to hold her. I would gently touch my fingers to the back of her head so she'd lay her cheek on my shoulder. I would stroke her matted hair and shush her as if she were my child although she was likely much older than me. I would whisper, "It's okay. Everything is going to be all right." And though she wouldn't speak a word of

English, she would *know* because I could see in her eyes that it was what she was dying to hear.

I would say, "You are not alone."

Since my Sunday school days, I have seen more pictures of women like her than I could ever begin to tally. And while I'd feel stabs of guilt followed quickly by an indescribable and unlikely fear, it was impossible for me to relate to those bone-thin children and desperate mothers when I was a little girl. What did we have in common? I ate three square meals a day and snuck Pringles in between—Oreos if I was lucky and Dad had felt indulgent at the grocery store. But tonight, with the look in her eyes matching the anxious pounding of my heart, she was my neighbor—my sister. If I wanted to, I could reach out and touch her weathered fingers. We inhabited the same space.

Of course, I realize that the vast oceans and sweeping continents of our stunningly fashioned earth span tens of thousands of square miles that I could never in all my life hope to explore. I have been taught that there are species of plants and animals that have been formed for nothing more than the pleasure of God as the human eye will never be blessed with the opportunity to perceive their beauty. I know there are corners of creation that remain as pure and untouched as a patch of newly fallen snow in the hollow of a tree where no one could ever hope to run a finger across its glistening splendor. I appreciate the fact that the world is a very big place indeed. I am little more than a gnat in the scope of such enormity. But *she* has caused me to believe that the world is a very small place. Ghana to Galapagos, India to my own pastoral Iowa, we are all the same. We all want the same thing. Don't we?

Her picture stayed with me for days, hidden discreetly against the backs of my eyelids so that she was with me when I slept. I thought of her baby when I tentatively placed my palm against my own bare belly. Did she have a husband? a mother? someone to help her carry the burden? A trembling thank-you swept through me at the thought of my own grandmother. And then I let myself utter the tiniest, gravest word I could fit my mind around: *help*. For me, for her. Just *help*. I suppose it was a sort of obsession, a surrender, the kind of fixation that would have had Grandma worrying far more than her blood pressure could allow if only she knew about it. Maybe it was unhealthy.

I was thinking of her later, when the wind was howling in the single-pane windows and a winter storm was brewing in the west. It was fierce outside, but inside the kitchen it was a balmy oasis and positively resplendent with the aroma of Indonesian rice, a childhood comfort food that had become my one pregnancy craving. Grandma indulged me at least once a week, and in anticipation of sambal oelek and diced pickles, I had already changed out of my work clothes and donned a pair of ratty sweatpants with an unraveling drawstring. The gray rope barely held together but made it possible for me to cinch the waistband below the baby curve that was beginning to make all my pants uncomfortably tight. The fluorescent lights of Value Foods made my eyes bloodshot and dry, and since we were in for the evening, I had gone so far as to remove my contacts, wash off my makeup, and sweep my hair into a bedtime ponytail. We had locked the doors, turned off the outside lights. Guests were not in the plan.

We were talking about unimportant, happy things, but my heart was heavy and I had to push away my thoughts with cheerful chit-chat and busy hands. I was almost relieved when a pair of headlights glared off the porch window and I could turn my head to watch.

"Is someone coming up our driveway?" Grandma asked. She made it sound as if we got visitors about as often as Sleeping Beauty snoring away decades with every breath in her impenetrable tower.

I laughed. "It's probably the Walkers. Mrs. Walker was so worried about your ankle."

Grandma hobbled around the table as if to prove my point. An oversize black bootie concealed the slim but sturdy cast beneath. She had said it was just a twist. Dr. Morales had assured us it was just a stress fracture.

"If she is bringing us food, so help me, I am sending her right home with it!" Grandma furrowed her eyebrows menacingly, but there was a blush in her cheeks that betrayed how very much she appreciated the attention.

"Sit down. I'll go see who it is. I promise if Mrs. Walker has brought over a banana bread, I'll toss it right back at her."

"Well, Julia, don't be rude—"

"Kidding, Grandma." I winked at her. As I made my way to the door, someone knocked twice—two determined, even raps instead of the friendly scuffle of hits that Mrs. Walker always showered on our leaded window.

Before I disappeared into the mudroom, I shot a bemused look at Grandma and shrugged as if to say, *Who, then?*

By the time I had switched on the porch light, she was already standing with her back to me. Her hand was on the banister above the five wide steps to the ground, and her head was angled toward her car as if she wished she were back inside it. The wind was making a tangle of what little hair peeked out from beneath her raised hood. From the rigid peak of her head, her shoulders visibly slumped and pointed forlornly to her toes as if her balled-up fists concealed weights that strained every muscle along her narrow arms. Her hands were empty.

There was surrender in her bearing, and though I didn't know the cause of her defeat, she cut such a sorry silhouette backlit by the half-moon that I wanted to take her inside, listen to her story. I had no idea who she was, but the need to help welled up in me so strong that I put my hand on the door to let her in. I wanted to do for her what I couldn't do for the woman with the dark eyes. I softened my face for her and opened the door.

She turned to me slowly, and before I had time to blink, I realized that I had seen this woman before. A little ripple of surprise tore through me. The dirty jean coat, the dishwater hair, the beaten posture—the woman from the store. The Braeburn apples. I made a little noise of confusion.

She glanced up at me, and her eyes in the glare of the porch light were inexpressibly sad.

Every gasp of air in my body drained from me in what can only be called a moan.

The woman smiled. A thin, tight-lipped, careful smile. She looked at the ground. "Julia."

I was mute, though my mind exploded on her name with blinding, throbbing force. *Janice*. And then, in its wake, another word—a word that hadn't passed my lips in a very, very long time: *Mom*.

reunion

"I SHOULDN'T HAVE COME," Janice said haltingly, stealing a glance at me. She waited a moment for me to respond, but whatever she was expecting from me, I did not deliver. I just stared.

In my memory, Janice remained the eternally lovely and incomprehensibly remote woman who smiled girlishly and waved good-bye with dancing fingertips even though she knew she was abandoning her only child. She had been an ice queen—perfectly chiseled, beautiful, cold. I could remember the indistinct outline of her lavender mohair sweater and the scent in her hair when the updraft from the almost-slammed door came over me: tobacco and Suave strawberry shampoo. Her face had been fresh and unlined, hard and cool in its powdered perfection.

It was forgivable that I had not recognized her in Value Foods. The ten years since I last laid eyes on her had not been kind ones. The woman who now stood before me was not the same one who had left. A part of me recoiled from the way she tore through my memories of her and left them as mere husks of pathetic, childish illusion. I was startled to find myself sorry at the loss of my carefully preserved remembrance of a young mother—because I hadn't allowed myself the luxury of looking back, I never realized that I regarded her with anything more than a fine and well-deserved contempt. But here she was and so changed I was unable to breathe. Limp hair, lined skin, gaunt shadows where attractive curves had once been. My lungs ached. I gasped shallowly, a fish drowning in the clear, cold air.

"I'm sorry; I shouldn't have come," she said again quietly, but she daringly searched my face as she said it. She seemed surprised at what she saw there, and her lips dipped and trembled. She started down the steps backward.

When she stepped away from me, I could feel the pull in my gut. It was as if in that one small moment of realization she had sunk a part of herself deep inside me, set a hook in my being so that we were held together by a thin but indissoluble strand of what should have been. I couldn't help but move with her, fall forward to match her withdrawal so there was no more space between us than before. I didn't want to follow her; I couldn't help it.

"Julia," she breathed, again trying out her faltering voice on my name as if tasting it—savoring it slowly while I was still close enough to hear it. There was a sudden boldness in her now that she was leaving, and as she slid slow-motion down the steps, her gaze took me in almost hungrily. She examined my hair, the curve of my cheek from chin to brow, my misshapen form beneath the baggy clothes.

Almost subconsciously I pulled at the wrists of my sweatshirt and looked away from her, grateful that the bulk of the fabric hid any evidence of my condition.

When I dared to steal a glance again, I found Janice smiling at me from the bottom of the steps. Her expression was a study in regret, though I was almost sure I could find something akin to pride mingling with the water in her eyes.

She would have left then with nothing said between us save an incomplete apology and the three soft syllables of my name. I would have let her go. I would have watched her car drive away and then stumbled back into the house a very different woman than I had left it. But in the seconds of standing with my long-lost mother and feeling her draw me toward her against my will, and even desire, there was a very small and hidden part of me that knew I would mourn if she left. I *wanted* her to go. I longed for her to turn around and disappear, to sever whatever cord she had tied me with in those few moments on the porch. And yet I wanted her to stay to do nothing more than answer the question that had burned inside me for ten years: *Why?*

Footsteps in the mudroom broke the spell that had been cast over me. Though Grandma had fled my mind the moment I opened the door, I suddenly, sinkingly understood that I was not the only one who would have to deal with the advent of Janice. I was filled with a need to protect the woman who had protected me, and I swung to the door, willing Grandma back into the house with every ounce of my being. I prayed silently, wordlessly, *vehemently*.

But there was the click of the rusty handle and then: "Julia, it's freezing! What are you doing out here in the cold?"

I moved so that I filled her vision and meant to smile nonchalantly at her. I tried to say something like, "Wrong house, Grandma. I'll be inside in a minute." But my voice would not be liberated, and the heat in my eyes betrayed that there were tears waiting there instead of the composure I had hoped to convey. My face was a contortion of disbelief and pain.

Grandma hardened and brushed past me with an almost fierce defensiveness. I tried to block her way, but she gripped my arm and stepped past me, ready to confront the person who had left my eyes so desperate. I watched my grandmother turn to stone, and when she had stared for far too long without blinking, I threw a look over my shoulder at Janice. The broken woman was rooted to the spot, and from the self-loathing hang of her head, I guessed that she was pleading with the frozen earth beneath her to split and swallow her whole.

Although I half expected the moon to fall from its orbit, the porch, the encounter, was momentous for us alone. Nothing more significant happened than the rustling movement of some animal in the grove. The storm continued its slow progress, erasing stars from the sky with a cruel, black line of threatening clouds. Dots of light peppered the horizon and defined the farms of our neighbors while the families inside—comfortable and warm—went about their lives none the wiser that ours would never be the same. We were small, forgettable points of life in a world much bigger than our personal sorrows. Yet I felt the ground beneath me as if it had been created for the sole purpose of holding me up in this one moment in time.

Finally, Grandma cleared her throat and said thinly, evenly, "Hello, Janice."

Janice inclined her head and, contrary to my estimations of her, gave my grandmother a solemn, contrite nod. "Hello, Nellie," she whispered in a voice that at the very least sounded respectful. It was a little token—an offering, maybe—to begin to repay the lifetime of debt she owed her ex-mother-in-law.

I swept automatically back to Grandma and tried to read her expression. Her eyes were great brown pools in the darkness, deep and bottomless and unsearchable. I couldn't begin to discern what she was feeling. Loathing, anger, resentment? Fear possibly? Regret? Whatever she was experiencing, my infinitely long-suffering and perpetually sweet-hearted grandmother was as implacable as chiseled granite.

There were a few beats of silence and Janice shrunk even more. Grandma cut a sharp shadow in the halo of porch light, and her outline seemed to carry with it an almost tangible presence. Janice would not look up, and though I felt slightly vindicated, something in me flashed quickly with unexpected compassion. I forced the feeling deep beneath my rising anger.

The weight of the stillness compelled Janice to try to explain. She started, "I'm sorry, Nellie. I should have—"

"What are you doing here?" Grandma interrupted. While her words were harsh, her voice was surprisingly not.

Janice looked taken aback. "Well, I . . . I just thought . . ." She stumbled painfully over her words. Glancing at me and then back to

Grandma before returning her attention to her feet, she tried again. "I just wanted to see Julia," she confessed almost inaudibly. "I saw her in the grocery store and—"

"You knew it was me?" I croaked. My unused voice sounded hollow to me and very, very far away.

Janice tore her gaze from the ground to square me in her vision and bravely admitted, "Not at first." She addressed me alone, leaving Grandma outside the borders of her confession as though she knew I would soften to her pleas.

I hardened my face for her, tried to prove I could not be so easily won.

"I suspected it was you," she continued, "so I came back a few times and watched you when you weren't looking. I followed you home once or twice."

A shudder passed through me—a shiver of pure shock—at the realization that I had been spied on without my knowledge. Janice had sought me out, followed and tracked me as though I were some rare, exotic bird and she was trying to catch a glimpse. My face warmed even as my skin quivered. *Why? Why now, after all these years?*

I couldn't help but gape at the woman who had once been my mother. I remembered every cold and callous word. I remembered how she took up space in our home without ever actually being there for us. I remembered the way the engine of her car revved as she drove away for the very last time. I wanted to cling to those things. I wanted to hate her.

But now, amid the disgust, the disillusionment, all the evidence of her guilt, there was something much like hope that threatened to rise to the surface. Somewhere in the dark recesses of my mind there was a preserved moment that inched its way into my consciousness. I remembered a forgotten morning.

A stolen hour.

I couldn't have been much older than five when I crawled into bed with Janice one lazy summer morning. For some reason, we were alone in the house—or at least alone in the closet-size master bedroom—and she was still mostly asleep in her overblanketed and sagging bed. One arm was draped thoughtlessly over her eyes to block out the sunrise streaming in through the window. Her skin looked soft and the freckles on her forearm were little sprinklings of color. I remembered standing by the bed and watching the yellow light make her hair glow. And then, because she was asleep and because I wanted to be close to her, I carefully peeled back the smooth white sheet and climbed in beside her.

Just thinking of it made my heart thump in a frantic echo of what it must have done all those years ago. I breathed shallowly, aware of the steam from my slightly parted lips, and was afraid for the child I had been. But on that sunny morning, I had been cautious. I had moved slowly. She hadn't stirred when I curled myself beside her. I recalled pulling my knees up to my chest and lying there with my back pressed lightly against her cool arm. I listened to her sigh in her sleep.

When she rolled over, I squeezed my eyes shut, pretended to be asleep as I waited for the groggy reprimand. But instead of hearing annoyance in her voice, I felt her arm slide around me. She curved herself along the length of my child body and rested her cheek against my head. She murmured something about the smell of my hair, then tightened her grip so that I was enveloped by her.

She was probably sleeping. It had most likely been pure instinct—an impulse born of thousands of years of genetic code—not an intentional act of tenderness.

But I remembered it.

And it made me illogically, uncontrollably angry.

Though it had been silent between us for only a moment or two, I longed to fill the empty space with ruthless words. I instantly distrusted her motives; it struck me that she had not yet explained why she was here at all. She probably needed money or a place to stay—or both. The thought made me sick. Any small hope I had, any childish flame of desire for a present, loving mother, was extinguished.

We stood, a trio of women like the points of a misshapen triangle, and I could feel the pull in each direction. It was an impossible situation. Janice was right; she never should have come. There was nothing that could possibly be said to erase the past ten years and make everything okay for either generation. Even if my estranged so-called mom could explain away her abandonment of me, there was still the issue of my father, her husband, Grandma's only son. Never mind the years without contact, the offensive indifference to my father's death, and her sudden, seemingly self-indulgent appearance at the least likely time. It was all too much. Nothing could fix what had been broken here.

"You need to leave, Janice." I tried to say the words unemotionally, but my voice betrayed the depth of my feelings.

Janice looked as if I had slapped her.

"Julia," Grandma said, and I was stunned to hear the firmness in her voice, "I think we need to—"

"No, Nellie," Janice cut in. "She's right. I'm going. I apologize for coming. I should have . . . I should have called . . . or . . ." She trailed off, raising her hands in supplication or maybe in defeat. I felt no sympathy for her.

Janice didn't turn as she left but continued to recede slowly as if unable to tear her gaze away from me until the absolute last possible minute. It made me queasy. I spared her a sappy good-bye and turned my back on her, sweeping past Grandma so I could retreat into the sanctuary of the house. But then two things happened at once and my refuge was deferred—if not forever destroyed.

First, Grandma grabbed my arm and held on with all the jurisdiction of an infuriated parent. I would have been stunned but for the second thing that happened: Janice's car door opened and a little voice called from inside, "Hey, I'm hungry!"

When I turned, he was standing in the doorframe of the car, gripping the top ledge of the window with mitten-clad hands. I could make out glossy brown hair beneath his rainbow stocking cap and matching dark eyes behind wire-rimmed glasses. They were slightly crooked on his petite, sloped nose. He brought his mitten to his face and pushed the glasses up, wrinkling his nose in the process and sniffling. His eyes seemed maybe a bit older, but his small stature disclosed that he could not have been a day over five.

Grandma and I surveyed him guardedly from the porch, still as though we had been frozen solid by the vicious wind. Suddenly I felt it—the wind. It was bitingly cold and growing in ferocity even as we watched the boy. Grandma let her hand drop, and I wrapped my arms around myself.

Janice had forgotten me. She was holding the child in her eyes with a look so tender and loving that I knew exactly what his next word would be.

"Mommy, are you almost done? I'm hungry."

I didn't even blink.

undone

HE WAS A LITTLE slip of a thing with cowlicks at the temples and glasses that were too big for his face. His skin was a creamy shade of milk chocolate, and his big brown eyes were nothing like my father's or grandmother's—they were exotic, lined with charcoal, densely lashed. At first I thought I had made a mistake. He was not my half brother. But then Janice gripped him under the arms and lifted him lightly to the ground. She pulled him beside her and wrapped herself around him so that only his furrowed brow peeked above her puffy coat. "I'd like you to meet my son," she said, her voice a curious mixture of reticence and pride.

"Mom, I can't breathe!" the boy yelled, pushing her arms off and jumping a pace away.

I can't either, I thought.

Grandma swallowed hard beside me. I reached for her blindly, hoping that facing him together would be easier than facing him alone. If he was my half brother, was he her half grandson? It changed the shape of the entire world. She was only a few feet away from me, but when I should have brushed up against her side, Grandma was gone. She had already taken a step toward the boy. I nearly stumbled over my own feet because I realized what she was doing. I had seen her do it a thousand times before.

Maybe it was because she had been a child immigrant—a little girl who spoke only Dutch in an English-speaking school, in a community that hadn't seen a family fresh off the boat for over a generation. Maybe it was because she had lived most of her hard life on the unpredictable prairie. Or maybe it was because she had lost much in her seventy-seven years. Whatever the reason, Grandma was an unequaled pro in the art of maintenance. When a situation threatened to tip off its axis and spin wildly out of control, Grandma laid aside her own feelings and best interests and simply *preserved*. She doled out great measures of peacekeeping control. She cooked or cleaned or talked, pushing through the crisis as if it were nothing out of the ordinary—nothing that couldn't be fixed with a mug of steaming coffee or a slice of freshly baked pie.

She would have that set look in her eye now. That determined, commanding, resolute look.

It hit me suddenly that she was going to ask them to come inside. She saw a child with a need and she could meet that need, even if there was nothing else she could do to fix the situation. Even if Janice was the woman she had to allow into her house to do it.

I took a quick, panicked stride after her and grasped at her sweater, clutching only displaced air as she started heavily down the steps. It looked painful for her to walk, but her back was straight and even, her stride steady.

Ignoring Janice entirely, she approached the child and said, "Are you hungry, honey?"

There is nothing like the gentle sound of a grandmother's voice, and he nodded at her with eyes so great and thankful that it was impossible not to be taken in. He was responding to her as though they were old friends. Warmly, he started, "I had pancakes at the café this morning for breakfast, but then—"

"Simon," Janice interrupted, "please, they don't need a play-by-play."

Grandma fixed her daughter-in-law with a brief, impervious stare. She turned back to the boy. "Simon?" she asked kindly.

He nodded almost shyly, peeking at her from beneath the sliding silver rims as though he knew she was someone with whom he wanted to be close.

Grandma's face melted when she smiled at him. "Simon, would you like to have supper with us?"

He glanced at his mom but looked away before he could see her shake her head. "Yes, thank you," he said politely, and without a moment's hesitation, he followed Grandma up the stairs. "Hey," he added guilelessly, as though he had just noticed, "what happened to your foot?"

"I broke my ankle," Grandma said conspiratorially. "I'll tell you all about it inside."

I didn't dare to stop her, or even to touch her, but when she was close enough, I whispered, *"Grandma."* My voice conveyed far more than that one word, and I didn't doubt that she heard my every fear and worry loud and clear. There was no way she could mistake the torment in my tone.

But she didn't look at me. "It can't be undone" was all she whispered back, though her words were thick and uncharacteristically gruff.

I watched her go, dumbstruck, and couldn't help but wonder if she even wanted it undone.

Grandma yanked open the screen door with a little too much force and pushed the storm door with her hip. Standing back to hold the screen open for Simon, she bowed her head and motioned him inside, every inch the obsequious porter with a smile that was a close approximation of genuine.

He tripped happily through the door, oblivious to the angles of emotion surrounding him. I watched him pull his stocking cap off with relish and remembered that Janice's car had not been on. He was probably half-frozen.

When I looked away, Grandma was waving me inside with such intent that it would have been distinctly unwise for me to do anything but comply. The house was almost stiflingly warm after braving the bitterness of the porch, and Simon had already stripped off his coat and was working on his shoes. The laces were in a wide double knot, and seeing his small fingers struggle with the graying cloth made me somehow dizzy. I froze on the threshold, paralyzed by the knowledge of who he was and my own inability to understand or even try to hold that truth in my mind. I struggled for air, turned back to the door, and found Janice framed darkly in the rectangle of windswept night.

"Come on, Janice," Grandma said. She waited as the woman stepped toward the house.

I fell past Simon into the kitchen, beyond feeling, mercifully numb. The smell of nasi goreng made me nearly reel with nausea, but I dutifully moved in the direction of the cupboards to set the table for two extra mouths. It was something that had not been done much in this house for more years than I cared to remember, and though I should have been happy to include guests around our table, I was anything but.

"I can help," Simon said unexpectedly. There was a ring of childish self-importance in his voice when he added, "I'm a good helper."

"Mm-hmm . . . ," I mumbled, averting my eyes from his sweet face. I heard rather than saw him approach me, and I glanced his way only when I felt him tug the plates from my white-knuckled hands.

"What's your name?" he asked, pulling the dishes to his chest.

I stole a glance at his arms and saw stout little fingers peeking around the blue delft rim of Grandma's ancient dinnerware. "Julia," I muttered absently, unable to tear myself away from the eight digits curled upward in some sort of accidental supplication. I was close enough to touch him. I could have reached out a finger and stroked the smooth, brown skin of his hands. His fingernails were half-moons, marred only by ragged white edges—evidence that he bit them. Something we had in common.

"That's a very nice name," he said and the hands disappeared. I looked up to watch the back of his head as he drew away from me. He nodded curtly and laid a plate on the table with an air of satisfaction. "A nice name," he repeated, as though my name required his approval.

For a moment, I almost grinned at him because I was filled with the certainty that there was no way under heaven he was Janice's child. She had to have kidnapped him, stolen him from some sitcom family that functioned according to the textbook and said things like "I love you" every single day. But even as the thought tried to take root, it wilted. He was hers and I knew it. It almost killed me.

"Thank you," I managed after a moment. "I like your name, too."

"Simon Eli Wentwood," he said proudly, situating the last dinner plate in front of an empty chair so it was perfectly centered. I wasn't surprised to hear that he bore Janice's maiden name. He continued, "I'm named after my dad and my grandpa, but I don't know my dad—he died when I was little. Grandpa, though—he sends me cards sometimes!"

"What are you talking about, Simon?" Janice's voice crept into the kitchen followed immediately by the rest of her. The only thing whiter than her face was the gallon of milk I was bringing to the table.

"Nothin' much," Simon confessed. "Hey, did you know her name is Julia?" He smiled between the two of us and began to make introductions. "Julia, this is my mom. Her name is Janice."

Oh, dear Lord, my soul exhaled. *He has no idea.*

Grandma's face was flint when she swept into the kitchen. She commanded the room, quashing our conversation and moving to the stove so she could stir the simmering pot of rice. Lifting the lid with a bit more than her usual flourish, she let a cloud of fragrant steam into the kitchen and muttered appreciatively as though everything was exactly as planned. "Do you like Chinese food?" she asked cheerfully, directing the question at Simon.

He wrinkled his nose, slipping into a chair. He had to perch on the very edge to rest his tiptoes on the linoleum floor. "Only fried rice," he stated. "Once I tried some orange chicken, and it almost made me throw up."

"Sweet-and-sour chicken," Janice clarified quietly. She glanced at me awkwardly and sank into the nearest chair as if she had been reprimanded.

Grandma struck the wooden spoon on the edge of the pot with a few hard cracks. "Good," she said firmly. "You'll like this, then, Simon, because it is nothing like sweet-and-sour chicken and quite a bit like fried rice. There are eggs in it and everything."

"If I don't like it, do you have PB and J?" Simon gave up on trying to be the big boy and slid onto his chair so that his feet dangled. He absently kicked his heels against the beveled legs. "I like PB and J, and most people have it."

"PB and J?" Grandma asked.

"Simon!" Janice chided.

"Peanut butter and jelly," I explained.

Both women blushed. "Well," Grandma said noncommittally, "you have to try this first."

I finished setting the table as Grandma approached with the pot of steaming rice. Avoiding her gaze, I placed a trivet for her and backed away. My chair was directly across from Janice, and I was excruciatingly aware of her proximity as I took my seat. I blinked in her direction and was unsettled to find her looking at me.

She mouthed, *I'm sorry.* It could have meant anything. She could have been apologizing for horning in on our supper for two. Or maybe she wanted forgiveness for something more. I looked away.

"It smells okay," Simon commented, sniffing the air. He took his dish and reached for the ladle, ready to scoop his plate full. So he wasn't perfect after all.

"Hang on," Grandma alerted him, reaching across the table and putting her hand over his. "We pray before we eat in my house."

"Oh," Simon replied innocently. "Okay." He dropped the spoon.

I was thankful then that we had never been the kind of family to hold hands when we prayed. The Walkers were hand holders, and at every meal—even an impromptu lunch of tomato soup and grilled cheese—we reached beside ourselves to grasp the hands of our neighbors, no matter who they were. When I was young and in love with Thomas, nothing made my heart beat harder than finding myself next to him at a meal, my clammy hand held tight in his. But most of the time, it just felt strange to me. I never knew if my hand was supposed to be on the top or the bottom or how I should respond if someone gave me a little squeeze at the end of the prayer. It was unnecessarily intimate. I thought about Simon's small hands and chewed fingernails and was grateful that I could clasp my fingers tight in my own lap. I dropped my head so I didn't have to watch them fumble around uncomfortably.

There was silence for a moment, a little shuffling, and then

Grandma began softly. "We thank You, Lord, for this day. For its blessings, its trials, and Your hand in it all. We pray now that You will bless this food to our bodies. Bless us in this night, in all . . . in all we . . . in . . ." She stopped. "Amen."

I echoed her in an inaudible whisper. At first we didn't talk about much—at least, nothing of importance. Although I half expected it all to come out in a torrent of things unsaid and feelings unearthed, we all kept our heads and spoke in placid tones about everyday things. We were polite strangers excelling in the art of small talk as though we had nothing more significant to say to one another.

Simon regaled us with stories of his exploits on the soccer field, though I doubted he often made contact with the ball much less took part in epic battles between the teams in the peewee league of the small town he said they were from. He breezed over the name of the town, and when I asked him to repeat it, Janice cut in and explained that it was a very tiny place near Chicago—we would surely have never heard of it. I just shrugged and let it go. We were, after all, being civilized.

Simon liked Grandma's Dutch-Indonesian, but he ate around the pickles and left a neat little pile of green on the table beside his plate. I watched him periodically make sure Janice wasn't looking and then slowly ease a piece of diced pickle over the edge, under the rim, and out of sight. All he had to do was offer to clear the dishes and slide the pickles into his hand for deposit in the garbage on his way to the sink. A foolproof plan. It was hard not to smile wryly; I clearly remembered doing the exact same thing.

Grandma studied Simon as he ate and looked very little at Janice or me. I could see the strain in her profile and the plastic smile that was beginning to get brittle. More than once, I touched her foot lightly under the table and tapped it comfortingly—a reminder that it would all be over soon and an olive branch to let her know that I wasn't about to hold a grudge. She had done the only thing she knew to do; who was I to blame her? Besides, the meal was almost over and then Janice could disappear from our lives for another decade. Maybe more. We could go back to forgetting. We could pretend there was no Simon.

Toward the end of the meal, it was Simon who mentioned his dad in a voice filled with the naive pride of someone who had not been told the entire truth. He clearly adored his allegedly deceased father, and he sat up straighter in his seat as though he was entreating us to ask him more.

Janice looked uncomfortable as her son beamed unreservedly. She obviously did not want her former lover to be a part of our conversation.

"My dad was a . . ." Simon looked confused for a moment and then quickly turned to his mother. "What's that word again? What did Dad do?"

Janice smiled a narrow, placating smile. "Nothing, honey; they don't want to hear about your dad right now."

"Yes, they do!" he insisted, and because I was gripped with a sort of morbid curiosity, I was glad he did. He ignored his mother and turned back to Grandma and me. "He built big buildings," Simon bragged, sweeping his arms up over his head. "Really big ones—like the giant ones in Chicago. But he didn't *work* on them. He *thought* of them. He . . ." Simon struggled for the right word. "He . . . *drawed* them." The little boy grinned, triumphant.

"He was an architect?" I suggested.

"Yes!" Frowning at Janice, he added, "See, I told you they were interested."

She dragged her fork across her plate, displacing more rice as though she could hide the fact that she had barely eaten a bite.

"That's very interesting," I told Simon, to fill the silence. He positively glowed. Then, though I hadn't planned on saying it—and as the words were escaping my mouth, I found them outrageously rude—I asked, "Was your dad from Chicago, Simon?"

Grandma's heel bounced off the bridge of my foot in shock and warning. I tried not to cringe.

But Simon didn't realize anything was amiss. "No, he was from *Casablanca*." He said the word slowly, carefully, as though he had practiced it with loving concentration many times before.

"Simon is half-Spanish," Janice interjected tiredly.

I couldn't help gawking at her. "Janice," I said evenly, "Casablanca is in Morocco. You know, the country in northern Africa? He's half-*Moroccan*."

Her face flushed an unbecoming pink from the apples of her cheeks to the very tips of her ears, but she didn't say a word.

All Simon said was, "Cool, *Morocco*." He seemed to like the way it rolled off his tongue. But there was a hint of a lisp left over from toddler years in his young voice, and it came out sounding slightly like *Mowocco*. He practiced it again.

I was about to ask more when Janice saw fit to change the conversation before it became far too personal. "We really lead a very boring life," she admitted. "Not much to tell."

Grandma and I both nodded in sync, effectively blocked from

pursuing that particular vein. I focused on my plate and tried to phrase the questions I was longing to ask. *Why are you here? What are you doing in Mason? Why did you show up on our doorstep? When are you leaving?* Each variation burned in my throat and refused to pass my lips.

But Janice had been practicing her own careful inquiry, and she cautiously threw out a showstopper. "What are you up to these days, Julia?"

It was my turn to blush. Obviously I worked at Value Foods, but the question implied much more. She knew I was out of high school; she wanted to know if I was in college, if I had a significant other, if my life was advancing through the official and approved stages of young adulthood.

"I work at Value Foods right now," I answered with what I hoped was dignity. "I plan to go back to school in the fall. Or maybe next year." The last part was a lie. I hadn't given school a second thought since I drove away from Brighton over three months ago. It was hard to think about anything beyond the baby right now, and though I hated to admit it, I couldn't be sure that once I was a mother I would have the time or money to ever return. It was a sobering thought. I felt Grandma staring at me, thinking the same things I was. Maybe she was mourning for me.

"Julia went to Brighton for a semester and took engineering," Grandma offered, asserting my intelligence and trying to bolster my self-worth a little. I immediately wished that she had said nothing at all.

But Janice bit. "Really?" Her voice was peculiarly soft. "You always were a smart girl. . . ."

My head jerked up at the unexpected praise, but Janice had a faraway look in her eyes. I exhaled slowly, grateful that the topic was going to be dropped, and self-consciously got up to start clearing the table. I was capping the milk when Janice stopped me in my tracks by asking the question I feared.

"Why did you drop out, Julia?"

It shouldn't have been a difficult thing to say. I mean, Janice had obviously been in my position more than once. And yet, admitting to her that I had made the exact same mistake she had made was somehow excruciating. I couldn't help feeling that it lessened my ability to be angry with her and gave us something in common that I didn't want to acknowledge. It stripped me of my identity and reduced me to little more than the object, and now subject, of generational sin—a fallen child of a fallen mother, capable of doing nothing more than what had already been done to me. It was cyclic and shameful. It made me feel unworthy. Small.

I shrunk, knowing that I would have to tell her.

Grandma broke in and tried to save me. "Julia is taking a little time off, Janice. She's working a few things out." It wasn't an outright lie, but it wasn't entirely honest, and I was surprised that my legalistic grandmother was bending the truth to salvage a shred of my dignity. The selfless gesture made me want to lay a kiss on the top of her silver head. It also made me achingly aware that I could not let her compromise any of her values for me. She had already given enough.

My frustration quickly found a target in Janice and began bringing up years of long-buried anger before I had any opportunity to accept that she wasn't the only person to blame on this bewildering night. All I could think was that it wasn't fair for Janice to believe she could march back into our lives and throw everything off the delicate balance we had worked so hard to restore. It wasn't fair that she sat at our table like a treasured guest instead of the cowardly deserter she was. It wasn't fair that she waltzed up to our door with my unheard-of half brother and expected to smooth things over without the years of penance and petition she deserved. It wasn't fair that she had come at all. I had been fine without her. The anger inside me that had been pushed down to make room for the anesthesia I needed to endure the night was rising furiously to the surface—a hot, roiling blast of self-righteous wind. It was time for her to leave my house.

"Actually, Janice . . ." I swallowed hard, looking her square in the eye. "I'm taking time off because I'm pregnant." The words were easier to say than I had expected. I lifted my chin indignantly, an act of defense despite the fact that she hadn't yet had a chance to respond. I was ready to fight.

Janice regarded me uncomprehendingly, her eyes blinking rhythmically as though gathering the information bit by tiny bit. Finally she muttered, "Excuse me?" Her mouth was gaping slightly in what seemed to be disbelief. "But are you married? engaged?" It was a blunt thing to ask, though I had expected as much. Her eyes darted to my left hand and registered a slim, bare ring finger. No sparkling solitaire, no simple gold band.

"Neither were you," I asserted bitterly. It was liberating to finally confront her, my heart pounding an impossible drumbeat in my throat. I knew I was baiting her. I knew I was being childish and immature, drawing her out systematically and waiting for an opportunity to say the things I had longed to say for years. *Ten* years to be exact. I was brilliant in my wrath.

She winced and slid her chair back a little. The legs screeched on the linoleum floor, and she jumped as if someone had struck her. "Julia, I . . . I'm just surprised, I guess."

"What are you basing that on? What on earth do you think you know about me?"

Grandma was distraught, trying desperately to get my attention, but I ignored her in my fury.

Janice was still scrambling. "I'm not trying to say anything about you—"

I rolled my eyes. "There's nothing you *could* say. It's been over ten years. What gives you the right to march in here and accuse me?"

"I'm not accusing. I just . . ." Janice trailed off hopelessly, studied her hands in her lap, and then suddenly looked back at me almost pleadingly as though she simply couldn't help herself. "But the father—"

"Parker is—the father is gone," I said acidly, "though you wouldn't know anything about that, would you? Dad actually stuck around, tried to take care of—"

"*Julia,*" Grandma broke in, catching my hand and holding it tight.

"Not now," Janice whispered. Her voice was choked and wretched.

"Did you know my dad?" Simon asked incredulously.

I clung to Grandma's wrinkled fingers, glared at Janice, tried to ignore Simon. I hated her; oh, I hated her. She was a pathetic excuse for a mother, and she had no right to try to force her way back into my life. And though her eyes were huge and hurting, I was about to tell her exactly that when Simon spoke and stilled my storm with a voice that bordered on ecstatic.

"Hey, Mom, I think Julia knew Dad!"

My head throbbed as I shook it. Just like that, I was spent, my rage poured out in some vile offering with nothing left to show for my outburst but the quiet horror in Janice's eyes and the expectant hope in Simon's. I couldn't even bring myself to look at Grandma; I knew her disappointment in me would be the hardest to face. I closed my eyes to block them all out. But he was waiting for me to say something. "No, Simon, I'm sorry. I didn't know your dad," I said wearily.

"You didn't?" he asked, visibly disappointed.

"No." I turned to him and tried to make my trembling lips curl in a smile. "It's just that your mom once knew *my* dad."

The little boy, my half brother, considered me for a moment. "Wow, Julia," he breathed happily. "That makes you almost like family!"

The room went still.

I didn't look at him when I gathered myself enough to address Janice. "I think it's time for you to leave."

"Me too," she agreed, slipping out of her chair. "Come, Simon; time to go." She reached for her son and gripped his shoulder tenderly. "Thank Mrs. DeSmit for the nice meal, please."

"Thank you, Mrs. DeSmit," Simon said, swiveling his head between the women towering over him. Though he didn't understand it, he knew that something bad had happened, and he kept shooting me looks that implored me to smooth things over before they left and were never invited back again. I turned my attention to the table.

"You're welcome, Simon," Grandma said, and her composure—or utter disbelief of all that had happened under her roof—was evident in the flat line of her voice. She tucked Simon into a brief hug, but I was thankful that she didn't tack on her usual nicety: *You can come to my house anytime.*

A dim flicker of worry for Simon lit up my consciousness, but mostly I was sickened to think of what Grandma would have to say to me when they were gone. And though I tried to hold my hurts like self-righteous badges to my bursting chest, I knew I would deserve whatever castigation she saw fit to share. I had almost seen the lines around Janice's mouth deepen with my malicious words. It made my skin feel too tight to know that I had done that to a person. Grandma was a gracious hostess and propped the door to the mudroom open so she could fill the chillingly thin air with soothing monologue. I doubted Janice heard any of it. Cleaning the kitchen occupied my hands as my estranged family buttoned up their coats and laced their shoes, and because it hurt to hear her, I ignored the murmur of Grandma's voice too. Only when Simon poked his head back into the kitchen and waved solemnly at me did I manage a halfhearted good-bye.

"Bye, Julia," he called. "It was very nice to meet you." His voice held little of the energy it had boasted before.

"Nice to meet you, too," I parroted. "Have a safe trip back to Illinois."

I should have expected it. The natural disaster that was posing as our evening should have alerted me to the fact that this was no small thing. This visit—these torturous moments with Janice close enough to touch—was the beginning of something much bigger. And in some ways I knew it the instant I realized who she was on the porch. But instead, it was the split-second pause when Simon should have said *thank you* that warned me my life would never be the same.

"Actually, Julia—" *akshually*—"we're not going back to Illinois."

Strangely, when the world implodes before you, it doesn't make a sound.

surrender

JANICE AND SIMON LEFT, but nothing went back to the way it had been. I had hoped that some semblance of normalcy could be achieved after a few days of trying to forget that they had ever taken up space in our already overcomplicated home. Pretending was a perfectly acceptable method of dealing as far as I was concerned, and at first I thought Grandma was also willing to leave that night buried somewhere deep and distant—somewhere we would never have to come across it again. But while I first mistook her silence for denial, I soon learned that the stillness behind our walls was actually directed at me.

My relationship with Grandma had always been exceptionally, almost unnaturally, good. I could count on one hand the times that she had ever been notably angry at me—times when I had willfully and often stupidly done things I had no business doing. It was impossible to forget the frantic, furious look in her eye when she caught me trying to nail a piece of plywood to the old propane tank out back. The monstrous, white-bellied, red-capped cylinder was my ship; I had only wanted to christen it with the appropriate name: the SS *Julia*.

Or the time I burned the few letters that my father had penned me before he died. "You will regret this for the rest of your life, Julia," she had said with quiet passion. I was hurting, incensed by the world and burning up inside, and it was a rash act of intention—I wrongfully believed that I could erase him. Her few words extinguished me instantly, and she left me to sob it out, only to return and fold me in her arms just before I began to believe I was hopelessly alone.

But as far back as I could remember, Grandma had never been upset enough with me to let her disappointment fester for more than a few hours. Until now.

It wasn't hard to understand that she thought I had made an enormous, potentially life-altering mistake. For days I allowed my own resentment of Janice to build a wall between Grandma and me. I hardened my heart. And though at first I counted my so-called mother forgotten, it wasn't long before I realized that I could no sooner forget Janice and Simon than I could ignore the unborn child that crouched at the corners of my every thought, threatening to derail any contemplation or conversation I embarked on. They were a part of us, Simon and Janice, whether we wanted them to be or not. If we couldn't forget, we would have to forge on.

"Don't be mad at me," I pleaded one day as I drove Grandma to a doctor's appointment. Her ankle was healing slowly, maybe too slowly, and Dr. Morales had squeezed her in on a Friday morning when the clinic was usually reserved for appointments that had been booked weeks ago and last-minute maladies that could not wait until Monday. Grandma was hunched over in the passenger seat, her wrist on the armrest of the door and her hand laced through the molded plastic handle. She could have been bracing herself for another disappointing diagnosis, but it felt like she was trying to get as far away from me as possible. The very thought made my throat tight.

I had tried to draw her out many different times over the days since Janice and Simon had walked into, and out of, our lives. But I had always been met with disappointed looks and the sorrowful downturn of her usually smiling and beautiful mouth. Granted, I had never tried to broach the one topic that was the only thing we really had to talk about. Maybe she was waiting for me to say something that mattered.

At any rate, we seemed to have lost the ability to talk about anything but the most trivial and mundane things. Other than the necessary exchanges of everyday life—*Do you want one egg for breakfast or two? What time will you be home tonight? I have a doctor's appointment tomorrow at nine*—we had barely said a word to each other. Not that we were necessarily angry or avoiding each other; we were simply too consumed with the effort of remembering to breathe to expend any energy on encouraging the other person to inhale and exhale.

She prayed a lot. I could tell by the distracted look in her eyes and the almost indiscernible movement of her lips. She also creased the pages of her Bible often, and if she found answers written there, she didn't share them with me. But then, I didn't ask.

Sometimes I wondered if Grandma had lost her point of reference when she gave me her Bible and if she was slowly learning to work with a new compass. To me, the crinkled pages of her treasured book were a seemingly random collection of charts and maps and directions in a language that I was only just beginning to understand. To Grandma, her Bible was as familiar as the lines on the back of her hand. I felt guilty every time I held her sacred book and found myself unable to fully appreciate the power at my fingertips.

When I spoke in the warm car, she was probably engrossed in a dialogue with God—the God I was fumblingly trying to know and seemingly failing at miserably—and her response was slow in coming and mildly confused. "Mad?" she asked absently, glancing sidelong at me. "I'm not mad at you."

"You have to be," I argued, sounding more despondent than I had hoped to come across. "We've hardly spoken in days."

She sighed, and I turned my eyes from the road to regard her as she stared out the windshield. We had just entered the outskirts of town, and I was relieved to know that there was no way we would have time for this conversation. I had wanted to bring up the topic with her, but I didn't feel prepared to resolve it, and I was grateful that she certainly didn't seem to be jumping at the chance to dive headfirst into the deep end either.

"There's a lot to say, Julia," she said cautiously. "Maybe I don't know where to begin. Maybe I don't know *how* to begin."

I bit my lip for a moment. "Fair enough."

"Are you ready to talk about it now?" Grandma asked. "Are you ready to at least say her name or even try to process what happened?"

It was my turn to sigh. "We have to, don't we?"

"Yes, we do."

I knew what I had to do and I measured my words, weighing each syllable and practicing brief phrases in my mind. "Grandma," I finally ventured, "I am so sorry. I know I—"

"You don't have to apologize to me." Grandma brought me up abruptly before I could launch into my well-rehearsed appeal for forgiveness. "You have to apologize to Janice. You and I have enough to deal with without throwing unnecessary apologies into the mix."

I hadn't expected that. I wanted *her* forgiveness, not Janice's. Besides, Janice needed *my* forgiveness, not the other way around. I longed to say as much. All at once I found the car stifling, but I resisted the urge to crack my window open and feel the healing breath of icy wind on my face. The storm that had been brewing the night of Janice's arrival had dropped a mere three inches of snow but plunged temperatures well below freezing. Fresh air was in short supply as it was simply too painful to wrap my lungs around the biting breeze. I ran from my car to Value Foods, back to my car, and home. But suddenly, arctic or not, I yearned to gulp a few splintering mouthfuls.

Hiding my inability to speak by focusing on making a left turn across traffic into the parking lot of Dr. Morales's clinic, I was both disappointed and relieved. Now that Grandma and I were finally talking, I didn't want to interrupt the steady trickle of words that, if left to flow, I was sure would increase into a torrent of all the pent-up things we had wanted to say in the days gone by. And yet they were hard things to say—and even harder to hear. I drove slowly to an empty space near the door and put the car into park, but I didn't kill the engine. I made no effort to move and neither did she. We were effectively trapped, though the doors were unlocked.

"What do we have to deal with?" I managed after a broken moment of staring at the brown brick exterior of the Mason Medical Clinic.

Grandma reached out to touch my leg and let her fingers rest above my knee. I liked it that she had bridged the space between us. "Why do you think Janice came?" she asked gently.

I had asked myself that question dozens, maybe hundreds, of times since Janice and Simon had swept out of our driveway, but I had not yet come up with an answer. Curiosity? Instinct? Sheer stupidity? She had nowhere else to go? Grandma had not seen her ex-daughter-in-law mouth an apology to me across the table, and I didn't mention it. I couldn't believe that Janice had come to make amends. I said nothing.

Grandma changed her tactic. "Where are they now?"

I had wondered myself. "Simon said they weren't going back to Illinois."

"Janice said they were staying around here for a while," Grandma confirmed.

"Why?" I blurted out, shutting off the car with an angry flick of my wrist.

"I don't know. But is this the way you want it to end? What if they leave and it's another ten years before you see them? What if you never see them again? You've already lost one parent."

My eyebrows arched in disbelief. "I've already lost *two* parents." I stuck two fingers in the air for emphasis, and though I wasn't angry at Grandma, she looked taken aback. But I couldn't stop. "Janice walked out of my life years ago, and her sudden appearance on our doorstep doesn't automatically make her my mother again. She's the name on my birth certificate, nothing more."

Grandma opened her mouth and then just as quickly closed it. She looked away from me and considered for a moment before she quietly said, "But, Julia, honey, Simon is your *brother*."

It was a loaded word and she knew it. From the time I was old enough to realize that my friends were the proud big brothers and sisters of chubby, babbling siblings, I had wanted one of my own. I had pestered Dad and Janice endlessly, begging for a little addition to our family that I could mother and boss and ignore. And when I was older and began to feel the solitariness of a home where mine was the only young voice, I redoubled my efforts, offering to care for the child as if this imaginary little person were a puppy that I could periodically feed and water and keep out of my parents' hair. When Janice left and all hope was lost, I took a babysitting class and pretended the neighbors' kids were not just the pests who lived down the road. Even now, Jacob and Simon, Emily and Maggie were more than friends to me. I couldn't help smiling wryly when I thought of Simon Walker, the blond-haired, football-loving early teen I had known and loved for years, and the Simon I had just met. One I considered my brother. The other actually was.

Brother. The word hung in the silence of the car and made the hum of the wind against the doors somehow malevolent. "I don't know what to do," I whispered and was horrified to feel a tear spill down my cheek and drip off my chin. "Stupid hormones!" I sniffed, frustrated. "I'm not a crier—you know I'm not. It's these hormones. My hair is practically too thick to fit into a ponytail, I'm hungry all the time, I get headaches from smells I didn't even notice before, and I cry at the drop of a hat!" Irritably, hastily, I wiped the salty streak with the palm of my hand. The wetness felt cool in the steadily dropping temperature of the still car.

"I know," Grandma consoled. She patted my leg.

"What do we do now?" I asked hesitantly, wanting to move forward but afraid to hear the answer.

"I don't know," Grandma admitted again, and it was more than a little unsettling to realize that she had very few answers and more likely just as many questions as I did. "But we could start by finding them. Janice said they were 'sticking around.' They couldn't have gone too far."

"Okay" was all I said.

We waited for a long time in the doctor's office—a preteen boy with what seemed like an extra joint in his forearm and a mechanic with black, greasy hands that were smeared in drying blood took precedence over a little old lady with her foot snugly held in a black orthopedic boot.

Though I felt conspicuous in the doctor's office, I was grateful that I had dressed in my work clothes first thing in the morning as it was uncertain whether or not we would make it home before my shift. But when Dr. Morales saw me with my Value Foods uniform on, he reminded me for the tenth time at least that being on my legs for such long stretches throughout my pregnancy would surely result in varicose veins. I groaned inwardly and glanced at the door to make sure it was firmly shut. I knew I wouldn't be able to hide my condition much longer, but it drove me crazy to hear my doctor mention it so casually, so dispassionately. Only a handful of people knew about my pregnancy, and I wanted to be the one to decide when the rest of the world could learn of my secret. Besides, what did I care about varicose veins? I didn't even know what they were.

Grandma's fracture seemed to be healing okay, and Dr. Morales gave her permission to drive—something she hadn't done in a few weeks. I had wondered at his instructions the first time we visited his office as the affected ankle was her left one and her car was an automatic. She didn't need her left foot to drive anyway. But Dr. Morales had been Grandma's physician for over twenty years, and she never questioned his advice or directives even if they were hard to follow. Not driving had been very difficult for her, and the moment we stepped out of the office, she held her hand out for the keys, smiling at me a little impishly.

I felt like a bit of an idiot when she drove right up to the door of Value Foods and enthusiastically waved me out. Just as we pulled up, Michael, who was even more good-looking than Alicia had implied, stepped out of the double doors pushing a cartload of shopping bags for an elderly gentleman and his grumpy-faced wife. When he saw me being dropped off for work by my grandmother, he grinned widely and winked. I raised my eyebrows helplessly and hoped that I looked nonchalant.

My shift at Value Foods started at eleven, just in time for the noon rush. In preparation for the weekend ahead, it seemed the whole town decided to get groceries at the same time every Friday—during their lunch hour. The carts were usually gone, the aisles were packed, and everyone was testy because of the inconvenience of waiting, but it was always the same. And Clark always scheduled our shifts to overlap for a three-hour slot during the middle of every madcap weekend rush.

"Five o'clock," I reminded Grandma gravely. I had worked a hectic Friday shift often enough to know that I would be worthless after six hours on my feet, and I had no intention of staying a second longer than I had to.

"Five o'clock," she repeated, nodding seriously. "I won't be a second late; I promise."

It was a little strange to watch her go, knowing that as I bagged groceries, performed price checks, and helped people recover unusual items from their forgettable dwellings on the very top shelves, Grandma would be playing the part of a detective. "I'll call the local hotels," she'd informed me before I slipped out of the car. "We'll see if anything comes up." I nodded, a little scared that she would find them and equally afraid that she wouldn't.

But I didn't have time to ponder what my grandmother was doing. True to experience, from eleven until two, I barely had time to blink. Denise was the shift manager—and in a pretty sour mood, even for her—and she ordered me around with more than a little irritation in her voice. We had worked together a few times before, and I had found her to be sullen and resentful. I could have been reading her wrong, but she seemed exasperated that she was still stuck in Mason when she so obviously deserved much better than this little coffee smudge on a map. She was older than me by a few years, and though I had briefly entertained modest daydreams that we would become good friends, it was clear there would be no such relationship between us. Graham had been extremely generous to her when he had told me on my very first day that she could be "a bear."

I tried to give her a genuine smile when I walked past on my way to the back room, and I very dutifully threw myself into my work. Unfortunately, while most employees were assigned a particular task—bagging groceries and helping people to their cars, manning the floor and restocking, running the till—by accident or by design I ended up being the only floater, the only person who played every part and filled in any resulting gaps. Because it was so busy, I quite literally ran, and when Denise caught me breathing a little too hard, she made some snide comment about how I needed to get in better shape.

I seethed. And I couldn't help regretting that I hadn't worked harder at making her my ally the first day I met her. It had only taken me a few hours of working with her to realize that those she liked were treated as royalty and those she disliked were treated as scum. Though it had never occurred to me that we had a bad relationship, apparently we were not close enough to warrant even common courtesy on crummy days. It was a bit of an act, but when I wanted to snap at her, I smiled and tried to be sweet. I decided life at Value Foods would be much more enjoyable if I could ingratiate myself to her at least a little.

The store died at two o'clock. The employees who had been working since eight politely checked with Denise before heading to

the back room. It sounded almost as if they were small children asking to be excused from the dinner table, and she made a big parental
display of glancing around the store and trying to determine if she
would be able to let them leave or not. In reality, she had no right to
make them stay, but in practice, she had done it many times before.
Today there was no visible reason to keep them around, and she
grudgingly said, "You may go," although it sounded like she thought
they had asked for the moon.

Catching me in the corner of her eye, Denise turned to see me
leaning against a closed counter. I had just finished cleaning up a
shattered baby food jar in aisle four and I was only awaiting further
instructions. But she thought I was slacking off. "Taking your break
already?" she asked. Looking at her watch, she warned me, "You
only have ten minutes left."

I had heard Alicia say the same thing before, but when she said it,
I wasn't possessed by a desire to strangle her scrawny little neck.

I bit off a smart retort and turned on my heel to find a folding chair to fall into in the break room. Rolling my eyes as I
walked away, I caught up with Michael and gave his shoulder a
little bump. He was stripping off his apron with a flourish and
unclamping his faded tie. Black-haired, blue-eyed Michael was
one of the few people Denise actually seemed to like, and I had
watched her try out a seductive grin on him when he touched base
with her before leaving.

But I wasn't so sure that he liked her. "The yeti came to work
today," he commented under his breath, referring to a week or so
ago when Denise had come into the store as a customer, dressed
head to toe in white. Even her sunglasses were white rimmed, and

while she was probably trying to appear ultra haute and fashionable, she just looked ridiculous. Some of the employees started joking that she was secretly the abominable snowman, and her job at Value Foods was nothing more than a clever disguise to throw people off her trail. She certainly was cold enough.

I gave him a devious look and tried to suppress a yawn.

"She worked you like a pack mule," Michael commented decently. "Too bad you have a few hours left."

"Take the rest of my shift," I suggested impulsively, knowing that there was no chance he would ever do so.

"Are you crazy? No way. Uh-uh."

"Come on," I begged halfheartedly. "I'm beat. . . ."

We chatted inconsequentially all the way to the back of the store, and I found myself enjoying his company against my better judgment. I didn't know much about him, other than he had to be out of high school since we sometimes worked days together. I guessed Michael was around my age, but he had a Faith Academy sticker in the back window of his car—evidence that he'd attended the private Christian school while I went to Mason Public. Rumor had it he was going to the local tech school for a year to save up money so he could go to the University of Iowa. I couldn't remember his alleged chosen field or anything else about him. *I don't want to know anything more about him*, I reminded myself quickly. Besides, even if I did want to know more, he would want nothing to do with me in a matter of weeks. Trying to strike up a friendship with him was an exercise in futility. What guy would want to be associated—in any capacity—with a pregnant girl?

The back room was bustling with activity as people piled on

coats and hats and punched time cards in the ancient metal clock on the wall. I grabbed the nearest chair and sank into it gratefully, closing my eyes for a moment as a handful of different conversations washed over me.

I heard, "What are you doing tonight?" a number of times, and when someone tacked *Julia* on the end, I promptly opened my eyes and tried to look interested.

Graham was sitting on the table in front of me, munching on a Butterfinger that left orange slivers on his white collared shirt. "So?" he asked pleasantly.

"Nothing much," I muttered. "How about you?"

"I feel like going to a movie, but nothing good is playing. There's nothing worse than a bad movie."

"Oh, I can think of a few worse things," I said but was thankful when he took my comment lightly.

Two girls whose names I didn't know had paused by the table, and Graham looked up to catch the tail end of their exchange. "What's the gossip today, girls?" he asked casually.

One of them flashed a sisterly smile at him. "Wouldn't you like to know," she teased. "Graham's got to be up-to-date on all the scandals so he can set us straight."

"Most of that stuff is usually hogwash," he stated.

I giggled out loud because it was something my grandfather would have said—a word I hadn't heard used in years. It was hard not to admire Graham for being his own person and pulling it off so well.

"So," he pressed, "what is it today?"

The girl with the pink Columbia jacket acquiesced. "There's

a homeless family wandering around Mason," she said, her eyes sparkling.

Graham considered this for a moment. "Nope. I don't believe it. Too cold."

"It's true," she contradicted. "My aunt owns the motel just outside of town, and she said they stayed there for a few nights. Most people pay their bills at the end of their visit, but my aunt had a bit of a funny feeling about them, you know? So she tried to collect after a few days. She told them that payment was expected every other day to secure the room."

Michael laughed. "Like the Mason Inn is so busy in March that the rooms need to be reserved!" He was right; it was rare to see even a single car parked outside the outdated orange and white motor inn.

"Oh, shut up," the other girl scolded him, but she pinched his arm flirtatiously and watched him through downcast lashes.

"*Anyway*," the girl in the pink jacket continued pointedly, "my aunt tried to collect the bill from them, and *they couldn't pay*." She paused to let us digest this shocking information. "What could she do? She had to kick them out."

There were a couple of murmurs of assent, but Graham was shaking his head. "Nice story, Monica; could be true, but that doesn't make these people homeless."

"It does if they were caught sleeping in their car by the gravel pit," Monica said, saving the best for last and savoring it with a satisfied smile.

"Those poor people!" Graham exclaimed, looking truly concerned. "It was freezing last night—how could they survive in their car?"

My mouth was dry, but I moistened my lips a little with my

tongue and managed to ask, "Are they a . . . a big family?" I was nauseous long before Monica ever responded. I knew exactly what she was going to say.

"Nah, just some mom and her kid. They don't even look alike— my aunt says the boy is practically black, and the mom's white."

I was able to stay upright in my seat, but when everyone was badgering Monica for more information, Michael moved beside me and quietly asked, "Are you okay, Julia?"

"Fine," I whispered, trying to look normal. "I'm fine."

"You don't look so good. If you still want me to cover the rest of your shift—"

"No." I stopped him hastily. "I'll be fine. I just have a little headache."

But it was much, much more than a headache. The thought of Janice and Simon huddled around each other in her cramped two-door car all night long was some pitiful scene from a low-grade tearjerker. It was not reality. It couldn't be. I felt sick and guilty and horrified at the same time. My mind flashed to Grandma and her afternoon role of gumshoe. Had she uncovered the truth that I was learning? I wanted to lunge for the telephone.

Apparently Monica had even convinced the skeptical Graham as to the reliability of her story. He broke into my reverie by jumping off the table and making it bang against the wall. "We have to do something! That's so terrible—I feel so bad for them."

"Don't feel bad for them," Denise said derisively from somewhere behind the group.

No one was even aware that she had slipped in, and we all went quiet as if we had been caught doing something forbidden.

"My pastor says every event carries a consequence," she continued haughtily, wagging her finger as if warning us about the dangers of immoral living. "They're sleeping in a car tonight because they deserve to. Somehow, somewhere along the way, she must have done something to warrant a practically homeless night. Decent, respectable people with decent, respectable lives don't end up curled in the backseat of some beater car for lack of a better place to lay their heads."

Six pairs of eyes blinked disbelievingly at her. Her theory was full of holes—and didn't say much about the inherent goodness of our lives if we were all working at Value Foods—but we were too stunned at her unexpected outburst to retaliate with anything intelligent. I was briefly thankful Grandma and I did not go to her church and wondered how her pastor reconciled his ideas of decent, respectable people living decent, respectable lives when Jesus Himself had been born in a barn.

Finally, to loosen the tension, Michael said, "Wow, Denise, that's pretty philosophical coming from you. I had no idea you were so opinionated."

Or so pitiless, I wanted to add.

No one knew how Denise would take Michael's comment, and you could almost hear the frightened heartbeats as we all held our breath in anticipation of her reprisal. But because Denise had a bit of a crush on him, she took Michael's remark as complimentary. She laughed a little, and everybody else followed suit. Swinging her hair over her shoulder as though the act would somehow entice the object of her affection, she said as diplomatically as she could, "Well, coffee break is over."

Everyone started to go their own directions, and it looked like

Denise was going to get away with her uninformed tirade until Graham cleared his throat. "I don't agree with you, Denise," he said softly but bravely. "This mom and her son could be having a hard time. They could be just having some problems. . . . For all we know, they're angels in disguise."

It may have been a bit of a silly thing to say, but judging from the earnestness in his eyes, Graham meant—and believed—every word. A part of me cringed to hear Janice referred to as an *angel*, but another part of me shuddered to hear them discussing my . . . *family* as if they were what many of my coworkers so courteously referred to as trailer trash—bottom-feeders, the lowest of the low, the kind of people gossip was invented for. What would they think if they knew Janice was my mother? Or that Simon was my half brother, the son of a man Janice had probably had some sordid affair with? In a few weeks, when I couldn't hide my pregnancy another day, would they nod sagely to themselves and assert that they'd known all along that the apple hadn't fallen far from the tree? I was torn between wanting to leave work in a sprint to save Simon—and, grudgingly, Janice—and wishing that I could forget I had ever heard the rumor that would bring me to them. But it was too late.

I finished work, feeling every moment pass as if God had plunged the world into slow motion. Grandma once told me that a life lived outside of the will of the Lord is like trying to climb a waterfall. Surrender, on the other hand, is peace—a flowing, moving calm that comes with letting His water, His way, carry you downstream.

"Okay, God," I whispered in a moment alone by the canned goods, "I give in. I'll go find Janice."

until

THE CAR WAS warm and quiet, the radio so low I couldn't make out the song that was playing. I had practiced what I would say to Grandma, how I would break the news of Janice and Simon's whereabouts to her, and the words were fresh on my tongue as I swung open the door and clicked my seat belt on. But I didn't have to say anything. The leaden feeling in the pine-scented interior of Grandma's car told me that she already knew.

When she didn't put the car in drive and didn't bother to greet me with her usual query—*How was work?*—I turned to face her. There was a shallow pucker in her cheek where she was biting it, and she looked hesitant, unsure. She was terrified to tell me, and I was about to make it easy for her when she spat out, "I know where they are."

"I do too," I confessed without preamble.

"You do?" Her eyebrows shot up almost comically.

"We live in Mason," I reminded Grandma grimly. "*Everyone* probably knows by now."

She exhaled disapprovingly and rubbed her temples with gloved hands. "Always gossip but rarely good," she mused. I couldn't help being cynical and instinctively rephrased her grievance in my mind: *Always gossip, never good.* "Why don't people ever *do* anything when they hear these sorts of rumors?" she wondered sadly.

I felt like I should respond, or at the very least shrug, but it seemed like altogether too much effort. I was exhausted. Instead, I reached over and turned the heater up. I had shivered all afternoon.

Grandma sighed and put the car in gear, heading cautiously out of the Value Foods parking lot. She pulled up to the stop sign on Main Street and put her blinker on to turn south. A little wave of apprehension swept over me. The farm was in the opposite direction.

"Where are we going?" I asked carefully, watching a handful of cars drift past. The roads were just slippery enough that cars appeared to float across them like drops of oil skimming along the surface of water. They were dangerous only if you didn't know what you were doing—if you accelerated too quickly, stopped too abruptly, switched lanes thoughtlessly. Though she had lived in Iowa nearly her entire life, these kinds of driving conditions always made Grandma nervous. I wished that I had offered to drive. I would point the car toward the farm, where we could talk things out before we did anything rash.

But Grandma had thought everything through. "We're going to get them," she said matter-of-factly.

I swallowed. "And . . . ?"

"And we're going to take them home," she finished. "What would you have us do? Rent them a room with all that extra money from my social security check?" Grandma wasn't being sarcastic; she really saw no other way.

I had hoped to go home, make myself a good hot cup of Mrs. Walker's homemade, pregnancy-friendly strawberry tea, and sit down with Grandma to meticulously go over every possible scenario. A wicked little corner of my heart wondered why we couldn't just leave them to their own devices. Janice had lived without my help—or even my very existence—for ten years. Surely she didn't need it now. But of course we couldn't leave them in the cold. And though I knew that with certainty, I had almost desperately schemed all afternoon, waiting for another option to present itself.

The first feasible one that had crossed my mind was the Walkers. They had an enormous house and hearts to match. . . . Yet somehow I couldn't imagine asking them to do something so monumental. Baking cookies together was one thing; taking in my hapless would-be mother and her unknown son was quite another. I couldn't bring myself to do it even if I thought it was the most viable solution.

The only other alternative I had come up with was contacting the pastor at Fellowship Community. Reverend Trenton was elderly and unpretentious—boring but docile and utterly harmless in a sweet and grandfatherly way—and I knew that his heart would shatter into a million pieces if he knew such a need existed in his small corner of creation. But what would he be able to do? Drum up enough money to keep them in the Mason Inn for a few more days? Bundle Janice and Simon off to some halfway home or maybe to one of the safe houses for victims of domestic abuse? None of those options felt right.

I opened my mouth to offer Grandma one of my grand ideas anyway. "What about . . . ?"

"You have another idea?"

"No."

We headed south.

"I fixed up the sewing room for them," Grandma informed me. "Everything is moved along one wall, and when we get home, you can help me pull the mattress downstairs from the attic. They can sleep on that until . . ." She broke off, letting the uncertain word hang in the close air of the car. It fluttered against the lids of my closed eyes, demanding consideration that I was unwilling to give. *Until.* Until when? She didn't say any more; she didn't have to.

I can't do this, I thought, shoving panic aside with hard, angry sweeps of steely concentration. The sewing room was directly beneath my attic bedroom; Janice would sleep a mere floor away, her body only feet below mine, a shadow of my own twisted limbs and pounding heart as I tried to sleep, tried to forget that she was there.

"Everything is going to be all right," Grandma assured me, reading my mind. I wanted to believe her, but her promise felt hollow.

Everything is going to be all right, I echoed silently, willing myself to have faith in words that sounded so easy, so trite.

There was no car at the gravel pit. In some preoccupied daydream I had imagined that we would drive up to the little lake and they would be there, needy and vulnerable, simply waiting for us. Like something out of a movie, we would glide onto the snow-packed lane and pull up behind them, reluctant heroes but heroes all the same. Janice would be penitent and tearful and, of course, forever indebted—as if she wasn't already. But Grandma and I drove around the empty lot a few times and eventually had to admit that our rescue was poorly planned at best and completely unnecessary at worst. Besides the crisscrossing tread marks of a few different vehicles in the snow, there was no sign of life whatsoever in the deserted, modest park. For a moment I imagined that they were already gone, that they had moved on and we had missed our chance. *I* had missed my chance.

"Five fifteen," Grandma observed, glancing at the clock on the dashboard.

"Maybe they've left." I tried to say it indifferently, but my words came out barely above a whisper.

"They haven't left," Grandma was quick to reassure. "Where would they go?"

The guilt I felt was immediate and churning. Where *could* they go? Though we could hardly consider ourselves acquaintances, much less family, Grandma and I were all Janice and Simon had in Mason, maybe in the world.

Janice's family—Eli and Margaret Wentwood and their only, very spoiled, daughter—had moved to Mason when Janice was in high school. Eli was the newly acquired philosophy professor at Glendale Hill University, a small liberal arts college a twenty-minute drive from Mason. The formidable Dr. Wentwood had his doctorate from Cambridge, and Glendale hadn't seen someone with credentials like that in all their fleeting sixty-some years of existence. The Wentwoods were practically celebrities in Glendale, though they had moved to Mason instead of settling in the quaint college town.

Their decision was based primarily on an enormous, turn-of-the-century three-story Victorian that graced the corner of Eleventh Street and Hamilton Road. I had been told that they worked magic on the house, restoring the sagging wraparound porch, stripping and repainting the gorgeous cedar siding, and otherwise breathing life into arguably one of the most beautiful buildings in town. But they'd had a much harder time carving a niche for themselves in the hearts of their neighbors and community.

Bluntly said, they were total snobs. In a close-knit, hardworking, and no-nonsense town like Mason, Eli and Margaret's superior attitudes and affectations did not endear them to many people. Maybe they regretted not settling in Glendale, where their welcome would have been much more enthusiastic. Maybe they would have stayed in Iowa if things had been different. But when they left after only three years, no one mourned or missed them. Almost twenty years later, I doubted many people even remembered them—or their lovely daughter. Even when Janice stayed behind to marry my father in complete opposition to her parents' compellingly voiced wishes, her actions did not assure her any friends. In fact, most lamented the fact that one of their own—the sweet and studious Daniel DeSmit—had fallen prey to her devious charms. Janice had no one in Mason, and while I wished it could remain that way, I couldn't escape the fact that she should, if nothing else, have us.

Grandma and I stared at the pond for a few minutes, watching the wind run trembling fingers through the barren branches of the trees along the water's edge. The shallow lake was nearly frozen solid, covered in peaked, diminutive waves that were whipped up by the wind and frozen in the same icy breath. I tried to picture Janice and Simon spending the night here, overlooking the water and following the moon's slow progression in flawed reflection across the uneven surface. It was a fate I couldn't resign even Janice to.

"Let's wait," I said.

Grandma shook her head. "Let's go have supper at the truck stop. We'll come back later."

The south edge of Mason boasted a dumpy little truck stop and café that was undoubtedly the very restaurant where Simon had had pancakes for breakfast. Had it been only two days ago? I pictured them sharing a booth in that greasy spoon, a dingy place with perpetually dirty windows and a menu full of fried foods and breakfast items. Even a side salad, the healthiest option available, came disguised beneath a mountain of shredded cheese, buttery homemade croutons, and great dollops of nearly any dressing imaginable. The house special was a local favorite: mayonnaise, sugar, and a little vinegar whisked into a thick and frothy substance that resembled vanilla pudding. It was delicious. In spite of myself, my mouth watered at the thought of the beer-battered onion rings, and I wondered if Simon had experienced the pleasure of tasting them.

Although I thought of Janice and Simon the entire way there, I wasn't ready for what we saw when we walked through the door. They were seated in one of the red vinyl booths only feet from where we stood on the soaked and grimy rug immediately inside

the grease-scented building. Grandma hummed a little note unconsciously—a distinctive mannerism alerting me that she had half
expected this all along. She always hummed a small note when she
was right. I felt stupid for not putting two and two together. It made
sense; the vagabond pair could hardly sit in their car all evening and
all night, and no one would ever dream to kick them out of the truck
stop as long as there was a cup of coffee in front of Janice. They had
probably half lived here for days.

Grandma reached for my hand and squeezed it briefly, asking me
with her eyes if we could proceed.

I took a deep breath, nodded.

When we stepped to the table, Janice slid her coffee cup toward
the edge and continued to look at the bifold dessert menu. "Just a
warm-up," she said softly.

I didn't know how to respond, but I didn't have to because Simon
looked up from ramming two Hot Wheels into each other and
exclaimed, "Mrs. DeSmit! Julia!"

Janice's head jerked up. Her eyes were defiant, full of suspicion,
and defensive all at once.

I remembered those eyes, and for a moment everything made
sense. This was how I knew Janice; this was what I had daydreamed
about before she appeared on our doorstep—melancholy daydreams
without closure, simple wonderings of what it would be like to see
her again. In my mind, we always circled each other like wary animals, testing and sniffing the air before admitting we would never
be able to do more than move around each other. Close enough
to touch, forever distant. I could deal with this woman. I did not
understand her, but I knew her.

I began to harden in response to her, but just as my soul shifted to accommodate the inflexible mother I thought I knew, her face fell. Immediately she looked defeated, sad—she was again the woman on the porch. I could see her more clearly after a few days of coming to terms with her return. Janice looked misused to me, her mistakes less her own than the sorry consequences of what had been done to her. But what had been done to her? Surely no hurt, no amount of misunderstanding could exonerate her, magically switch her role from offender to victim. I could not bring myself to pity her.

"Nellie," Janice said slowly, blinking as though she had just come in from the dark. "Julia, hi. Please have a seat." She slid deeper into the booth and motioned for Simon to do the same.

Grandma shook her head. "No, thank you, Janice. It looks like you two are about done."

"I had a glass of chocolate milk," Simon said proudly, tipping the empty Styrofoam cup toward us as evidence of how much he had enjoyed the treat.

"Aren't you lucky?" Grandma smiled. "When Julia was little, we only had chocolate milk on special occasions: birthdays, Christmas. . . ."

"Mom says I can have chocolate milk whenever I want," Simon boasted. "It may be chocolate, but it's still milk."

"I guess calcium is calcium no matter how you get it," I muttered. Janice had not bothered to buy me chocolate milk when I was five.

Janice cleared her throat almost as if I had spoken my silent contemplation. "What can I do for you ladies?" she asked politely. "Are you here for supper?"

Grandma reached out to touch the scruff of Simon's unkempt hair. She rubbed it absently as she looked meaningfully at Janice and said, "Actually, I wanted to talk to you. I'm glad we found you here."

"You want to talk to me?" Janice repeated uncertainly.

"Alone," Grandma clarified, turning to smile at Simon. "Can you stay here with Julia? I'd like to talk to your mom alone for a minute."

Simon nodded seriously. "Here, Julia," he said, handing me one of the toy cars. "I'll use the red one and you take this one. It's called the Gov'ner. That's what it says on the bottom."

I accepted the car hesitantly. I hadn't planned on Grandma and Janice working this whole thing out on their own. The conversation should have included me. I should have had the opportunity to speak my mind, to let Janice know that though we were inviting her into our home, she had not been forgiven—all had not been forgotten. But I couldn't make a scene in front of Simon. Janice crept tentatively out of her seat and I resentfully took her place.

"We'll be back in no time," Grandma assured us. By the slant of her half smile I could almost believe that they were going to speak of pleasant things—surprise parties or occasions for chocolate milk, maybe. But I knew better.

I watched them walk away and was stunned to see Grandma grip Janice's elbow as though she were supporting the younger woman. Their heads were almost exactly the same height, and from my angle they could have been any mother and daughter, silver head tilted toward fair. They looked almost comfortable.

"How are you doing?" Simon said conversationally, jerking my head back to the table and the boy that shared my blood.

"I'm okay," I answered, cocking an eyebrow at him. He was unusually mature for his age. It was a little disconcerting. "How are you doing?" It was only polite to return the question, even if he was just a preschooler.

Simon thought for a minute. "I'm okay too. Mom says I should tell people that I'm good when they ask me how I am. She says that they don't *really* want to hear how I'm doing. But you said that you were okay, so I can say that I'm okay too."

Part of me wanted to laugh, but another part found his explanation somehow depressing. "I'm sorry that you're just okay," I eventually offered. "I hope that next time we see each other you are doing very, very good."

"Me too!" Simon chimed brightly. "Wanna see how fast my car can race down the ramp?" The somewhat somber mood instantly forgotten, he propped a laminated menu against the windowsill and perched his car at the top. "You catch it before it falls off the table."

We had only raced the cars down the makeshift slope four or five times when Grandma and Janice returned. I hadn't expected them to come to a conclusion so quickly. I tried to read either woman, but Grandma's smile was fixed and Janice refused to look at me.

"Simon, honey," Janice said, crouching down, "let's go, all right? I have something to ask you."

"I want to play with Julia," Simon complained. It was the first time I had heard his voice border on whiny.

"Later, buddy." Janice reached for his coat and helped him into it. She stole a glance at me over her shoulder, and in that one look I knew she had accepted Grandma's offer. I didn't know whether to be disappointed or happy.

"I gotta go, Julia," Simon said. "You can keep the Gov'ner until I see you next time."

I was disarmed by his generosity. "No, Simon, you keep it. It wouldn't be fun to play with it without you."

"Okay." He gave in without much of a fight, accepting the car from my hand. "Next time we'll make an obstacle course."

"Next time," I agreed.

When they were gone, Grandma took my hand and led me out to the car. "Janice is going to tell Simon and meet us at home in a half hour or so."

"She agreed to stay with us?" I asked pointlessly.

Grandma didn't even bother to answer. The same silence accompanied us as we drove the cold highway home.

I insisted on getting the mattress down from the attic myself. A few minutes alone in the chilly air of the poorly insulated loft sounded like a tropical getaway to me. It would be easy, I convinced Grandma. All I had to do was tilt the monstrosity on its side and push it down the stairs. I could tell she wanted to argue, but there was no disagreeing with the edge in my voice. She let me go.

The closed-off storage room was just down the hallway from my bedroom. We nailed an ancient quilt across the door in the wintertime and laid old boards against the bottom to stop drafts from seeping into the house. I pulled the quilt aside and set the boards against it to hold it in place. The room was cold and dry and dusty smelling. I sank to the floor in the middle of it, neglecting to even pull the chain on the single-bulb light and dispel the darkness. Though I should have planned or prepared myself or even prayed, I did nothing. I breathed.

It wasn't long before I heard movement downstairs. Voices carried up the hollow belly of the stairwell and slid under the door of my makeshift prison. I got up then because I had to and pulled on the light so I could drag the mattress through the maze of junk.

Simon heard me coming down the stairs and threw open the door at the bottom. "Julia!" he called enthusiastically. "We're going to stay with you for a while!"

I forced a smile at him. "Surprise," I said weakly.

"This is so awesome!" he whooped and disappeared from sight.

Janice came to help me haul the mattress around the corner and into the room Grandma had prepared for them. She looked as if she wanted to say something to me, but I focused on the mattress, denying her an opportunity to speak. We placed the improvised bed against the wall and together wordlessly covered it with the sheets and blankets that Grandma had laid out.

When we were done, Janice smiled feebly at me and moved toward the door. I blocked it. I had rehearsed what I would say over and over on my way down from the attic—I would not be deceived and I would not live with her if she refused to meet me in some way. She would answer me or they would leave, I had decided. It was intolerable to think of sharing a roof with her if she didn't have the decency to at least satisfy two small uncertainties that were eating me up inside.

"I have two questions for you, Janice. I need you to answer them." My voice was reedy and my fists were clenched. I stared her down.

She looked trapped, but there was resignation in her bearing. I believed she would answer me honestly. "Okay" was all she said.

I wasted no time. "What did Grandma say to you?" I demanded frostily.

Janice nodded as if she had expected that question. She thought for a moment, and I was about to insist on the truth when her eyes went expressionless and she answered almost obediently, "Nellie told me that this might be my last chance. My only chance. She told me I was a fool if I passed it up."

One more last chance. I suddenly felt sick and hot. We were far from second chances, and every step toward some pathetic and patched-up form of reconciliation was an unprecedented gamble, a risk that I was not convinced I was willing to take. But as I watched Janice in the closeted airlessness of the sewing room turned bedroom, I finally understood that she was at least willing to try. The pain in her eyes as I'd stood on the porch and asked her to leave only days ago had been the reflection of what she believed was her final, failed opportunity. She had hoped I would see her and say, *I wanted you to stay. I've waited for you.* Did I? Had I? I didn't know. I didn't know if there could be another chance.

"One more question," she prompted me. There were tears in her voice.

"Why are you here?" I whispered achingly, afraid to hear the answer.

She didn't even pause. "I had a dream that you forgave me."

believe

GRANDMA ONCE TOLD ME that belief is the suspension of disbelief.

I didn't understand her at first. I smiled and mumbled my agreement, apparently discarding her words of wisdom somewhere that they could grow undisturbed—seeds tossed carelessly on unexpectedly thorny soil. Though I suppose the earth of my soul was always fertile and ready for whatever Grandma chose to sow, even if the gestation period was sometimes a process of many long and seemingly fruitless years. And while her definition of belief was nothing I pondered at the time, that first night, with Janice and Simon inside my house—trying to find a place inside my life—I remembered Grandma's words as though she had whispered them in the darkness of my room.

Believe. It's a scary word. *Believe in me* is even worse. And wasn't Janice asking me to do exactly that? *Believe in me. I won't let you down this time.* She hadn't said those words, but then again, they didn't need to be said. And neither did I have to clarify my answer. Janice knew how I felt, though I wasn't exactly sure I could trust my own feelings anymore. I couldn't shake a sense of guilt when I thought of her agonized tears and the way she almost asked for my forgiveness.

The truth was, I couldn't forgive her. I didn't trust her. I didn't have faith in her. I didn't even like her that much. But I also wasn't ready for the look on her face, the tremble in her voice. Against my will, a small part of me wanted to believe.

I pressed my eyes closed, willing myself to rest, but I knew my impatient efforts only forced sleep farther and farther away. The house was still and silent, and the alarm clock beside my bed read 3:24. I wondered if I was singularly awake and tossing with the knowledge that life could never go back to the way it had been. That I would make choices—*we* would make choices—in the coming days and weeks that would change us in ways that could not be undone. I thought of Janice staring at the ceiling with one child beside her and the other only a floor above her, and I knew it was my decision that would affect us most of all.

In the darkness and quiet, I sought to unravel the act of believing and attempted to find a way to believe *her*. It comforted me somehow to begin to understand that belief was far less a jump of faith than I ever realized: Disbelief did not have to be eradicated. I did not have to reach a point of complete and utter faith in Janice to believe that she, in her own way, wanted to try. *The suspension of disbelief,* Grandma had said. Like a time-out, an interruption. A brief interlude during which decisions can be made, trust can be tested.

Abandoning my disbelief was impossible; shelving it seemed to be a workable option. I could do that. I could suspend my doubt, tuck it away for a little while and see if Janice could be someone new. It helped to know that my skepticism could be used as a security blanket of sorts—a way of tiptoeing into the unknown with the knowledge that one small step could be quickly reversed, that I could go back to where I started. If I didn't see Janice taking steps toward me, I could retreat into the reassurance of my utter disbelief. I could rest vindicated, knowing I was right.

It was cold in my room, but I was hot underneath the pile of blankets. Shoving them aside, I let the draft from my window snake cool fingers around my bare feet. The chill was somehow clarifying. With shadows from the almost-full moon slipping around the sides of my curtains and dancing on the ceiling above me, it struck me that I could at least try. I could try to believe. A little. Maybe one day at a time.

My effort would make Grandma proud.

Suddenly, like a flash of phantom pain, I wondered if my effort would have made Dad proud. Would he want me to invite Janice back into my life? Or was I betraying him by giving her a chance that she so obviously did not deserve?

We had rarely, if ever, talked about Janice after she left, but there was something raw and broken in my father whenever we were reminded of the woman who used to share our home. The very thought of her used to incense me, as if I were the parent and Dad were my child, as if he needed my protection and I were the only one who could shelter him from her memory. And now he was gone and Janice was here. Something in me sank and folded, bowed to the weight of his loss, but I couldn't think about Dad now. I thrust the man I loved out of my mind and tried to focus on the woman I thought I hated.

I pictured her on the steps of our porch, staring at me with an emotion that could have been mistaken for grief. But grief over what? Over losing me? Over coming back? Whether or not she regretted what she had done, I let myself grasp what it meant that she had traveled back. Cautiously, I let my heart wrap around the idea that Janice, my *mother*, had come home. She had come home to me. It was a small admission, but it crushed my chest so I struggled to breathe.

"Don't let her mess it up this time," I whispered into the darkness. "Don't make me believe for nothing." I didn't know who I was talking to, but I realized too late that if I was praying, I was doing it all wrong. "Amen," I said quickly. I covered my face with my hands.

When I stumbled into the kitchen in an exhausted haze the next morning, I wasn't the only one for whom it looked like sleep had proven to be elusive. Janice had ugly lines under her eyes so deep and obvious that it looked like she had mistakenly applied eye shadow below instead of above her eyes. Grandma was barely concealing a series of jaw-cracking yawns behind the back of her hand. Only Simon looked as if he had gotten any sleep. In fact, he looked so rested and cheerful it seemed he was glowing from the inside out. His eyes positively sparkled.

"Morning, Julia!" he called louder than necessary.

"Good morning," I muttered back. I pulled a chair away from the table and sat opposite the bouncing bundle of five-year-old energy.

"Sleep well?" Grandma asked from the stove.

It was an unfair question because she absolutely knew the answer. I had no choice but to answer her with a half-truth. "I slept okay. You?"

"Same," she said noncommittally. "Cup of coffee?"

I blinked incredulously and nodded. Though my doctor had okayed a cup of coffee a day, I hadn't had one in months. The very thought made my mouth water. Grandma must have realized how badly I needed it. I forgave her for her absentminded question.

"I slept great," Simon informed us out of the blue. "I slept like a baby!"

We all ignored him.

Grandma passed me a full mug of coffee, and I huddled over it as if the fragrant steam was therapy. I snuck a peek at Janice, who was leaning against the sink, and found that she too was lost in the depths of a cup of her own. The resolutions of my restless night were clinging stubbornly to me, and my stomach did a little spin as I took in the angles of her profile, the way her ponytail exposed the sagging line of her chin. She was so different from how I remembered her.

She felt like a stranger. I imagined for a moment that she looked up at me and smiled. I imagined what it would feel like if she had never left.

"That bed was so comfortable, Mrs. DeSmit," Simon said into the silence. It was obvious he was trying to draw us out and more obvious that we were not in the mood.

"I'm glad you liked it," Grandma replied distractedly.

"It wasn't little at all. There was plenty of room for me and Mom." Simon caught my eye from across the table. "You could fit in there too, Julia!"

I smiled dryly. "No thanks. I have my own bed."

"Sweetheart, tone it down a bit, okay?" Janice shook her head slightly at her son.

"I'm just *happy*."

"I know. Just cool it a little. We're still waking up."

"He's fine, Janice," Grandma cut in. "Ready for some oatmeal?" she asked, directing the inquiry at Simon.

He wrinkled his nose, but butter and brown sugar went far to restoring his faith in Grandma's cooking. Simon gobbled his breakfast while Grandma, Janice, and I picked at our food and drove it around our bowls like spoiled little girls who wished for four-minute eggs and Belgian waffles instead of hot cereal. Surprisingly, it wasn't that the room was filled with an inordinate amount of tension. In some slight way we had already moved past the shock of finding ourselves together. But now we had to make it work. Simply existing side by side was baffling our every attempt at normalcy. We didn't know which way was up.

And though my lack of appetite was no different from anybody else's, Grandma singled me out. "Julia, you have to eat something."

"I did. I am." I lifted a spoonful as evidence and dropped it back to the bowl when she moved to clear the table.

"Your body needs the nutrition," Grandma warned.

"Please eat something," Janice added.

My head shot up at her unsolicited advice. "I'm not hungry," I defended, appalled that they thought they could gang up on me.

Lowering her voice, Janice entreated me, "Don't skip breakfast because of me. If this whole thing is going to make you lose your appetite . . ."

"I'm fine," I huffed.

"Why does Julia have to eat her breakfast but you don't, Mom?"

I wanted to give Simon a high five for sticking up for me. But just as quickly as I was filled with warmth toward him, I realized that someone would have to explain to him that I was pregnant. I tried to replay past conversations in my mind. What did he know? What did he understand? Had Janice told him everything?

The uneasy silence betrayed Simon's ignorance. Before Grandma or Janice could try to enlighten him, I decided, for once, to take control. "Well, Simon, I should eat breakfast because there is a baby in my tummy, and she needs food to grow healthy and strong."

Grandma and Janice gawked at me.

Simon looked unimpressed. "Oh, I know that," he said offhandedly.

"How do you know that?" Janice demanded.

"I know what that *pennant* word means."

"Pennant?"

"Pregnant," I said. "Did you hear us use that word the other night, Simon?"

"How in the world do you know that word?" Janice asked.

Simon rolled his eyes. "Duh, Mom. I'm not a little kid."

"Apparently." Raising her eyebrows at me, she smiled.

The lines of Janice's face became the memories of past happiness, and for a moment it flashed through my mind that if she looked like this forever, with love like burnished gold lighting up her cheeks, I could believe. I grinned back. "You are a very smart young man," I told Simon, trying to sound serious.

And then Grandma started to giggle.

"What?" Simon asked. His eyes were eager little moons as he waited for the joke to be explained.

I heard a sputtering from beside me and turned to see Janice clap both of her hands over her mouth. She laughed so hard I could see tears gather in the corners of her eyes.

"What?"

Simon's voice was so filled with anticipation I couldn't stop myself. When I started to giggle, Simon joined in excitedly and within minutes his belly laugh was utterly sincere and intoxicating. It was a beautiful sound, the four of us laughing. Something within me seized the moment hungrily, folding it deep inside so I could remember it always, no matter where we went from here. If Simon and Janice stole out of our lives and it was indeed another ten years until we met again, I would always have this one secreted crease in the fabric of my memory.

"Oh, that's funny," Simon said after we had calmed down a bit.

He stuck out his tongue to be silly and got the desired effect—I laughed again.

"*You're* funny," I corrected him.

"Mom says I'm silly. Maybe I can teach your baby how to be silly too."

I sighed, my stomach pleasantly sore from laughter, and pushed back from the table to help Grandma with the dishes. "That's a great idea."

"I can teach *you* how to make funny faces, if you'd like."

"He's a master," Janice informed us, reaching over to tickle the soft spot above his collarbone.

"I would love a few lessons," I said. "But not today. I have to run into town."

Grandma gave me a sidelong look as I stood beside her at the sink. "What do you have to do today? I thought you had the day off."

"I do," I admitted hesitantly, wondering what she had planned for me. "But it's payday, and I was going to go pick up my check and then spend a little time at the library."

By the way Grandma stared so intently at the soapsuds I could tell she was about to spring something on me. I wanted to stop her, but I didn't know how. "Why don't you take Simon along?" she asked innocently, loud enough for Janice and Simon to hear.

I tried to give her a meaningful look, but she was avoiding my gaze. Besides, it was too late.

"Really?" Simon yelped. "I'd like to go with you, Julia! I like going to the library."

Glancing back at them, I saw Janice lay her hand on Simon's shoulder. She shook her head at him gently and mouthed something, probably admonishing him to wait for a proper invitation from me. His face crumpled enough to convince me that there was no way I could leave him behind now that he had his heart set on it.

Though I had wanted to be alone, it struck me suddenly that Simon was an easy companion to walk with on the road to Janice. I had a lifetime of reasons to distrust her. But there was nothing in sweet, uncomplicated Simon that I needed to fear. When I saw the way she looked at him and ran her fingers over his body as if somehow sealing him against every hurt, I found it significantly easier to want to try. Simon was a fantastic place to start practicing belief.

"He can come," I told Janice. "You can come," I assured Simon. "The library is pretty small, but they have a lot of neat picture books."

"I don't need picture books," Simon said. "I can read."

"No, you can't," Janice shushed him.

"I can read my Clifford books!"

She smiled indulgently at him and then winked at us. I took it to mean he had his Clifford books memorized.

"Maybe I can help you with your reading if you help me with my funny faces," I offered, hoping Simon wouldn't see Janice's patronizing look.

"Okay," he agreed lightly. "I'll go get my sweater on." Simon practically skipped out of the room.

Janice watched him go and then came to stand at the sink. She held out her hands, and as though it were the most natural thing in the world, Grandma squeezed out a washcloth and gave it to her. I had forgotten that table washing had been Janice's role all those years ago. Evidently Grandma had not.

I froze for a moment, and in my mind the house was full again. Grandpa pushed his chair away from the table and balanced on the back two legs, chewing on his unlit pipe. Dad spun a towel into a tight cord of fabric and whipped it at my legs as I giggled and danced out of the way. Grandma laughed, plunging her hands in and out of the sink. We were happy. Janice was the shadow in the sunlit room, halfheartedly wiping the table, ignoring us with a distant look in her eyes.

But this Janice was not the same one who had grudgingly participated in the rites of our family over ten years ago. I watched now as she swept the cloth over the table, head bent, eyes downcast. She washed as though everything depended on each calculated flick of her wrist. As though she could atone for all that had happened by wiping away the hurt and the years with suds from a wet washcloth. It felt wrong to observe her somehow, but I couldn't tear myself away.

It was quiet with Simon gone, and once or twice Janice looked toward the living room as if she was wary of his return. Finally she cleared her throat. Keeping her back turned to me, she said, "Simon doesn't know that . . ." Her voice dropped. "He doesn't know that you are his sister."

I followed the movement of her hand, forgetting the glass that I clutched in my own. "I won't tell him."

Janice seemed relieved. "We'll tell him, Julia." She tumbled over her words, looking up at me with relief in her eyes. "Just not yet. The right time will come."

"Okay," I agreed. It struck me that I complied as easily as Simon had.

We had to move Simon's booster seat from Janice's car to mine. I could have just driven her car—she offered to let me take it—but something inside me balked at the idea of sitting in the seat that she occupied.

When we were buckled in and on our way down the highway, I let myself stare in the rearview mirror and take in the boy who was my brother. He really was adorable. I decided it was impossible for me to be biased, as I hardly knew the skinny little rascal in my backseat. Anyway, we had absolutely nothing in common, so it couldn't be an affinity for my own genes that drew me to him. If he was chocolate, sweet and rich and handsomely dark, I was vanilla—bland and tepid, dull against the animated glimmer of his eyes.

Simon looked out the window as I drove, talking quietly to his reflection and occasionally singing a line or two from a song that I couldn't quite determine. It would have been melodramatic to say that I loved him, but in those minutes between the farm and Mason, I felt that loving him wouldn't be nearly as much work as I thought it might have been.

Mostly I realized that I trusted him and his guileless motives for wanting me to be a part of his life. He didn't know who I was, yet he believed me with the willing innocence of a child who has known no reason to mistrust. For a moment, I wished that I could wipe myself clean of those experiences that had jaded me. I wished that Janice with her washcloth could make me forget, make me new and trusting and ready to believe that everything would once again be as it should have always been. But then again, I didn't really want that. I possessed a wisdom that Simon would soon enough know too. There was safety in knowing. There was safety in being prepared.

"Is this where you work?" he cried when we pulled up to Value Foods. "Can you have all the candy bars you want?"

"Yes, I work here," I answered, happy to find that Simon could elicit more laughter from me. "And no, I can't have all the candy bars I want." It had never occurred to me that working in a grocery store was nearly the equivalent of working at Disney World for a five-year-old. What preschooler wouldn't want to be among the rows of Ding Dongs and Doritos day in and day out?

I parked near the store, intending to leave the car running while I popped in for my paycheck. "Can you wait in the car for me, Simon? I'll just be a minute."

"No." He shook his head vehemently. "I want to come in with you. Mommy says it's dangerous to stay in the car by yourself."

I wanted to explain to him that Mason was safe, that I routinely left my car running when it was cold outside, and Grandma hadn't used a house key in ages. But he looked wide-eyed and scared in the rearview mirror. I decided it wasn't that big of a deal to take him in. "Fine," I said, turning off the car. I reached over the front seat and unbuckled him. "Can you get out by yourself?"

Simon furrowed his brow at me. "I told you I wasn't a baby."

"Okay, okay." I threw up my hands. "Climb out and come around to my side. I don't want you walking through the parking lot by yourself."

We entered Value Foods hand in hand, and when we were through the doors, Simon made no movement to extract his hand from mine. I held his warm fingers and was proud to have him by my side.

Alicia and Michael were lounging by the first checkout lane, and the store looked nearly dead. Catching sight of me and my pint-size buddy, Alicia smiled and raised her arms in question. "Who is this, Julia? I didn't know we had a new employee."

"He's a good worker," I teased, pulling Simon along with me. "He's also very good at making silly faces."

"I am," Simon asserted and jutted out his jaw as if to prove it.

Alicia and Michael laughed. "Seriously, who is this little guy? He's a hoot."

I hadn't really planned an answer since I had intended to leave Simon in the car. But I only paused for a second before I replied, "This is Simon. He's the son of a family friend."

Alicia crouched down and extended her arm in greeting. "I'm Alicia. It's very nice to meet you, Simon."

"Nice to meet you," he said politely. He shook her hand but did not let go of mine.

Michael waved at Simon. "I'm Michael. You've got cool hair, buddy." Michael ran his fingers through his own hair as if to replicate Simon's mussed-up waves.

Simon grinned.

"You're here for your paycheck, aren't you?" Alicia asked, straightening up. "I brought them to the front so everyone doesn't have to run all the way to the storeroom. Clark's back there." She smiled meaningfully.

"Thanks, Alicia." I pulled away from Simon and gave him a reassuring smile, pointing him in the direction of the candy. "Go pick out a chocolate bar, Simon. I'll buy you one if you promise not to tell your mom."

"Really?" Simon gushed. Not waiting for an answer, he took off in the direction I had indicated.

I couldn't help but laugh at the bob of his receding head. I was in a fantastic mood considering the events of the last few days, and, even better, Michael was across the lane from me and we were more or less alone. It frustrated me that this dark-haired guy could make my heart skip a beat. The timing was all wrong. My life was all wrong. And yet here he was, watching me with a sly smile that made me want to smile back. I was seized by a desire to flirt with him a bit, be coy and playful and fun—just to see if he would respond even a little.

Michael beat me to it. "We haven't worked together in a while," he said, frowning slightly to show his disappointment.

"Who makes the schedule?" I demanded, my hands going clammy and cold in spite of the flush in my cheeks. "We have to have a talk with him."

"Or *her*," Alicia said, handing me my check. "I make the schedule."

I started, feeling like we had been caught in the act. Of flirting? What was so wrong with that? Trying to explain away my blush, I unzipped my coat and leaned against the high counter in front of the cigarettes. I bent over, resting my arms on the smooth top and feeling unusually safe and hidden with my stomach pressed tightly against the side, well below eye level.

Michael watched me with a glint in his eye before turning to Alicia. "Julia and I have lots to talk about," he complained. "We should work together more often."

Alicia rolled her eyes. "Yeah, I'll get right on that."

"That'd be great," Michael said without skipping a beat. "I'm also due for a raise. Could you bring that up with Clark for me?"

We joked and laughed until I could almost pretend that my life was as normal and mundane as nearly every other person's in this sleepy town. It was a soothing mirage, and I wasn't quite ready to face my reality when Simon came bounding back.

"Look! I found a Twix! It's my favorite candy bar. . . ." He trailed off, staring at me. His face had transformed so completely that even Alicia and Michael looked concerned.

"Simon, what is it?" Worry fractured my voice.

Simon raised a thin finger and pointed at me. "The baby!" he almost yelled. "You're going to hurt the baby if you squish her like that!"

I could feel the color drain from my face. He didn't say that. He couldn't have just said that. But Alicia's expression told me that I hadn't dreamed it. Her mouth was open, and her eyes were round in disbelief. I couldn't bring myself to look at Michael.

"Julia! Don't do that!"

Startled, I straightened and backed away from the counter. "Simon, it'll be okay," I assured him quietly, willing him not to say more. My fingers fumbled with the zipper of my coat as I tried to hide any evidence that would support Simon's claim.

"You didn't have breakfast this morning either," Simon accused. "You have to take good care of the baby."

"Enough." The word was as hard and final as a guilty verdict. I pulled a dollar from my coat pocket and laid it on the counter. "That's for the Twix."

Taking Simon's hand, I led him away. I could feel their eyes boring into my back and the force of their unsaid questions virtually pushing me out the door. This wasn't the way it was supposed to be. This wasn't what I had planned. They would have understood if only I could have been the one to tell them. They would have known that there was much more to me than this one misstep.

I was almost gone when I turned around and looked back toward Alicia and Michael, not at them. I couldn't make my eyes meet theirs. "I was going to tell everyone soon," I tried to defend myself. As if that would explain everything.

I buckled Simon in wordlessly and got behind the wheel.

"What's wrong?" Simon's voice was small and faraway.

I glanced up at the mirror and studied him as he stared into his lap. I watched him mangle the candy bar. "Nothing," I said. But he wasn't a baby. He knew.

I skipped the library and drove straight home, heartsick and utterly worn. My mind spun; it assaulted me from every direction and I couldn't make any sense of what I was thinking or feeling. It was all too horrifying. A part of me couldn't believe that it had happened, that Simon had blurted out the one secret I had guarded so carefully for four months. What was supposed to be understated and discreet was now crude and trashy. I saw myself through their eyes, and I hated what I saw.

Simon was as quiet as a mouse in the backseat, but he recognized the farm as we crested the hill and murmured something I couldn't discern. Then he said audibly, "I didn't mean to make you mad."

I bit my lip, not knowing how to respond. Finally, because his face was so drawn with disappointment, I glanced over my shoulder to force a weary smile at him. "I'm not mad."

Simon studied me seriously. "Yes, you are."

How could I lie to him? I looked away.

"I'm sorry," he said sadly.

"I believe you," I whispered. I didn't know what else to say.

Grandma was wrong. Belief has nothing to do with suspension. It is all about *suppression*. Forcing things down, deep down, where you hope that they will die and not grow in the darkness to emerge someday as a tree with bitter fruit.

stronghold

WHEN SIMON AND I returned from Value Foods, it was clear to everyone that something had happened. Simon was pale and reserved, stealing glances at me as if he thought I might tell on him like some playground tattletale. Of course, I would never do such a thing, but he avoided me like a whipped puppy, and I didn't give him any reason to behave differently. In fact, I may have contributed to his anxiety, because it rankled me a bit that Grandma and Janice gave *him* concerned looks. My attitude turned more and more sour with each minute we were home—*I* was the one they should have been worried about. Simon may have been only five, but he had ruined me in ways that I could hardly begin to grasp.

I retreated into my own world, where I could nurse my injuries and collect the sins that had been committed against me as proof of my persecution. Obviously any relationship at all with Michael was completely, indisputably over—not that I really expected anything from our flirtations. It just killed me to know that he probably cringed now when he thought of any attention he had directed at me. And the tenuous respect that bordered on friendship with Alicia was annihilated. Never mind that the entire store would most likely know by tomorrow and, consequently, the rest of the town within hours of that.

Janice sensed something dark and brooding in me and ushered Simon out the door not long after we walked in it. She claimed they had errands to run, a Wal-Mart stop to make, plus she wanted to drop off a few job applications around town. I almost made some snide comment about her qualifications or lack thereof but managed to bite my tongue before I said something we would all regret. It had been difficult for me to be mad at Simon, but with Janice in the room, my frustrations had an outlet. If I had felt beaten in the car, I felt ready to fight back when I had a worthy opponent in the house.

After they were gone, I was ready to talk—nearly bursting with pent-up disappointment and righteous condemnation—but Grandma chose to overlook the heaviness that clung to me and went about her routine as if by sheer will alone she could bring peace to our tumultuous home. I lingered wherever she was for most of the day, dropping hints and feeling sorry for myself. By the time *Jeopardy!* came on at four thirty, I was sullen and moody and well aware that Grandma was treating me as she would any petulant child: she was ignoring me.

I knew better than to talk during *Jeopardy!* but Janice and Simon had been gone for hours and my time was limited. They had been in our house for only a day, but time alone with Grandma already felt like a precious commodity, and I was conscious of every minute passing on the clock. I had no choice but to interrupt her favorite half hour of relaxation. Besides, she should have expected that I would need to get a few things off my chest. I couldn't hold it in a second longer.

"They know," I said, studying Grandma from where I sat buried under an afghan on the couch. The words sounded fateful to me, but my grandmother didn't flinch.

Instead, Grandma looked up from her knitting to glance at the TV. "What is daylight savings time?" she asked, clasping the yarn in anticipation.

I followed her gaze and watched Alex Trebek smile right at her from the framed glow of the dusty screen.

Grandma grinned back. "I got one! I never get the questions right!" She laughed a little to herself and turned her attention back to the soft, nursery-green blanket. Though she hadn't said as much, I knew that the lovingly fashioned stitches were formed for my baby. I hadn't seen her use the delicate yarn intended for children since our neighbors had their last little boy. He was about Simon's age now.

I sighed, and when her head jerked up, I realized that I had done so out loud. It had been a private exhalation, though it got the desired effect.

"Oh, honey, I'm sorry. You said something."

I bit my lip in self-pity and waited for Grandma to turn down the volume on the TV. She did, then watched me expectantly.

"At the store today, Simon told Alicia and Michael that I'm pregnant." It was a grave proclamation, and I waited for shock to register on Grandma's sweet face.

She studied me for a moment and then pursed her lips and shrugged. "They were going to find out sooner or later. Maybe Simon simplified things." She turned back to her blanket.

I realized that I was gaping at her and made a distinct effort to shut my mouth. She didn't understand. I closed my eyes to shut out the hum of the TV, the click of her oversize needles. There were too many feelings stirring just below the surface to single one out and offer it to her as evidence of how I had been wronged. I felt lost in a breeze of indefinable numbness—battered and spent.

A part of me wanted to cry at the injustice of it all, but I was too affronted.

Grandma moved to turn up the volume again, and I cut in quickly before Alex could take her attention away from me. "You know, I thought that I could do this, but I can't."

"Can't do what?" Grandma asked absently, squinting at the TV before turning again to me.

"I don't think Janice and Simon should stay here."

Grandma's smile was indulgent. "They've only been here for a day! I know it's not ideal, but we're going to work through this. You know that, don't you?"

"I was willing to try—I even prayed about it last night—but now . . ." I pulled the end of my ponytail over my shoulder and curled my hair around my fingers. It was a childhood habit, and when I realized I was doing it, I quickly flicked the ponytail over my shoulder and dropped my hands.

"Is this all because Simon told your secret? Julia, you had to know that you couldn't keep it quiet much longer. People may have already guessed."

The thought hit me like a splash of ice water. How delusional was I in my little house of glass? I glanced down at the growing roundness of my belly and knew that she was probably right. Surely some had at least speculated. Everyone knew that I had dropped out of college, and though the reason was a mystery, it wouldn't take much deductive power to assume that my expanding waist was why. I had tried hard to hide it, but the five-month mark was not far off, and when I wasn't consciously sucking in, there was a tight little arc that would be obvious to the keen eye.

I could have deflated right there. All the angst and sorrow could have melted into a wave of tears that left me tired and broken. But I wanted to be angry. Whether or not people already knew, whether or not they would have known sooner rather than later, it wasn't enough to excuse what had happened. I clung to the bitterness that rose thick and thorny around my heart.

"He ruined everything," I muttered.

"This has nothing to do with Simon," Grandma assured me quietly. She laid her knitting beside the rocking chair and got up to sit on the couch with me. "This is old anger. You're mad at Janice, and you're taking it out on Simon because he did a silly, childish thing. He *is* a child. Don't be upset with him."

"I have every right to be mad at him! And Janice. I was right—I never should have trusted her. *Him*. Them. Whatever."

Grandma reached out to touch my face but thought better of it and stopped. She clutched her hands in her lap, and my cheek ached where her fingers should have stroked it.

I felt so far from her. There should have been a chasm between us in the beginning, when my pregnancy was new and we had to learn how to deal with what I had done and the ensuing consequences. But Grandma had been gracious with me in ways I never imagined possible. We had been comfortable. We were dealing just fine with what had happened. It was *now* that things were starting to unravel; now nothing was as it should be. And the only difference was the arrival of Janice and Simon. They were the off frequency that filled our lives with static.

"I wanted to believe her. I wanted to see if there could be another chance for us, but it's been *one day* and already I've been hurt again!"

"Julia, it was an accident. Simon didn't mean—"

"They shouldn't be here. They're making a mess of everything," I fumed. Angrily thrusting the blanket off me, I nearly jumped to my feet. There was resentment coursing through my veins, and when Grandma clutched my wrist, I almost shook her off. "I was right," I repeated with venom in my voice.

"It's not about being right," Grandma said suddenly. Her voice was a cool chip of chiseled stone. I looked down at her, and her eyes were as black as coal in the dimness—intense and unreadable. Her fingers trembled against my skin, and though I had seen the vibrations from time to time when she wrote out a check or lifted a pan from the stove, tonight the stirring in her bones had nothing to do with age.

My breath stayed locked in my chest.

Her fingers tightened. "Who cares if you're right, Julia Anne DeSmit? Maybe you shouldn't have trusted Janice and Simon. Maybe you should have left them in their car at Crescent Lake. Maybe if you guarded yourself more carefully, Simon would never have come along with you today and your secret would still be safe." Grandma caught my other wrist in her free hand and pulled me down until I had no choice but to kneel in front of her. "But maybe you're wrong. Because this has nothing to do with being right. It's about being *free*."

Immediately my eyes stung with hot tears and I frantically blinked them away. My throat closed. I wanted to be angry. I wanted to have a place to unleash the hurt that was inside me. I didn't want to cry. Twisting my arms, I made a little move to pull away.

Grandma hung on tight. "I didn't know you were still so wounded." She was resolute, but she searched my face tenderly, and her eyes were as wide and wet as my own. "I'm so sorry. It's my fault for not realizing how hard this would be for you. We'll get through it together, okay? I'm here; I've always been here for you."

I turned away from her.

"Do you want to be free, sweet girl? Do you want to let go of all this—" Grandma cast around for the right word—"all of these *shadows* inside you?"

Out of the blue, I felt her hands warm on my cheeks. She turned my face toward hers, and without my wrists shackled by her fingers, I was aware of how easy it would be to get up and walk out of the room, retreat somewhere that I could be alone to sob and sulk. I almost did. But I couldn't leave her.

"You have to forgive Janice."

I wasn't ready for those words, and I recoiled from her expectations.

Grandma held me fast with her gaze. "You want to know why life has been so hard? It's not that you lost your dad or that you lost Thomas or even the fact that you're having a baby now. It's hard because you have spent more than a decade of your life clinging to a bitter root. Janice is here because you have to let it go. I invited her into our home because *you have to let it go*."

"I think I've earned the right to hate her," I said through clenched teeth.

Grandma let her hands drop as though I had hit them away. We stared at each other for a moment, and it felt as though I was looking at a stranger.

"Sweetheart, don't do this," Grandma whispered. "Don't wall yourself behind some unquenchable hate. Don't you know that you're only building a stronghold around yourself? Janice and Simon may not be able to get in, but don't forget that when you build a fortress this impenetrable, *you* won't be able to get *out*."

My legs shook when I stood up. Grandma watched me with something akin to fear in her eyes, but I disregarded it. What did she know about the depth of my misery? Who could understand the burden of pain that I had to carry? Forgiveness was for those who deserved it.

I gathered the walls of my stronghold around me as I walked away. At least in there I was protected. I was safe. And I had no intention of coming out.

Part 2

quicken

I FELT THE BABY move for the first time on an unseasonably warm morning in the middle of April.

At first I didn't realize what was happening. There was a flutter in my abdomen, a feeling like falling from a great height. A dip and turn deep inside me that caused me to reach out and grab the porch railing as if Iowa had just experienced the tremors of some far-flung coastal earthquake and I needed to ground myself. I stayed there, splinters of peeling paint digging into the soft palms of my hands, and thought, *We really need to put a new coat on the porch this summer.*

And then it happened again. There was the faintest, cosmic beat of hummingbird wings at the very center of my being. This time, steadied by the thick cedar rail and quiet in my thoughts, I knew what it was.

I held my breath and waited to feel her once more. She didn't disappoint, and a grin burst across my face to match the sunrise I had witnessed only moments earlier. I laughed out loud and pressed my hands to my stomach, hoping to feel her there, awed that she had finally made herself known to me.

I was twenty-two weeks along, give or take, and Dr. Morales had expressed only mild concern that it seemed to be taking so long for me to become aware of the child growing inside. However, I wasn't worried. Grandma had bought me *What to Expect When You're Expecting*, and it suggested that eighteen to twenty-four weeks was a perfectly acceptable timeframe in which to experience "the quickening."

The quickening. I was dubious upon reading it, confused at first because I didn't know what it meant and then downright skeptical because it seemed such a portentous title for something that was surely rather small and routine. But when she first twirled circles inside me, I understood that her inaugural movements were any-thing but small and decidedly not routine. She introduced herself to me with all the eloquence of a rehearsed speech, all the passion of a lover's embrace. Surely the earth itself must have paused in its orbit to acknowledge the celestial movement at my core.

Suddenly, I very fully appreciated that there could not be a more perfect term for what I had just experienced than *quickening*. My breath quickened. My pulse quickened. My fingertips hummed with significance. Even the very life that coursed through me accelerated abruptly toward some distant goal and blurred forward with new meaning and purpose. It was indescribably exhilarating.

And it was the perfect morning for such a momentous event. The horizon was filled with the growing bands of a golden peach sunrise, like a slice of fresh nectarine with the honeyed sun a glistening pit at its center. The earth below was yielding and warm; a green tractor across the field from where I stood dug a silver disc across the fertile surface and made hillocks and furrows of the rich, soggy dirt. Best of all, the scent in the air was of spring and newness. Everything seemed crisp and clean, ready for renewal.

As I surveyed the landscape before me, there was an unexpected swelling beneath my collarbone, a full and happy ache that made me think of prayer. I fought to ignore the compulsion. In my mind, prayer was a habitual thing, a matter of necessity, not beauty. And the loveliness of this morning—the watercolor spring sky, the almost-warm southern breeze, the child dancing inside me—left no room for the tedium of "Our Father, who art in heaven."

But I didn't want to say, *Our Father, who art in heaven*. I wanted to say, *thank You*. For moments alone; for the dark, loamy scent of earth being tilled; for letting me feel her touch me inside. When I thought I would burst, when this thing that filled my chest to overflowing and threatened to pull me apart bone by bone became too much to bear, I said it out loud. "Thank You."

It wasn't that I had ceased trying to chase God and trap Him in some darkened corner where I could hold Him under a careful magnifying glass. I still sought Him. I still believed in Him. I probably always had. But I didn't know how to translate that belief into more than a stoic acceptance of something greater than myself. How did that differ from anybody else? How did that connect me to a God who was as important, as dear, to my grandmother as every measure of breath she inhaled moment by moment?

For now, the irrepressible prayer was enough. The reality of my daughter quickly left room for nothing else in my heart and mind. I wanted to run into the house and throw my arms around Grandma and tell her what I had just experienced. But the thought of what waited inside dampened my spirits a bit, and instead I went to sit at the bottom of the steps.

As soon as the snow had melted and the weather turned, I had become an early riser. The house was too laden with unmet expectations, unresolved hurts. I felt isolated and alone, even though it was my own choice to be so. And, thankfully, things had been tenuously calm. No, not calm. Passive. As though we were all breathing shallowly, afraid that even the smallest exhalation could shatter whatever unspoken agreement we had come to. We were polite to each other, like solicitous but uncomfortable strangers, and though I knew I had the power to change everything, I did nothing.

The anger that had carried me for weeks after Simon's impulsive—though I could now admit *un*intentional—disclosure had faded somewhat with time. I rolled that term around in my mind for many days before finally deciding that *faded* was actually a very good word to use in relation to how I felt about my mother and her son. They drained me, drew me out of myself, made me feel less of everything that I wanted to be. And though the coarse, viscous resentment that I felt toward Janice in particular had thinned and dulled with each day that I woke with her in my home, the color of my unforgiveness was still raw and red, maybe just a little less intense. Instead of fighting, I drew away. Instead of enduring the burden of our dissatisfying togetherness, I became an entity unto myself. The sole survivor in my own empty universe.

The porch became a retreat of sorts, a place where no one would bother me in the minutes before breakfast. We sat down together for meals, and though we went our separate ways the instant the last dish was tucked away in its proper cupboard, I found that I still needed time to prepare for the presence of Janice and Simon at my table. No one bothered me or tried to join me when I slipped out the door early every morning. Sometimes Grandma even wordlessly handed me a cup of coffee as I left the house.

I wished for one now, a celebratory cup of something as dark and black as the earth being turned.

Almost as if I had made the wish aloud, the door opened behind me. I didn't turn around because I knew it was Grandma, and I smiled softly to myself, glad that she had come. In the last weeks, I had hoped often for some sort of compromise to be made. I wanted to reconcile with her after the trauma of the day my pregnancy became public knowledge. Though we had not outwardly fought, we had not resolved the argument of that afternoon when she had tried to talk me into forgiveness, and I longed to go back to the way we were. I missed the unity of our relationship when we were of one accord, two strings plucked in harmony. Quite simply, I missed my grandmother. But I also needed her to know where I stood. I was tolerating Janice and Simon because I had to, not because I wanted to. I was past the point of even contemplating forgiving my mother, and Grandma and I could not patch up the damage that had been done between us until she fully understood and accepted that fact.

I was in a generous mood on such a lovely morning, and when Grandma sat down next to me, I planned to put my arm around her and tell her that I loved her. It would be a start. A place we could move forward from.

But the footsteps on the porch were wrong.

Surprised, I whipped my head around and found Simon making his way across the knotty boards to me. He was wearing his pajama bottoms—rainbow-colored dinosaurs against a blue backdrop—and a slick, green coat with a drawstring hood, unzipped over his bare, narrow chest. The air was easily fifty degrees, even in the shade, and I had to prevent myself from telling him to zip up. That was Janice's job, not mine. Simon clutched a mug filled to the brim with steaming coffee, and his eyes were so trained on it I was worried he would trip.

I scrambled up the steps to him. "Careful," I warned. "You're going to drop that."

"That's what I was afraid of," he said when I eased the mug out of his hands. He looked at me thankfully for a moment before his eyes glazed over with the guardedness that reminded me nothing had changed between us. However, instead of going back into the house as I expected, he started distractedly toward the steps and plopped himself down where I had just been sitting.

Grandma would have been welcome this morning, but I wasn't much in the mood for Simon. Then again, he had brought me coffee, and I wasn't yet willing to give up the morning and go inside. I sighed a little and plodded heavily down the steps to join him.

We sat in silence, me with my back propped against one banister and Simon as far away from me as he could get against the other. At first I considered my hands warming around the mug of coffee. Then I turned my attention to the sun slowly climbing the sky. When I had followed the path of the John Deere until it crowned a distant hill and continued out of sight, I ended up stealing a peek at Simon. He was watching me.

"Why do you get up so early?" Simon asked, looking quickly away. He picked at a sliver of white paint that was curling beside his knee.

"Why do *you* get up so early?" I replied. Though I was often awake by six and out the door in time for the light show around six thirty, Simon was usually on the couch by the time I made it downstairs. He never turned the TV on—even though I knew he had a fondness for early morning cartoons—but instead sat cross-legged with a pile of library books stacked in his lap. I watched him once when he didn't know I was there, and I was astounded at how long he could study a single page. Simon's eyes swept over every square inch of the paper, taking in the minutest detail of the illustrations and carefully examining the words, though I knew he couldn't read.

When I turned the question around, Simon chewed his bottom lip and considered the rutted field on the horizon before looking at me. "Can you keep a secret?"

I didn't really want to like him, to become attached to him so he could leave with Janice someday and break my heart, but his earnestness made me smile in spite of my efforts otherwise. "Yes, I can keep a secret."

Simon glanced over his shoulder to make sure no one had slipped out of the house to hear his proclamation. Satisfied that the coast was clear, he leaned in close and whispered, "I'm learning how to read."

"You are?" I said, trying not to sound amused.

"Yes, but you can't tell my mom. I want to surprise her. When I go to kindergarten next year, I want to be the smartest kid in the class."

"I'm sure you will be," I assured him with all the condescension of a seasoned adult. I didn't believe he could teach himself to read, but I was instantly embarrassed by my own disdain and his innocent acceptance of my phony approval. Simon was looking at me so sweetly—shy eyes behind long lashes and a small, tight-lipped smile—and I was being a jerk. He thought we were making friends. I was surviving his presence. It made me sick with myself, and all at once I was repentant. I blurted out without thinking, "I'll teach you how to read. I think I remember that you were going to help me with my funny faces and I was going to help you with your reading."

If it was possible for his eyes to get any bigger, they did. "Really? Are you really going to teach me how to read?"

Trapped. What in the world was I thinking? "You bet," I said benevolently, but in my mind I yelled, *You idiot!* I laughed nervously, and Simon mistook it for glee at our little conspiracy.

"It's going to be so cool!" he cheered, warming to me as though nothing had happened between us. As though I hadn't been distant and miserable for over a month. He put out his hand for me to slap and waited to see how I would respond.

I gave him a high five and then followed his small hand through a few more hits before he punched me excitedly on the shoulder.

I understood it to mean I was forgiven. If only everything were that easy.

"Do you even know your alphabet?" I wondered, a little nervous now about following through with my promise. Simon was someone I tried to avoid, not someone I sought out time with. How could I make it through private study sessions with him? Besides, I had never taught anyone anything before. What could he possibly learn from me?

But Simon didn't pick up on my hesitance and frowned at me as though I had asked him the dumbest question ever. "Yes, I know my alphabet. I knew that when I was *three*."

"Can you read letters?"

Simon tilted his head, slightly confused, before he figured out what I meant and exclaimed, "Oh yes! I know *M* looks like two mountains and *S* looks like a snake. And *S* is for Simon and *M* is for Mom. *O* is a circle. . . ." He put his finger in his mouth to think. "*J* is a hook, *Z* is a squiggly zigzag, and—"

"Good enough," I interrupted him. "You know your letters."

I turned away from him, but he wasn't done with me. "When can we start, Julia? Will you help me today?"

Moaning inwardly, I managed, "We'll start tomorrow, okay?"

"What time?"

I considered for a moment. "I'll come downstairs in the morning before Janice and Grandma get up."

"It'll be our secret, right?"

"Right."

Simon seemed thrilled with our minor intrigue, and I had to admit that it was nice to see him regard me with something other than caution. I still wasn't ecstatic to have him tangled in the already snarled web of my world, but he definitely was an adorable thing. He was looking out toward the low line of clouds in the east, and I was filled with the sudden urge to lean down and kiss the line of smooth, brown skin above the collar of his coat. I had never felt such a strong motherly—*sisterly*—impulse, and though I certainly didn't dare to follow through, I did lift my hand to ruffle his unkempt hair. Maybe reading lessons wouldn't be so bad. Maybe I could pretend he was just a cute little boy and I was just his tutor. Anything at all but his sister.

"Hey," he started when I touched him, "now you have to tell me a secret."

"I do?" I was not well versed in the rules of childhood etiquette, and had I known this disturbing tenet, I never would have allowed him to spill the beans about his reading scheme to me.

"Yup." Simon stared at me expectantly.

I buried my nose in my coffee to buy a few seconds. What in the world could I possibly tell him? He had already proven himself to be a lousy confidant. A part of me wanted to point this out, but how can you reason with a five-year-old? He was waiting for me to pull him into my inner circle, to entrust him with something as precious to me as his reading lessons were to him.

And then I felt her like a hiccup buried within.

I smiled genuinely at him. What possible harm could come from him knowing this small thing? "All right," I said. "But you can't tell anyone. Not yet."

Simon nodded solemnly.

Taking a deep breath, I locked his eyes in mine and tried to give him the impression of gravity. "I felt the baby move this morning."

"You did?" He bounced off the step in excitement before hopping back down to regard me with curious eyes. "What does that mean?"

I laughed. "Well, the baby is in my tummy, you know? And now that she's getting bigger, she likes to move around. And I can feel her moving."

"You can?"

"Today, for the very first time, I can."

"Does it hurt?"

"Not even a tiny bit. I love it."

"You do? May I feel it?"

"No, I already tried. Only I can feel her right now. But I promise that when she starts kicking harder, I'll let you feel her whenever you want to."

"Cool!"

"Very cool," I agreed.

We fell into silence, a pair of conspirators, maybe even on the road to being friends.

The breeze shifted a bit and Simon stifled a shiver. Zipping up his coat with clumsy hands, he stood and turned toward the house. I was startled to find myself disappointed that he was leaving.

"I'm hungry," he explained, though I had guessed as much. By the amount of food he put away, one would assume Simon had a hollow leg.

I almost laughed at my own thought, but he was hovering over me. He didn't move. "I'll be in soon," I assured him.

I thought my dismissal would be enough, but he waited as if there was something more to say. I arched my eyebrows.

Simon hung his head and scuffed at the edge of a step with his bare feet. Refusing to look at me, he said quietly, "I promise I won't tell your secret this time."

I didn't care if he told the whole world my so-called secret. But it shamed me to see him so contrite and I rushed to relieve him. "I know you won't. And don't worry. I won't tell yours either."

Simon shot me a grateful smile. I held out my hand and he wound up with relish, slapping my palm on his way up the steps.

out of
the blue

THE FOLLOWING MORNING, the day of my first scheduled reading lesson with Simon, I woke with a headache so all consuming I could not lift my head off the pillow.

It was strange for me to wake in a fog of pain; I rarely had headaches, even of the typical garden variety. Migraines were a thing of mystery to me, something that people complained about on television, and I wasn't ready for the throbbing band of steel around the crown of my head like some macabre circlet of misery. Feeling gently with my fingertips, I explored my temples, my aching forehead, the usually warm hollow at the back of my neck, where my hairline formed the top of a heart. It felt like my brain was engulfed in flames, but my skin was almost cold and decidedly clammy.

I squinted, barely making out the numbers on my alarm clock, and was shocked to find that it was already quarter to seven. My first thought was that I had missed my minutes alone on the porch. And then I remembered Simon.

Gripped with a need to explain why I hadn't shown up when we had agreed to meet, I rolled hastily onto my side. I couldn't bear the thought of Simon concluding that I had betrayed him, that I had made promises I did not intend to keep. Throwing the blankets off, I moved to stand and instantly felt myself anchored to the bed as if a rope were tied securely around my skull and the line was pulled too tight. My body bowed back and my heartbeat pulsed behind my eyes. The sheer force of it, a growing, swelling pressure that dotted my vision with sparkling points of ghost light, made me understand for the first time how Jesus could have shed tears of blood in the garden of Gethsemane. Surprise at the unexpected bits of information tucked away in my aching head was quickly replaced by the realization that I would not be getting out of bed anytime soon.

I let my head sink back into the warm pillow and, nauseated by the heat and the lavender and vanilla scent of my shampooed hair, carefully turned it over to press my cheek into the cool, unused underbelly. A contradiction of too hot and remarkably chilly, I pulled the blankets up to the bottom of my nose and suppressed a shiver. I squeezed my eyes shut, knowing that I could not navigate the stairs and apologize to Simon. It would have to wait. I would have to sit him down later, make him understand, do whatever was necessary to restore any confidence he had lost in me.

Somewhere in the murky basin of my throbbing mind, I also remembered that I was expected at Value Foods by eight o'clock. But I was too deep in a fog of agony to care, and I promised myself that five more minutes of shut-eye would do wonders. I would get up and make the world right then.

When I felt a gentle hand on my forehead, I started.

"Shhh . . . ," Grandma whispered. "Are you feeling okay, honey? You didn't come down for breakfast, and when I opened the door at the bottom of the steps, I could hear you moaning."

Moaning? A flash of embarrassment washed over me. "Headache," I said, and though my mind formed more words of explanation, I found them impossible to say.

"Oh, I'm sorry," Grandma consoled.

"Time?" I asked.

"Almost seven thirty."

My eyes flew open, but the morning light was excruciating. I covered my face with my hands. "I'm going to be late for work."

"Forget work. You can't go to Value Foods like this."

I hadn't taken a single sick day since starting at the grocery store, and the idea of indulging in one now both appealed to me and frightened me. The thought of pulling the blankets up over my head and going back to sleep was almost blissfully comforting, but I didn't want to give anyone reason to speculate about my absence. Never mind that Clark seemed to hold sick days and absences against his employees as evidence of their utter lack of work ethic. Only a month ago Graham—innocent, adorable, likable Graham—had been out for a week with the flu. He had almost been hospitalized, but Clark made it seem as if Graham had staged the entire thing to get a few days off.

"No, I'll go," I said, attempting to make my voice sound normal. "A couple of Tylenol and I'll be just fine." My mind stuck on the name of the pain reliever, trying desperately to remember if I was allowed to have ibuprofen or acetaminophen and which was which. "Advil?" I asked.

"We have a generic brand," Grandma clarified, "and it's perfectly safe for you to take. But I don't want you to go to work if you feel like this."

"But—"

"Don't argue. There are more important things than perfect attendance at Value Foods." Grandma's voice was firm, but her hand trailed softly along my cheek, the hard line of my jaw. Her fingers brushed mine where my hand still lay across my eyes.

I dropped my arm and melted into the bed, grateful to bend to her authority and even more thankful for the loving way she touched me. It had been too many weeks since we had allowed a chasm to separate us, and her presence at my side, the compassion in her fingers, felt like the beginnings of a bridge.

We had a ways to go, but I was ready to reach for her.

Though I was nineteen years old and soon to be a mother myself, for this one brief moment on a pain-filled morning I felt like a helpless child. I almost wished I were still small enough to climb into her lap and be encompassed by the loving ring of her arms.

And like an unanticipated fragrance—a whiff of wild strawberries in a ditch full of weeds—I remembered the last time I had been a child on my father's lap.

We found out that he had cancer a week after Christmas. I was fifteen years old, self-absorbed, I suppose, and convinced that my world would never be any different from what it was at that safe and comfortable time. The news hit me with the force of a nuclear bomb. Of course, I knew something was wrong; Dad had been circling in and out of the doctor's office for weeks. But I told myself that he would be diagnosed with high blood pressure or high cholesterol or something else appropriately run-of-the-mill and treatable with mild diet exchanges that we would joke over. Grandma would fry bacon and eggs for me in the morning, and I'd tease him about his pasty bowl of oatmeal.

When he sat me down in the living room on New Year's Eve, my heart knew that the heaviness in his eyes carried something much more fateful than a few uncomplicated diet alterations. The news was not good.

"Baby girl . . . ," he started and couldn't continue.

My hands began to sweat as soon as he called me by that special name, a nickname he only used once every great while because I had asked him not to call me by it. I wasn't a baby anymore, and I definitely considered myself more woman than girl. But sometimes, when he loved me so intensely he could think of nothing else, he didn't remember my request and called me *baby girl* anyway.

I waited, breathless, and he said a lot of things before finally getting to the *C* word, *cancer*, and another one, *colon*, which inexplicably made me blush because I was young and could not imagine a more horrible manifestation of such an awful disease. I was shocked and suddenly freezing, and when my teeth started to chatter, I made them stop by saying, "No." I said it over and over and over again: *No, no, no, no, no, no* . . . A quiet drone, an intonation that quickly became a chant, as if the right mantra could tame and trap the words that he had released into the room.

I jumped up from the couch at one point and began to pace, but before I could take five steps, Dad was behind me, putting his hands on my shoulders and choking back a sob. He sat down in the recliner, pulling me with him until I was curled on his lap, my head on his trembling shoulder. He cried and stroked my hair, wetting it with his tears. I didn't have tears, not yet, but I felt my heart pounding behind my rib cage, straining against the bones that held it in place and beating wildly as if I had just run the two-mile in gym class. Dad just rocked and rocked.

He lived only nine and a half months after the diagnosis.

I remember wishing near the end that I had sat on his lap more. But after the revelation, there hadn't been any time to. Chemo and radiation happened simultaneously, a drastic approach recommended because Dad was young and seemingly healthy. He was left a wasted man. While the narrow bones of his legs would never support me, and the crushing weight of my hundred-pound frame would have been unbearable, I held his hand or stroked his head, remembering what it felt like when his arms were strong around me.

From the cloudy haze of my headache, I was comforted by the fact that if Grandma felt tears on my cheeks, she would most likely attribute them to pain. I turned my face into her hand almost imperceptibly and gave in. "Okay. I'll stay home."

"Good." Immediately Grandma was all business. She gently tapped her knuckle under my chin and then straightened out my bedclothes, folding the sheet over my down comforter and bringing the satiny fabric up around my neck. "I'll call Value Foods and tell them that you're sick today. Who should I ask to speak with?"

"Clark," I muttered, wishing that there were someone else I could direct her to. He would not be gracious or accommodating.

"All right. I'll let him know, and then I'll be right back with something for the pain. Are you hungry? Maybe a slice of toast?"

"No, thank you," I said, unwilling to even think about chewing as it would mean moving my head. An undulating roll of nausea also added protest to the topic of eating.

I heard rather than saw Grandma get up to leave. Her footsteps stopped at the top of the stairs and I opened my eyes a crack. "I'm going to make an appointment for you with Dr. Morales."

My heart seized at her proclamation. It hadn't occurred to me that this was anything more than a headache, but apparently the thought had crossed her mind.

"Do you think there's something wrong with the baby?" I whispered, barely able to get the words out around the fear that had suddenly lodged tightly in my throat.

"No," Grandma assured me. "Headaches are often part of pregnancy." She started down the steps and just before her head disappeared she added, "But we want to be sure."

I held my mind still while she was gone, suspending any movement or thought so I wouldn't panic. And in the stillness, I noticed that something was missing. I didn't feel her moving. Anxious, I tried to remember the last time I had felt her twirl inside me and realized that she had wobbled shortly after supper last night. I had not felt her again. A slow horror raked gnarled fingers against the thickness in my chest. But because I could not deal with my fears,

I pressed them down and down until this worry was a caged animal, thrashing and wild but contained.

Against my wishes, Grandma returned with a tray of orange juice, water with three square ice cubes, and a plate that was still steaming with hot scrambled eggs and buttered toast topped with her homemade strawberry jelly. I had helped her put up the neat jars of garnet-colored jam myself in early June. Last summer. It seemed a world away. Before Brighton. Before Thomas's rejection. Before Parker. I hadn't thought of him in many weeks, and just his name in my aching mind startled me wide-awake. My fears and shortcomings lined up like accusers at the foot of my bed. I stifled a groan.

Grandma smiled at me and left the tray on my bedside table. "Everything is taken care of. Clark sounded a bit put out, but I told him you were very ill. Dr. Morales is going to squeeze you in at eleven." She slipped out as unobtrusively as she had come.

Eleven o'clock seemed far away, and my heart grew featherless little wings when I thought of my baby in distress. I could feel the weak fluttering throughout my entire body, but I held myself from the verge of full-fledged terror by focusing on my afflicted head. Purposefully, in an act of resolute self-preservation, I pushed the dismal possibilities out of my mind and propped myself up on my elbow to reach for the water and the two neat little pills beside it. I willed myself to start feeling better and drank the entire glass without stopping. For some reason, the ice appealed to me and I let each cube melt slowly on the desert of my tongue.

I wanted to lie back down, but I forced myself to nibble at the corners of my toast. I even tried a forkful of eggs, but they turned out to be limp and unappetizing, so I swallowed them quickly without chewing. Though I was still nauseous and dizzy, I felt that I had at least made some progress. Surely I would be healthy and whole in no time. Surely this headache was nothing more than exactly that.

I fell back into my pillow and promptly drifted into a sleep like shallow tide pools; I wanted to dive in but couldn't.

I did feel a little better when Grandma woke me after ten. The headache that had exploded like fireworks in the dark caverns of my brain was diffused and insubstantial, trails of that formerly unbearable intensity trickling from the top of my head, down my neck, and across my shoulders in ashy lines of washed-out color. A mere watermark of what had come before. But the echo of pain remained and I was spent and exhausted, worn and weary as if I had just run a marathon.

The steamy spray of a hot shower felt disproportionately wonderful, and I let the jets pulse against my closed eyes, washing away the clinging remnants of the agony I had felt. I told myself that this day was a gift, that after a reassuring appointment with Dr. Morales, I would actually have the entire house to myself for an afternoon. Janice would be at work, Simon at preschool, and Grandma at Ladies' Aid. I could read books, tune the radio to my favorite station, maybe even bake cookies and have them ready with a tall glass of cold milk for Simon when the bus dropped him off at three thirty. It would be a peace offering to make up for the disappointment of our missed morning together.

Though it was the middle of spring and there were only a few weeks of school left, when Janice and Simon were finally settled in our home, the first thing she had done was enroll her son in the community preschool. It was really nothing more than a portable trailer parked outside the overcrowded elementary school, and every time I drove past the drab grayness, I thought of Simon and cringed for him. I was sure it was a fine school, sure the teachers were kind and competent, but Simon was so gentle, so tender, I felt like I had to protect him somehow. I think we all felt that way.

I decided he would feast on peanut butter chocolate chip cookies still warm from the oven when he came home today.

Janice was no longer able to do those sorts of motherly things for him. She worked Monday through Friday, nine to five. It was still astonishing to me that she had gotten her old job at the dentist's office back. The day that Janice went job hunting, her very first stop was her old place of employ, and she secured the position without having to inquire anywhere else. It was kind of a freak thing that the secretary had quit only three days previous, but I couldn't help wondering what it said about Janice that the good doctor was so eager and willing to take her back. I didn't know whether to readjust my perception of her or assume that the doctor was a poor judge of character.

But uncertainties aside, Janice's job paid relatively well and she was even able to afford a small rent. The day after her first paycheck, Janice had opened a bank account and written Nellie DeSmit a tidy check for two hundred dollars. She laid it on Grandma's plate before breakfast, and Grandma wasn't the only one who did a double take when she saw the unanticipated, carefully penned numbers. At first she stared at it indecisively, her mouth opening and closing as she thought of things to say and quickly dismissed them. Finally she looked straight up at Janice and said, "Thank you." Then she folded the check and slipped it in the front cover of her Bible.

"Are you about ready, honey?" Grandma's voice floated through the closed bathroom door and the hum of cascading water.

Guiltily, I turned off the slippery tap and called back, "I'll be just a minute yet."

"We need to leave in ten."

I toweled off and wrapped my hair turban-style so I could work some color into my pale cheeks. My blush was called New Bride, which always gave my sensibilities an awkward little twist when I swept my brush across it in the morning. But it was a good color on me, and with a bit of mascara and pearly lip gloss, I didn't look so haggard, so ashen and depleted.

Grandma smiled at me when I emerged moments later. My hair was still wet and pulled into a loose braid, and I wore a comfy T-shirt with three-quarter-length sleeves over jeans that had to be secured with a hair tie. I felt sloppy and sleepy, but I must have looked much better than I had a mere hour ago.

"He'll listen for the heartbeat and then send you on your way," Grandma assured me.

But Dr. Morales wanted to do more.

"There's the heartbeat," he said, pressing a Doppler to a spot just above my right hip bone. The room filled with the gallop and swish of blood coursing through my baby's veins. I had heard her heartbeat before; I knew well the pounding of each throb as if a tiny horse ran furious circles in my belly. But it awed me every time, and I let go of a shuddering breath when I realized that she was well. Her heart beat and beat and beat.

A pulse of static filled the air, and Dr. Morales commented as if to himself, "The baby is kicking."

I felt it.

"She's fine," I exhaled.

"I'd like to do an ultrasound," Dr. Morales said.

"What?"

My voice must have betrayed my alarm because Dr. Morales looked up sharply. "Don't worry, Julia; I'm just being overcautious." He flipped my chart open on his lap and extracted a sheet of paper. "Look at these heartbeats: 150 beats per minute, 155, 160, 150. . . . Every heartbeat we've ever had for your baby has been 150 or over. Today she's clocking in at 120."

"Is that bad?" I asked, aware of how desperate I sounded.

"No, it's perfectly normal. But we're going to do an ultrasound anyway. I didn't schedule one earlier because you're young and healthy. There was no reason to perform an unnecessary procedure. But now, with your headache and the change in the baby's pulse, I'd like to just take a peek." Dr. Morales dropped the medical file on a low counter and grabbed a fistful of paper towels to wipe the lotion off my stomach. "Hey—" he smiled, catching my eye—"don't look so worried. Most women beg me for an ultrasound. You'll get to see the baby."

That was a nice thought, but my hands quivered anyway when Dr. Morales's nurse handed me the sheet for the radiology department at the hospital.

Grandma stood when I walked into the waiting room and gripped my elbow in support and concern. She must have read my apprehension in the downturn of my wavering mouth. "Julia?"

"I need an ultrasound."

"Is something wrong?" Her fingers tightened on my arm, and

I realized, maybe for the first time, how much this baby meant to her, too.

I swallowed. "No, she's fine. Dr. Morales just wants to check things out."

Mason Community Hospital, a small, low-lying building with a covered roundabout entrance, shared a parking lot with the medical clinic. It was less than a block from one entrance to the other, and though we could have used the glassed-in walkway, I hated the antiseptic smell that hung in the halls and elected to take the outdoor route. As we passed through the neat rows of cars, a sharp breeze played with our hair and drove leftover gravel from the winter roads against our shins. I hurried, wanting to escape the wind but also driven by a nervous energy that tried to persuade me to keep walking. No news was good news. It would be so easy to hop back in my car and pretend that everything was okay. But as I pulled even with my means of escape, I kept right on walking. I had to know.

We paused beneath a Japanese cherry tree on the boulevard flanking the hospital to let a car pass. The branches hung bare and brown, but hundreds upon hundreds of buds were tiny acorns of promise filling the tree with possibility. I fingered one and tried to calm the pulsing doubts in my mind. My breath was short and anxious, and it stopped in my chest altogether when Grandma curled an arm around me and said, "Pray with me."

Of course, we prayed together often. In church, before meals, and sometimes when Grandma heard news that needed to be addressed immediately instead of tucked away for mention later, we bowed our heads and brought our petitions before the God who Grandma was convinced heard every word we uttered. But an uncertain discomfort usually niggled at the corners of my mind, and though I tried to understand, tried to believe, I often felt my voice was being raised in an echoless vacuum. I spilled thoughts, dreams, requests, and they melted into some great expanse of nothingness as if they died the moment they left my lips. I was afraid to voice my plea now. What if the answer was not what I hoped for?

But Grandma took my silence as assent and held me close for a moment as she prayed over the baby and me. I let her words graze me, trickling against my skin and dripping off in some ancient rite of blessing. A mild sense of comfort rushed through me when she said, "Amen," as if I had zipped up a jacket against the dipping temperatures of an autumn night, and my soul stirred beneath the unexpected. I tried to hold the feeling around me, but it was fleeting and gone before I could raise my face to thank my grandmother for her kindness.

The radiology department was more or less abandoned, and we were ushered in almost immediately. Grandma hung back for a moment, and when I felt her slip from my side, I stopped and whipped around, afraid that she did not want to come. Her face told me that she hoped to follow me but didn't quite dare. She wasn't sure if she was invited. I closed the space between us and slid my arm through hers, pulling her with me wordlessly.

It was dark and warm in the ultrasound room, and I couldn't decide if it was too close and somehow ominous or enveloping and cozy. Following the technician's instructions, I bared my tummy and curled my arm under my head so I could see the black-and-white screen that would afford me the very first glimpses of my child.

Grandma stood beside the low gurney, holding my other hand

and alternating between gently rubbing it and thoughtlessly clutching it. It occurred to me that she had not really allowed herself to think there was anything wrong with the baby. Though she seemed collected, together, I knew she was well aware that God didn't answer every prayer exactly as we hoped He would.

"Twenty-two, almost twenty-three weeks?" the technician asked cheerfully, glancing at my chart. "This will be a fun one—you'll get to see the baby so clearly!" She was probably forty, with dark, straight hair that swept up and out stylishly above her chin. Her smile was infectious, and when she fixed me with a particularly merry one, I couldn't help but smile back wanly.

Fine. Everything would be just fine.

"We've got a low heartbeat and a migraine?" she queried.

"I guess," I replied, wondering why she was asking me if my information was laid before her on the paper from Dr. Morales.

But then she wrinkled her nose amicably, and I realized that she was only trying to loosen me up a bit. "You know, migraines can't really be diagnosed," she said. "But with all the extra blood in your system, plus the added stress of baby-growing on your body . . . even if you've never had a migraine it's not uncommon to start getting them when you're pregnant." She patted the low, tight arc of my belly, apparent now even when I was lying flat on my back. "Hey, don't look so worried."

She turned the screen away from Grandma and me, explaining that she had a lot of measurements to take and she'd let us see everything when she was done. As she squirted warm lotion just under my belly button, I watched her face settle and focus. She got to work.

I followed her eyes as they studied the screen and tried to read her expression. But she was good at what she did, and her features remained utterly blank as she pressed my stomach over and over, pausing here and there to key in something one-handed amid the clicks and beeps of the machine. I was thankful for her unqualified friendliness and the fact that she didn't seem at all perturbed that my grandmother stood beside me instead of an apprehensive but doting husband. She made me feel safe somehow, as if she could rewrite whatever was happening inside me with a few strokes of the instrument she held in her steady hand. I relaxed somewhat against the pillows.

Finally, she stopped and spun her chair so she could regard Grandma and me. She took a deep breath, and I could feel tears rise from somewhere far away and hidden to collect at the corners of my eyes. She was going to tell me something was wrong. The baby was ill, somehow malformed, or worse. The room went still with the burden of my fear, and I felt it weighing on us, filling every square inch of space with a quiet dread. I closed my eyes.

"You have a beautiful, healthy baby!" The voice was disembodied, almost meaningless, and it took me a moment to hold it in my mind before it made sense.

My eyes flew open and found Grandma. We sputtered in accord and then laughed as the news sunk in.

"I couldn't help being a little worried," Grandma admitted, touching a finger below each eye and sniffling. She bent to give me an impromptu kiss on the forehead.

"Me too," I said, relief washing over me—the deep, cool, soulful sea that had eluded me as I lay buried in the pain of what I now knew was a migraine.

"Would you like to see?"

Of course! It was an unwarranted question, and Grandma and I cried sweet, happy tears as we counted ten fingers and ten toes and marveled over the upturned slope of a tiny nose in perfect profile.

The technician grinned at us and spent a few moments pointing out the details of my child's delicate frame. As she moved the wand across my skin, the baby drifted in and out of focus, offering glimpses of herself before retreating almost shyly into the shadows. My breath caught at the sight of her carefully crossed ankles and prettily shaped arms curled beneath the curve of her cheek. I could imagine those limbs, long and tanned, on the little girl that she would someday be.

"Everything looks great," the technician assured me as she pointed out vital organs and shared important measurements. "And it looks like you're pretty much right on track with your due date. Does August 7 sound right?"

I nodded absently, happy that she was coming at all and rather indifferent to the specifics of when.

It hadn't occurred to me to ask or even wonder, and when the technician clapped mischievously, it took me a minute to realize what she was going to offer. "Would you like to know if it's a boy or a girl?"

A little sound from Grandma told me that she was delighted at the idea of knowing.

But I waffled. I already knew my baby. It would be fun to surprise everyone at the birth, to be right after all this time that my daughter had been so connected to me, so much a part of me, from day one. But certainty meant that I could buy something pink. There was a little sleeper in Wal-Mart, a soft, rosy, impossibly small thing with a row of white, doe-eyed bunnies across the chest. I thought of stopping there on our way home to buy my baby her very first gift.

"How sure are you?" I asked, aware that these things weren't always so black-and-white.

"Oh, I'd say 100 percent." The technician winked.

invitations

KNOWING WHO MY CHILD WAS carried a certain weight that I had not anticipated and was not prepared for. There were photographs of a sort, fuzzy black-and-white things with alien features that swam out of the darkness and aligned themselves into bent legs and lines of curved ribs before fading back into obscurity. Grandma wanted to put them on the refrigerator, but I balked at the idea and instead cut the six pictures apart and stacked them like note cards that I could study and examine at will. It was hard to focus on much else, and when Mrs. Walker caught me off work one morning and invited me over for tea, just the two of us, I jumped at the idea. I wanted someone to talk to.

The day was overcast but warmish, and I was still peeling off my light sweatshirt when Mrs. Walker gestured at the stacks of envelopes and beribboned invitations on her dining room table. She gave me a wry smile. "Thomas is busy writing a big unit for his class on teaching history, and Francesca has her last round of clinicals. Guess who gets to address all 350 of their wedding invitations?"

I nodded in what I hoped looked like sympathy and waited for the familiar falling feeling that I associated with Thomas and Francesca's impending wedding. It wasn't that I was still pining for Thomas or that I was jealous of Francesca. Rather, when I thought of the future Mr. and Mrs. Thomas Walker, I had a sense of being cut loose, of finding myself floating and anchorless and not at all sure of how to plant my feet on solid ground again.

Thomas was what I had always planned for myself, and although I thought I had let him go long ago, when he and Francesca announced their engagement in the beginning of April, I didn't know what else to hope for. But as Mrs. Walker showed me the pearl-colored rectangles of paper with their pink and apple green striped ribbons, they seemed inconsequential to me. I realized I was already flying, pushed forward, upward, by a completely different current. The dream I once had of Thomas was nothing more than a memory. It had been replaced when I wasn't paying attention.

I settled my sweatshirt over the back of one of the tall chairs and pulled down the edges of my short-sleeved shirt, self-consciously making sure that it wasn't too short to cover my ill-fitting khakis. Trying to appear interested, I made a little noise of appreciation.

"They're beautiful," I said, vaguely admiring the exquisitely lettered cards. There was a sheer piece of embossed vellum over the heavy paper of the formal invitation. The grosgrain ribbon holding the two pieces of paper together was tied in a perfect, tiny bow, and I fingered it absently, knowing that Francesca had been painstaking with each and every one. It was just her style.

Strangely, I had thought of doing something similar for birth announcements. But who announces the birth of an illegitimate baby? Who would I send such cards to?

And yet, I would have written her name across the top of the vellum, just her name, with the rest of her information—weight, length, time of arrival—printed on the inside. *Ellie Danielle,* the announcement would have read. Ellie for Grandma—her name without the *N*—and Danielle for Dad. Ellie Danielle DeSmit. It was perfect.

But she was a he.

"Just perfect," I said, startling myself with the sound of my own voice. I hadn't intended to say anything aloud. I wasn't even sure what I meant.

Mrs. Walker assumed I was talking about the invitations. "They certainly are pretty," she agreed, picking one up and then tossing it back on the teetering pile. "But what a pain! Be glad that you didn't get roped into helping."

I almost said, "Believe me, I am." Instead I murmured a meaning-less nicety: "They were worth it."

Mrs. Walker pursed her lips. "I don't know about that."

The teakettle on the stove began to whistle its shrill note, and Mrs. Walker disappeared into the kitchen. "Back in a sec," she called.

I pulled out a chair and was about to sink into it when I noticed a framed photograph across the table. It was a portrait of Thomas and Francesca. Their engagement picture. I walked around the enormous harvest table and picked it up.

The couple was staring directly at the camera, so no matter which angle I surveyed them from, their eyes seemed locked on mine. Francesca's head was tilted toward Thomas, and her chin was slanted down a little too far, giving her an almost sinister look. Thomas didn't fare much better. His smile was wooden, and one eye was open slightly wider than the other. He had never been very photogenic. But I was being critical. They were a lovely pair.

Mostly I was just thankful that I didn't have to worry about any residual feelings for Thomas Walker. My life had been consumed with the pregnancy, and any longing that I had for Thomas had been placed like billowing robes of consequence on my anticipated Ellie Danielle. A daughter that didn't exist.

It bothered me that I mourned her so much. In the ultrasound room, after the technician told us the news, Grandma had squealed with delight and buried me in a hug that hid the disappointment—no, *shock*—on my own face. I had been so sure; I had left room in my heart for nothing else, and it was almost frighteningly disconcerting to know that I had been dead wrong all along. It was so stupid, but I couldn't help feeling like a stranger occupied my body instead of the tiny soul mate that I had thought I'd known for five months.

In the days after the revelation, I forced myself to confront my desire for a daughter. I had to admit that she was the child who was supposed to complete the broken trinity of generations under

Grandma's roof: mother, daughter, granddaughter. Janice had vacated her place in our family tree so long ago that it was almost as if she had never existed—and yet something was missing; something was not as it should be. So I had risen to take her place. And my little girl would have finished it. She would have made things right, steadied the scale and mended the chain that Janice had broken when she walked out of our lives.

But now Janice was home. I still couldn't really accept that she had returned to take her own role, and I half blamed her for the presence of my son. I was angry with her—she had upset the balance, insufficiently plugged a hole that my daughter was supposed to fill. But I also knew that I was being ridiculous. I was a silly little fool. And though I knew it, accepted it, I couldn't help missing the young woman who would have been the smallest sliver of my very soul. She would have been an extension of me, a part of me somehow and yet altogether separate. She would *not* have made the mistakes that my mother had made. That I had made. She was my freckled, ponytailed redemption. She was a dream.

"Strawberry tea with a squirt of honey and an almond-cranberry scone. I baked them fresh this morning." Mrs. Walker set a wicker tray right on top of some scattered envelopes. "Don't know if they're any good, but we'll see. You're my guinea pig."

"Everything you bake is good." I put the picture down and found a chair that had access to an open plot of table. "I promise not to spill on the invitations."

"And I promise to *try* not to spill on the invitations," Mrs. Walker countered. "Maggie already made a mess of one of the stacks by tipping a glass of orange juice. She promised she wouldn't, but . . ."

The thought made me smile a little. I could picture Maggie's eyes flashing as she defended herself to Francesca. No, she wouldn't defend. She'd just shrug as if to say, *Oops*. Maybe a sassy half apology would follow. Maybe not.

"Do you care if I address some envelopes while you're here?" Her question surprised me because Mrs. Walker was one to tell, not one to ask. I wondered that she bothered to secure my approval at all. It made me feel self-conscious, like she was afraid it would hurt me to watch her mail invitations to her son's wedding.

"Of course not," I replied quickly. "In fact, I'll help you. Grandma and I took a calligraphy class together when I was in middle school, and I still have a pretty neat hand."

Mrs. Walker sighed with relief. "Thank you. I think it's absurd that Francesca insists on handwritten envelopes. I have a computer program that would do this all in minutes! And it's not like we have tons of time, either. Have you ever heard of such a short engagement?"

"When is the wedding?" I asked absently.

"July 14. Three months to plan, prepare, and pull off the wedding of the century." Mrs. Walker sipped her tea and pursed her lips abruptly because it was too hot. "I still can't believe that they're having the wedding here. Francesca's from California, you know. I'm the mother of the groom! I'm supposed to be taking it easy, flying out to sunny San Diego instead of worrying if the Glendale Golf and Country Club is going to be swanky enough for the *familia* Hernandez." She rubbed her thumb and fingers together as if to show me the extent of their wealth.

I shrugged evasively because I had always thought of the Walkers as well-to-do. "Do you have an extra calligraphy pen?"

"Silver ink," Mrs. Walker said with a dry edge in her voice. She fumbled through the piles of papers to find a sleek pen. "The postal workers are going to love her."

It was healing to copy out line after line of distant dwellings in the clean, steady hand that I had learned all those years ago. The first few envelopes would probably be considered substandard, but by the time I had written out a dozen addresses, there was a certain flair to each capital letter, a swivel and sweep of arching lines that became bigger and bolder with each stroke of the pen.

Mrs. Walker and I talked about everyday things, work and weather and her girls, and when she began to slip references to Janice and Simon into our conversation, I didn't object. We had been down this road before; in fact the entire Walker clan had met Janice and Simon at Sunday dinner one week. Simon Walker had been a little overwhelmed by the utter adoration of the younger boy who shared his name, but other than his deer-in-the-headlights look by the end of the meal, everything had gone relatively well. I had expected the meeting to be colossally awkward. Instead, the Walkers seemed somehow respectful, maybe even reverential, as if something significant was happening in our home. Something rare and beautiful, something that should not be undermined. The whole thing left me mildly confused.

But I respected Mrs. Walker's advice and found her insight helpful. After our less than disastrous Sunday dinner, I was particularly grateful for her grace when it came to my unconventional family. I didn't mind when, after approaching the topic every way but head-on, Mrs. Walker finally gave in and said, "How are things with Janice and Simon these days?"

"Fine," I said matter-of-factly. She wanted more than that, but there wasn't much more to say. Janice and I orbited each other as always, and while Simon and I were getting closer, it was hardly momentous. "I'm teaching Simon how to read," I offered and immediately chastised myself because I had broken his confidence.

"That's sweet," Mrs. Walker said, obviously happy that my half brother and I were doing something together.

"It's a secret," I clarified. "Please don't tell Grandma or Janice. Or anyone, for that matter. I know he's five, but he trusted me with this."

Mrs. Walker laughed. "Don't worry; my lips are sealed. Besides, I'm much more interested in your other secret."

My hand stopped dead on the page. "Other secret?" I asked, not looking up.

"Something's going on. I've known you long enough to know something is eating you up. And for once I don't think it's my son."

I would have been mortified, but it was Mrs. Walker. "That obvious?" I asked, a little numb that she could see through me so easily. "I don't know what I should be more upset about: that you know I loved Thomas or that you know I have a secret."

She reached across the table to give my arm a friendly pinch. "I love it that you loved Thomas. It's no secret that we all adore you. But God has something different planned for you, honey. Something better."

My skepticism must have been etched across my face when I glanced at Mrs. Walker because she suddenly got serious. "I don't believe that, Julia DeSmit. I *know* that."

Her declaration made me feel equally guilty and indignant; it both bewildered me and enticed me to wonder at the path she took to know so much about the road that God had laid out for me. I knew so little about it myself. I had gone to church with Grandma faithfully every single week. I had read my Bible almost daily, even when the words swam together on the page and made about as much sense to me as the list of side effects in small print at the bottom of pharmaceutical advertisements. I was doing my part. And nothing had changed. The eternal *He* did not seem to be doing His part. But then again, maybe I was doing something wrong. Maybe I hadn't yet figured out the formula.

Still, Mrs. Walker's interest touched me. She could almost make me believe that what she said was true: there was something better for me.

Thankfully, Mrs. Walker couldn't know the emotions that her words had stirred up, and she made her voice light again to continue her gentle probing. "Anyway, I think you just admitted that there is another secret."

I thought of my baby boy and my deal with Grandma that we would keep it between the two of us. I knew Grandma would keep her end of the bargain. "It has to stay a secret," I said apologetically.

She had a wonderful way of curving her eyebrow so high it was almost comical in its stature and expression. I had to look away from her to stop myself from laughing. "Big secret?" she asked, knowing the effect she had on me.

"I'm full of big secrets," I teased back, but somehow it didn't sound very funny. It sounded rather real. "But this is a small one," I added. "Not a big deal at all."

"Hmmm," Mrs. Walker intoned. "I wouldn't want to pry it out of you."

But I wanted it out. I wanted to let Mrs. Walker see a little bit of my disappointment because I couldn't let Grandma know how I felt. She was so happy.

Mrs. Walker saw me crack and instantly reined herself in. "You absolutely do not have to tell me. I was only kidding around." She turned back to her envelopes.

I took a deep breath. "I'm having a boy," I said, staring at her soft, short curls. There were more gray strands than I remembered.

Mrs. Walker's head popped up. "A boy?" she exclaimed, obviously thrilled. The look on my face pulled her up short. "That's not a good thing?"

"Of course it's a good thing," I said in a rush. "I just . . . I just thought I was having a little girl." Once I had said it out loud, I realized how incredibly dumb it sounded. I was acting like a selfish child, and it was downright embarrassing. Flustered, I capped and uncapped my pen, fumbling as I exposed the gleaming gray nub and tried to focus on the next address.

"Julia," Mrs. Walker broke in softly, "it's okay." I opened my mouth to make nothing of it, but she hadn't paused. "You know, I had a friend who had three baby girls in a row. When she got pregnant a fourth time, she prayed every single day that it would be a boy. She was convinced that God had answered her prayers."

I already knew the outcome of the story from the tone of her voice, but I listened anyway because I wanted to know what the friend did with her disappointment.

"When the baby was born, it was a girl," Mrs. Walker finished, confirming what I had suspected. She stopped, didn't say anything more.

I looked up. "And . . . ," I prompted.

"And it was very, very hard on her."

I was mystified. Where was the moral to this story? "Is that supposed to make me feel better?" I asked, struggling not to sound indignant.

"No. I'm just trying to let you know that it's all right to feel whatever you feel. Do I think that you'll get over this? Yes. Do I think that you'll fall crazy in love with this baby the moment he's put in your arms and it won't matter that he is a he? Yes. But for now, don't beat yourself up for feeling sad."

It was the last thing I expected to hear. But somehow I felt the tension between my shoulders ease at Mrs. Walker's reassurances. "Thank you," I said.

"Don't thank me," Mrs. Walker demurred. "Any mother would tell you the exact same thing. We all go through moments when our children are not who we hoped they would be."

It was a slow and lazy morning once I had unburdened myself. Mrs. Walker's scones were indeed incredibly good, and I had a second, effectively ruining my lunch, before I headed home. Tea alone with Mrs. Walker had been a much-needed reprieve, and I nearly crushed her in an unreserved embrace as I got ready to go.

"Hey, what did I do to deserve that?" She laughed.

"You listened," I told her earnestly. "Sometimes I don't feel like I have anyone to talk to. Lately Grandma and I have had a hard time connecting. . . ." It was true that Janice and Simon got in the way of my time with Grandma, but there was more to it than that, and Mrs. Walker guessed as much.

She frowned. "Nellie loves you so much."

"I know." I smiled slowly. "We're working on it."

"Good. Glad to hear it."

We stepped onto the porch together, and I turned my face to the sun, reveling in the warmth of its rays. It was decidedly spring and the ensuing softness of the world seemed to gentle everything else in turn. My problems seemed lesser. My worries not as urgent. I was so glad I had come.

"Thanks so much," I said, smiling at Mrs. Walker and starting down the steps. "It's been a great morning."

I thought she would respond in kind, thank me for coming or wish me a good day, but when she said my name, it was tight and unexpectedly urgent. "Julia?"

Somewhat taken aback, I turned.

Mrs. Walker was watching me with an uncertain line deepening a shadow across the length of her forehead. I was surprised to see her troubled and took a step back toward her. "What's wrong?"

"Nothing's wrong," she assured me, but the cheer in her voice seemed forced. "It's just . . . remember that friend I was telling you about? The one with four daughters?"

I nodded, perplexed.

"Here." Mrs. Walker held out a postcard-size piece of paper.

I took it without hesitation but did not look at it, focusing instead on her distressed gaze. I waited for her to explain.

"She's a counselor. I thought about giving you her number so many times, but it felt out of place. Well, it still feels out of place, but I guess I was ready to do it today." Her words tumbled over one another, restless and eager to be out of her mouth.

"Counselor?" I asked, not understanding.

"She's an adoption counselor. I don't know if you ever thought about giving the baby up for adoption—and I'm not suggesting that you do—but she'd love to talk to you. It's free. You don't have to commit to anything. . . ." Mrs. Walker wrung her hands.

I tried to swallow around the dryness in my throat. "Adoption?" I managed after a moment. "You mean abandon my baby?"

Mrs. Walker's eyes got wide. "No, of course not. Not *abandon*. Give the baby up for *adoption*."

I knew exactly what I had said, but I smiled thinly and tipped the postcard at her. "I'll take a look at it."

"Don't be mad. This is why I never gave it to you before. I didn't want you to misunderstand my intentions." Mrs. Walker reached for me and grasped my shoulders with her lovely hands. Her perfectly manicured nails dug into the fabric of my shirt. "I'm not suggesting anything. I just want you to know all your options." A bottomless compassion radiated through her fingers, and though I knew she meant well, I felt she was badly misguided.

Closing my eyes, I tried to calm the mistrust that rose up in response to her concern. Mrs. Walker was looking out for me. It was an act of friendship, of love even. "I'll think about it," I said, hoping to sound more receptive than I felt.

"That's all I ask," she conceded. Pulling me into a quick hug, she kissed my cheek. "You're going to be just fine, Julia DeSmit. Just fine."

I nodded once before walking away.

In the grove, I pressed my back against a budding tree and examined the glossy card. There was a picture of a handsome young man and a cute, curly-haired woman cradling a baby whose face was hidden by a fluffy, white blanket. They were huddled over the infant, and it didn't matter that no one could see the child. The faces of the happy couple said it all. *All His Children*, the card read. *We will find a loving home for your baby.*

"She—*he*—already has one," I said. I tore the card once and then again and again until I couldn't tear it anymore. When I held up my hand, the many pieces scattered in the wind, odds and ends destined for squirrels' nests and tree hollows and forgotten burrows. Nothing more.

blue moon

I WANTED SO MUCH when I was young. I was an endless abyss of want, of need, of desperate dreams for myself that defied logic. The promise of what was to come hung like rings around the moon on clear autumn nights; the future was unmistakable. It was always there, glistening in the dark and suggesting that life was little more than climbing a ladder into the sky, where I could reach up with one hand and secure everything that I had ever hoped for in my grasping fingers.

Oh, I dreamed.

And they are not easy to give up, these dreams.

When I learned that I was having a baby, those lavish promises fell like moonbeams that flickered with ephemeral light and quickly died against the backdrop of my much-changed life. I was a modern woman; we were decades past the days when girls were sent to distant relatives to have babies in secret and return as if nothing had ever happened. Nor did I have to stand in front of my church to admit before the entire congregation that I had committed the sin of fornication. But none of that changed the fact that I would be a single mom before the age of twenty. I was a college dropout. My patient, enduring grandmother wouldn't live forever. I couldn't support a child on my wages at a dumpy little grocery store, and no decent man in his right mind would be interested in such damaged goods. Janice was living proof. And, frighteningly, unlike Janice, I didn't have a saintly ex-mother-in-law to fall home to. The stark reality was sobering.

Better things, Mrs. Walker had said. Better than what? Better than those ornamental wishes that shimmered from my childhood moon? I doubted it. Not for me.

I had effectively relinquished those romantic ideas long ago—with Dad, with Thomas and then Parker, with my schooling and that measureless hope that I could be *more*—yanked them from the night with one angry sweep of an arm, no longer believing in such nonsense. Or so I thought.

But while I tried to be sensible, realistic, even prosaic, I found that hope rose like sweet cream to the surface. I still dreamed. And after the word—*adoption*—had been spoken aloud by someone I respected and loved, I dreamed haunting dreams of clean slates and fresh starts. In my sleep, in that hazy moment between oblivion and waking, my mind would form the most unfathomable of thoughts: *Maybe I can pretend that nothing ever happened. Maybe I can let him go, be free.*

Then a nearly frantic horror would overtake me. No. *No*. He was mine. I was his. Our lives were interwoven in a way that excluded anything less than his life mingled with mine. I could not erase him from my future. I could not give him away as if he were no more important than a trinket to be passed from hand to hand. Nor did I want to bequeath him a legacy of leaving. A legacy like Janice's.

But I was being theatrical. "Adoption is a beautiful, necessary thing," I would whisper to myself. The ultimate sacrifice of love. Maybe my problem was that I did not love him enough.

Or that I loved myself too much.

When the long nights drifted into day, I watched Janice and Simon and wondered if I would wax slowly into the same harried woman my mother had become: unkempt hair, defeated eyes, low-hung head like a puppy waiting to be whipped, though trying to hide the truth behind glossy lipstick and secondhand suits. It made me want to weep with the possibility. With the *lack* of possibility. And yet, watching Janice hold her son in a gaze so fierce and loyal and loving, I knew that she would not change her situation for all the vast and breathtaking world. She wouldn't change a thing.

I clung to that thought when nightmares danced between the steps of my faltering dreams.

The bland sense of well-being that I worked so hard to cultivate at home evaporated like water on asphalt in the middle of July every time I made the short drive to Value Foods. The weight on my shoulders, the sense of being trapped, a reluctant prisoner, became heavier and heavier as I drew closer to the scrutinizing eyes at the grocery store. *My life*, I would think, pulling into the parking lot. And the years stretched out before me as long and gray and solemn as the highway unfurling in the distance. There was nothing ahead but more tired towns, more of the same limited opportunities for a woman in my position.

At work, I found it difficult to hold myself so delicately all day long, to live with the understanding that this was my present and my future. It was hard to accept that everyone knew what I had done and assigned value to me as a person because of my stupid mistake. I was effectively labeled, with or without the scarlet letter. So in the beginning I tried to make myself invisible, avoiding conversations and even eye contact, feeling sorry for myself and regretting the decision that was really not a decision at all.

Sadly, it didn't take a degree in engineering to know that my attempts at invisibility were about as effective as trying to stop the tide with outstretched hands. At the six-month mark, I gave up trying. I stopped sucking in, let my shirt hang loose, and tied my apron in a slack knot above the round ball of my belly. The effect was almost silly: the stiff canvas of my royal blue apron hung in a straight-edged A-line that could have been the front of a sandwich board. I almost wanted to write cryptic messages across the fabric. Maybe "Abstinence Makes the Heart Grow Fonder." Or "True Love Waits." But then again, such sayings made my heart snag as if pricked by a barbed hook.

Graham was the only person at Value Foods who treated me as if nothing had changed, as if I was the same Julia he had met back in February. And I suppose I was the same person, though I couldn't help but find it strange that fourteen-year-old Graham, mature beyond his years, could look past what I had done to still see who I was. I don't know if he asked Alicia to arrange it or not, but we seemed to work together all the time. And his simple decency was the one thing that got me through every day.

Once he said to me, "You look pretty today," and I shrank defensively because I was sure he was rubbing salt in a wound. But his smile was authentic and his eyes reassuring, and I had to accept that he meant what he said.

"Thank you," I managed after a moment. It struck me that it had been a very long time since I had heard such gracious words.

"You think I don't mean it," Graham said. "But I do." And then he offered to stock shelves for me so that I could take his position bagging groceries behind Alicia. I was forced to interact with more people that way, but it was much easier on my back. I gave him the sort of smile that is intended as a gift.

That Thursday evening seemed to commence a tradition, and for many Thursdays to come, Graham, Alicia, and I worked together with Alicia and me handling customers up front while Graham bent and stood, lifting boxes in my place. Alicia acted a bit weird around me, but she didn't avoid me the way some other employees did. I knew that malice had nothing to do with how they dodged my company; what does one say to someone in my position? I could barely think a thought to myself without becoming sad or offended or at the very least reminded of the many concessions I would have to make. I wasn't bitter that my coworkers steered clear of me. I would have done the same thing in their shoes.

But Alicia, like Graham, was different somehow. She wasn't overly friendly like he was, but she also didn't act as if she were afraid of me, as if pregnancy were contagious and I might infect her with an ill-timed sneeze. Instead, Alicia seemed wary and a little too cheerful and bright, almost forcefully irreproachable and full of wide-eyed naiveté. Maybe I was being far too presumptuous, but she gave off the impression that my situation hit a bit too close to home for her comfort. She exuded a generic fear, a feeling of *it could have been me*. But she was courteous; she chatted with me between customers and never stared at my stomach, and working with her came in second only to working beside Graham.

When I showed up for work the last Thursday in May, I had forgotten that Graham would be playing his tuba in the band at his high school's graduation ceremonies and that Alicia was off for the entire week. The sight of Michael feeding a new roll of cash register tape through the till in the first aisle made my step falter. A wish like quicksilver sparked through me, and I yearned to race home and call in sick before he saw me. But the hum of the automatic door betrayed me as I entered, and Michael looked up from his task, fixing me in his gaze and giving me a slow, uncertain smile.

Michael was the one person I had rarely worked with since the day my pregnancy was brought to light. It seemed his face would forever be fixed in my mind with the blank, stunned expression he had shot my way as I dragged Simon out of Value Foods all those weeks ago. Rumor had it that he was very busy with the classes he was taking at the local tech school, and Graham told me that Michael had secured a scholarship at the University of Iowa for the coming fall. Apparently he was entering the premed program.

Those outrageous dreams that I tried to silence surged quickly, wildly, at the news, and without pausing to think, I imagined what it would be like to go with him. In a different world, one without a baby, a place where there was such a thing as a new beginning, I wondered if Michael could have ever seen something worth pursuing in me. Maybe we would have clutched hands like Thomas and Francesca, made plans for the future as we worked side by side toward individual goals. But we barely knew each other; there had never been anything between us. It was pathetic to let such a thought flash through my mind.

I hoped my random musings hadn't made me blush, and I tried to make myself smile decorously when Michael lifted his hand in a halfhearted wave. "Hey, Julia," he called. "Long time, no see."

Not knowing what to say, I merely nodded in agreement and kept walking toward the back of the store to punch in and hang up my purse. I wondered who else would be working with us and hoped earnestly that it wasn't Denise. Contrary to my experience the first night I worked at Value Foods, there were only four people who were typically scheduled to work the evening shift. The wrong mix of people could make for a miserable couple of hours. I had become dependent on my nonthreatening Thursday routine.

Walking through the aisles, I caught a glimpse of Monica, the Value Foods gossip, standing with a new worker, someone I had never met before. He was heavyset with huge, timid eyes behind plastic-framed glasses, and I startled him nearly out of his skin when I passed the aisle he was crouched in.

"Hi," I said, offering him my hand. "I'm Julia."

"Hi," he said back, but he did not tell me his name. His fingers were soft and limp, and he pulled his hand away quickly. When he slipped away from me and disappeared around a corner, I let myself chuckle. I could tell that he wasn't disturbed by me; he was just high-strung or maybe a little intimidated, as I had been when I started at Value Foods.

So no Denise, no Alicia. And no Clark as far as I could tell.

"Who's the shift manager tonight?" I asked Michael softly, approaching him after I was settled in. I hated to do it, but there was no one else to go to.

He was giving a middle-aged woman correct change, and when he had counted the last dollar into her outstretched palm, he turned to face me. "I am."

It was impossible to hide my surprise.

Michael shrugged casually. "Denise quit; didn't you hear? I guess she's going to live with her aunt in New York. Thinks she's going to get some gig off Broadway."

I smiled at that.

"Off *off* Broadway. Way off," Michael joked, then stopped himself with a thoughtful tip of his head. "She was a nice enough girl, just had some crazy ideas."

Though I didn't think Denise needed him to defend her, I found it charming that he wanted so badly to find the good in people. Maybe he would do the same for me.

"Anyway, they asked me if I'd like the position. Pays more, who would say no?"

"Not me," I said, sounding as stupid as I felt.

The conversation abruptly came to a halt. We stood in awkward silence for a few moments as we glanced around the store and tried to think of more to say. Other than a brief hello in passing, we hadn't really talked since our short-lived flirtations, and I felt clumsy and confused trying to reconnect now. Trying not to feel embarrassed for extending my attentions as I kept my secrets, my shame, to myself.

"Well," I finally said, deferring to his authority and hoping to put an end to such an uncomfortable encounter, "what would you like me to do?"

To my utter surprise, Michael patted the counter in front of him. "Stay up front with me. I mean, not *with* me, just up front. And I'll be here too. . . ." He looked uncharacteristically shy for a moment, but he shook it off with an easy smile. "When it's not busy, I'll start mopping the aisles and you can work the counter, and when it is busy, I'll bag groceries and you can ring people in." His gaze dropped for a moment, and then he peeked up and added, "I thought that scenario might be easier on you."

A little flustered, I cleared my throat. "Thanks, Michael. That's very thoughtful of you."

He waved off my gratitude. "Not at all. Somebody has to run the cash register. Besides—" he patted his stomach—"it's almost swimsuit season. I gotta take whatever form of exercise I can get." He meant it to be funny, and he smirked at his own joke. Then his eyes registered the shape of my abs, the body that wouldn't see a swimming suit this summer, and he froze. "Oh, Julia, I'm—"

I laughed a lighthearted little laugh and brushed off his attempt at an apology. "Don't be ridiculous. If you want to look like me by the time you're invited to your first pool party, you'd better get started. It's not easy maintaining this awesome bod."

Michael looked shocked for a moment, and then a grin unfolded across his face. "You are something else." He was shaking his head at me, but there was a quiet admiration in his eyes. "Sorry I'm such an idiot."

"You're not," I assured him.

I tried not to be, but I was even more attracted to Michael because of his sweet consideration. And though I felt somewhat guilty about doing it, I allowed myself the odd glance at him as he mopped the floors and slid groceries into clear plastic bags. He wasn't like Thomas at all—there was no posturing self-assurance, no promise of protection that elicited both comfort and a feeling of vulnerability in me. Nor was he like Parker—determined and overly confident, capable of making me believe that I, too, could be as driven and successful as he planned to be. Instead, Michael was himself, separate from me and yet not unconcerned or indifferent toward me. He was kind. He treated me like I was worth something in and of myself. I didn't feel manipulated or needy. I felt respected. I felt . . . nice.

We closed up together, and I stayed longer than I needed to because I was content and not in a hurry to leave Michael's company. We didn't talk much, but it was all right to just know that whether or not he thought I had made the biggest, dumbest mistake of my life, he didn't plan to hold it against me. Though I had avoided him more than anyone else at Value Foods, he was turning out to be more perceptive, more genuine, than even the sensitive Graham. Graham had a way of making me feel that deep in the very heart of his kindness he held the smallest seed of pity. I didn't get that from Michael.

When we locked the front doors and emerged into the night, the air was warm and moist, the humidity prophetic of what was to come: a summer of unseasonable heat, of blistering asphalt and sweat that beaded like an otherworldly crown along damp hairlines. It felt wonderful. The night wrapped itself around me, soft against my skin, and when a breeze stirred the leaves that were still silky and pistachio-colored in their newness, I looked up. Smiled.

"Night, Julia," Michael said.

Swinging my purse from the very tips of my fingers, I tossed it upward in a carefree salute and tried to thank him without words. "Good night, Michael."

I thought about trying to say more, about letting him know how much I appreciated his kindness, but I wasn't ready. Not yet. It was more than enough to have had a few hours to feel like myself: Julia, just *Julia*, without any addendums, postscripts, or footnotes.

He whistled as he walked away, waving over his shoulder and melting into the shadows of the parking lot.

I watched him go until he disappeared completely and then turned my face to the sky, hunting for the light that had leaped out of the darkness at me only a few heartbeats ago. And there it was, between the countless blossoming branches: the moon. It was far away and small, but also full and bright, and though there were no shadows, no halos of hope in the light, it was gleaming and brilliant and gloriously white.

secrets

"'Hi. I'm Emily Elizabeth and this is my dog, Clifford.'"

I could see by the way Simon's eyes brushed over the pictures that he wasn't reading at all, wasn't even looking at the words. "Hey," I said. "You have that line memorized."

Simon glanced up at me with a look of disdain. "*All* the Clifford books start that way. I don't have to read the first page."

"But I don't care if they all start that way or not, Simon. I want you to be able to read the words."

He snorted as if taking great offense and turned the page with a sharp toss of his fingers. "Just watch," he asserted. "I know how to read the whole book."

Though it was true that there were certain words Simon always got right—*Clifford, dog, the, and, to*—the list of vocabulary that he could routinely recognize was actually still very small. During our morning sessions there were a few words that we could sound out together, but most of them I had to flat out tell him. I doubted if we were making any progress, and I could see his frustration beginning to show as we plodded through book after book.

We had barely turned the page when Simon came across *emergency*, long and baffling, and he didn't even try to tackle it. He shrugged a little self-consciously and skipped right over it, probably hoping that I wasn't following along and wouldn't notice.

"Emergency," I said, stopping him. I pulled apart each syllable and moved my index finger under the word as I carefully repeated it. "E-mer-gen-cy."

When Simon didn't parrot me, I wrapped an arm around his dark head and gave his hair a quick kiss. It smelled sweet, like he had touched his messy mane with syrupy fingers. We had feasted on waffles for breakfast yesterday. I smiled and breathed him in. "Sick of it?" I asked.

Simon flipped the book closed. "No, but why can't we read *my* Clifford books?" he complained, scraping at the library sticker on the back cover of the book he held.

"Because you know them by heart," I answered. "I thought you wanted to learn how to read." Then, flicking his fingers lightly, I added, "Don't do that. You're going to pull it off."

He sighed and wrinkled his nose at me, abandoning the book

and instead scratching a spot near his temple with ferocious energy. "I do, but it's very hard. I don't know lots of words yet. How many words are there, Julia?"

I laughed, dumbfounded at his question. "I have no idea. Lots and lots. Thousands. Hundreds of thousands, I suppose. Maybe millions."

Simon's face crumpled at such an unachievable number.

I rushed to soothe him. "Oh, don't worry, Simon. You don't have to know them all."

"Do you know them all?"

"Absolutely not. I have a terrible vocabulary."

"Vocabulary?"

I narrowed my eyes at him good-naturedly. "You know the word *pregnant,* but you don't know *vocabulary*?"

My half brother shook his head solemnly and dropped the book on the floor so he could fold his legs underneath him and face me on the couch. He took a strand of my hair between his fingers and began to twist it from the base all the way to the tip of his pinky. It was a strange habit that he had picked up during our informal reading lessons. I usually showered before bed, twisting my hair into a loose bun while I slept and letting it down to air-dry when I woke. In the morning my hair was still slightly damp. It had grown outrageously thick as my pregnancy progressed, and the limp natural wave in my usually boring brown tresses had tightened into gentle curls that I hoped remained even after I gave birth. One morning Simon had touched a lock as it hung over my shoulder, and apparently he liked the heavy, cool feeling of the dampness in his hands, because he reached for my hair more often now.

"*Vocabulary* means 'all the words you know,'" I said, trying to explain. "Does that make sense?"

"Yup," Simon said, but I doubted he was paying attention anymore. I let it go. One of the things I had learned early on about trying to teach a preschooler was that his attention span lasted for about the duration of a single book. Much more and he became silly and unreasonable.

"Come on. What letter does *vocabulary* start with?" I prodded. "Get it right and I'll make you a smoothie. V-v-v-vocabulary."

"*V,*" Simon said with relish, hopping off the couch. "Do we have peaches or raspberries? 'Cause I want a peach smoothie."

I followed him into the kitchen in time to see Grandma emerge from the hallway that led to the rest of the house. Simon wrapped himself around her middle in a brief, tight hug and then all but leaped toward the freezer, flinging it open and searching for the bag of frozen peaches.

"Good morning," Grandma laughed. "What's the hurry?"

"Peach smoothies," he informed her. "Want one?"

"Yes, actually, that sounds great." Grandma smiled at me over Simon's head. She was falling in love with him by degrees; her affection growing exponentially as she learned more about him, as he slowly revealed himself to her. It wasn't that Simon tried to be enigmatic—he was too young to let such duplicity even cross his mind—but his young personality was angled and full of unknown corners. It was like wandering through a maze, exploring hidden paths and finding yourself in uncharted territory, mysterious and exciting in some inexplicable way. It wasn't too far below the surface that our sweet Simon became rather complicated.

And Grandma wasn't the only one who cared for him more with each passing day. My morning routine with Simon had become the highlight of most of my days, whether or not he was becoming bored with our intrigue. He was fierce and determined underneath his sensitive exterior, and I wanted so desperately to learn all the details that had made him who he was. I wanted to experience everything I had missed, take back the years when I should have been a part of his life and was instead a stranger. Sometimes it felt like I couldn't possibly know him today until I knew who he had been yesterday.

I pulled the blender down from the cupboard above the stove and set it on the counter beside the bag of peaches Simon had tossed there. "We need juice, buddy. And a container of yogurt."

"We don't have peach juice," Simon called, standing in the yellow glow of the open refrigerator.

"We don't need peach juice," I assured him. "Anything will do. Orange? Apple?"

"Apple," Grandma cut in. "Way in the back, Simon, behind the gallon of milk."

"Got it!" He grinned, emerging with the paper carton of juice held high in triumph. There were goose bumps on his bare arms.

Grandma leaned against the sink for a moment, watching the smoothie production unfold. She grinned at Simon's excitement and pulled a banana from the curved wooden stand to her left when he tried to scramble up on the counter to get one himself. "What is going on with you two?" Grandma asked merrily. She dug a fingernail into the stem of the banana and then gave it to Simon so he could peel it himself. He loved peeling bananas; though he would

often claim that he wanted one, then proceed to peel it and sur-
reptitiously abandon it with only two small bites gone. I found and
finished many browning bananas left that way.

"Nothing," Simon said quickly, tossing me a sloppy wink that
Grandma couldn't have missed even without her glasses.

"Nothing at all," I agreed, winking back.

Grandma laughed. "Okay, whatever you say. But just for the
record, I don't buy it."

Simon looked confused. "What don't you buy?"

"I don't believe that there is nothing going on," Grandma clarified. She moved to start a pot of coffee, turning on the cold water
and testing it with her finger until it was acceptably brisk.

"Well, we're not telling you anyway," Simon gushed happily. "It's
our secret."

"Absolutely," I agreed.

"What is it with secrets in this house?" Janice said from the
hallway.

I hadn't expected her voice, and I swung around to regard her.
She stood squarely in the oversize doorframe, arms hanging at her
sides as if she didn't know what to do with them and a half smile
on her lips that seemed forced and unnatural. It was obvious to me
that she was trying to edge in, trying to be a part of the lighthearted
chitchat of our morning, but she hovered at the boundaries of our
miniature community and did not step into it. Janice waited for
my invitation, but as far as I was concerned she was unwelcome.
An outsider.

I turned the blender on.

When the pink-orange foam was frothy and light, I poured out three careful glasses, making sure each one held exactly the same amount of smoothie as the one before it.

"Red straw?" I asked Simon, knowing the answer.

"Yup," he said, reaching for his special drink.

I took the last two smoothies in hand and gave one to Grandma, sipping out of the other one myself.

Grandma held me in an indefinable look for the span of a breath and then turned away and smiled broadly at Janice. "This one is for you," she said, holding out the cold glass. "I'm having a cup of coffee."

Janice hesitated in the shadows, her bare toes curling into the carpet of the hallway before she stepped carefully onto the checkerboard linoleum. She smiled again, thinner this time. "Thank you," she said, taking the drink. Then she made a point of looking me square in the eye. "Thank you, Julia."

I searched her face for animosity, but her expression was blank, unreadable. "Anytime," I muttered.

Though I liked to think that Janice deserved it, I wasn't always so mean to her. There were just certain times when I was so overwhelmed by the scope of my own anger toward her that a rough stone of malice would rumble loose and escape. Occasionally that rage seemed vast and unplumbed, and I fell into it unexpectedly—a booby-trapped, bottomless pit that I slid into without intention or even desire to do so. Most of the time I more or less ignored her and then, out of the blue, something inside me would click and I would tumble head over heels, taking her with me as if the fall would serve to punish her somehow.

When I pulled out a chair across from her at the table, some civil part of me knew that I should apologize for being rude and childish, but consideration for Janice wasn't part of my repertoire. I held my tongue.

Grandma scrambled eggs for breakfast and even sprinkled a few pinches of fresh Parmesan cheese in the skillet just before serving them. Janice loved Parmesan, and she smiled almost timidly at Grandma when she brought the eggs to the table. To my utter astonishment, Grandma gave Janice's wrist a little squeeze, and the younger woman closed her eyes for a moment in what looked like pure, unadulterated gratitude.

There was something going on between them, too.

I knew it instantly. If Simon and I had a little secret, Grandma and Janice definitely had one of their own. My defenses rose like battlements, and I glanced back and forth between them, trying to guess at the riddle of their alliance. I felt betrayed.

Simon raved about the eggs, but I avoided them out of spite and nibbled instead on day-old bran muffins that Grandma and Simon had made together the morning before. My good day was disintegrating quickly and I hated it, though I knew it was my own fault for being so cynical and bitter. But knowing something and being able to change it are two completely different things.

Only a week ago, Grandma had directed me to a passage in her tattered Bible that had something to do with wanting to do good but not being able to follow through with it. I could feel the writer's angst and it made aggravating, perfect sense to me. I knew well the ceaseless battle between the two women of my psyche: the woman I wanted to be and the woman I was. Unfortunately, the author had not in his infinite wisdom told me how to change. There was nothing for me to do but continue to plod along a path that I was beginning to know very well.

I had to be at work by eight o'clock, so I left the table before everyone else and went upstairs to mope and get ready.

Depressingly, the size-medium uniform that I had started work in had been traded for a large, and I knew it would not be much longer before I would need the extra large. I wasn't particularly huge—my pregnant belly was by no means outrageously out of proportion—but the shirts were cut slim and I couldn't stand it when the buttons pulled and the fabric gapped open. Grandma was an excellent seamstress, and she tailored the shirts to fit me, allowing room up front and shaping the seams in the back to help combat the tent look. Though it helped, altered seams were not enough to make something so sadly unflattering look good.

I cheered a little, though, as I pulled the sides of my hair back in a silver clip. Dr. Morales had warned me at the beginning of my pregnancy that some women have a difficult time carrying a baby, not just because of the extra weight and stress on their bodies but because the little one leeches every good thing out of blood, marrow, and bone. Thin hair, he warned. Acne, brittle fingernails, pallor. However, it didn't take me long to learn that the opposite could also be true: glowing skin, vibrant hair, an overall outward manifestation of all that is beautiful and secreted inside.

I was one of the lucky few to be far lovelier in pregnancy than I had ever been before. I knew it wouldn't last, so I relished my moments of glory, letting my hair hang loose and full and wearing pink on my eyelids and lips to match the color in my cheeks.

Once I had caught a glimpse of myself in profile as I slipped through the glass doors of Value Foods and been stunned by how familiar I looked. I stopped and stared, wondering what had caused such powerful déjà vu. It wasn't until I'd turned my head slightly right and left that it hit me: I looked like Janice. Not the Janice I knew today but the one who had for a few short years been a caricature of a mother. When I was a little girl, I had heard more than one person refer to my mother as *gorgeous*, and though I was certainly nothing of the sort, there was an unmistakable similarity in the arch of my neck, the curve of my heavy-lashed eyes, the fullness of my face as it shone from within.

I didn't know whether to be happy (I was marginally pretty!) or devastated (I looked like Janice?). But it was what it was and I couldn't change it. What could I do but accept it?

Everyone was still sitting around the kitchen table when I emerged from my room at quarter to eight. Janice had to be at work by eight thirty, and she dropped off Simon at preschool on her way. Usually they lingered at the table while Grandma puttered around, Janice occupying herself with a newspaper and a cup of coffee and Simon racing his Hot Wheels cars or maybe drawing with chunky crayons if he was in the mood. They were together but engaged in the affairs of their own personal worlds. There was little conversation, rare amusement. Today, however, the dishes had not been moved an inch, and the members of my unorthodox family sat laughing and talking as if there was nothing more comfortable, more wonderful and fun than the three of them huddled around the table.

Simon looked up when I walked into the room and clapped enthusiastically. "Guess what?" he practically yelled.

I opened my mouth to humor him, but he didn't give me a chance to.

"Grandma Nellie is going to take me on a date tonight!"

Grandma Nellie? As far as I knew, Simon had always called my grandmother Mrs. DeSmit. Since when had she become Grandma Nellie? Simon and I might be siblings, but my grandmother certainly was not his—not ever, actually. And what was this about a date?

"I think you're too young for a date," I said with a tight-lipped smile. "And I think Grandma Nellie might be a bit old for you."

Simon squinted at me uncomprehendingly.

Grandma tsked. "Come on, Julia. Don't be a party pooper. I'm taking Simon to the A&W, and then we're going bowling."

"I've never been bowling before!" Simon interjected. "I'm going to get three strikes. Grandma Nellie and Mom say that's a chicken."

"Turkey," Janice corrected.

"Yeah, a turkey," Simon repeated, still staring at me excitedly.

"Sounds like fun," I said, trying to feel indifferent. It would be good for Simon to have some time one-on-one with Grandma. Then it hit me that if Grandma and Simon were gone, Janice and I would be home alone together. I schemed quickly. Maybe I could stay late at work, pick up an extra half shift or something.

But Janice cleared her throat and looked right at me, putting a halt to my hasty plans. "Why don't we go out, too, Julia?" She asked the question hesitantly, but once it was out of her mouth she seemed to gain confidence and began to list arguments in favor of her idea. "The house will be empty. We might as well get out. We can go somewhere nice . . . my treat," she added hurriedly, lest I use money as an excuse.

I didn't know what to say, and I couldn't think fast enough to come up with a reason not to. I sputtered for a moment.

"Sounds like fun," Grandma said encouragingly. "You know, there is a new restaurant that just opened last week in Glendale. I hear it's really good."

"Mediterranean cuisine," Janice offered, though she was looking at Grandma now instead of me. "I don't really know what that means, but it sounds good."

"It got a rave review in the *Herald*."

"Very elegant."

"When's the last time you went out, Julia?" Grandma asked. She was trying to help Janice's cause, and between the two of them I couldn't get a word in edgewise.

"It would be good for you."

"Who can say no to a night out?"

It all sounded pretty good to Simon, too. "Hey, I know!" he said. "We can all go bowling together tonight and then to that new restaurant tomorrow!"

Grandma and Janice turned to him as one. "No, honey." Janice stopped him. "Grandma Nellie wants to take you out by yourself. Just the two of you."

"It's our special night," Grandma added.

"Okay." Simon shrugged.

The room went quiet, and I tried to slip toward the door.

But Grandma caught my arm as I walked past. She swung it gently, her fingers a bracelet on my narrow wrist and her eyes almost pleading. "What do you say? How about having supper with Janice?"

I wanted to glare at her for putting me in such a position, but as always, I knew she was only doing what she thought would be best for me. And Janice. That's the part that bugged me the most: that Grandma was worried about what was best for Janice, too. I realized that the two of them had not had to keep their secret very long. Any plotting between my grandmother and my mother had to do with this. They were trying to orchestrate a few hours so Janice and I could be alone. Together.

Pursing my lips, I studied Janice. She was watching me, but when I met her eyes, she looked at her lap. Played with her fingers. Waited for my reply.

What could I do? "Fine," I said.

There was an almost audible exhalation in the room. Grandma and Janice exchanged quick smiles, and Simon laughed the fake little giggle of a five-year-old, trying to fit in though he didn't understand the ripple of electricity crackling in the air around us.

"What time do you get off work tonight?" Janice asked, bolder now that I had said yes.

For a second I entertained the idea of lying to her, of saying that I had an extra-long shift today and would not be home until late. But this was all rather inevitable. If not tonight, another night. Grandma and Janice would scheme and plan, maybe even pulling Simon into their operation if I proved to be recalcitrant. I didn't need him pitted against me too.

"I'm off at five," I answered.

Janice's lips curled slightly. There was a time; five o'clock was concrete, a moment on the short linear procession of our lives that was singled out for us. Her plans were being realized. "Okay. Can you be ready to leave at six?"

"Whatever," I said, pulling my arm from Grandma's gentle grip. "I've got to go or I'm going to be late."

The room buzzed with energy behind me, and I knew Grandma and Janice were silently celebrating. I rolled my eyes and had swung the door open a little too forcefully when suddenly Janice's voice drifted from the kitchen.

"Wear something pretty, Julia. It's a really nice restaurant." I didn't bother to look at her, but her voice fell soft on my ears. Soft and pleased.

Maybe even hopeful.

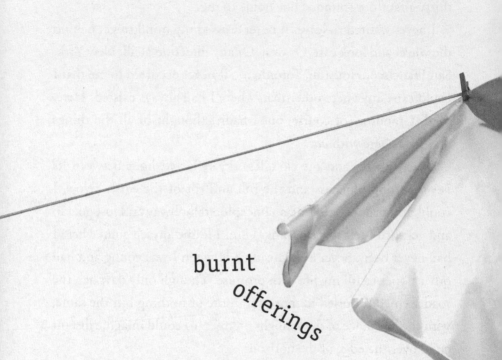

burnt
offerings

ON THE WAY HOME from work I heard a song on the radio that pierced me as if unseen arrows filtered through the speakers instead of innocent sound waves. It made me feel open somehow, exposed, as if the songwriter knew my heart and had captured it, caged it, and conferred it upon any ear open enough to hear. It was disconcerting. It left me cold, because I hadn't even known myself that I felt this way until the words washed over me in the still air of the car. *April back in New York. The thirty-first floor. It seems somehow everything's changed. . . .* It was probably supposed to be sad. The vocalist probably sang of sorrowful things and deep longing, but the thirty-first floor sounded like home to me.

I never wanted to leave. It never crossed my mind to get behind the wheel and look east. Or west. Or any direction at all. New York, San Francisco, Houston, Toronto . . . it never occurred to me that I could exist anywhere other than where I had always existed. Here. With Grandma, of course, but I hadn't thought of all the things that I was here with*out*.

It was warm, and the cloudless sky reflected light between its never-ending blueness and the roll and tilt of the earth below. I could drive on. I could find an unexplored highway and just go. Go and go until I felt like stopping. Until I found myself somewhere I had never been, never even dreamed of when I was young and had other hopes to fill my life with promise. Though only days ago the road seemed unfurled to more and more of nothing but the same, with the brilliance of the sunlight on my car I could imagine distant cities over the edge of the horizon.

But the way home was automatic; I drove the roads without thinking of where I was going. When the gravel of the farm drive-way crunched beneath my tires, I startled with the reality of where my roots ran deep. Leaving here would be a digging, burrowing, nearly impossible thing. I would almost have to cut and run, take whatever semblance of self I could rip out of the ground and pray that new roots would grow before everything within me withered and died. But trees don't take well to the shock of being uprooted, and neither did I. Or at least that's what I figured.

Not now, I told myself, thinking that maybe someday I could whisper, "Not *quite* yet."

It wasn't nearly as thrilling as the pull of the open road, but I was relieved that Janice's car was not parked beside the unattached garage, and Grandma and Simon were already gone. The house was empty, and I looked forward to spreading myself across my bed, stretching out my back, and pointing my toes to the far corners of my mattress for a few moments before I had to curl into my designated sleeping position. I longed to sleep on my back, my stomach, in any position but on my left side. I thought of blood flowing to feed and strengthen my son and the inconvenience seemed lesser, but my muscles still stiffened in protest when I folded them into the same position every night.

The house was warm and stagnant, a little musty after the freshness of a late spring afternoon, and I stifled a yawn. Planning to throw open a few windows before my quick presupper nap, I stepped into the kitchen and was stopped in my tracks. I forgot about the windows, the heat. Any sleepiness was extinguished and surprise turned my feet to lead.

Hanging from one of the cupboard doors was a dress. It was black with a narrow V-neck that was outlined in a tasteful pewter-colored ribbon. The narrow bands of silvery charcoal crisscrossed the bodice of the dress, resting off to one side in a neat knot that ended in a stylishly uneven wave of extra fabric. It had a snug empire waist, and by the way the skirt draped from the cupboard and over the counter, I imagined the full folds would probably fall just below knee length. It was gorgeous. And I knew instinctively that it was intended for me.

I glanced around, half expecting someone to emerge from the shadows of the hallway, but the only sound in the house was the soft pat from the leaky faucet over the kitchen sink. It dripped in syncopation to my pounding heart. Shaking myself a little, I kicked off my shoes and went to examine the dress. The fabric was cool and sleek in my fingers, finer and softer than anything I had ever worn before—including the hand-me-down prom dress that I had forced myself into my junior year of high school. Though I couldn't blame Grandma for trying, that dress had been as uncomfortable as the prom itself—a lopsided event that left me with no desire to attend my senior year.

Up close, the black dress was even more breathtaking than it had been from a distance. It wasn't a formal dress by any means, just exquisitely tailored, well made, and classy. I could also see that there was a necklace slung around the hanger, a pretty platinum chain with a single black pearl dangling from the very end. And on the floor was a pair of shoes: strappy black sandals with small, slim heels. Tucked between the shoes was a card.

I picked it up hesitantly, wondering who would do this, fearing the answer, and somehow also afraid that I was mistaken—that all this extravagance was not meant for me. But the envelope read *Julia*. I tore it open with unsteady hands. There were only four short lines:

I know this does not make up for everything I missed.

But I do hope you like it.

Please wear it tonight.

—Janice

Something indefinable and nebulous gnawed at me. I had never been the recipient of such an expensive gift. The dress alone was luxurious in a way that convinced me it had not come from JCPenney. And it made me giddy, almost dizzy, to catch the necklace in my palm and realize that the pearl, with its rainbow iridescence and slightly misshapen sphere, was unquestionably real. Janice must have been saving an enormous chunk of every paycheck for such opulence.

But though I was strangely enchanted, deep in my chest something thudded angrily at what could only be considered a bribe. Janice was trying to buy me, win my affection as if I were a naive child to be wooed. A mindless imp easily swayed by something lovely. The only thing missing from her kitchen display was a box of chocolates, maybe a single red rose.

I tried to talk myself into going upstairs and lying down as if I hadn't seen her backhanded offering. But maybe I was being melodramatic. Maybe her intentions were pure. The card was open in my hands, and I didn't know how to explain that I could not, would not, take her gift. I wanted to accept it almost as much as I wanted to reject it.

Leaning against the counter beside the dress, I unclasped the necklace from the hanger. *Just for a moment*, I told myself. *Just to see what it feels like*. I hooked the chain around my neck with clammy fingers. The pearl rested precisely below the hollow of my collarbone, and I could feel the slight weight of it roll against the warmth of my skin.

Wiggling my toes, I studied the shoes. My feet were still slender, not at all swollen, and I stepped into the heels without pausing to think. I promised myself I was only sampling the goods, proving that they wouldn't work anyway, but the sandals were a perfect fit. I knew the dress would be too. Grandma must have helped Janice raid my closet and research my shoes and clothes, averaging everything out until they were left with the right sizes. It was obvious that the two of them had given their secret much thought.

I sighed and took the dress from the cupboard handle, pressing the billowing fabric against the length of my body. What should I do? Leave everything untouched? Walk away and refuse not only the gift but also Janice's none-too-subtle offer of reconciliation? Or could I accept what had been given, even if it was not freely given? Could I take this one small peace offering without somehow communicating to Janice that I had a price? that all could be forgiven and forgotten for nothing more than the cost of a pretty dress with all the trimmings?

Standing in the kitchen, I felt my mind freeze, my body solidify against the chipped countertop as I came to an impasse and did not know where to turn. I blinked in the half-light of the kitchen, sliding the dress through my fingers and trying not to think, until I saw Janice's car coming up the long driveway.

Feeling like I had been caught in the act of doing something forbidden, I cast around looking for an escape and an explanation. I fumbled with the necklace, trying to get it off as I twisted my foot out of one of the shoes and hung the black dress back where it had been. When I heard the slam of her car door, I jumped and started toward the stairs, necklace forgotten and lone shoe abandoned. I still wore the heeled sandal on my right foot, and I hobbled, almost tripping, and then changed my mind in an instant and reached suddenly for the dress, the other shoe.

I scrambled out of the kitchen and hopped into the stairwell, pulling the door closed behind me but not hard enough to latch it. I waited on the second step, knowing that Janice would be in the house any second and unwilling to betray my position by starting up the creaky stairs. She always went straight to the bathroom when she got home from work. She ran the water, so I assumed she washed her hands and face, but mostly I figured she wanted to be alone for a few minutes. As soon as my movements were hidden beneath the muffled gush and purr of water in the pipes, I could escape to my room and decide what to do.

The front door protested loudly as Janice opened it, and I heard her footsteps on the dull tile of the mudroom floor. Then there was nothing more for a long moment, and I imagined her standing on the threshold of the kitchen, surveying the empty spot where the dress had hung like a trophy. Had she intended for it to be a baited thing? In my mind's eye, I watched a slow smile blossom across her face and I was torn as if my soul was perforated into two incomplete halves.

Something in me rose at the thought of a gate swinging wide in the walls I had so carefully built. And another something tugged me down, chaining me to doubts and fears and disbelief that anything could be any different from what it had always been. I felt ashamed and vulnerable at the same time.

I should have kept driving, I thought in the darkness of the stairwell. I pressed my eyes shut. *I should have gone off to find my thirty-first floor.*

The swish and flow of water in the faraway bathroom spurred me up the stairs, and I stumbled into my room, still uneven on one lone shoe. *Cinderella*, I thought, tossing the dress on my bed and rubbing my head with trembling hands. Only there was no Prince Charming. Just a wicked ex-mother.

I got ready unenthusiastically, freshening my makeup by rote and pulling my hair into a loose French knot with little concern for the wisps of curls that struck out on their own. Going through the motions was soothing somehow, normal, even though I felt drawn forward, pulled into this evening against my will and utterly helpless to do anything about it. At some point I knew I would wear the dress; I resigned myself to it. I wasn't sure what such an action would suggest to Janice, but I decided that I didn't care. Whatever the night held, I might as well look good enduring it.

When I emerged from the staircase at exactly six o'clock, Janice was waiting for me at the kitchen table. She stood as I entered, pushing back and up expectantly, fluidly, as if she had waited a very long time for this moment and had practiced how she would rise to the occasion.

"Julia." Janice blinked quickly, and for a split second I thought that she had teared up, but then she smiled broadly and exclaimed, "You could have just walked out of my high school graduation photo!"

I didn't know how to begin to respond.

Janice read my indecision, and the smile wavered and slid off her carefully made-up face. "I should have said, 'You look so beautiful.' I guess that sounds pretty self-serving now, doesn't it? Though you do." She stopped, started again. "You look very beautiful."

Silence grew between us, a small hill of misunderstanding that would soon be an impassable mountain. Janice laughed a little self-consciously, trying to beat back the growing peak. "Hasn't anyone ever told you that you look like me?"

"No," I said, my voice a shard of ice chipped from the block I held close inside.

"A younger me," Janice clarified. She smoothed the coat of her pastel pink suit and sighed. "We're not off to a very good start, are we? Let's try again. Can we start over?"

I just shrugged, swallowing the many things I wanted to say and maintaining my icy calm.

But Janice would not be so easily deterred. She covered her eyes with her hands and took a steadying breath. Then she quickly uncovered her face, like a child unveiling some marvelous surprise, and smiled. "Julia!" she cooed, her voice different this time around. "You look gorgeous! That dress is a perfect fit on you. How are the shoes?"

"Perfect," I said. Unconsciously, I brought my hand to my neck and rolled the smooth, black pearl between my thumb and forefinger. When her eyes followed the path of my arm, I dropped my hand almost guiltily. But Janice's gaze was warm, inviting.

"I mean it. You are stunning," she whispered.

The words fought to stay in my throat, but I forced them out before I could lose my nerve to say them entirely. "Thank you." My recognition came out slow and heavy.

"No need to thank me for stating the simple truth."

I cleared my throat. "I meant thank you for—"

Janice waved away my costly gratitude and turned toward the door. "You don't have to thank me for anything. Shall we go?"

The hook was set.

She was already mostly gone, and I had no choice but to follow. The night had been launched into motion, and all that it would contain was foggy and uncertain, hovering at the edge of my consciousness like a mist that chilled and clung.

We drove in relative silence, partly because we did not know what to say to each other and partly because I found a jazz station on the radio and turned it up a smidge too loud. I effectively ruined any conversations that Janice feebly tried to start, smiling blandly at her and trying to tap my fingers to the music in a show of my disinterest. I didn't even ask her whether or not she liked jazz, and the truth was that I certainly could not count myself an avid fan. In fact, I could probably number on one hand the times I had even heard a jazz song in my life. But there was something about the off rhythm, the sudden bursts of sound and unpredictability that appealed to me on this indeterminate night.

The restaurant was called Sebastian's, and it boasted a white-washed exterior that was reminiscent of Greece. But the sunken brick walkways lined with a profusion of potted plants seemed French, and the stone columns and sweeping archways reminded me of a Spanish villa. The whole place had a slightly schizophrenic feel, as if the designer had never actually been to the Mediterranean and merely borrowed from every known cliché to create a far-removed, Midwestern tribute to some southern European ideal. But bewildering design aside, it was a very nice place, resplendent with crisp linen tablecloths and flickering candles on intimately apportioned tables.

It was busy but not so crowded that we had to wait to be seated. When a graceful hostess with earrings that dangled halfway down her long neck led us to a quiet corner in the back, I was both relieved at the privacy and flustered at the proximity that I would have to share with Janice. The night already seemed to be stretching, extending slowly outward as if the hours for this one small nugget of time had been lengthened. If it was true that God had held the sun still in His hands, maybe it was also true that He was lingering along the minutes of our evening, making sure that Janice and I had the time we needed to say those things that had to be said.

Janice ordered hummus as an appetizer with an almost relieved flair. It was obviously a dish she recognized and liked, and suddenly the unfamiliarity of such a night, the foreign, almost alien feel of being together, was minimally less strange. She also studied the wine list intently, squinting over four pages of exotic varieties and vintages with a furrowed brow.

"Have a glass of wine," I told her because she seemed to need permission. Her hesitancy to order in front of me was an unbearable facade. "I don't care if you drink."

"Oh no." She laughed, snapping the leather-bound menu closed and aligning it carefully beside the almost equally extensive dessert menu. "I don't drink."

Sure, I thought, *and I'm not pregnant.*

"When did you stop smoking?" I blurted out abruptly, shocking even myself. For some reason I could see her bringing a chalky white cigarette to her lips and lighting it, her eyes pressed shut in anticipation. I wondered if she longed for one now.

Janice looked taken aback, and she fumbled to begin. "Well," she said evenly, "I suppose I haven't touched a cigarette since the day I found out that I was pregnant with Simon." She held her fingers in front of her, calculating, and I could see that she had recently painted her nails. For tonight? For me? "Simon will be six in October, and it's the beginning of June now. . . . It's been over six years, I guess." She laughed self-deprecatingly and shrugged in a show of modest pride.

I nodded. Then, to my utter astonishment, I said, "I used to smoke too."

Janice's eyes got wide as she regarded me. She obviously didn't know how to respond, and I couldn't find fault with her delay. What did I hope to gain by divulging such a useless bit of information? But before the moment became awkward, Janice erupted in a giggle, hitting the table lightly as if I had just told a marvelous joke. "You are absolutely kidding me!"

Embarrassed, I shook my head.

"I can't believe it. I would have never, *never* guessed."

Her response shamed me somehow and I chastised myself, wondering what I had hoped to accomplish with such a senseless statement, such an unnecessary and unasked-for revelation. Why was I making small talk with her? Was I trying to earn her approval? Or did I hope to shock her? Did I want to prove to her that we had something, any small thing, in common? We had *nothing* in common.

"It was a stupid phase," I muttered. *It was only a handful of times*, I thought.

"Oh yes." Janice nodded, serious now. "Smoking is so stupid. Such a nasty habit and so bad for you. Good thing we both quit."

"Good thing," I echoed mindlessly, wishing that I had kept my big mouth shut.

Janice was looking at me differently now. I could tell that in her mind we were even on this one score, and it was a start. My confession had served as an olive branch, a small but stable corner of common ground where I had stepped aside to make room for her. She leaned in toward the table, visibly relaxing and ready for more of this counterfeit intimacy. "You know, Julia, this is exactly what I hoped for tonight."

"Confessions?" I asked, trying to be obtuse. I would have loved to hear a few of her confessions. Or maybe that was exactly what I feared.

"No, of course not," she assured me quickly, unaware that I was intentionally being pert. "I just wanted a chance for us to get to know each other a bit." She swallowed, and I could see that she wanted to say more but didn't know if she dared. When I had watched her expectantly long enough to make the hush uncomfortable, she added tentatively, "You are my daughter, and I barely know you. I want to know you."

So she had the nerve to say it. She called me *daughter* and almost brought herself to admit in the very same breath that she had failed me, that she was no mother. *"I barely know you,"* she had said, but we both knew that it was her own fault, that she had ruined anything good between us. That she had left.

I was about to remind her of this, to set it free into the tense air surrounding us so we could stop tiptoeing around the issue, pretending that everything was okay.

But our waiter appeared just then, bearing a square, turquoise plate with gold-filigreed edges overflowing with an assortment of crisp vegetables and seasoned triangles of toasted pita bread. The hummus was thick and fragrant, nestled in a curved leaf of iceberg lettuce, and after we had ordered dinner—roast leg of lamb for Janice and paella minus the shellfish for me—we ate and sampled and Janice filled the space between bites with nervous, mindless chatter.

"Yummy," she said eventually, crunching a spear of green pepper. "Do you like it?" she asked, pointing at me with the half-curled end of the slender vegetable.

"Mm-hmm," I mumbled, subdued, though I did indeed like it very much.

"Ben loved hummus." Janice smiled a private little smile and dug into the dip.

I stared at her, stunned that she would have the audacity to mention the name of another man to me. I was the daughter of the man she should have been faithful to forever. We were not friends; we were not confidantes. I did not want to hear about her exploits. My displeasure must have been tangible because Janice suddenly looked up and her eyes were startled, maybe a little afraid.

"Who's Ben?" I inquired nonchalantly, trying to sound casual and disinterested in spite of the hard edge in my voice. "Don't forget that I hardly know you either."

Janice groaned softly and threw her hands up in entreaty. "I am so bad at this. You have to give me one freebie, one chance to erase something dumb that I never should have said in the first place."

"I have to?"

Her eyes dropped. "I would like you to."

"Who's Ben?" I asked again.

Instead of answering me, Janice said, "I knew this wouldn't be easy, but I didn't know it would be this hard."

Much to my consternation, I actually enjoyed her discomfort. How could she bring out such cruelty in me? "It doesn't have to be this hard." I sighed. "But we have got to stop pretending. Either you are totally, completely, *brutally* honest with me, and I'm the same with you, or we might as well waste the night asking each other about our favorite colors."

"Pink," Janice offered almost shyly. "You?"

"Yellow, but that's not the point."

"Food?"

I narrowed my eyes at her but acquiesced. "Watermelon."

"A hamburger, medium rare, with everything on it. And extra onions if it's a red onion. I don't like Vidalias. Sport?"

"I'm not athletic," I muttered.

"I used to play volleyball, but that was years ago. I like to watch football."

We studied each other with nothing more than the table between us. But hovering and invisible above the wavering heat of the lone candle, there were ghosts. Ten years of conversations that should have been, experiences we should have shared, rose and lingered and reminded. Taunted us with what we could have had.

The hint of a smile played at the corners of Janice's mouth. "Who was your first kiss?" she dared me, breaking into territory that smacked of motherly affection.

Although I didn't want to play her little game, I was learning things about her that I had only imagined as a child. My mother, a stranger, was taking shape before my very eyes. I cooperated. "A boy named Brandon. You?"

Janice bit her bottom lip. "Your father," she admitted, and the two words were measured and timid.

I couldn't go there. I couldn't talk about Dad with her. Not now, maybe not ever. I clung to the name that had incensed me only moments ago. "Who is Ben?" I demanded.

"Simon's father."

And it was released. There was an almost soundless puff, a sniper's bullet loosed at some well-defined target, and though I waited for the slashing pain, there was none. Instead I felt a rush like relief. We were actually getting somewhere. Yet beneath my subtle relief, disappointment swam just below the surface—she had lied to Simon. "He's not dead," I stated dully. "Simon said—"

"I know what Simon said," Janice interrupted. "I know I shouldn't have . . . I shouldn't have told him that. But what would you have me tell him? How can you explain . . . *that* to a little boy?"

I didn't know what she meant by *that*, nor did I necessarily want to know. Apparently Ben wasn't very excited about being a parent. Something he and Janice had in common. What was different this time around? Why did Janice try to be a mother again when she had failed so miserably the first time?

But Simon's story was his to uncover. I wanted to learn more about mine. Shoving thoughts of my wronged little brother aside, I pressed on. "Did you leave us for Ben?"

Janice laughed. "Absolutely not. I didn't meet Ben until much, much later."

"Was he the first?"

It was a bit of an ambiguous question, but Janice knew exactly what I meant. I was being bold, maybe too bold. But she gave me a hard, unreadable look and finally admitted, "No. He was the last."

I didn't even want to know how many had come before. Obviously Ben had been different. He had meant something to Janice; he was more than just one of the many names that had paraded in and out of her life. I needed to know if he was still a part of her and how he would affect Simon and, in some mysterious way, *us*. I pushed forward, though I almost wanted to end the conversation right there and talk about safer, less risky things. But she was answering my questions, and I couldn't bring myself to stop now. Even if the answers were wild, unexpected things, things that could bite even as I tried to tame them. "Were you married to him?"

"No."

"Is he an architect like Simon said?"

Janice pursed her lips as if it pained her to admit the truth. "He's a construction worker." Watching me carefully, she went on, adding information in a growing pile of words like they were a collection of small gifts that she could extend to me. An extra helping. A little understanding. "He has a thick accent. Ben is a nickname. His real name is Benret or Benmet or something else that I can never remember."

I nodded, a reporter merely collecting the facts as analytically and impassively as possible. I detached myself from the conversation and plodded on. "Why did you leave him?"

The stranger across from me opened her hands on the table, palms up, as if she had hidden the answer inside. "He left me." Her voice splintered on those three short words.

I felt no pity for her. "Kind of like you left Dad and me?"

Janice didn't answer.

The question hung like a threat in the air between us, and at that exact, inopportune moment our food arrived. I wanted to scream. Janice looked shell-shocked, and her hands were still gaping, prostrate and ready to accept the proffered plate as if she had seen our waiter coming from a long way off. But it wasn't food that she was waiting for. Janice flushed and looked up at the waiter's starchy white shirt and black tie with a sheepish, down-turned mouth.

"The lamb is exquisite," he assured her with an indulgent smile.

I watched her snake her hands from the table, folding them in her lap and peering at the waiter through lashes heavy with mascara. There was something changed in her hazel eyes, and all at once I imagined that she was flirting with him. Only moments ago we had been making progress, cutting a path through the impenetrable jungle of our lives and our relationship, and she had switched it off to share coy smiles with a stranger. Our waiter. A man ten years younger than her with what I now considered to be a greasy smile and bad hair.

A steaming plate of paella was set in front of me, and though I had longed for it when I saw it on the menu, the scent of it now turned my stomach. I pushed it slightly away from me and watched as Janice followed the waiter with her eyes and then turned eagerly to her meal. My question, only seconds old, was forgotten. She dug in with her knife and fork without glancing at me again, without acknowledging once what we had just experienced, her disclosure drained of all value and importance.

"Is that why you left?" I finally asked, sickened by her obvious pleasure in the perfectly done lamb.

Janice laid down her utensils and touched a napkin to the corners of her mouth. Still chewing, she surveyed me mildly, taking in my untouched entrée and the angry slant of my eyebrows. A mixture of bland concern and uncertainty washed over her features, softened and indistinct in the candlelight. She swallowed. "Excuse me?"

"Some sort of an addiction?" I prodded. "An unquenchable need for a man in your life? The next best thing? The grass is greener on the other side or something dumb like that?"

She looked genuinely confused, maybe even offended. "What in the world are you talking about?"

But I was fuming. I wasn't about to play games or hint at what I meant when we had more or less agreed to be honest, brutal if need be. "You were flirting with him," I accused caustically. "We came here to work on us, to try to find some way to make this ridiculous arrangement work, and you were just making eyes at our waiter."

"I was being nice!" Janice countered, surprised and sharply defensive.

The heat in her voice evoked old, buried feelings in me. I was reduced in an instant to the child I had been, cowering and perplexed by her coldness but also increasingly unaffected by her disinterest, her distance that often translated into unmistakable resentment. I glared at her, rolling around a dozen bitter comments in my mind before I finally spat out, "You are unbelievable."

"Well—," Janice began, and then cut herself off as quickly as she had started. She took a deep breath, visibly stilling herself and attempting to fight back the defensiveness that prompted her to meet me insult for insult. I wanted her to strike back, but instead she said gently, "I am not going to be like this."

"Like what?" I tested.

Janice narrowed her eyes at me, and I saw her anger rise, cool and controlled. "Look, I am trying so hard. You have to cut me a little slack, Julia. I know I'm not perfect, I know I'm not good at this, and the whole world knows that I've made mistakes, but at least I'm *trying*." She was visibly trembling when she added in a whisper, "You're being impossible."

Affronted, I opened my mouth to respond but found I had nothing to say. Was she right? Though I had felt vindicated all along, suddenly there was a swelling guilt, a knowledge that we could be so much more and I was preventing any healing that might take place. But didn't I deserve to hate her?

Janice refused to look at me when she continued, "You know the whole house walks on eggshells around you. You're moody and difficult, and though you try to direct your anger at me, it spills over onto Simon and Nellie. They feel it. They're affected by it."

I rushed to stand up for myself. "That's not true. Grandma knows how I feel about her, and Simon and I are . . . we're friends," I finished lamely.

"Believe what you want." As quickly as the words were out of her mouth, Janice caught her head in her hands. She spat out a quiet curse. "Sorry. I'm sorry. It's just . . . we're not supposed to be fighting!" She looked at me desperately. "I'm sorry. I really am. Please don't fight with me anymore." Her face was drawn and sad, pale and etched with shadows as if her makeup was slowly peeling away from the aging skin beneath. "Eat your meal," Janice entreated me. "It looks delicious."

My appetite had fled, and more than anything I just wanted to go home and strip off the dress that came with such a cost. But at the same time, Janice's words stung me, and, despairingly, I realized that they rang true. Was I like that? Was I the person she described? It horrified me enough to make me pick up my fork and try a bite of paella. The rice was sand on my tongue. I took a sip of ice water and said to my plate, "You were right about one thing. This is very, very hard."

"There isn't a textbook for this sort of thing."

"I guess I'm glad that there isn't," I admitted.

"Truce?" Janice asked.

What could I possibly do? I nodded.

We ate in silence for a few moments, and I put bites of food into my mouth mechanically, chewing minimally and swallowing quickly. My jaw ached with the pain of wanting to cry, but I resolutely held back the tears.

I was startled when Janice offered, "Maybe we should go to counseling together."

Counseling? I dismissed the thought without even considering it. "We don't need counseling, Janice; we just need to talk this through."

"Then let's talk. I want to work this out. What do you need to know?"

It was a simple question with a complicated answer. "Why did you leave?"

Janice sighed. "You don't really want to hear it. But I'm going to tell you the truth since that's what we've agreed to do." She paused, collected herself. Looking me square in the eye, she confessed bleakly, "I should never have married Daniel."

My father was my hero, my best friend, almost supernaturally perfect and preserved in my memory without the flaws and foibles that were so human when he lived. How could any woman not want to be his wife? How could she be so cold?

Apparently my disgust was obvious, because Janice rushed to explain. "Don't look so insulted—hear me out. I was young and I was rebelling against my parents. I liked Daniel well enough—he was kind and generous and he loved me, I think—but I know now that *I* certainly didn't love *him*." She stopped to regard me seriously. "Don't get me wrong. He was a wonderful, wonderful man. I didn't deserve him. The fact that I left had nothing to do with him and everything to do with me." Then Janice shrugged, waved her hands in front of her a little as if the rest of the story was obvious. "And, well, the next thing you know I was pregnant and essentially trapped."

Trapped.

Janice pressed her fingers to her temples and made a little noise that sounded like surrender. "I know that sounds terrible. I know I should have been happy. I should have settled down and had three more kids, but I *couldn't*. I just couldn't. I'm not built that way, Julia. I'm a terrible mother. I failed with you; I'm failing with Simon. . . ."

"And running away fixes everything," I said softly.

Her eyebrows shot up in surprise. "No, of course not. Of course not." She faltered. "It's just . . . you were better off without me."

"I was?" It was something I had wondered many times myself. Life without her had been hard enough. Would it have been even worse with her? It was tempting to accuse her of the things she missed, but I wouldn't let myself get dragged down that tired old road. Janice had not been a part of my life, and no amount of moaning would change that.

But there was one last thing to ask, one last question that had the potential to bring everything into focus. My head ached; my emotions surged and sputtered like a downed power line. I had energy for no more than this. Throbbing with the strain of the evening, I finally managed, "What do you want from me?"

She studied me for a long moment. At some point she had put her hands on the table, and she slid them forward now, toward me, as if she wanted to touch my fingers with her own.

I withdrew the hand that clutched and crumpled a heavy linen napkin and balled it on my lap.

Something fierce and unanticipated flashed across Janice's face, and then understanding like a sudden explosion lit up her eyes. She gasped, a small, choked inhalation that ended in a whisper. "You think I don't love you."

"What?" I croaked.

"Oh, Julia, you think I don't love you. I can see it in your face." Janice was crying a little now, as though she finally got it and whatever it was had been entirely preventable and all her fault. She shed resigned, mournful tears for something—or maybe someone—already long gone. "You have to believe me," she said. "I have always, always loved you. I know that you might find that hard to understand, but in my own, broken way I have loved you. I still do."

It was an admission that I hadn't planned for and wasn't ready to hear. She loved me? Janice was right: I found that very hard to understand, almost impossible to believe. Leaving was a love language that I would probably never get. If she cared for me at all, why let ten years slip away into oblivion? And why try to make things right after all this time? Hadn't someone once sung, "If you love me, let me go?" I wanted to say, *"Let me go."* But I couldn't speak.

Instead, Janice answered my question. "What do I want from you, Julia?" She bit her lip, closed her eyes as if it was difficult to admit. "I want . . . I want—I *wanted* you to love me, too. Just a bit. Just enough for me to know that that one thing, all those years ago, is not completely unforgivable."

Somewhere, veiled behind the anger and the regret and the self-righteous indignation, I heard myself say, *"I did. I did love you very much."* And then the unexpected: *"Maybe I still do."* But the Julia that would say something like that, the Julia that actually felt that way, was very small and very far away.

She was riding the elevator to the thirty-first floor.

seeds

FOR DAYS I FELT like there were words on the tip of my tongue, things I longed to say that filled my mouth but refused to spill past my lips. Maybe I was still processing, working through the many conflicting emotions Janice had unearthed the night we tried to connect. Maybe I was waiting for the right person to talk to. No one seemed quite ready, quite suited to hear everything I wanted to say.

Or maybe it was simply a timing thing.

Either way, something had changed between Janice and me. Though anger still gnawed, though it was still difficult for me to look her in the eye, she had said something that I hadn't planned on. I wavered between disgust at her obvious and pathetic attempt to win me over and a reeling, floating, wishful feeling of *maybe*. Maybe Janice really did love me in her own incomprehensible way. Maybe we would be able to come to an understanding. Maybe my life would be more than I ever imagined it could be. Maybe. But then again, I had learned enough to know not to give in to such immature dreams.

We all went to church together on Sunday morning with Simon sandwiched between Janice and me on the hard-backed pew and Grandma tight against my other side, and though we had done so nearly every week since Janice and Simon had arrived, everything felt different. There was an urgency that nagged at the corners of my consciousness, a feeling of determination, of *now, now, now*. I couldn't escape the sensation that something was about to happen. It was almost as if a stranger had whispered my name just out of earshot. *Julia* from an unfamiliar mouth. My ears pricked. My skin tingled. But nothing extraordinary happened. We sat. We sang. The pastor preached. I listened, but there was nothing for me to hear.

When we got home, Janice tried her hand at grilling hamburgers for lunch. Grandma and I made a warm potato salad, letting Simon snitch crispy pieces of bacon as we fried it and leaving a small bowl without onions so that he, too, could enjoy Grandma's signature side dish. I followed her careful instructions blindly, oblivious to their cheerful conversation as I chopped potatoes and sliced fresh radishes that snapped when the knife slid through them. Each red-rimmed disk was a word I ached to say. But I said nothing.

It was gorgeous outside, the sort of still and softly warm afternoon that makes you want to find a place, any place on God's green earth, that can boast such loveliness more than one or two days a year. The breeze was from the south and more of a breath than a breeze. It lifted the very edges of each leaf, merely to steal a peek at the veined underbelly, then rested, leaving nothing between the earth and the sun but distance. Birds warbled and sang. And winding along the ditch, the creek that would be nothing more than a trickle by midsummer was a burbling, laughing thing.

We ate on the porch, balancing our plates on our laps and scooping potato salad with ruffled chips when we dropped our forks and found ourselves too lazy to reach for them. Grandma and Janice talked and laughed while Simon watched us all, smiling as he swung his head from face to face. Every so often Janice would glance at me, and her eyes would be tender, inviting. But I didn't know what to say, and I didn't know how to feel, so I dropped my gaze and ate.

Simon inhaled his hamburger, leaving the bun untouched, and grabbed a handful of chips so he could join me on the porch swing. My plate was beside me as my lap was steadily disappearing and I flat-out refused to use my belly as a makeshift table. Scraping up the last of the potato salad with my finger, I moved my dish to an antique milk crate on the floor of the porch so Simon could tuck in close like I knew he wanted to.

"May I touch the baby?" he asked, shifting his potato chips to one hand. He examined his empty palm and, seeing crumbs there, quickly wiped it on his shorts. "My hands are clean," he added.

Normally I would tease him about grubby fingers or at least laugh at his childish attempt at hygiene, but there was still something insistent and unreadable resonating just below the surface. I merely said, "Sure." I took him by the wrist and laid his hand against the hard roundness below my ribs. There was a knee or a foot or an elbow curiously prodding, trying to escape. I put my hand over Simon's.

"Ouch!" he yelped gleefully. "The baby's kicking me!"

"That happens every time." I smiled wanly.

"He's tough. We gotta name him something cool like Bubba or . . . or Duke."

"Duke?" I arched an eyebrow at him.

"His best friend's dog," Janice explained around a mouthful of hamburger.

"Yup. Duke was big. Big, big, big!" Simon enthused, gesturing with his arms to create a dog large enough to encompass the whole of the porch. "And tough." It sounded like he could think of no finer trait.

"Duke is a nice name for a dog. But I don't think we should call the baby Duke. Besides, what if it's a girl? We couldn't possibly call her that." I tried not to sound so tired, but I could feel a headache creeping up the back of my neck. There was a grease spot on my T-shirt where Simon's hand had been, and I picked at it absently.

Simon didn't notice my lack of interest—he was too busy laughing at the thought of calling a little girl Duke. "What are you going to name the baby, Julia?"

I looked up to see everyone's eyes glued to me. Grandma looked curious, Simon excited, Janice unreadable. "I don't know," I said slowly. "I hadn't really thought about it."

Janice opened her mouth to say something but closed it before the words could pass her lips.

I studied her for a silent moment, wondering if I should pursue it, but gave up because I wasn't sure that I wanted to hear what she had to say.

Grandma very deliberately forked a tart grape, and it burst when the tines pierced the plump, ruby-colored skin. She turned to look over the low rail of the porch. Simon was already on to something else.

The glorious pull of such a beautiful day lulled Simon into a sleepy daze by midafternoon. By the time we had cleaned up lunch, he was curled on the porch swing, eyes half-closed and gently swaying from the push I had given him with my hip when I walked past with the last of our lunch things.

"Naptime," Janice announced, emerging from the mudroom with an old quilt.

"No," Simon protested weakly. "I'm too big for a nap."

"I'm not," Janice chirped, holding out her arms to him.

Simon complied without further protest and wrapped his legs around her waist, his head resting on the blanket she had slung over her shoulder. I was struck by his long, slender limbs—dark, willowy branches that draped behind Janice's ponytailed head and hung halfway down her legs. He looked so big in her arms. Simon was such a baby to me, such a little boy, and yet he had grown in the months that I had known him. He was not the same child who had almost magically appeared from the depths of Janice's car that wintry March night.

Though I hadn't planned on loving him, I did. Fiercely. I realized with a start that part of the funk I was in had to do with the thought of losing Simon. Janice had told me next to nothing about Ben, yet I couldn't shake the feeling that she was hiding something, that there was something inexact, maybe even dangerous, right beneath the surface. I could see it in her eyes when she said his name. The thought made me shiver in spite of the warm summer sun. If she left again, if things didn't work out between us the way she had envisioned, she would take Simon with her. I couldn't bear the thought.

Janice spread the blanket beneath the three dwarf apple trees that made up our meager orchard. Every other year the apples were so worm-eaten and miserable that even the horses wouldn't touch them. But on the alternating years, those three little trees produced the most delicious apples I had ever tasted. Though we couldn't remember which variety they were, the apples were small and crisp with a marbled red and green peel. The flesh was strikingly white and more sour than sweet, just the way we liked it. I could remember many early fall nights sitting on the porch steps with my dad, an old ice-cream bucket of apples between us. We shined them on our shirtsleeves and admired the perfectly shaped orbs. And while I took my apples straight, he always had a saltshaker beside him and he sprinkled a little before every bite. We ate until our stomachs ached.

This fall would be a good season for apples. I couldn't quite imagine October with Janice still in my home, but I also couldn't help hoping that Simon would be around to taste our extraordinary fruit. It was a double-edged longing, both bitter and sweet.

When Grandma came out of the house wearing an old pair of jeans and carrying her gardening gloves, I did a double take. I had assumed that she had gone inside to curl up on her bed for a little Sunday afternoon nap.

"What are you doing?" I asked, and though I didn't mean to sound so surprised, I did.

Grandma laughed. "I'm going to weed the garden," she announced happily.

I gaped. "It's Sunday." Grandma was usually very rigid about Sabbath observance, and I had never before seen her do any sort of work on what she referred to as the Lord's Day.

"I know," she said with a smile. But she saw the utter disbelief on my face and kindly went on. "What is my favorite thing to do in all the world?"

"Besides hanging out with me?" I kidded.

Grandma flicked her floral-print gloves at me. "Nothing makes me feel closer to God. I can't think of a more beautiful day to sit in my garden. Can you?"

I shook my head as she started down the stairs.

"Besides," Grandma shot over her shoulder, "unless you tell someone, no one will ever be the wiser that I once gardened on a Sunday!"

Although I had thought about disappearing upstairs for a little shut-eye myself, watching her walk across the ocean of blue-green lawn had an almost tangible effect on me. The grass was resplendent in a striking June gown of emerald and sapphire, and I craved the subtle touch of it between my bare toes. I wanted to sit beside my grandmother, a black half-moon of cool earth arching beneath each of my fingernails.

I changed quickly and left my shoes in the mudroom, stepping onto the boards of the porch barefoot for the first time since last summer. Smiling, I tossed an old beach towel around my neck and waved at Grandma, who was already halfway through a row of lettuces.

"You came!" she exclaimed with a grin.

"I couldn't think of a better thing to do today," I replied.

Because my belly was in the way, I had to sit sidesaddle on the towel between the rows. The garden was still very new, and plants like diminutive trees vaulted out of the ground, casting curved necks heavenward and spreading several small leaves toward the sun. A few things—the radishes, the lettuces—were more mature, and in their leafing greenness I could imagine the splendor that Grandma's garden would become by the middle of July.

The weeds were easy to spot amid the freshness of a newly growing garden: they were big and sprawling, greedily taking up space that did not belong to them and staking daring claims with roots that choked and spread far beyond the extent of their foliage. I dug viciously with a trowel, attacking thistles and crabgrass that appeared to have been growing since March. The odd button weed was an easy-to-extract treat, and I relished unearthing the volunteer maples that sprouted from the profusion of helicopters that had fallen the previous autumn.

"Good idea," I assured Grandma after we had worked in peace for the length of two rows.

"It's all I wanted to do today," Grandma agreed, wiping her cheek with the back of her wrist. There was a smear of dirt along her jaw like some ancient tribal mark. "Is it sacrilegious to say that I think gardening should be considered one of the sacraments?"

"I'm the last person to ask," I admitted with a laugh. "What are the sacraments again?"

Grandma narrowed her eyes at me good-naturedly. "You know exactly what they are. And I know that you're not nearly as lost as you sometimes think you are."

Her comment jarred somehow, and the uneasy feeling that had rested on me for days returned like a tidal wave surging over a dry expanse of beach. It was uncanny how Grandma could understand me better than I understood myself sometimes. I wanted to press her, ask her what she meant by such a statement, but I didn't know how to be inquisitive without staging an inquisition. So instead I said nothing and inched along the rows, pulling more weeds in silence.

When we reached the carrots—nothing more than a line of sea-green fuzz tickling gently at the sky—Grandma spread out her towel and sat cross-legged to regard me. "Did you have a good night with Janice?" she asked out of the blue.

I had been anticipating this question, maybe even hoping for it. I had so much to say, so many things to examine, poke, and prod before I could claim at least a bit of understanding. But as soon as the query was out of her mouth, I found myself speechless. I had so much bottled up inside, so much that wanted to come out, and yet what was there to say? Truthfully, it had been neither good nor bad. It was an experience, a collection of moments to store away and spend the next months, maybe even years, deciphering.

"Did I have a good night?" I repeated to myself. All my words had melted away beneath the warmth of the sun.

Grandma saw me fumbling. She peeled off her gardening gloves to massage her arthritic knuckles and sighed. "I know it probably wasn't a *good* night, but did it go okay?"

"I suppose so," I answered slowly. "I think I learned some things about her. I think she learned some things about me."

"That's a good thing," Grandma encouraged. "Making progress?"

"Maybe," I said. "It was very hard."

"Nothing wrong with hard." Grandma put her gloves back on, a finger at a time, and turned her attention to the dirt.

But I didn't want the conversation to be over. "You know," I began, "I was wondering about something."

Grandma didn't look up, but she murmured a little under her breath.

I continued. "Where did Janice get the money for all those things? The dress, the shoes . . . The necklace alone must have been, what, over a hundred dollars? *Hundreds* of dollars?"

Without giving it any thought, Grandma came out with the truth. "Janice bought the dress on sale. I paid for the shoes. And the necklace had been Janice's—she wanted to give it to you."

I stopped with my fingers in the soil, grasping the root of a small maple that could only be considered a sapling. "*You* bought the shoes?"

Grandma pursed her lips at me. "Janice wanted everything to be special. I offered to help out and buy one small thing."

"But she made me believe that they were from her!"

"Did she? Did you ever ask her?"

"No," I conceded.

"Maybe you just assumed." Grandma's attention turned back to her task. "Janice would have told you the truth if you asked, just like I did now. It's not like we were trying to keep a secret from you."

"What about the necklace?" I asked after a moment. "I don't want a hand-me-down gift from . . . from . . ." I faltered. I almost said, *from one of her boyfriends*, but that was simply too harsh, too black-and-white for a day of such delicate and muted color.

Grandma exhaled heavily. "Why do you care where the necklace came from? It was obviously special to Janice, and she wanted to give you some little, meaningful piece of herself. She's trying, Julia."

"So am I," I said quickly.

"Are you?" Grandma stared at me hard, holding my eyes captive in her own before sighing a bit and turning to the soil at her fingertips. She picked up a handful of earth and let it fall through her fingers, breaking the chunks so they tumbled down gently and hit the ground with the softest of thuds.

I watched her, wondering if she was waiting for me to say something, to defend myself somehow.

Before I could open my mouth, Grandma spoke again. "I don't think there is anything quite so beautiful as grace," she said almost to herself. "Problem is, we can easily see when others are withholding it, but we are blind to the times we clutch it greedily to ourselves." She brushed her hands together, ridding her palms of the last of the dirt.

Grace. It was a word I had heard often, and yet I wasn't sure that I could accurately define it. *Freely given* came to mind. *Undeserved. Extravagant. Easier said than done*, I thought.

The maple had deep, mature roots, and I needed leverage to wrench it out of the ground. Rising to my knees, I plunged my hands into the dirt and secured the plant in an iron grip. I pulled on the woody root of the maple until my palms burned. I yanked and tore and jerked. My fingers began to sting.

Grandma watched my efforts. "You know, there is a parable about soil. And grace, too, I think."

I gave the sapling one last mighty heave and fell back on my haunches, angry red lines of torn skin intersecting my dirty palms. I peered at my hands and didn't respond to Grandma's comment, which she took as permission to proceed.

"God is a generous gardener. Liberal even." Grandma gestured at the neat rows of vegetables that we had planted weeks before. "We like things neat and orderly. But God scatters seed enthusiastically."

Of course I knew the parable. I had heard it in Sunday school and caught snippets of the familiar verses in many different sermons and lectures when I was older. But I always skipped straight to the part about the soil, more or less ignoring the metaphor of the seed. It never occurred to me that when God sowed, it looked nothing like the way we planted. I remembered preparing the garden with Grandma only weeks ago and the painstaking way we found a home for each and every seed. We staked out perfect rows and positioned everything carefully with our fingers. There was nothing extravagant about the way we planted.

"Seed that falls on the path or in rocky places will never grow," Grandma continued. "It can't. But we're never told that the seeds fallen among the thorns *die*; they are just *choked*." She held up a dandelion thistle in her grimy hands. "If God is the gardener, what do you think He does?" She dropped the thistle and reached across the row to grasp my wrist. She squeezed. "I think that sometimes He weeds. He gives us room to grow."

I remembered a year when the field across from our farm had been sown with soybeans. Someone had been renting the land from a recent widow, and he lived a few hours away. He rarely checked on his investment, making long-distance decisions and hiring the work out locally. When the time came to weed the field, he didn't bother to set up a crew to walk his beans and pull the weeds. I heard that when the renter finally came to survey his crop, it was so over-run and filthy with thorns that he counted the harvest a complete loss. I wondered at what point does God consider one of His seeds a complete loss?

But I wasn't in the mood to be philosophical or theological. So I left. "I need something to get this out," I said, motioning at the small tree. Maneuvering around my belly, I hoisted myself up so I could get the garden hoe from the shed. Grandma let me go.

As I walked away, my feet swished through the long grass and seemed to whisper with each step: *grace, grace, grace, grace.* I glanced at the apple trees, the bodies entwined beneath it, and wondered what it would feel like to curl up beside them, to nap beneath a canopy of grace so sweet and tart it stung.

"I'm not good enough," I whispered. "I don't have it in me."

And somewhere, deep in my heart, there was an echo: *But I have it in Me.*

summer snow

ON MONDAY MORNING, my car didn't start. It clicked. No matter how many times I turned the key, no matter how earnestly I hoped, the only sound I could coax from the engine was a shallow, definitive click, click, click. It felt like I was being reprimanded.

You too? I thought, twisting the ignition one last time. *What did I ever do to you?*

And then I couldn't help but smile when I thought of driving with Thomas years ago, back when my crummy little car had been newly acquired, though far from new.

"You drive it like you stole it," Thomas teased.

It was true. I wasn't a bad driver, but I certainly wasn't easy on my car. In some ways it was miraculous that I had driven it for over three years without a hitch. Too bad it couldn't have chosen a more appropriate time to break down. As I wiggled out of the driver's seat, I felt one fresh, small burden fall upon my already overladen shoulders. It was almost possible to hear my back creak beneath the weight. I repressed a defeated sigh.

"Starter," Grandma guessed with some certainty in her voice when I marched heavily back into the house. "Your grandpa loved anything and everything that ran on an engine, and I remember a few of the terms he used to throw around."

"Could it be the battery?" Janice offered, taking a stab in the dark.

Grandma tipped her head in assent. "Could be. Or the alternator, maybe."

"Gas!" Simon contributed happily. "Diesel?"

"I don't care what's wrong with it," I cut in with a wan smile. I held out my wristwatch with the smooth face bulging forward. "I care about getting to work. I'm going to be late."

"Oh, of course." Janice downed the last gulp of her coffee and grimaced as if the dregs had settled into a bitter sludge. "I'll take you." She pushed back from the table and tugged gently on Simon's ear. "Come on; let's quick brush our teeth. We'll be two minutes, tops."

The last comment was directed at me, and I saluted in response, sinking into the chair that she had just vacated. "Will it be expensive to fix?" I asked Grandma.

"I don't know," she admitted. "But there are some men at church who do this sort of thing to help people. I'll see what I can find out."

Charity.

Thinking of the ever-dwindling number in my bank account, I swallowed my pride and said, "All right."

Simon chattered all the way into town, and I was grateful that I didn't have to do anything more than murmur the occasional "Mm-hmm." I was trying to do the math in my head: Did the money I had set aside in savings offset the cost of fixing my car? Would I still have enough to cover the doctors' bills that would pile up by August?

I was cutting corners and being as careful as I could with the small amount of money that came in every month. Based on my income, Grandma had even tried to sign me up for some government program, but I flat-out refused. Supposedly I was eligible to receive a certain amount of healthy food every month: milk, cheese, grains, peanut butter. Peanut butter? Since when was that considered healthy? But though I had seen women in the grocery store eagerly hauling out their coupons and I knew there was no shame in it, I couldn't bring myself to add one more thing to the list of differences that made me stand out from everyone else I knew.

I had to make it work on my own.

"I'll pick you up tonight," Janice offered cheerfully when we turned into the parking lot of Value Foods. "What time do you get off?"

"Five," I said. "But I'll see if I can catch a ride home with someone. You have to pick up Simon before that, don't you?"

"It's no bother. I can come back."

"No. I'll work something out." I hopped out of the car and reached in through the open back window to give Simon five. "Have a good day, buddy. See you tonight."

"Let's play Yahtzee after supper," Simon cajoled, catching my fingers when I tried to pull away. His eyes were each a sparkling chip of black onyx, and they glinted at me mischievously from behind his slipping glasses. I knew he wouldn't let me go until I agreed, so I nodded quickly and pretended to try to wrestle my way out of his grip. "Promise," he demanded with a giggle as I flapped his arm.

"I promise." I laughed, finally yanking my hand away.

Simon had a way of making me forget myself, but by the time their car had pulled out of view and I was surrounded by the overly cool air of the dim grocery store, worry was beginning to pluck at the corners of my mouth. Only yesterday I had stopped in the shade of the garden shed and wondered if the God of heaven and earth was talking to me. But in the reality of a day gone wrong, it was easy to imagine that the only voice I had heard mingling among the warmth of a perfect afternoon was the whisper of my own conscience, my own deep-down desire to make everything work out. I was on my own. Grandma might stand beside me, Simon might fill my days with laughter, but I was essentially alone—the car, the baby, the muddle of relationships, and even the ambiguous future were entirely mine to disentangle.

The roller coaster of it all was making me dizzy and sick. *I can. I can't. I'll try. It's too hard.* The constant teetering seesaw of emotions was nauseating, and as my footsteps echoed on the scratched linoleum of the grocery store, I decided once and for all to cut myself a little slack. No promises. No guarantees. Taking it one day at a time was more than enough drama for me. And a broken-down car first thing on a Monday morning was the only proof I needed to assure me that my resolution was timely and well made. Dealing with Janice and everything that entailed would simply have to wait. I had other things to worry about: Thomas and Francesca's wedding was mere weeks away and the baby was following not far behind. But before facing any of that, I had a car to fix. It was a manageable problem; even better, it gave me something specific to concentrate on.

My car so consumed my thoughts that when the clock read 5:05 and I finally slowed down enough to realize that the day had flown by, it struck me that I had not secured a way to get home. I collected my purse slowly and took a few minutes to freshen up in the bathroom to buy myself a little time to think.

It seemed hopeless. The one person I felt comfortable asking for a ride, Alicia, had already left, and though Graham had arrived at Value Foods after school, his shift wasn't over until close. I barely knew Monica and certainly wasn't confident about petitioning her for a lift, and besides, she had skipped cheerfully out of the back room moments before I entered it. I would have to chase her to catch her—if she was still in the parking lot. There was no one else; my options were exhausted. I was stranded.

For a moment I tossed around the idea of calling Janice or Grandma and asking them to come and pick me up, but I had been so insistent when Janice dropped me off only hours ago. I wasn't willing to recant my earlier assurances that it would be no problem whatsoever to find a ride home. Or maybe I wasn't willing to admit that I couldn't manage even this one small thing on my own.

I walked aimlessly to the front of the store, waving unenthusiastically at Clark when I passed him. He grunted back. I wondered how long five miles would feel to my pregnant feet.

The air was startlingly warm after a long day of working in an air-conditioned store, and goose bumps sprang up on my arms instantly. The breeze lifted my hair off my neck, and the sun spread like a blanket across my back. It felt wonderful. All at once I didn't care about the car. It didn't matter that I couldn't simply drive home. I found myself actually thankful to be more or less marooned in Mason. It was *Mason* after all, not New York, and if nothing else I could enjoy an hour to myself before breaking down and phoning home. *One day at a time*, I reiterated. Even, *one moment at a time.*

I remembered that the used-book store was open until six and that the bakery was only two doors down. People often joked that Mason had been founded around Lily Spencer's kitchen. Apparently she had been such a well-known baker that when she opened a shop and tried to call it Stone Ground, everyone ignored her chosen name and called the bakery Lily's instead. Two generations later, Lily's remained. Their specialty was sweet breads, and the thought of a thick slice of lemon-blueberry bread and a new book seemed like the smallest piece of heaven to me. I would treat myself to two indulgences, guilt over car expenses repressed, and find a bench in the park for an hour or so. I could call from the gas station when I was ready to go home. Though my plan would give Grandma ammunition for her dogged allegation that I needed a cell phone, I decided it would be well worth the short argument. I liked the thought of dropping off the radar for a while.

But my well-laid plans crumbled long before I even made it out of the Value Foods parking lot.

"Hi!" a voice called as I stepped onto the sidewalk at the entrance to the grocery store. I looked around for the source of the sound, wondering if the greeting had been directed at me. But pretty girls got shouted at in parking lots, not pregnant ones. I blushed and concentrated on the path in front of me, embarrassed that I had reacted until I heard someone tease, "Work is that way!"

I turned around to see Michael sitting in an ancient, rusted-out Volkswagen Bug. Shielding my eyes from the sun, I watched him as he pulled his car up beside me and let it idle. The engine sounded like it was full of gravel, and I raised an eyebrow quizzically. "My shift is just over," I assured him. Then I added playfully, "Nice car. It looks about as reliable as mine."

"Hey now, don't knock the Bug," Michael said, feigning offense. "I've seen your car. Herbie here is one fine machine compared to that."

"Apparently so," I consented. I didn't mean to roll my eyes.

But Michael looked at me and then swiveled around in his seat to survey the parking lot. "Where is your car?"

"I gave it the day off." I shrugged. "It was being rude—wouldn't start."

Michael gave a low whistle. "That doesn't sound good. Did it go *rrrr-rrrr*?"

"*Rrrr-rrrr?*" I mimicked with a laugh. "Nice sound effects. But no, actually, it sounded more like *click-click.*"

"Good thing you make the big bucks, Julia. *Click-click* is not cheap to fix."

I sighed. "Go figure."

The conversation lulled and Michael and I exchanged weak smiles before it hit him. "You're not walking home, are you? I thought you lived in the country."

"I'm not and I do," I said. But I didn't really know how to explain what I was doing, so I motioned rather lamely in the direction of Main Street and shrugged again.

"I can give you a ride somewhere, you know. Do you need a ride?" Michael's smile was candid and his eyes were amiable, intense even. He was wearing a T-shirt that said *Eagles Lacrosse* in faded lettering across the chest, and through the open window I could see that he had on baggy jean shorts and flip-flops. I had never seen Michael wear anything other than his Value Foods uniform. It was a bit like running into my teacher at the swimming pool in second grade and realizing that she did not actually live at school—she had a house, a husband, a life. Shocking.

"Uh . . . ," I wavered, trying to think of a polite way to say no.

But Michael reached over to the passenger door and swung it open. "Get in," he said, nodding at the seat beside him. "You need a ride and I know it. I have one quick thing I need to do, and then I'll take you wherever you want to go."

"How much gas do you have in the tank?" I muttered, surprising myself.

"Not nearly enough," Michael replied with a good-natured grin.

I felt conspicuous and awkward, but I also felt committed, and I crossed in front of the car slowly. My apron caught on a sharp edge of the license plate, and my ears burned as it became obvious that I hadn't even bothered to take off the most hideous aspect of my ugly uniform. What was Michael doing offering me a ride? He might as well have picked up the fat lady from the circus sideshow I was so conspicuous in the tenting royal blue fabric. I bit my lip and caught Michael's eye through the windshield, making a sheepish face as if to show how stupid I was to not ditch the apron the second my shift was over.

Humiliated, I quickly undid the strings and pulled the piece of fabric over my head. I hustled into the car and yanked the door shut. "Thanks," I said shyly. "I was going to go to the bakery and then call for a ride later, but this is more convenient."

"Good idea," Michael shot back, driving out of the parking lot. "The bakery, I mean. Still want to go?"

Too much information, I thought, wishing I had kept my mouth shut. He probably thought that the last thing I needed was a baked goodie. "No," I demurred.

Michael stopped in front of Lily's anyway.

I lunged for my purse and was out the door before he had a chance to undo his seat belt. "If you're driving, this is my treat. Don't move."

He put both hands on the steering wheel as if he had been warned, but he seemed pleased.

It was inexpressibly strange to be surrounded by the smell of baking bread in Lily's as I picked out a snack for Michael as if it were the most natural thing in the world. I didn't know what he liked, so I bought a slice of lemon-blueberry bread and one of cinnamon coffee cake as well as two strawberry lemonades in Coke cups. The cashier asked me if I wanted the strawberries that usually adorned the glasses of Lily's hand-squeezed drinks, but I declined. Somehow strawberries made a drive home seem like a date.

Michael happily chose the cinnamon coffee cake and then made a U-turn in the middle of the street to head south out of town.

"I promised to drop something off for my brother, and he was expecting me over a half hour ago," he said around a mouthful of coffee cake. "But after that I'll take you wherever you need to go, okay?"

I almost replied, "Take as long as you need," but I caught myself in time. Somehow that sounded smarmy, desperate. Instead I said, "Deal."

Talking to Michael was like walking in sand: it was easy and comfortable, even calming somehow. At first I tried to guard my answers, think about what I was saying before I let words pass my lips, but there was nothing to fear in his questions. His affability was sincere and I lost myself in it.

I didn't notice how far we had come until Michael drove down the long driveway of a farm that was over ten minutes south of town. There was a small huddle of people around an extended-cab pickup beside the barn, and Michael waved at them as he yanked hard on the rusty parking break. "Back in a sec. If the brake doesn't hold, you do know how to drive a stick shift, right?" He winked. Reaching into the backseat, he grabbed what was obviously a tractor part and let himself out of the car.

When Michael was gone, I came to as if rousing myself from a deep sleep. Late-afternoon drives down country roads? Cake and conversation? What was I thinking? Or, more accurately, what was I hoping for? What good could come from chasing impossible dreams down dead-end roads? I liked Michael. I liked him too much to be satisfied with the occasional ingenuous encounter. I didn't need an intermittent friend or another reason to stay up at night. I needed answers, help, a little understanding. I needed a savior. Incredible as he was, Michael didn't seem the superhero type to me.

"I want to make one more stop," Michael announced, sliding back behind the wheel only moments later. I could hardly complain—it was his car after all. But some of the magic of the afternoon had worn off for me, and Michael noticed my hesitation. He elbowed me with a conspiratorial smile. "You'll like it. I promise. It's a season thing."

I was utterly bewildered by his proclamation and not much in the mood for surprises, but I participated in friendly chitchat almost automatically as we drove back toward Mason.

"Are you in a rush?" Michael asked, though he had already gotten me to agree to his extra pit stop.

I shook my head.

"Good, 'cause this is so cool. It only happens once a year for a couple of days."

My interest was piqued, but he wouldn't answer any questions about his subterfuge, and before long our destination was revealed when Michael turned onto the tree-lined road that led to the gravel pit. It looked like an entirely different place from the last time I had overlooked the small lake, but that didn't stop my stomach from lurching painfully when I realized where we were going. Though the verdant swatch of wooded terrain was barely recognizable as the barren wasteland it had been only months ago, in my mind's eye I could still see Janice and Simon curled up in her car. The thought made my vision blur.

"It's the perfect day for it," Michael assured me as he cut the engine.

We stepped out of the car wordlessly, and immediately the warm June air slid around me. It seemed a little too close for comfort, like an unwelcome embrace, and I pushed up my long sleeves wishing that I were wearing shorts.

"The perfect time of day," Michael continued, watching the sky. He turned away from me and stretched in the sun-soaked shade of an immense tree as if we had been driving for hours. Light fanned through the flutter of leaves and cast wavering lines of radiance across his skin, his dark hair. I realized that I was staring and looked quickly away.

"You are about to witness a once-a-year phenomenon, Julia. Maybe even once-in-a-lifetime if the temperature and wind and lighting are just right."

Michael's excitement was endearing, and when he spun around to grin at me, I tried to grin back, pushing the blackened remnants of bad memories out of my mind. He was right—it was a beautiful day. And though I didn't know what he had planned, there was no reason for me not to enjoy it. When he motioned me to follow, I willingly trailed him single file across the parking lot, down a small hill, and through a copse of lithe trees. Within moments we emerged at a short precipice above the lake, and Michael spread out a hand to encompass it as if to say, *Take it in.*

The sun was sinking on the horizon, and it bathed the lake in golden light that made the surface of the water glitter with an ethereal iridescence. I had to squint to look at it. Even more impressive than the play of light on water was the airy show above it. Dancing and buoyant on the exhalation of a soft wind were thousands upon thousands of cottony snowflakes. They spun and floated and fell only to be swept up and away before descending once more to flirt with the coolness below. After a pause to admire their reflection in the lake, the wisps of white settled down gently to glide along the glistening wetness. It was indescribable.

And it took me a moment to understand what was happening: the cottonwoods were shedding puffs of down in an impressive display all over the tranquil lake. I had never seen anything like it. Summer snow.

"I feel like I'm in a fairy tale," I breathed. A sense of sudden and acute self-awareness told me that I should feel embarrassed for saying something so silly, and yet I didn't. Michael had brought me here; he obviously felt something akin to what I was experiencing amid the torrent of white. He didn't say anything.

Evening was approaching, and there were pockets of coolness in the air. A gust of wind rose over the knoll behind us, and in an instant the atmosphere changed. Without warning, a chill shivered down my spine, and across the lake the trees responded in kind: they shuddered and trembled, nodding to the current in graceful submission. For a moment the shower of cotton swept into a frenzy of stormlike proportions, and my breath caught in my throat. It was so beautiful. It was so unexpected and bright.

Hopeful somehow.

Michael must have turned to regard me, and he witnessed first-hand the affected look on my face. I felt him touch my arm in an almost paternal gesture, and just as quickly as his fingers made contact with my skin, I felt them withdraw. In the corner of my vision I could see him bury his hands deep into his pockets. I blinked and held my eyes closed for the space of one deep breath, watching the waltz of white and gold on the backs of my eyelids. Then, smiling, I tried to focus my attention on Michael. I wanted to say something to dispel the crystalline quality of the moment, but nothing seemed right.

"You're going to be okay, you know." His voice came out of nowhere, and though I didn't know exactly what he meant, something inside me clutched at those words and pulled them close as if he had offered me a talisman.

Really? Do you really think so? I felt an almost reckless hunger to hear him say more. What did Michael know about my situation? What comfort could he possibly offer me to soothe the ache of Janice and Simon? the baby? all my unanswered questions? Yet there was something wise in his statement, some nugget of truth that felt real and definable. I clung to it.

And then, though he had given me enough, though he had helped me forget for a while, shown me beauty, even spoken truth over my life, Michael opened his mouth again. "You're not alone."

It was what I longed to hear.

possibility

I HAD HEARD IT BEFORE.

From Grandma, from Mrs. Walker, and even from Janice: *"You'll be okay. It's fine. Everything is going to be all right. This too shall pass."* But to hear it from Michael's lips— *"You're not alone"*—was incalculably different.

From the moment I knew I was pregnant, a gap had opened in the earth. It was a wide, bottomless fissure that slashed through the center of everything and stranded me on unstable ground. It left me wandering, unbalanced. Alone. And Michael reached for me. He didn't have to do it—he wasn't bound to me by genetic code, history, or obligation—and yet he extended an arm, a bridge of blood and bone. I took it.

When Michael finally drove me home, it was nearly six thirty and the house was in a bit of an uproar about my alleged disappearance. But my face had changed somehow—I could feel it—and though Grandma looked like she wanted to berate me for being late, she simply smiled a mystified little smile that slowly took on a decidedly pleased edge.

"Where have you been?" Grandma rose from the supper table as if to come to me, maybe take me in her arms, but the legs of her chair caught and she was trapped in a half-standing position.

"I'm a big girl," I assured her with a laugh. "A friend drove me home and we got sidetracked. No big deal."

Grandma looked on the verge of demanding to know more, but then she shot a bemused look at Janice and sank back into her seat. "Well, supper is cold."

"I'm sorry," I said with all sincerity as I took my spot in front of an empty plate. "I should have called. We just lost track of time."

Maintaining a schedule had been a nearly impossible endeavor back in the days when Thomas and I were two sides of the same coin. But it had been a long time since I last had to apologize for causing my grandmother to worry about my whereabouts. Though I didn't agree with it, I certainly couldn't blame her for her apprehension, and already any annoyance at my lack of consideration was being quickly replaced in her demeanor by a rare satisfaction that I had been out with a friend.

"You should have a time-out," Simon scolded, pointing his fork at me as though provoked.

"I'm kind of old for time-outs," I told him. "Besides, when I was your age I didn't get time-outs; I got spankings. Please pass the asparagus."

Simon grudgingly passed me the greens, but I felt buoyant, at ease, and it was hard for the rest of the table not to follow suit. The tone in the room seemed to lighten with every bite of tepid food I cheerfully lifted to my mouth. We talked and laughed. I even smiled at Janice—directly at her, a smile meant specifically for her—and she swelled as if something inside had filled to overflowing and burst whatever banks had held it at bay.

And because of the untroubled weightlessness of the air around us, I was reckless and hasty and agreed to something I would have never consented to do only days ago.

"Dr. Morales's office called," Grandma told me at an easy break in the conversation. "They wanted to remind you about the hospital orientation tomorrow night."

My understanding of the birth process was limited to books and hearsay, and when I learned that Lamaze was outdated and that birthing classes had been relegated to one evening crash course, I had been surprised. But not disappointed. It suited me just fine that instead of weekly meetings with adoring couples wrapped around each other I would only have to endure a few hours of public learning. Apparently first-time moms got little more than a tour of the facilities and a rundown of pain management options.

I swallowed a mouthful of chicken. "You're coming with me, right?" I downed the last of my milk, not really even waiting for Grandma's answer. It was a given. We had decided months ago that she would be in the delivery room with me. Dr. Morales had told me that I would need a birth coach, and though I was determined to take care of myself more and more, I also knew that childbirth was something no one should have to do alone. I looked forward to sharing the experience with Grandma.

But the room filled with silence.

I looked up with a half smile pinned to my face. "I can't do this without you," I faltered, fixing my eyes on her. Grandma was biting her lower lip in a gesture of distinct discomfort. "You can't come?" I asked incredulously.

"I'm still your birth coach," Grandma rushed to reassure me. "But I am *so sorry* I can't make it tomorrow night. I got the dates mixed up on my calendar, and I have to be at a memorial service."

All at once I remembered. Grandma volunteered at the yearly hospice memorial service, and it was always held the third Tuesday in June. This year she was going to be director of the volunteer staff. Why hadn't we thought of it when we signed up for the class in the first place? "We'll just reschedule the hospital visit," I said. "No big deal."

Grandma still looked distressed. "I already asked, honey. We can't. They only offer the birthing class every few months. The next one is too late."

"I can't go alone!" I yelped. *She'll have to skip the memorial service this year*, I reasoned silently. Surely Grandma wouldn't leave me stranded at such an event.

"You don't have to go alone." Janice's voice surprised me, and I turned to her as if in a daze. She was looking at me expectantly, eyebrows lifted as if she was waiting for me to understand her meaning.

I did at once. "But Grandma is my birth coach," I told Janice, leaving no room for discussion.

"She is," Janice agreed. "But you just *have* to go tomorrow night. You'll get to meet the nurses and see the birthing rooms. . . . They'll tell you what to expect, and you'll learn how to cope with the different stages of labor. . . ." She waved her hands as if to pluck more reasons out of the air. "It's so important. And you shouldn't go alone. You don't have to go alone." She tapped her own chest with two hesitant fingers, then shrugged at me awkwardly.

I opened my mouth to argue, but I couldn't think of a single thing to say that wouldn't come out insulting. How could I tell Janice, *I don't want you there*?

"What about Simon?" I said. "He can't come along. Someone has to stay home with him."

"I'm going to have a babysitter," Simon chimed in happily. "Mom says that a babysitter is *paid* to play with me."

I snorted involuntarily.

Grandma and Janice watched me for a split second, and then they laughed, too, though they seemed too intent on my response to find Simon's declaration very funny.

"What?" Simon implored. "What are you laughing at?"

"Nothing," I muttered. Quiet fell around the table again, and I picked at the remnants of my potatoes with the tines of my fork. Nobody said a word, and I could feel three pairs of eyes studying me as I scraped my plate. "Okay, fine," I finally said. "Janice can come with me. But *you*—" I pointed the fork at Grandma—"are going to be in that delivery room with me."

"I wouldn't miss it for the world," Grandma promised, relief in her voice.

"Thank you," Janice said.

I looked at her and was somewhat startled to find that she truly, deeply wanted to be a part of this process in some small way. It was unnerving but also strangely touching, and I decided that a few hours at the hospital with her would hardly be the end of the world. Besides, a tour of the maternity ward was far from intimate, and moreover, I was feeling benevolent, gracious even, after witnessing Michael's enchanted snowfall.

The following night Janice and I had a quick supper with Simon and then dropped him off at the babysitter's early so we could be among the first to arrive at the two-and-a-half-hour class. It felt peculiar to walk the empty hallways of the hospital with Janice, my right hand planted firmly below the swell of my belly, where the baby was beginning to feel a tad too heavy. Janice had walked this same path with my father over nineteen years ago. Did she clutch his arm? Was she afraid? excited? Did she know even before I was born that she wasn't ready to be a mother? It hadn't occurred to me to be nervous about the practicalities of the impending birth of my child, but with the clinical smell of hospital disinfectant in the air and the strange juxtaposition of past and present as Janice strode beside me, an abrupt wave of disquiet rushed through my soul.

We had hoped to be early, but when we neared conference room two—unnecessarily demarcated with pink and blue streamers twirling around the door—we heard voices inside.

"Guess we're not the first," Janice said nervously.

I grunted in response and stepped gingerly through the door.

The room was nearly full already, and couples sat in folding chairs that formed a tight circle around the perimeter of the small room. Though I knew my response was the result of oversensitivity, all those young faces seemed attractive to me—happy and confident, with big, white smiles and an air of poise and accomplished ease. They turned as one to survey the newcomers, and as quickly as I had formed an opinion about them, they appraised me. Maybe I was being cynical, but it seemed that something altered in their eyes when Janice appeared behind me—Janice instead of a handsome husband to hold my hand and gaze at me tenderly. There was an almost imperceptible twinge of discomfort before the room dissolved into conversation once again.

"Welcome," a nurse in uniform greeted us. "Are you together?" She motioned between Janice and me, and when I nodded, she handed me a clipboard and gave Janice a red folder. "This is information for you to keep and go over together at home."

I almost blurted out, "She's not my birth coach." But my tongue was thick and uncooperative, and I merely smiled weakly instead.

The nurse pointed to the clipboard in my arms. "Please find your name and check it off the list." She paused while I located *Julia DeSmit* at the very top of the short spreadsheet. A glance at the rest of the names told me that I was the only single mom. Every other entry was twofold: *Andrew and Darci Dragstra, Luke and Elizabeth Fennema, Benji and Kim Menning*.

"Done?" the nurse asked. I quickly tore my eyes from the clipboard and handed it back. She indicated the chairs with a rehearsed smile. "Go ahead and find a seat."

It was stiflingly hot, and I wished that I had taken a bottle of water along. None of the other women seemed bothered by the heat, and they stroked their tummies lovingly, catching their husbands' hands now and then to let Daddy feel the little kicks and movements of Junior. They laughed serenely and talked of nursery decorations and layettes.

"What is a layette?" I whispered desperately in Janice's ear. Suddenly she felt safe to me, familiar amid the exoticness of such a foreign, even hostile landscape.

"It's just a fancy term for all the things you need for a baby," Janice explained quietly. "You know, clothes, blankets, diapers . . ."

I had a few sleepers and Mrs. Walker's old crib. There was nothing else. There was no nursery to decorate. The baby would sleep in my room; we simply had no more space. Janice and Simon had taken over the sewing room, and the only extra room in the house was the other half of the attic. It was completely uninhabitable. I thought of the plain white walls of my bedroom and the neat collages of old photographs that I had hung in any available space. It was a far cry from what I envisioned a nursery to be.

When I overheard the woman to my left ramble on about an oak changing table and a new glider rocker, my heart cringed for the things that my baby already lacked. We hadn't been rich when I was growing up, and I knew well what it felt like to buy my clothes at Wal-Mart instead of in the mall shops where the jeans sported tags with catchy brand names. My heart plummeted at the thought of my son feeling what I felt: *You are not enough.*

But *stuff*—nurseries, expensive labels, layettes—was nothing in comparison to the one fundamental thing that I could not provide for my son, and I abruptly, achingly came face-to-face with the insufficiency of my role as a mother.

It was a tremendously depressing evening. When the nurse explained the stages of labor, she kept slipping up and saying "your spouse" whenever she referenced techniques that the birth coach could use to ease the pain. Most of the time she caught herself the moment the words escaped her lips and threw me a quick, obvious look that made my spirit sink a little lower in my abdomen with every glance.

Janice must have felt me stiffen beside her because she laid a hand on my knee for the briefest of moments. It was an act of support, a gesture of solidarity, and while I appreciated her indication of encouragement, in some ways it made me feel even worse. Not only did I have to face this without a husband, the person accompanying me was a virtual stranger.

The last thing we did before the nurse dismissed us was take a tour of the birthing rooms. There were only three rooms, but they were large and modern with suede-colored walls and cream moldings. Peaceful landscape prints adorned the walls, and any medical equipment was discreetly concealed behind large cabinets with shapely pewter pulls. The effect was clean and sophisticated; this one little area of the hospital had been transformed into an upscale hotel.

"Oh, honey," one woman gushed, pulling her husband into the spacious bathroom, "there's a Jacuzzi tub. Maybe we could have a water birth."

Water birth? I wanted to curl up in a corner and hide my face in my hands. Everyone seemed completely taken with the newly redecorated maternity ward, but I longed for a cold operating room. This was all too much: too lavish, too indulgent, too *romantic* somehow. It was intended for gentle kisses, warm embraces, blissful *families*. I didn't fit the demographic. Not at all.

Janice and I stepped into the starry night a few minutes before ten. Many of the couples were still chatting and asking the nurse questions, but the moment she thanked us for coming, the two of us blazed a path to the door. Janice hadn't said much of anything throughout the entire evening, and when the hospital was behind us, she seemed to come to her senses. She looked at me out of the corner of her eye, and I assumed from the brisk pace she set to the car that she was embarrassed by the lack of guidance she had offered. For some reason I wanted to tell her that I hadn't come with any expectations, but she spoke first.

"A little overwhelmed?" Janice asked lightly, as if this was nothing more monumental than an upcoming science test. But her voice was strained, and it was obvious to me that she knew the class had been more than just a little overwhelming for me. It seemed to have been difficult for her, too.

Yes didn't begin to encompass what I felt, so I said nothing.

We entered the distinct circle of light cast by a streetlamp, and I saw a smooth, round stone. I kicked it absently, and it skidded unevenly across the pavement before bumping into the curb and flipping into the grass beyond.

Janice trailed the movement of the rock and, watching it disappear into the darkness of the well-kept hospital lawn, followed its path and sat down heavily on the ground. She ran her fingers through the grass and heaved a loud sigh.

Because I was exhausted and didn't know what else to do, I joined her. The grass was cool and smelled like summer. Without thinking, I lay back until my vision was filled with a sky full of stars and nothing more. "That was awful," I said quietly into the blackness.

Janice fell back too. "I know."

Then, because I needed consolation, I voiced the fear that I had shared so many times before: "I don't know if I can do this."

Janice didn't respond. I waited for a few words of comfort, for a confirmation of my ability to do this well, to be an excellent mother, but none came. The seconds stretched into a minute and then two. Completely stunned, I indignantly rolled my head to survey her. She owed me that much at least. After all she had done to me, after all we had been through, the least she could do was muster up a couple of reassuring words.

Janice was watching the sky, but when she sensed me move, she turned her head to face me. Her cheeks were pinched and pale, her lips a slight, hard line. "Julia," she said quickly, ignoring the heat in my glare, "you're going to hate me for this, but I have to say it." She pressed her eyes shut but kept her face turned toward me. Her words tumbled out like a pent-up confession. "It's not too late. I know that you think you love this baby, and I'm sure that you do, but you don't have to do this. You can let the baby go. There are so many families out there who just *long* for a child, and you can make their dreams come true." Janice's eyes flashed open. "You can make *your* dreams come true. You can start over."

The last bit made her voice climb a notch, and I understood in an instant that *starting over* was probably the dearest dream enclosed in the depths of Janice's heart. But even as a chink of insight into

Janice's soul fell into place, my defenses inflated at her words. "It's a little late for advice," I said frostily, articulating each syllable with careful precision.

"It's *not* too late," Janice replied. She pushed herself up on her elbow.

I didn't like her above me, and I sat up with difficulty. "I don't want to give my baby up for adoption. I am his mother. *Her* mother," I added quickly, hoping that Janice hadn't noticed how accustomed I had become to the thought of a son.

Janice didn't catch on. Instead, she groaned and sat up too. "I hate that phrase *give up*. It sounds so negative. Think of it as giving an incredible gift—an extravagant, expensive, *priceless* gift. It's a gift to the adoptive parents; it's a gift to your child." She searched my face earnestly. "It's a gift to *you*."

Her words burned because I knew they were true. I had wrestled with my own thoughts along the exact same lines, and it shattered my world as I knew it to hear them voiced so clearly outside of my own mind. Mrs. Walker had offered her own suggestion, but it was easy to dismiss because I had never entertained such a thought before. Now, after the seeds had already been planted, I felt them grow as Janice watered them with her deliberate opinions.

"I can't do that," I said, even though some small sliver of me wished that I could.

"Yes, you can."

"The baby is due in six weeks."

"Think of the joy you would give some family. They wouldn't even have to wait for their baby."

Their baby. No. He was *my* baby. And yet underneath the burning resentment of my possessiveness, there was the icy reality of what my jealousy would mean for my son: He would grow up without a father. Like I grew up without a mother. Somewhere inside my chest the truth thudded painfully.

"Tell me you'll think about it," Janice pleaded.

"I have thought about it."

"Think about it some more. Please. You don't understand."

"I *do* understand. I can do this," I said, sounding more confident than I felt. "You're a single mom; why do you think I can't pull it off?"

Janice looked stricken. "I know you can do it. But don't you get it? Keeping the baby is the easy thing to do. I'm asking you to do the impossible. Do what I couldn't do: Be strong. Be selfless." She fumbled for more words, sighing and groaning. But the task of conveying all that she was feeling was either beyond her or simply too painful, and finally Janice finished feebly, "I love Simon, but what kind of life have I given him?" The dim glow of the streetlamp was a fine, reflected point of light in the tears collecting along her lower lashes. "Julia, believe me, you don't really have a choice. This is no way to live."

I should have pitied her, but I had a hard time relating or even understanding. Maybe Janice had forgotten that I, too, was her child. Maybe she couldn't stand back far enough to see that she had experienced it both ways: she had left and she had stayed. Neither solution was perfect, but at least Simon knew that his mother loved him. At least he would grow up knowing that he was worth holding on to.

If she ever expected me to breathe again, Janice had to know that I could not possibly let my baby go. But as we sat in the dark-ness, the front doors of the hospital slid open and the rest of the childbirth class spilled out into the night, laughing animatedly and waving good-bye to each other. The couples held hands on the way to their cars, and I watched them from our patch of earth, feel-ing like an invisible spectator peering into some impossibly perfect universe. Had I been happy only twenty-four hours ago? Had the world seemed full, maybe even limitless?

I watched them all disappear into the night, each half completing the whole, and felt that I could not possibly be more alone.

life without

WEEKS AGO, I HAD torn up the postcard that Mrs. Walker had given me and left it to litter the grove. I never intended to give it a second thought. But though I tried to forget, though I tried to force it far, far away when Janice breathed new life into the possibility, I remembered the name of the adoption agency anyway: All His Children.

I typed the name into Google late one night when everyone was in bed and found the Web site almost too easily. The agency was the very first search result, and I stared at the description for a moment before gathering up enough nerve to click on the blue-lettered link. Our Internet connection was dial-up, and the site itself loaded painstakingly slowly. Holding my breath prisoner in my rigid throat, I watched as a relaxing sage and honey background gradually melted into view. The tabs were done in a willowy font along the left edge of the home page, and a large picture frame materialized front and center. A few minutes later, an unhurried parade of potential adoptive families faded in and out of view in the middle of the computer screen, each taking a turn to try and grab my attention.

"We are athletic and outdoorsy," one caption announced. The couple was perched on a boulder with a rugged swath of snow-capped mountains in the background. Their faces were tanned and their legs were lean and muscled, their feet planted firmly in khaki hiking boots. "We can't wait to share our love of creation with a son or a daughter. Your baby will see the world!"

Next, an older couple filled the black-rimmed frame. "Mature, stable, financially secure," the caption proclaimed. "We long for a baby to make our home complete."

Then there was a family of six with a robust-looking father and a slim, redheaded mother whose four children looked like miniature copies of her. "Big families mean lots of love. Your child will grow up with adoring brothers and sisters on our large acreage in the country. We laugh hard, work hard, and play hard."

They marched across the screen one at a time: twenty-something and nearing the end of middle age, childless and teeming with an entourage of other kids. Multiracial families. Obviously wealthy families. Every shape, every size families. Each photograph and description was a different life, a different future that would open unforeseeable doors for my baby. He could live in any locale throughout the country with one of a myriad of unique families that all promised to love him as if he were their own.

I didn't doubt their ability to love. One look at the eager faces, the willing, open set of their eyes, and I knew my son would be a treasure to any of the couples in the handsome photographs. I wanted to be selfless enough to see a specific picture and know, *Here they are. This is the family.*

As I tried to be receptive to the possibilities, I went so far as to envision a sleeping blue bundle in the arms of a woman who inexplicably reminded me of myself. She was petite with razor-cut blonde hair that just skimmed the curve of her shoulders, and she had enormous blue eyes. We looked nothing alike. But the similarity I saw had nothing to do with appearance and everything to do with her expression. She was a contradiction in terms: timid but hopeful, defiant yet afraid, weary and somehow eager. Her emotions clashed in her eyes, but I felt like I understood her. I had seen the exact same look months ago in the visage of the dark-eyed woman on TV. *That's me*, I thought. *That's what I look like.*

And then, with an abrupt swell of understanding, I knew that I could give the blonde woman what she needed. I could end the anxious war in her face. But try as I might to imagine what it would feel like to release my baby into her arms, I couldn't do it. My insides snaked. I put a protective hand over my belly and clicked the computer off.

If earlier I had felt like I was finally getting somewhere, after the childbirth class it seemed as though someone had pushed pause on my life. Michael and I entered a holding pattern; he was kind but made no indication whatsoever that our afternoon ride had touched him in any way. For her part, Janice retreated somewhat in her pursuit of a relationship with me. And I found myself at a complete standstill. August loomed like a shadow obliterating the sun, and any answers I thought I had claimed faded into obscurity against the opaque backdrop of doubt.

Grandma and Simon knew nothing of my conversation with Janice on the hospital lawn. They had no idea of the turmoil that Janice had stirred up, though in her uncannily perceptive way I could tell that Grandma suspected the hospital orientation had been less than fabulous. But she didn't ask and I didn't tell. We carried on exactly as we had before, talking about the baby as if he was already a part of our makeshift family. I didn't have the courage to say anything to the contrary, to let her in on the battle that raged between what I *wanted* to do and what I felt I *should* do.

Days turned into weeks and nothing changed at all. I circled the possibilities and impossibilities of my life with increasing restlessness and uncertainty until one morning I woke up and looked at the calendar. July 14. Thomas and Francesca's wedding.

Thankfully, they had not asked me to do anything during the ceremony or at the reception. I had been fearful that in an act of friendship that would feel like condescension—to prove to himself that we were fine, that everything between us had ended amicably, happily even—Thomas would insist that I sit by the guest book or hand out small envelopes of birdseed to toss at the couple as they ran to their getaway car. But enduring Thomas's wedding would require nothing more of me than sitting politely during the ceremony and appearing to enjoy myself at the catered reception. I figured that even in my muddled state I could at least pull that off.

The wedding was in the middle of a particularly balmy Saturday afternoon. It was a scorching day; the humidity and the temperature were twins, both hovering right at ninety on Grandma's multipurpose thermometer that hung beside the garage door. I went outside to enjoy some alone time on the porch before breakfast in the morning and almost immediately turned around and went straight back into the house. I was actually glad that my afternoon and evening would be spent in the nearly frigid air-conditioning of the church and then the Glendale Golf and Country Club. And though I held no grudges against either Thomas or Francesca, though the thought of their wedding didn't make my heart thump painfully, I had to repress a little surge of glee when I thought of the bridal party sweating through outdoor wedding pictures on such a blistering day.

Janice and Simon had also been invited to the wedding, but Janice declined politely, telling Mrs. Walker that they already had plans and then confiding in Grandma and me that it felt like a pity invite. Janice assured us that she had no desire to try to fit in at a wedding where she would hardly know a soul.

Instead of joining us in wedding preparations, after lunch Janice surprised Simon by hauling out a packed picnic basket and beach bag and informing him that they were going to drive to the lake for the afternoon. He hooted in delight and skipped around the house for five whole minutes while his mother loaded the cooler with ice packs and juice boxes. I shot a regretful look at my black dress hanging in the doorway to the bathroom and decided that air-conditioned buildings ran a distant second to cooling myself in the lake. Though I wouldn't put on a swimming suit, it would be fun to wade in with Simon. But it wasn't like I had a choice.

When the screen door slammed behind them, Grandma turned and gave me a slow, gentle smile. "The house to ourselves . . . ," she said with a glimmer in her eye. "Why don't you take a nice, long shower, honey? When you're done, I'll paint your toenails for you and take you out for an iced latte before the wedding."

I tried to look at my toenails and found that I had to step my foot to the side in order to accomplish the task. "Pretty bad, huh?"

"Not so bad," Grandma protested with a laugh. "I just know that you can't do it yourself right now. I thought it would be nice since we're getting dressed up."

"It's very nice," I assured her, leaning over to give her cheek a quick kiss. "I'd love to have my toenails painted. Are you sure you don't mind?"

"I want to."

Grandma put some old records on while I was showering, and we took our time getting ready. For a few hours it felt like we lived alone again—there was no stomp and shuffle of Simon racing around the house and no Janice, sad-mouthed and somnolent, lurking in the rooms we frequented. I reveled in the opportunity to have my grandmother all to myself, and more than once I was on the verge of telling her about those happy families, the ones that promised to make my son their own. But the peace of the afternoon was tenuous and rare, and I was loath to disrupt it with such weighty, bewildering things.

Not only did she paint my toenails, but Grandma also gave me a full foot massage and pedicure while we chatted on the couch. I sat on one end of the overstuffed piece of furniture, and she sat on the other with first my right and then my left foot in her lap. It was restorative to let her words wash over me, and I leaned my head back to close my eyes as she kneaded my feet. I hadn't even realized how much they ached.

Although she knew that I had been burdened for weeks, Grandma didn't press me and instead kept the conversation easy and light as we prepared ourselves for Thomas's wedding. We spoke of the garden, funny things that Simon had said, the incredibly hot weather. I was struck again by the gracious, selfless way my grandmother lived and her ability to know what I needed in nearly every situation.

By the time we stepped into the car—both of us scented and powdered and pretty—I felt more relaxed than I had in a long time, even though I was wearing the expensive black dress I had received from Janice. I felt ready to watch Thomas get married.

It turned out that we didn't have time for a latte stop before the ceremony, but I didn't mind. Grandma had equipped me for the day, given me the tools I needed to watch yet another display of the things I didn't—and feared I would never—have. I was simply ready to get it over with. And as we pulled into the church parking lot and I caught sight of the white stretch limo, I was even able to earnestly wish Thomas well. Thomas was an amazing man. He deserved to be happy. He deserved to drive off into his own sunset, Franny in hand.

The church was richly decorated and dazzling with dozens of candles and massive urns that overflowed in cascades of green hydrangeas and bursts of perfect roses the color of strawberries and cream. A string quartet sent classical music spinning through the fragrant air, and well-dressed couples spoke quietly as they bent over the guest book and scrawled quick notes of blessing.

We weren't late, but the pews were already nearly full and I noted without much surprise that Francesca's side contained even more people than Thomas's. Never mind that her relatives lived all over the country. I knew that Mr. Hernandez had offered to fly out anyone who wanted to come to Iowa for the wedding, and it seemed that the entire clan had taken him up on his generosity.

Grandma and I flowed wordlessly with the crowd and were just ready to join a short queue of people lining up before one of the aisles when I felt a hand on my arm. Someone spun me into a tight hug.

"Oh, I'm so glad you're here!" Mrs. Walker gushed into my hair.

I pulled back and held her at arm's length, smiling at her lacquered hair and professionally done face. "Bit of a crazy day?" I asked, knowing the answer by the harried look in her eyes. "You look beautiful, by the way."

"You don't know the half of it," Mrs. Walker groaned. And then, smoothing her dress, she shrugged almost shyly. "Do you think so?"

"Absolutely," Grandma agreed, wrapping Mrs. Walker in a hug of her own. "And everything looks great."

"I think they like it," Mrs. Walker whispered, giving us a discreet thumbs-up. We didn't have to ask who *they* were. "They are very nice," she assured us. "*Very* nice. Why am I so nervous?"

"Probably because your son is getting married today," Grandma said. "It's a big day."

Mrs. Walker sighed dramatically. "I know. I know. I'm a mess. I can't imagine what I'll be like when they tell me I'm going to be a grandma!"

I wasn't offended, but suddenly Mrs. Walker glanced down at my belly, and beneath her dusty rouge her cheeks went white. "I'm sorry, Julia," she said quietly.

"Don't worry about it," I said sincerely, but her horrified air made me feel like maybe I should be insulted.

"I didn't mean—," Mrs. Walker tried to continue but was interrupted by a frenzied Maggie bursting into our little group. She was wearing a soft pink dress with a chocolate sash, and her hair was pulled up in a pile of curls on top of her head. I wanted to tell her that she looked lovely, but she barely glanced in my direction.

"Get behind the dividing wall, Mom!" Maggie barked, yanking her mother's arm. "You're not supposed to be seen yet! The seating of the parents won't happen for another—" she glanced at the clock on the wall—"four minutes." She huffed crossly. "And now people have seen me, too!"

Mrs. Walker rolled her eyes at Grandma and me and let herself be dragged away, mouthing something to us that I couldn't make out. When they were a few paces away and she finally gave Maggie her full attention, I overheard her say, "It's not like I'm the *bride*. Who cares if I'm seen?"

Grandma and I giggled a bit at the drama, but I couldn't suppress a feeling of disappointment that Maggie had hardly even noticed me. We used to be so close, but ever since the night I teased her about having a boyfriend, her loyalties had slowly shifted from me to Francesca. I told myself it was better this way. After all, Francesca was going to be Maggie's sister-in-law; I was merely the next-door neighbor. But that didn't change the fact that I missed Maggie and I couldn't help mourning the way things used to be. She had been right in her accusation all those nights ago: I had changed. Everything had changed.

Francesca walked down the aisle to a song I had never heard before. It wasn't the traditional wedding march, but it was bright and joyful and so stunningly beautiful that I felt myself choke up, though I'd promised myself it was the last thing I would do. We stood for the bride's entrance and she was a vision in white, a sparkling angel floating on the arm of her equally handsome father.

He will never walk me down the aisle, I thought with a raw stab of loss.

Strangely, it was one of the first things I had thought of when my dad passed away—that quintessential moment in the relationship between a father and his daughter, the act of giving your baby away—and I thought that I had dealt with it. But watching Francesca walk down the aisle with her dad made it seem very real and very new. I let myself cry.

Though I had felt more or less indifferent when we stepped into the church, by the end of the wedding ceremony I was a hopeless mess of crude emotion. It was like watching my life flash before my eyes: the life I was *supposed* to have. But my reality was a life without.

Without Dad, without Thomas or a white dress, a wedding ring, a father for my baby. I wanted to close my eyes when the pastor told Thomas, "You may kiss your bride," but it was like watching an accident in slow motion. I couldn't look away.

The wedding program informed us that the receiving line would take place at the reception hall, and I was thankful that I wouldn't have to greet Thomas and Francesca in my current state. There would be time for a bathroom stop, a tall glass of water, and best of all, a half-hour drive with Grandma so I could clear my head and arrange my face to survive the rest of the festivities.

We clapped and cheered when the bride and groom ran down the aisle arm in arm, exuberantly laughing and crying in the same shared breath, and then the ushers stood to tell us that we could depart at our leisure. Three hundred guests rose as one, and I quickly tried to pull myself together, feeling lost in the melee and yet also exposed as the crowd began to talk animatedly and survey the sanctuary full of their peers.

"You okay?" Grandma whispered, sliding her arm around my waist to give me a gentle squeeze.

I attempted a smile. "I'm fine. It was a beautiful ceremony."

Grandma nodded in agreement. "Weddings always make me cry."

"Apparently me too." I laughed self-consciously and pressed a tissue beneath my eyes. Taking a calming breath, I tried to relax my face. "Can you tell I've been crying?"

"Maybe a little," Grandma said honestly. "But look around you—nearly everyone looks like they've been crying."

It was true. The knot between my shoulder blades loosened

slightly when I glanced around and saw a number of people still dabbing tears.

The church emptied quickly, guests making a beeline for their cars to steal a few moments of peace before the reception started in an hour. Grandma and I melted into the crowd, eager to be swept outside and thinking maybe we could still grab a latte, when for the second time that day someone grabbed my arm from behind.

I turned promptly, ready to see Mrs. Walker and prepared to compliment her on the beautiful ceremony. On the marriage of her son. On her new daughter-in-law. I had rehearsed what I would say, and I was afraid I could say it only once if I hoped to be sincere. The words were on the very tip of my tongue.

But Mrs. Walker wasn't standing before me. It was Michael.

Surprise must have been written all over my face because Michael said with a smile, "Didn't expect to see me here, did you?"

"N-no," I stammered, trying to recover. There was nothing I could do about the state of my face, but I touched my hair insecurely and wished that I could disappear into thin air. I managed to choke out, "I didn't know that you knew the Walkers."

Michael dropped my arm and pointed over the crowd to where Thomas's siblings stood clustered around Francesca's extended family. "I played on a summer league slow-pitch team with Thomas and Jacob a few years ago. We hung out a bit. How do you know them?"

"Next-door neighbors," I explained. "We've known each other for years."

Michael snapped his fingers. "Of course. I thought of that when I dropped you off that night your car was going _click_."

I smiled a little in spite of myself and was about to attempt some comment about his obvious grasp of mechanics or lack thereof when I felt Grandma beside me.

"Is this the young man who brought you home?" she asked, a sweet look twinkling in her eyes.

"Oh, Grandma, I'm so sorry." I put my arm through hers and motioned at Michael. "Grandma, this is Michael Vermeer. We work together at Value Foods. Michael, my grandmother, Nellie DeSmit."

It was nice to have somewhere to look other than at the man in front of me. For slightly longer than necessary, I studied Grandma's profile so I didn't have to acknowledge the tailored lines of Michael's charcoal suit or the lay of his sky blue tie. I tried not to notice that the pin-striped tie was the exact same color as his eyes.

"Nice to meet you, Mrs. DeSmit," Michael said politely, shaking her hand.

"Call me Nellie," Grandma insisted. "Mrs. DeSmit is my mother-in-law, and she's been gone for almost thirty years."

Michael laughed. "Okay, Nellie. You can call me Mr. Vermeer."

Grandma's eyes widened. "He's cheeky, isn't he?" she said, elbowing me. Her voice was light, pleased somehow.

Because it was the complete opposite of the truth and because I felt more comfortable teasing him than having a real conversation, I quipped, "I'll say. He's a pain to work with."

Michael feigned indignation. "Hey now. We were being nice."

We chuckled for a moment, but then there was a gap in the conversation, a moment when we all looked at each other but could think of nothing more to say. I stole a peek at Michael, and he raised his eyebrows at me. Caught in the act, I turned to Grandma and found that she was staring at Michael. The silence was about to become uncomfortable, and I opened my mouth to wish Michael a good evening and slip back into the crowd.

But he spoke first. "Nice wedding, wasn't it?"

Grandma and I nodded.

"Beautiful," Grandma said.

"I've been to lots of weddings," Michael told us, "but you don't always see two people who are so obviously meant for each other."

I tried not to look skeptical thinking of the bumpy road that Thomas and Francesca had traveled to this day. I wasn't even sure that Thomas's family would agree with Michael's assessment of the now blissfully wedded couple. But then again, they had seemed like the happy ending of a fairy tale as they repeated their vows to each other. I smiled tactfully in agreement with Michael's proclamation and found myself earnestly wishing that, from now until death do us part, his assessment would be true for Thomas and Francesca.

"They have an incredible life ahead of them," Michael continued. "A happy home."

I knew he was just making small talk, trying to say the right things because it was the solicitous thing to do. I also knew that every group scattered around the church was having the same flattering conversation as though they could will each word into being by saying it aloud. But Michael's statements felt like little assaults. I told myself that he couldn't know what Thomas's wedding meant to me. He couldn't understand that each reference was a reminder. A glimpse of what could have been. A happy home. Together forever.

Grandma said something back to Michael, and I listened to them chat for a few more moments, their niceties washing over me but not sinking in, before someone suddenly called Michael's name. I was relieved and disappointed to see him look past us and wave, pointing out a group of young people lingering near the door.

"That's my ride," Michael said apologetically. "Guess I gotta go. See you at the reception?"

I nodded but wasn't entirely sure that I wanted to see Michael at the reception. The guys at the door were attractive and laughing, jock types with broad shoulders and matching smiles, and the girls spun on their high heels to give me an appraising look. It didn't seem that they were very impressed with what they saw. I wondered which one of them was vying for the position of Michael's girlfriend.

"Nice to meet you, Nellie," Michael said, taking off in the direction of his friends. "Talk to you later, Julia."

I smiled my good-bye and then turned away as if there were someone else I wanted to talk to. In reality, I just didn't want to watch him go.

And I also didn't want to deal with the thought he had inadvertently solidified in my mind: a baby was intended for a happy home. A home like the one Thomas and Francesca had just created.

The kind of home I couldn't provide.

christening

WHILE GRANDMA AND I were at the wedding, Janice and Simon were having so much fun at the beach that they commandeered the following Saturday and insisted that we all go to the lake together. Grandma loved the idea, and she immediately and enthusiastically jumped on board by planning a picnic that would send every ant within a five-mile radius into a fit of pure, unadulterated joy. It was going to be the family event of the summer.

But I couldn't stop myself from wondering if Janice had ulterior motives.

Twice before Saturday I caught her on the phone when no one else was around. She seemed secretive, cagey, and she looked at me with barely concealed guilt at being caught doing something that she should not have been doing. Had she ended the conversations with a smile and a simple good-bye, I wouldn't have thought anything of it. But she didn't. It made me very suspicious.

The first time was shortly after ten on Wednesday night. The weather was beyond hot—energy sapping, strength draining, exhaustion inducing—and by nine thirty everyone in our little farmhouse had gone to bed. The television was turned off, lights were extinguished, and we flopped into our beds, sweaty and sleepy.

Although I was asleep within minutes, I had started to get up more and more during the night as my pregnancy wore on, and I often stumbled through the kitchen a handful of times nightly on my way to the bathroom. Usually I was half-asleep and hoping to remain semiconscious, but that night I emerged from the stairs to the sound of a voice in the mudroom. Shocked and startled wide-awake, I crept toward the door and peeked cautiously through the leaded window. A small square of clear glass in the very center afforded me a glimpse of Janice, pacing the floor with the telephone pressed securely to her ear. She was framed and indistinct, a shadow of softly blurred color in the darkness.

Janice's voice was muffled and unclear, but I was quite sure I heard her say, "No! Not yet. She can't know."

And then, that woman's intuition, that subtle little prick at the back of your neck that tells you someone is watching you, must have alerted Janice to my presence. She turned suddenly, and I was caught staring at her through the transparent see-though in the door. From her perspective I must have been nothing more than a disembodied eye.

"I gotta go," she blurted out. Then, "What are you doing up, Julia? I thought you went to bed."

I left without saying a word.

The second time I wasn't lucky enough to hear any of the conversation. Janice was more cautious, fearful of getting caught, maybe. I stepped into the kitchen after work one night to hear her mutter an awkward good-bye and slip the telephone into its cradle shiftily, as if putting it down gently would stop me from realizing that she had been on the phone. The utter silence in the house told me that Grandma and Simon were not home.

"Who were you talking to?" I questioned Janice without preamble.

"Oh, no one," she murmured dumbly, forcing herself to smile at me. It was so unnatural, so fake, that I was afraid it would crumble off her face.

I continued to pursue her with my eyes.

"Just an old friend," Janice finally admitted, unable to stand up beneath my wilting stare. "No one you would know."

To say that her covert conversations made me apprehensive would be an understatement. Janice's behavior didn't change at all; she was no different than she had always been around Grandma and Simon, but I felt like I could sense something brewing just out of view. There was a brooding, indecipherable shift in her manner. It was as if I could feel her expression alter the moment I left the room.

I was sure she was conspiring against me. It occurred to me that Janice was so bent on getting me to give up my baby that she was ready to take matters into her own hands. I just didn't know how far she was willing to go. Not that there was anything she really *could* do about it—I was no longer a minor—but I still had a difficult time shaking the feeling that she was hiding something from me. What could it possibly be about but the baby?

And for some reason, I balked at the idea of going to the lake with her. It seemed like the perfect opportunity for her to poison my thoughts, to talk me into what she thought was my only real option. Maybe even to try to win Grandma over to her side. I wanted to beg her to leave me alone. I needed to figure this out by myself, without the shadow of her own broken past hanging menacingly over me.

But there was no way out of it. Simon was single-minded and even Grandma exuded a feeling of magnitude, as if this act of togetherness, of normal family behavior, was the culmination of four months of struggle, sweat, and tears. It seemed significant to me, too, though somewhat less promising.

We all piled into Janice's car on Saturday and left for the lake with Simon making up songs to the tune of "The Itsy-Bitsy Spider" in the backseat. His words rarely rhymed or fit the meter of the song, but he more than made up for his lack of skill with an abundance of intoxicating gusto. Grandma and Janice giggled from the front seat and I sat next to Simon, shooting him sidelong glances of theatrical annoyance that only egged him on to grander verses and exaggerated accompanying arm gestures.

Mill Lake was a forty-minute drive north, and by the time we had entered the outskirts of the nearest town, I was enjoying myself far more than I had anticipated. Even the cloud of Janice's clandestine late-night conversations seemed to evaporate in the elation of

Simon's singing and the blissfully warm sun that blazed through the back window of the car.

Not today, I told myself determinedly. *Today is a cease-fire, a rare oasis of peace in this seemingly endless journey.*

Though we were probably the only group of people at the lake that didn't drive up with some form of water entertainment hitched to the back of our car, we didn't mind. We spread our oversize blanket on the sand near the water, taking advantage of the sprawling shade of a burr oak that would have required at least three of us linking arms to reach all the way around it. Half of the blanket was draped in sun so that the already yellow-toned quilt took on the appearance of melted lemon sorbet. A fluttering division of leafy shadows flung the rest of our little island into tones of hushed blue-gray, and Grandma parked the cooler and picnic basket deep in the shade, where there were almost no coins of golden light glittering between the leaves.

We were set up in less than five minutes. With a contented sigh, Grandma bunched up a couple of beach towels and positioned herself against the cooler, gazing out at the water. The rest of us took to the sun. Simon looked to his mother for permission and, seeing the slight nod that he'd hoped for, kicked off his shoes and ran for the water, trailing a bucket in one hand and a long-handled scoop in the other. Janice plunked down on the blanket, rolling up her shorts instead of taking them off, even though I could see the lime green strap of a swimming suit peeking out from underneath her tank top. Consulting the sky, she aligned herself perfectly to the arc of the sun and lay back with her eyes closed. I found a comfy spot to sit cross-legged in the middle, Grandma's foot resting lightly against my knee on one side and Janice stretched out beside me on the other.

The lake spread out before me, a sheet of rippled, stone-blue steel that was dotted with boats and Jet Skis. All along the shoreline, trees stepped right up to the edge and hung dropping branches over the water so that the cove we were in was soft and rolling, spreading gracefully out to disappear around the bend almost a mile away in both directions. There were a few people on the beach, a handful of kids splashing in the water, but Simon alone could have been a portrait at the edge of it all.

He stood up to his ankles in the tiny, lapping waves, the red bucket at his side and his other arm still clutching the yellow scoop as it swept across his forehead to shield his eyes from the sun. His swimming trunks were almost exactly the same color as the water, and his white T-shirt popped as if cut out against the immense blue backdrop. I could see the breeze rake invisible fingers through the dark curls at the nape of his neck.

"Perfect," Grandma exhaled.

I turned to look at her and found her eyes closed, her head thrown back in surrender to the luxury of the day. The dancing shadows cast her wrinkled profile into relief, the angles sharp and chiseled, a reminder of the beauty she had once been.

"It is," Janice agreed, not moving. "It's why we wanted to take you here so badly." She popped her head up to shoot me a phony dirty look. "Why haven't we been here every weekend this summer?"

"Don't look at me." I raised my arms as if to fend her off. "Why is it my fault it took us half the summer to make it to Mill Lake?"

"Because you're young and cool, Julia. You should think about these things. You know, be our social coordinator and such." Janice flopped back down and raised her chin just so to take full advantage of the hot rays.

I made a noise of dissent but didn't bother to defend myself. Young and cool. Yeah right. More like old beyond my years and experiencing a pregnancy hot flash. I moved into the shade.

There was a boat pulling into the dock at the opposite end of the beach, and I watched wistfully as a guy in board shorts and dark sunglasses hopped barefoot onto the smooth planks. He ran both of his hands through his longish hair and then reached out an arm to help a number of young women climb out of the boat. They were all bikini clad and wet, the last one still removing her life jacket after what I assumed was a stint on the kneeboard. I could see another guy lifting the board onto the wide, flat back of the ski boat, wrestling with the long Velcro straps as he tried to reposition them for the next rider. Somehow they all reminded me of Michael and his group of friends at Thomas and Francesca's wedding.

It had been easy to avoid them throughout most of the reception because Francesca hadn't overlooked a single detail and our seats were meticulously assigned. Grandma and I sat around a table with six other adults who were all at least thirty years older than me, while most of the people my age were across the room from us, crowded around a few tables near two towers of stacked speakers. When the deejay put on something fast and loud after the first few slow dances, I watched Michael and his friends hop to their feet and loosen their ties as they flooded the dance floor. Grandma and her companions laughed and seemed ready to settle in for a long night of observing their flailing attempts at the actions to "Y.M.C.A." and

"Stayin' Alive." But I wanted to leave so badly that I could hardly make myself sit still.

After a few dances, some desperate look in my eye finally alerted Grandma to my suffering. We said our good-byes, picking our way through the maze of tables and haphazard clusters of people. We had almost made it to the door when the song switched again and a few strains of piano music filled the air. A row of line dancers dispersed, and people melted into pairs or slipped quietly away in search of a partner. The polished wooden dance floor was only feet from the door, and though I didn't want to notice, I was very aware that Michael was walking right toward us. He was alone. If I turned to him, if I smiled, would he smile back? Would he ask me to dance?

I hadn't turned to him. I had grabbed Grandma and ducked out the door too afraid that some silly dream was exactly that instead of a sweet possibility. In lieu of the real thing, I had gone home and imagined what it would have been like to dance with Michael. And on the beach I did the same thing. I imagined that my life was different.

The Walkers had a boat, and back in the days when Thomas and I were close, I had spent many scorching summer afternoons on the water with them. Thomas taught me to ski and wakeboard, but I never got the hang of kneeboarding no matter how many times I tried. It made my knees ache.

I wondered if I would even remember how to do those things if I ever had the opportunity again. Was it like riding a bike? Or had the person that I used to be disappeared as completely as I felt she had? Maybe the new me knew nothing about water sports.

As the driver of the boat looped a thick rope around one of

the poles sticking out of the dock, I made a distinct effort to look away.

For lunch we ate sandwiches piled high with turkey and provolone that were dressed up with generous slices of tomatoes from Grandma's garden, lettuce, and spicy homemade dill and garlic pickles. Simon had peanut butter and jelly but barely wolfed down two bites before claiming that he wasn't hungry and racing back to the water.

Grandma laughed. "He's a little frog, isn't he? One foot on dry ground and the other soaking wet."

Sure enough, Simon was crouched right at the water's edge, half in the hot sand and half in the water. He was scooping great shovelfuls of soggy sand into his bucket, one leg of his shorts hanging in the water and wet halfway to the waistband.

"He's always liked the water," Janice told us. "I took him to the pool a few times when he was a baby and he just adored it. Even at that age! I would've thought he'd have hated it."

"You should enroll him in swimming lessons," Grandma encouraged. "It's too late for the summer session, but I know that they start again in the fall."

Janice gave Grandma a hesitant smile and looked quickly away. "Yeah, maybe."

She wasn't the only one who didn't know how to respond to Grandma's suggestion. Swimming lessons in the fall? Long-term plans to stay? I was torn between wanting to get on with my life and worrying about what it would be like when Janice and Simon were gone. Though it should have been easy to know the answer, I couldn't discern which ending I hoped for. I had to keep reminding myself that this couldn't last forever; they couldn't share the tiny sewing room indefinitely, nor had Janice made any indication that she intended to stay permanently. Sometimes that thought comforted me. Other times it plucked uncomfortably at my heart.

Grandma also picked up on Janice's reluctance and cleared her throat quietly. She stared out at the cobalt water for a time, and I knew that she was feeling the same way I was. At what point had Janice and Simon become a part of our lives? At what point had we begun to wonder if we wanted them to slip out of it again or not? But such musings seemed out of place with the lake sparkling before us.

Leaving talk of our future behind, Grandma turned the conversation around 180 degrees. "You know, Julia, technically you could have the baby any day now. Have you figured out a name?"

The gloom in Janice's face deepened. She looked at me pointedly and bit the inside of her lower lip. For a second I thought she was going to be brash and come straight out with her recommendations for my baby and my future. But then she tore off another bite of her sandwich and turned her eyes to Simon.

"I think so," I said carefully. "I want it to be a surprise, though."

"Of course." Grandma smiled. "I wouldn't have it any other way. It would be like telling someone your birthday wish after you've blown out all your candles."

"What about you, Janice?" I blurted out, desperately wanting to shift the topic away from me and my baby. "I know I was named after my great-grandmother, but where did you get Simon's name from? Family too?" Some wicked little corner of my soul wanted Janice to feel just the tiniest bit ill at ease. Better her than me.

But although Janice blushed, she didn't say what I thought she would say. "No, actually. Simon's not a family name."

Grandma and I looked at her quizzically, waiting for the story. I almost reminded Janice that Simon thought he was named after his dad and his grandpa, but the set of her jaw made me think that I might be treading on volatile ground if I mentioned such a thing. Janice certainly didn't seem inclined to say another word, but Grandma pressed her.

"You can't just stop there. Sounds intriguing." Grandma leaned in, a good-humored grin on her face. "Where'd you get the name from?"

The ruddiness in Janice's cheeks spread to the tips of her ears. We were all hot, and her flush could have been attributed to the sun, the wind, the rising temperature. But I knew better.

"It's really quite silly," Janice said firmly.

"Oh, seriously." Grandma dismissed Janice's timidity with a wave of her hand. "No, it's not. If it's significant to you, it's not silly."

Janice studied her hands, still wrapped around a half-eaten sand-wich. A fly landed on it, and she flicked it away absently. "I got his name from the Bible," she admitted. Her voice was sheepish, and she refused to look at us.

"That's not silly at all!" Grandma concluded forcefully.

"Come on, Nellie. You know I'm not exactly the churchgoing type." Janice turned her head to regard Grandma full in the face with something like defiance flashing behind her hazel eyes. They were more green than brown in the bright summer sun, spunky some-how, and for a second it looked like she was challenging Grandma. Like she was willing her to say more, to openly contradict her. But then Janice crumpled a little and she sighed. "I mean, I go to church now, and I used to go to church when . . ." She trailed off.

I finished the sentence for her in my mind: *when I was married to Daniel.*

"It's just . . . I don't . . ." Janice tried again but couldn't—or wouldn't—finish what she started.

Strangely, I felt like I knew exactly what she meant.

Grandma didn't say any more and neither did I, but suddenly Janice muttered something I couldn't make out. Then she deposited the remainder of her sandwich in the grocery bag we were using for garbage and took a deep breath. "Right before Simon was born, I was at a very bad place in my life," she began, the words coming quickly now that she had decided to get them out. "I don't know why, but I wandered into a church one Sunday morning and I heard the pastor preach about Simon Peter. He told the story of this nobody fisherman Simon and how Jesus Himself came and called him. Jesus called him Peter. The Rock." Janice humphed as if she had discovered that in the retelling, her story was indeed rather silly.

We didn't say anything for a few minutes, each of us considering Simon as he emptied sloppy sand in bucketfuls all over his little stake of beach. I decided Simon Peter was a nice name, a meaningful, solid name, but then I remembered that Simon's middle name was Eli. Confused, I turned to voice my question.

Grandma beat me to it. "Why didn't you name him Peter, then?"

Janice's laugh was shallow. "That would be pretty audacious, wouldn't it? *Me* naming my son after the rock of the Christian church?"

I watched my grandmother open her mouth to say something wise, but she clamped her lips down as quickly as she parted them.

"I named him Simon," Janice finished, "because maybe . . . well, maybe he's waiting to be called."

Her explanation rang in my head. I understood that the name Simon was the best Janice could do. It was her version of reaching out a tentative hand, though I could also tell that she didn't think she deserved to do even that. "What does Simon mean?" I asked, almost unaware of the question until it filled the air between us.

"Listening."

All at once I knew exactly why Janice had returned to Mason. It was her last-ditch effort, her attempt at redemption, if not for herself, at least for her son. It made me inexplicably sad for who we all were. Broken, disappointing, flawed. Well, except for Grandma, and it seemed that she stood in the middle of our riotous little storms, trying desperately to gather us in and calm the gales that blew us from sorrow to sorrow. How could she stand us, group of Simons that we were? It felt as though in every trial, in every situation, we were *not enough, not enough, not enough.* Trying but failing. Listening but never hearing the call that would make us living stones.

"Well," Grandma said quietly, interrupting my sad reverie, "I know that God has placed an amazing call on Simon's life." She smiled at us softly, blessing both mother and daughter with a tender sweep of her knowing gaze. Then Grandma got carefully to her feet and stepped off the blanket into the sand. "I'm going to see if Simon is interested in getting an ice-cream cone with me at the concession stand. Would either of you like to join us?"

I shook my head at her, and though I didn't see Janice's reaction, I knew that she was doing the same. We watched Grandma walk over to Simon, and when he looked up at her, there was love in his eyes. As far as he was concerned, she was his grandmother. He trusted her implicitly, and it struck me that of all the people in his life, she was the only one who truly deserved it. Simon happily abandoned his water toys and slipped his hand in hers to follow her down the beach.

Janice and I trailed them with our eyes until they became lost in the small crowd around the concession stand near the dock. It was uncomfortable to be alone with her, knowing that she had revealed far more than she intended to and not quite aware of what I should do with the weight of such knowledge. I felt sorry for Janice, for us, and yet I was also afraid that she would use this mood against me. I was afraid that her failures would make her doubt my ability to make this work. And I wasn't entirely convinced that she was wrong.

When Janice started to talk, I knew that she had been waiting all day for a chance to dive into her rehearsed adoption speech. What better time, when we were contemplative and melancholy? What better time, when we were immersed in the bittersweet tale of the Simon who would never quite be Peter? But I was ready for her.

"You know, Janice," I cut in before she could utter two syllables, "I don't know who you've been talking to lately, but I do think that it has something to do with me and the baby. Have you contacted an adoption counselor? Mrs. Walker's friend?" I paused for less than a second before hastily fluttering my hands in front of me, fending off her response. "No, wait; don't answer that. I don't want to know."

"Julia, I—"

"Look, I know that it's going to be hard. I know that figuring this out, making it work, is as close to impossible as I'll ever experience. But it really has nothing to do with you. I don't need you interfering in any way." It felt good to get this off my chest, and although Janice was looking at me with distress written all over her face, I went on. "In some ways I appreciate what you are trying to do. I mean, you've been there, and I suppose you are trying to protect me. But you're not. And it really bugs me that you would go behind my back, sneak around and—" I stopped abruptly. "What exactly is it that you're doing? Are you trying to find a family for my baby? Are you gathering information so you can try to convince me?"

I didn't mean to sound so accusatory. I just wanted to firmly, confidently let Janice know that her so-called help wasn't solicited or appreciated. After her unanticipated disclosure, that peek into her motives and her mind, maybe even her heart, I felt a certain tenuous connection to her. I too felt inadequate, grasping. I too wondered if I would ever be able to listen hard enough to hear what I was supposed to hear. Lurking in the shadows of our relationship was a growing link that I couldn't help wanting to explore even as my heart rebelled against such knowledge. I set aside any feelings of amity because I didn't need Janice muddling things up any more than they already were, and more importantly, I needed her to know that.

But Janice didn't try to defend herself or argue with me like I thought she would. Instead her shoulders slumped and her head hung for the briefest of moments before she visibly gathered herself and looked up, past me. "I wasn't talking to an adoption counselor," she said in a voice that was barely more than a whisper.

Something cold spilled through my chest at the gravity of her words. Janice had revealed nothing, but her tone was so significant as to assure me that whoever she *was* talking to posed far greater implications than some random adoption counselor. Who? What? What had Janice done?

"You have to tell me," I demanded around the ice that was slowly forming painful crystals in my throat. "Who have you been talking to?"

Janice swallowed with difficulty, and I suddenly realized that whatever she had to say was far worse than what I had imagined.

"What?" I cried.

"I was talking to Ben. He's been calling me for about a week now."

Her admission tumbled out so fast I had to repeat the words silently to myself to make sure that I had heard her correctly. *Ben? He's been calling?* It took me the span of a few unsteady breaths to recognize that the pounding sound that had filled my head was coming from the uneven cadence of my own heart. I held myself rigid, dreading what Janice was going to say next but guessing at the general gist of the words long before she worked up the courage to say them.

"He wants me to come home."

Part 3

timing

I HAD MY FIRST genuine experience with the feelings of labor nine days before my projected due date. Grandma had warned me about Braxton Hicks, deceptive contractions that would seem as if I was beginning labor even though my body was doing nothing more than carefully preparing me for the eventual real thing. I figured I had been undergoing the symptoms of false labor for weeks—a painless tightening of my stomach that I often didn't notice until I put my hand on my abdomen and realized how insanely hard it had become.

But when I woke up shortly after falling asleep the last Sunday in

July, I knew that something very different was happening. At first I assumed that I had merely stirred because I needed to make another trek to the bathroom or shift to a different, slightly less unpleasant position. And then, before I could even force myself to peel my eyes open, I felt it: a tightening, gripping, aching vise that compressed itself around my middle until my very core was rigid and my lungs struggled to fill with air.

I panted a little, trying not to hold myself too tense, and rolled onto my back to make an effort to ease what felt like the most intense muscle spasm I had ever suffered through. The sound of my own confusion filled the air, a fast succession of tiny exhalations, and in the sudden stillness of the night the sound seemed deafening. I was mystified to find that I was able to drift outside myself and observe what was happening, as if a part of me had detached from the situation. Thankfully, it was over quickly, leaving me a bit breathless and completely alert, sleep utterly forgotten. *Labor,* I thought as a helpless wave of nausea passed through me. *I'm going into labor.*

The very notion sent me into a nearly mindless tailspin, a frantic, desperate state of fear and even grief. I wasn't ready. I wasn't anywhere *near* ready for this. I hadn't really made a decision yet, and I wasn't prepared to face all the consequences of my vacillation. Should I go with my heart? Should I go with my head? If I was supposed to give up the baby, it would be much, much harder—if not *impossible*—to do so after he was born and I had had a chance to cradle him against my chest. But if I was supposed to keep my son, I didn't want him to enter the world amid my own irresolution and doubt. I wanted to welcome him with arms wide open, with the knowledge, the absolute assurance, that he was—and always would be—*mine.*

I lay awake for over an hour and a half, watching the numbers on my alarm clock approach midnight and then march right past it. The contractions continued to attack erratically, clenching down at unexpected times and bringing with them a certain sense of irrepressible fate. Though I couldn't exactly call them painful, I was definitely uncomfortable and made more so by the interfering thoughts that seeped from my yearning mind and filtered through the rest of my now trembling body.

What am I supposed to do? I cried silently. *Tell me what to do!*

Around one thirty, I had so eaten my insides to shreds that I had no choice but to go and wake Grandma or face the prospect of losing my mind completely.

I crept down the stairs quietly, grateful that I did not find Janice huddling in the kitchen, wrapped protectively around the telephone. Just the idea of her there, talking to *him,* made the knots in my stomach redouble. I strained to push such images from my mind and focused instead on the swelling wave of a new contraction. I walked through it, but the floorboards creaked as I passed Janice and Simon's little sewing room turned apartment. I paused there with my hand flat against the smooth wall, waiting out the contraction and listening for any signs of movement. There were none.

Grandma's door squeaked a soft, high note when I opened it, and almost simultaneously I heard her whisper, "Julia?"

"How did you know it was me?" I whispered back. "What are you doing awake?"

"I have a hard time sleeping somctimes," Grandma explained

simply. I could hear her sheets ruffle as she shifted in bed. "What are you doing up, honey?"

There was no point in being coy, so I blurted it out, a little louder than I intended to. "I think I'm in labor."

A sharp intake of breath told me that Grandma was as surprised as I was at my seemingly early delivery. Dr. Morales had assured me that most first-time moms go late, not early, and he even went so far as to sternly warn me that he had no plans whatsoever to induce me if I did become overdue: "For the most part, babies know exactly when it's time to come out. We unnecessarily start labor way too often in this country."

But just as I was on the verge of panic, assuming that Grandma was about as ready for this as I was—not at all—I heard her move again. She seemed to draw apart from me to the far side of the bed away from the door.

"Come lay by me," she invited. A glint of moonlight on the white sheets told me that she had slid over and pulled the covers back for me.

I hadn't shared Grandma's bed since I was a very little girl and Grandpa still occupied it too. Before Dad and I moved in with Grandma, I used to sleep over on the couch in the living room nearly every week. Grandma would wrap a fitted sheet around the couch cushions and make a narrow bed for me, hauling out a special Indian blanket that was so thick as to be suffocating. For the first few hours I would sleep in peace. But inevitably I would wake up at some point and creep to my grandparents' bedroom in search of a little comfort and reassurance. Grandpa, who slept nearest to the door, would wordlessly grip me under the arms and lift me clear over his own body, depositing me between him and Grandma. She would roll over to face me, still mostly asleep, and curl her arms around me protectively. I'd wake up the next morning, alone in the bed but warm and contented, smiling to myself.

After Grandpa died, it felt wrong to be in his bed. It was so big and empty without him, so different. Altered somehow. I stayed on the couch, even when I woke up in the night and wanted to pad barefoot to the bedroom Grandma now occupied alone.

As I crawled under the covers beside Grandma, a grown woman with fears that far eclipsed those of my youth, I was hit with a twinge of regret. How lonely must she have been in that queen-size bed all by herself? How selfish was I to abandon her there? It made me sad that I had missed countless nights when we could have slept soundly to the tune of each other's breath in the darkness.

"Are the contractions regular?" Grandma asked, oblivious to the memories that were filling my heart and making me forget my situation. She reached a hand across the bed and laid it softly against my belly, breaking the spell that held me.

"No, I don't think so," I replied, any tremor in my voice disguised by the fact that I was whispering. "I haven't really been timing them or anything."

"Are they close together?"

"I'll get a couple in a row and then suddenly have a long break," I explained. "Oh! I'm having one now. Can you feel it?"

There were a few seconds of silence while my stomach hardened until I could barely make out the pressure of Grandma's hand on me. Then she said, "Yes, I can feel it. But I don't think you're in labor—not if you can talk during a contraction."

Relief poured through me, making my fingers numb as a shiver tingled through my bones. "Thank goodness," I exhaled. Suddenly the severity of the spasm seemed reduced, unimportant.

"Not ready yet?" Grandma didn't sound surprised or accusatorial, so I didn't bother answering. "That's okay," she murmured when the tightness in my tummy had passed. "You don't have to be quite ready yet—soon but not just now. I don't think you'll be having a baby today."

I lay in the blackness of her room, loving the warmth of my grandmother beside me and basking in the knowledge that I wasn't in labor. It was dark and still and cool downstairs—the attic always got a tad too hot in the summer in spite of the air-conditioning—and I wished all at once that I did not have to go back upstairs alone.

Grandma read my mind. "Why don't you stay here, Julia? I don't think you're in labor, but we'll time the contractions for a while anyway. If we fall asleep, so be it."

My head sank deeper into the pillow, and I barely stifled a gratified sigh. The weight of Grandma's blankets against my legs and her light hand still resting on my stomach made me feel safe. This was a haven, a place of protection. It crossed my mind that now, right now, would be the perfect time to confide in Grandma about some of the fears that were slowly burying me alive. She didn't know about Janice and Ben. She didn't know that I was plagued by doubt about whether or not I could be a good mother to my baby. Doubt about whether or not I could be a mother at all.

But I was suddenly overwhelmed by exhaustion. Instead of

speaking, I glanced cursorily at the clock, planning on trying to time just one contraction before letting myself drift into oblivion. It was 1:48. I knew no more.

❧

When I woke in the morning, it was to the sound of voices in the kitchen. Grandma's clock read 7:04, and I pushed myself up on my elbows hastily, confused and wondering what time I was supposed to be in for work. *Eight o'clock*, I remembered with a sigh, and I let myself sink back into the rumpled bed, relishing the feeling of over five hours of uninterrupted rest. It had been weeks, if not months, since I had enjoyed such a long block of restorative sleep. My body felt light, even a little tingly, as if I could float right out of bed. I decided that it had been way too long since I had spent a night beside my grandma.

After a quick trip to the bathroom, I waltzed into the kitchen and showered Grandma and Simon with generous smiles. I carefully avoided Janice's gaze, as I knew she possessed the ability to erase the fine feeling of all that blissful sleep with a single look.

"Feeling better?" Grandma asked, flipping a buckwheat pancake off the hot griddle and onto my plate.

"Much," I assured her. Taking my seat, I asked Simon, "Please pass the syrup."

Simon quickly gave his half-eaten pancake one last squirt. "Were you sick last night?" he inquired. "I got sick once when I was little, and I threw up all over my blanket." Forgetting to cap the syrup bottle, he slid it to me bartender-style.

I barely grabbed it before it tipped off the edge and spilled maple goop all over the floor. "Not *really* sick," I said, giving Simon what I hoped was a stern look as I held up the just-caught bottle. I considered admonishing him lightly—Janice rarely did it herself these days. But I was in a tenuously good mood and had no desire to unbalance my careful contentment by playing mom. Besides, it wasn't like the syrup actually spilled. Any chastisement would be for what might have been instead of what was.

"So, you feel good enough for work, then?" Grandma eased the last pancake onto her own plate and joined us at the table. "I thought maybe it was about time for you to start your maternity leave."

"No way," I told her quickly. "I only get six weeks of paid leave. After that I either have to go back full-time or take another week or two unpaid. I'm going to work until the last possible minute."

I felt Janice shift beside me, but she didn't say anything. Though the reason for her increasing silence made me sick to my stomach, I was thankful that she was too wrapped up in troubles of her own to worry much about mine. I was also grateful that if Grandma had noticed a change in Janice's behavior, she kept her concerns to herself. We were able to have a breakfast that, if nothing else, was routine and even tranquil on the surface.

The contractions of the night before had completely disappeared, and with my impending labor sliding farther away, I was able to somewhat enjoy the drive to work. The team of mechanics from our church had finally fixed my car, and though it irked me that the work had been done for free, the cost of parts alone was almost more than my budget could handle. Alongside the obvious embarrassment, there was a certain humble sense of keen recognition, of appreciation for the small acts of kindness that my world wouldn't be worth occupying without.

Small things, I thought as I drove. Like the corn standing tall in the fields and the swaying motion of the leaves as a soft wind rushed down the rows. It was hypnotic. And I knew that if I could see the long, lined vegetation up close, there would yet be droplets of dew on some. It was a humid day. So much so that the road was still damp in shady places, and as I crested hills I could see steam rise off the blacktop as if the earth were exhaling. From the air-conditioned interior of my car, it was all a sight to behold, a world wrapped in an extravagance of green: growing, breathing, alive.

As I pulled into the Value Foods parking lot, I remembered that my shift coincided with Michael's, and a matched pang of uncertainty and excitement swept through me. In many ways he was as confusing to me as Janice. Both were relationships that I tentatively longed to cultivate yet feared to watch grow. No matter how hard I tried, I couldn't determine where I stood with either person. It was complicated and messy and indecipherable. But in spite of all that, Michael was still one of those small things that made me smile. I looked forward to seeing him more than I worried about it.

It was unusually slow for a Monday, and though I had felt fantastic emerging from bed only hours ago, I was weary by midmorning and thankful that the flow of customers was an intermittent trickle instead of a steady stream. True to his word, Michael stationed me at the front, making my duties relatively easy and manageable. He worked the odd jobs, though I caught him studying me on more than one occasion and concern was apparent on his face, even at a distance.

When Michael approached me before noon and asked me to take my lunch break with him, I gladly abandoned my spot at the cash register and let Graham take my place.

"You look lovely today," Graham said, giving my arm a quick squeeze as I brushed past. "Sleepy but lovely."

I had grown accustomed to Graham's extravagant compliments by now, and instead of making me uneasy, they were a welcome diversion. I mustered up a smile for him and reached out to give his arm a squeeze back. "Thank you, Graham. You are always so nice to me."

Much to my surprise, Graham's cheeks went just the tiniest bit pink. He shrugged with an uncharacteristic shyness and, trying to take the focus off himself, blurted out, "Isn't it about time for us to meet that baby?"

"Soon," I promised him ruefully. "It can't be long now."

I followed Michael to the back room and grabbed my brown bag, ready to wilt into a chair at the table. But Michael motioned over his shoulder at me and walked deeper into the storage room, leading me past shelves of canned goods, dog food, and boxed cereals that all had a shelf life of untold years.

"Did you know that there's a picnic area?" Michael asked conversationally.

"A picnic area? You've got to be kidding."

"It's not much," he warned me, "but at least you can grab a little fresh air. And it's shaded."

There was a heavy metal door that I had never bothered to notice before set in the wall at the very end of the long hall. Michael backed into it and pushed it open, revealing the loading dock and beyond that the alfalfa field that bordered the back of the store. There was a cracked cement pad and a crooked picnic table with peeling red paint. But it was in the shade, like he promised, and while the air was hot and close, it wasn't still, and the breeze was just enough to make it comfortable. I far preferred the nearly rotten picnic table outside to the cold metal one inside.

"Looks great," I said, slumping onto the bench. It tilted and wobbled for a moment before coming to rest at a slant. I sat with my back to the tabletop, looking out over the field and placing my lunch beside me.

Michael sat down, jostling the table again, and extracted a twelve-inch sub from a clear plastic Subway bag.

"Wow," I joked. "I wish I was a shift manager. Then maybe I could afford Subway for lunch instead of . . ." I rummaged in my bag. "Peanut butter and jelly?" I sighed. "Grandma gave me the wrong lunch."

"Whoa, wait a minute!" Michael laughed. "Your grandmother makes your lunch?"

"Not all the time," I said, shooting him a slanting glance. "Besides, we were talking about you and your big bucks."

"Not quite," Michael grunted, taking a bite of his sandwich. He chewed and swallowed quickly, talking around his food. "Besides, you can have my job. I'll only be here for another three weeks."

I tried to stop my heart from sinking a little. In three weeks he'd be gone. There was nothing for me to be disappointed about, and yet it was impossible not to feel just the smallest bit jilted. I would miss him. As soon as the thought entered my mind, I found I had to amend it. I had to admit to myself that I didn't exactly know if

I would miss *him* or simply the *possibility* of him. Michael offered me the chance to hope.

To cover up my regret, I tore into my own sandwich. "I don't want your job. I want to get out of here as soon as I can."

Michael's eyebrows shot up. "Really? I always had you pegged as a small town girl."

"Ouch," I said, feigning hurt. "You think I want to work at this little dump forever?"

He smiled slowly, taking me in as his eyes worked over my face. "Oh, I don't know if it's a 'little dump.' I kind of like it here. The people are nice. The pay isn't terrible. . . ."

"It's Value Foods," I argued. "There's got to be something better than this. Besides, who says the people are nice? You must not have met Clark."

Still smiling that frustratingly indecipherable smile, Michael nodded once and looked off over the alfalfa field. It had already been mowed twice this season, and the new crop was young and lush with tiny purple flowers. "I have met Clark, but I think—" he studied the sea of lavender and green—"I think that a job is what you make of it. Just like anything else."

I fixed him with a disbelieving stare. "Seriously." I let the clipped word hang in the air for a moment. "So why aren't you staying? If Value Foods is so great . . ."

Michael shrugged. "I think I could. I think I could be perfectly happy working here, settling down not far from home, starting a family. . . ." He trailed off and then realized what he had said. Though it was obvious that he wasn't proposing a single thing, Michael had just uncovered something that was intended for his mind, his heart, alone. I quickly looked away as a flush began to creep up his neck. "But I have no reason to stay. And I've always wanted to be a doctor. Always."

"I wondered what you were going for."

"Internal medicine," Michael said with a definitive edge in his voice.

"Why that?"

I could tell that he was wrestling with exactly how much to share. Dreams, no matter how old, are sacred things, and whatever prodded Michael into a future of internal medicine meant a lot to him. It struck me that I had been nosy, and I rushed to retract the question.

But Michael was already answering it. "My dad died when I was really young. It was a car accident. We were all in the vehicle—my mom, my dad, my brothers, and me—but he was the only one who died." He looked like he was about to say more, but he stopped, ate more of his sandwich.

I didn't quite know what to say. At first I almost told him that I had lost my dad too. But that seemed manipulative somehow, like a game of one-up. Maybe he wanted to talk about it more—I could ask him for more details. But that seemed wrong too. I waffled and hesitated and finally said the only thing I could get past my lips: "I'm sorry."

"Oh—" Michael brushed away my condolence with a smile—"it was a long, *long* time ago. I was only three. Besides, my mom got remarried when I was nine, and my stepdad is a great guy. It's not like my life has been entirely fatherless."

I smiled back, because it was not like my life had been entirely fatherless either. Fifteen years was nowhere near enough, but it was better than nothing.

We ate in silence for a while, considering the field, the clouds that were gathering on the horizon as if a storm was welling up in the distance. The towering spires of white were hedged in by hues of blue and black, and they were being whipped into different shapes and configurations as cream stiffens when beat. I wondered how long it would take for them to sweep across the expanse of sky and drop a thunderstorm on Mason. And then, like a bolt of lightning leaves an incandescent inscription across a dark sky, it hit me. I suddenly knew why Michael was so nice to me, why he continued to reach out to me in ways that were both baffling and almost painfully sweet.

"Your mother was a single mom for six years," I said almost to myself.

"Huh?" Michael replied, wiping his mouth with the back of his hand. "Oh yeah, I guess she was. So what?"

I didn't mean to seem irascible, but my mind was putting two and two together faster than I could keep up. "That's why you are always so kind to me. You remember what it was like when she was a single mom, and somehow that makes you feel sorry for me." The moment the words were out of my mouth, I wished I could snatch them out of the thick air and swallow them as quickly as I had said them. But it was too late, and I found that I couldn't even look at Michael as I waited for his reaction, for his anger. I deserved it. His kindness was irreproachable; the reasons behind it were his and his alone. I had no right to diminish his consideration with my own insecurities.

But though I waited for a reprimand, a furious exit, and a

slammed door, none came. Michael sat quietly. I stole an impulsive peek at him.

He was watching me. "I guess you're probably right. My mom was an amazing woman, and I know that it must have been very hard for her to make it all those years on her own. I suppose I have a bit of a soft spot for single moms."

I didn't know what to say. It all came down to pity? Michael's thoughtfulness, the way he treated me like an equal, his offering the afternoon he showed me a summer snow? This was worse than his anger. This was far, far worse than watching him go and spending the rest of my life wondering what was behind the tiny seed of our purported friendship. At least then I could dream that maybe it could have been more if the timing were different. It crushed me.

My fingers felt unattached to my body as I reached for my bag, the remnants of food I had sampled and discarded. Without looking again at Michael, I placed my hands beside me to push myself off the peeling bench.

But he grabbed my wrist.

Surprised, I spun to glance at his hand. He held me fast; his tanned, calloused fingers wrapped clean around the narrow bones of my pale arm. Michael's arm was browned by the sun, and flecks of dark hair peeked from beneath the white long-sleeved shirt that he had casually cuffed twice. He just held me, waiting, as I watched the inexplicable embrace of his fingers. I slowly, bit by bit, dared myself to look at his face.

Michael was smiling tentatively at me. "Hey, don't think that's the only reason I'm kind to you. I don't like you because I have some deep down desire to reach out to unwed mothers. I'm not running a charity house here." He laughed a little at his own attempt at a joke but abandoned his mirth when he saw the look on my face.

"I don't understand," I said quietly.

Michael sighed. "Julia, I like you because I like you. Can't it be that simple? I think you're funny and intelligent. I admire you for your gentleness. I like your easy smile, even when it looks like the last thing you want to do is smile." He paused, and I could see the dispute unravel across his face as he decided whether or not to say one last thing. He gave in. "*And* I think you're incredibly brave for doing what you're doing. But that has nothing to do with my mother."

I stared at him for what felt like a full minute. Michael stared back, holding my hesitant eyes in his own warm gaze and bidding me with his open smile to believe the uncomplicated truth he offered. It was that simple. He liked me for me. Why was that so hard to believe?

"But I'm . . ."

"Pregnant?" Michael asked. "So what? You think that changes who you are?"

We sat in silence, listening to the rush of the wind through the alfalfa and what I believed to be the distant rumblings of the storm on the edge of the horizon. I wanted to argue with Michael, to inform him that he was acting in a manner completely counter-cultural and beyond my own comprehension. I didn't know how to deal with his offer of friendship, his easy acceptance of who I was, or his apparent ability to see me for who I someday could be. Would be? He saw things in me that I didn't see in myself.

I didn't know what to say. But finally, because I couldn't stand to look at him for another moment and because something *had* to be said, I choked out, "Thank you."

Michael appeared to think that I could have said nothing finer. "You're welcome," he said back. And then with a subtle, unassuming gesture that asked for nothing in return, he pulled my wrist toward him and held my hand lightly in his own. He considered it for a moment, turning it over so that the back of my hand rested in his, my palm exposed to the air. I watched the intersecting lines of my translucent skin, wondering what Michael was looking for and hoping he would find it.

He did. In one unhurried movement, Michael brought my hand to his face and brushed his lips against the thin, blue vein that pulsed in the inside of my wrist, just beneath the skin.

surprises

IT WASN'T A ROMANTIC KISS. Nor was it merely friendly. It was an affirmation, a tender acknowledgment of Julia Anne DeSmit as a person. A woman. Valuable. Significant. Maybe even lovely. But it was also not enough.

In the moment that Michael released my hand and led me back into the chill air of Value Foods, I knew that there was nothing he could do to be enough of what I needed. He could have swept me into his arms, kissed my mouth in a fit of passion, and begged me to be his bride, and whatever deep thirst I had hidden in the heart of me still would not be slaked. Amazing, unfathomable man that he was, I had hoped that he could breathe life into me. It took the touch of his lips to convince me that he was only a man.

True, he stirred something in me—sweetly, tenderly, even graciously—but when his kindness brushed up against my soul, it did not begin to ease the ache of the seemingly bottomless fissure that still gaped. The realization leveled me.

What then? Oh, God, what then?

Did my peace rest in making a decision about the baby? Should I keep him? let him go?

Or maybe satisfaction could be found in Janice. Maybe, like Grandma had said so long ago, it was all a matter of forgiveness. Of love? What if I called Janice "Mother" and pleaded with her to put Ben out of her mind, to start over?

But then again, what could I build with the strength of my own wounded hands?

I was no more aware of what I should do than I was sure of Michael's motives. But though I wanted to bury my head in my arms and cry, retreat from the world and the imminent decisions that crept closer with every day, immobility had never been an option. I gathered up Michael's words, his almost brotherly kiss, and tucked them somewhere that they would never be forgotten. I moved on.

And time was gracious to me. Though my due date tiptoed ever nearer, nothing happened. Though I caught Janice in the middle of yet another furtive telephone call, she stayed. I tutored Simon, went to work, talked with Grandma, allowed myself to dream a little about Michael. Life went on as it had all summer long, and if we were on the brink of falling apart, we kept our composure admirably.

As if verifying the solidarity of our unspoken pact to exist and be happy, Grandma celebrated her seventy-eighth birthday a few days after Michael's enigmatic gesture.

Simon helped me bake a golden yellow cake with chocolate fudge frosting, from a box and a jar respectively, and we decorated the house with pink and white streamers. I even let him use a chair to climb on the countertop and affix numerous ends of the gauzy paper to the tops of the oak cupboards, in spite of the fact that it was against my better judgment.

"I won't fall," Simon chided me, as if I was the one who had suggested something ridiculous. He had the handle of a cupboard door in one hand and was pushing pink strands of paper out of his face with the other.

"Make sure you don't," I retorted. Although my heart clenched to see him so high, so vulnerable and unwitting when he turned his back, I stood directly behind him, ready to catch him should he stumble.

We had gone earlier to pick out a birthday present and some cards, and Simon insisted on scrutinizing every single possibility in the birthday section before settling on what he considered to be good enough for Grandma Nellie. He had a very particular idea of what he wanted the card to look like and say, and nothing but his carefully imagined perfection would do. A rosy card with pale yellow flowers came close, and because I was more than ready to call it a day, I snatched it out of Simon's hands and tried to hurry him down the aisle before he could be distracted by more sappy couplets and doe-eyed birds.

But just before we rounded the corner, he saw it: the one. It was a pale green card with a cluster of intricate birdhouses along the left edge. They were bordered by an abundant flower garden that sprawled roses, gladiolas, and wispy ivy with purple flowers across the bottom and up the opposite side. The paper was laser cut so the flowers cast a looping shadow on the blue interior beneath.

"'Happy birthday,'" Simon read. He flipped the card open with an almost peculiar intensity and continued very slowly, precisely: "'I hope your birthday is as love . . . love-lee'?"

I peered over his shoulder. "You got it right: lovely."

"'I hope your birthday is as lovely as you are.'" Simon wrinkled his nose. "What does *lovely* mean?"

"Pretty," I said. "Beautiful." But somehow that didn't quite encompass it. "I don't know, soft somehow and gentle. . . . The word *lovely* makes me think of a lady. And love, I suppose. There's something lovable in it."

"Grandma's a lady," Simon breathed. "And I love her. It's perfect. Look, it even has a garden—and birdhouses!"

"It is perfect," I agreed, thinking of the birdhouse we had bought only an hour ago. One of our neighbors, a retired farmer who should have been a woodworker, had recently begun setting his little projects by the road with a For Sale sign stuck in the ground nearby. There was a pair of Adirondack chairs, a painted lighthouse, a long, low planter's bench, and three tall, white birdhouses on beveled poles. Simon chose the smallest one because it was the most detailed: the birdhouse was fashioned to look like a white, two-story Victorian complete with a wraparound porch and turreted tower. There was even a tiny painted sign affixed to the right of the circular door: The Wild Rose Inn.

But the card made me think of other things too. Of Graham's sweet praise and Michael's chaste kiss. Of seeing things in myself that I hadn't previously seen. I took Simon's hand, holding his card in the other, and hoped that I would find whatever it was inside me that made them think me lovely.

Grandma acted surprised when she came home from delivering Meals on Wheels, though we knew that she knew we were planning a party. She stepped through the door, taking in the streamers, the layered cake swathed in folds of chocolate, and her haphazard family blowing absurdly on children's noisemakers. They had been Simon's idea. I thought they made us look a bit silly, but from the other side of the room it seemed as though Grandma's eyes misted over a little.

"Happy birthday!" Simon yelled. He gave his noisemaker one last, triumphant wheeze, then skittered across the kitchen floor to hug my grandmother around the middle. She was radiant in her joy.

"Thank you, Simon," Grandma said, hugging him back. "Did you do this? Did you decorate and make that—that *amazing* cake?"

"Yup, but Julia helped. And she let me climb on the counter."

"Simon!" I yelped.

"Julia!" Grandma cried.

"He was fine," I stated quickly. I glanced at Janice, afraid that she would be furious with me, but she was busy with the pizza boxes, opening them and laying them out on the counter now that Grandma was home.

"We ordered pizza," Simon told Grandma, ushering her to her chair. "We didn't want you to think about cooking or cleaning or anything!"

"We thought it would be relaxing," I added, dropping a kiss on my grandmother's cheek. "Happy birthday."

She touched my hand as it lay on her shoulder. "Thank you, Julia. This is so sweet. So fun."

"That's the idea."

"We have everything for a party. There's cake," Simon enthused, needlessly pointing out the dessert that graced the center of the table, "and cards and presents. . . ." He swept his arms over the little pile by Grandma's plate. "And Julia said we could probably play a game later."

I winked at him. "It's up to Grandma, remember? Whatever she wants to play."

"Well," Grandma said slowly, "I think I could take you on in a game of Yahtzee."

Even Janice laughed at Simon's whoop.

We ate slowly and lingered over root beer floats, and though Janice was quiet, she wasn't unpleasant. The conversation darted around her, taking off in a million different directions as Simon's imagination was sparked. He even got Grandma to tell us stories about when she was a little girl, and her account of helping her mother make home-made laundry detergent and scrubbing their clothes on a washboard on the front porch made everyone's jaw drop.

"But we have washing machines," Simon remarked, confused.

"We didn't back then," Grandma told him.

Simon still looked like he was at a loss. "But, Grandma, you're not *that* old." He pulled his knees underneath him and stretched impulsively across the table, grabbing Grandma's hand where it rested beside her plate. Simon turned her hand over in his fingers, studying the lines with as much concentration as Michael had considered mine. Grandma's fingers looked gnarled in Simon's small, dark hands. They seemed much older when embraced by his straight bones and smooth skin.

"You're right," Grandma said eventually, giving Simon's hands a loving squeeze. "I'm not that old at all."

My oversensitive spirit was sobered by the obvious untruth of such a statement, but Simon was already on to something else. "We have a present for you!" he exclaimed. "And a card!"

The card was significant, and I tried to release my anxiety as Simon reached for the pebble green envelope. We had decided that the time was right for his little revelation, for Grandma and Janice to finally discover what we had been secretly working on for months. Like he'd hoped, Simon was indeed able to read at least a bit, and though I could really take no credit for his learning, nearly everything he had managed to pick up had come from our morning sessions. It was true that a number of words he simply had memorized, but still I was proud of him in a way that I couldn't really understand. When I heard him read, when I watched his thoughtful forefinger follow words across a page, I was overcome with a gentle elation that rose up and up until I found myself grinning and wishing big things for Simon that went far beyond stringing together his ABC's.

"Here." Simon scooted out of his chair and went around the table to hand Grandma the card. The second she touched the envelope he changed his mind, snatching it back quickly and ripping it open. "I can do it for you."

"Okay." Grandma giggled.

"Look." Simon showed her the card. "It's a garden—just like yours. And it says, 'Happy birthday.'"

Grandma smiled at Simon, but he was looking at the card. She caught my eye, giving me a funny look.

I shook my head, casting off her attention and nodding back at the little boy who stood with his arm just touching hers.

"And on the inside—" Simon opened the card—"it says, 'I hope your birthday is as lovely as you are. Love, Simon.'"

He had written his name at the bottom, each letter round and neat, painstakingly drawn and perfected as he chewed his tongue. "Look there, Grandma." He pointed. "I wrote my name. And I read this whole card."

"You did?" she asked, a grin lighting up her face.

"I did," Simon said gravely. "Julia taught me how."

"Surprise." I waved my hands sheepishly.

"I know how to read!" Simon threw his arms in the air and yelled again, "Happy birthday, Grandma!"

Laughing, Grandma caught him in another hug. "That's a wonderful surprise. What a great birthday present."

"It's kind of for all of us," Simon said earnestly.

"Oh, of course," Grandma responded, equally serious. "I wouldn't want to keep something like that to myself."

I tore my eyes away from them to see Janice's reaction. Clearly she knew that Simon had learned his letters in preschool, but wasn't she impressed that he was able to thread at least some of them together?

that he was able to read? Simon had, in fact, done it for her. He had wanted to amaze his mother, make her proud.

But when my gaze found Janice, the look in her eyes was resigned, as if she was steeling herself to follow through with a decision that had already been made. She sat across from them, watching my grandmother rub a gentle hand across her son's back. Their heads were bowed together over the special card, and Simon's lips moved a mile a minute, explaining enthusiastically. Grandma wasn't looking at the card. She was studying Simon, a mixture of love and pride battling cheerfully across her face. Janice observed them with a tired smile tugging at the downturn of her lips.

Stop! I wanted to yell. *You don't understand!*

It was like watching a train wreck unfold: I could see the engine, barreling down and oblivious, and Janice, on the middle of the tracks, trapped in the glare of the headlights, panic-stricken and pale. But it was all a misunderstanding. A mistake. Janice was supposed to be Simon's mother; he was supposed to be her son. Yet I could tell by the look on her face that she was regretting the decision she had made nearly six years ago.

Watching Simon interact with my grandmother, easily, openly, as if it was the most comfortable and natural thing in the world, I could see that Janice was berating herself for her own self-perceived weakness. In her mind at least, Simon would have been happier in a more stable family. In a family where a woman like my grandmother called him "Son." Where there was a devoted father, maybe even siblings, a dog. It was why she wanted me to give my baby up for adoption so desperately.

In an instant, I knew that Janice was hating herself for not having the strength to let Simon go when she had the chance. She was trying to figure out how to make it right.

"Simon," I said suddenly, my voice high and uneven, "why don't you show your mom how you can read?"

The little boy yanked the card away from Grandma and bounded around the table to bring it to Janice.

See? I longed to say. *He loves you.*

Janice opened her arms for him and lifted Simon's slight frame onto her lap. She rested her chin on his shoulder and watched as he opened the card and read it yet again. "Great job," Janice murmured when he was finished. She kissed the side of his head, breathing in his little boy smell. "You are so smart."

"I know," Simon quipped back. Then he slipped off her lap and came to tug on my arm, telling me it was time for cake.

Although everyone seemed happy and light, I rose to get the cake knife with a deep sense of dread pinching my chest. What would Janice do with these feelings, these beliefs that were written across her face as plain as day? I knew she considered herself a failure as a mother. I knew she regretted many of the decisions that she had made regarding Simon and, I suppose, regarding me. But what was she going to do to right her mistakes? I hoped that I didn't know Janice as well as I thought I did.

The cake was perfectly moist and gooey with chocolate fudge, but I barely tasted it. Instead of enjoying it, I continued to watch Janice watch Simon and allowed myself to become ever more morose, feeling guilty because it was my grandmother's birthday party.

After Grandma had opened her presents—the birdhouse from Simon and me and a pretty deep-dish pie plate with frilled edges from Janice—I got up to clear the table. My legs were heavy, and I wished that there were something I could do to erase the disquiet that hung around Janice like an almost tangible mist. I felt like we were finally doing okay; we were finally getting somewhere. And now she was going to talk herself into more feelings of failure, of inadequacy.

I couldn't let her topple everything we had been working so hard to create. I would have a talk with her later, I decided. Sit her down and try to undo some of the lies she had told herself. I would even listen to all she had to say to me about adoption, about letting go. If nothing else, I owed her the chance to get it off her chest, to have the conversation with me that she should have had with herself years ago. Though it made a sob catch in my throat just to think of it, I wondered if, given the chance, Janice would be able to convince me.

But before I had the opportunity to give my plan any more thought, Janice opened her mouth and changed our world. "Simon, honey, come here a sec." She scooted back from the table and pushed her knees apart, welcoming Simon when he came to stand by her by pulling him in between her legs and closing them tight. "Gotcha!" she said quietly, hugging him fervently for a moment.

"Mom." Simon wiggled against her grasp, but Janice did not let go.

"I have a surprise for you, Simon," she said, refusing to look at either Grandma or me.

I was standing behind Grandma, holding a stack of dirty plates that I quickly put on the countertop. My hands were shaking.

"But it's Grandma's birthday," Simon said, eyeing his mother warily. His nose was only inches from hers.

"I said a *surprise*, not a present," Janice clarified. There was a little smile on her face, but I was sure that her eyes were wet in the dimly reflected light of the kitchen.

Simon shrugged. Waited.

Janice took a deep breath and tightened her arms. "Do you know why we came here, Simon?"

"So that we'd have a place to stay," Simon answered simply.

I was surprised that he could answer the question without any clarification. At first I didn't even know what Janice was asking. It was hard for me to believe that Simon could even remember a time without us or why he and Janice had journeyed to Mason over five months ago. I had a very hard time picturing my life without him.

"You're right. But why did we come to Grandma Nellie and Julia's house?"

All at once I knew what she was going to do, and Grandma must have realized it too because she collapsed a little in front of me. I saw her shoulders wither, and a tiny exhalation deflated her enough to cause me to put my hands along the sides of her arms, holding her together, holding her up.

"They're our friends," Simon explained.

Janice nodded. "Yes, they are. But you know what? They're more than that too."

I didn't know what Simon was capable of grasping at the age of five, but his eyes darted to mine and then sought out Grandma's, and there was something sparkling and enchanted in them. Whatever Janice was going to say, he believed that it was a wonderful secret, something sweet and unexpected and delightfully mysterious. It was all a magnificent game.

Still refusing to look at me, Janice said the thing that I had been longing to admit since the day she and Simon showed up on our doorstep. "You know how you've always wanted a little sister, Simon? Well, you don't have a *little* sister, but you do have a *big* sister. Julia is your big sister, sweetheart."

The punch line was a bit confusing for Simon, and although I could tell he wanted to laugh, to celebrate, he didn't quite get it. His eyebrows furrowed together in uncertainty. "But you're *my* mommy," he said.

"I'm Julia's mommy too," Janice replied slowly, as if measuring her words would make them easier to digest.

"But . . ." Simon's head turned from his mother to me, trying to connect the dots and apparently failing.

Janice tried again. "A long time ago, I lived here in Mason, and I had a beautiful baby girl. I named her Julia. And then I . . ." She trailed off, struggling to find the right words to cover all that had happened and then condense them into a format suited for an almost-kindergartner. I didn't envy her in her task. "Then I had to go away for a while and . . . and find *you*." Janice cupped Simon's face in her hands. "But now you're home, and I can tell you that Julia is your sister."

Her words were nowhere near sufficient. They didn't begin to scratch the surface of the truth, of all the things that would need to be revealed to my younger brother. But for now, for this night of birthday cake and surprises, Janice had said enough. It was a beginning, and finally Simon knew that I was his sister.

He was studying me with his great, dark eyes, the color of damp earth under an overturned rock, half-hidden behind his perpetually crooked glasses. I studied him back. And then, as though seeing me for the very first time, Simon's face sparked to life and he waved at me from between his mother's arms. "Hey, Julia! Did you know that you're my sister?"

I nodded mutely, beaming at him in contradiction to the sick feeling crawling around in my stomach, loving him, even as I began to understand what Janice had just done. "*You're* home," she had said. Not "*We're* home."

letting go

JANICE LEFT THE FOLLOWING DAY.

She packed a very small bag and left her favorite shirt hanging on Grandma's clothesline, flapping softly in the wind as if waving good-bye. I knew that it was her way of assuring us that she would come back, that this little trip was indeed nothing more than an opportunity to "tie up a few loose ends." But I also knew that Janice's doubts and inadequacies ran deep, and she hadn't yet figured out that running away was no solution at all.

It was funny. I had wanted this from day one. I had looked forward with an almost desperate anticipation to the day that her car would pull out of our dusty driveway. But when Janice actually threw her soft-sided suitcase in the back of her car, I felt like I had been sucker punched. Out of the blue. Completely unexpected. Unfair. This wasn't the way things were supposed to end *again*, and although Janice assured us she wouldn't be longer than a week, something about her departure felt very, very permanent.

She was leaving so much behind.

She left Simon behind.

Grandma and I never had a chance to say no because Janice never formally asked us if we would take care of him. We were thunderstruck. We were utterly speechless. Not that we could have forced ourselves to deny Simon anyway, but it would have at least given us an opportunity to dissuade her. As it turned out, when Janice walked into the kitchen the morning after Grandma's party with a suitcase in her hands and a wary smile running a thin line across her mouth, Grandma and I could barely muster enough energy to move past our shock and part our lips to say good-bye.

We all followed her out the door after she chased down a fresh muffin with a cup of coffee so hot it made her wince as she gulped it.

"I have to make a quick trip," she said, forcing cheerfulness as she wrenched open the car door. "I'll be back in no time."

"What about your job?" Grandma asked, dismay making her reach out to touch the hood as if her fingers could stop the vehicle from backing away.

"Oh yeah," Janice said, smacking her forehead with her palm. "Can you call the office and tell them I'll be out of town for a few days? That would be so great."

"What about Simon?" I asked, ruffling his hair absently as

he stood beside me, apparently unconcerned with his mother's departure.

"I'm going to stay here with you," he said, looking up at me. "My *sister*."

I tried to smile at him but my lips would not comply.

"I'll be back soon," Janice repeated. "It just doesn't make sense for me to lug Simon along when he'd rather stay here with you anyway. Right, buddy?"

"Right," Simon agreed, giving her two thumbs-up. It was obvious that they had already spoken about Janice's little plan, and Simon was completely on board. However, he was also oblivious to the way Janice's eyes darted frantically away from his, the way her hands trembled so that her car keys filled the air with a quiet jangling sound. He knew what she wanted him to know, nothing more.

Janice took a shallow, shaky breath. "Well," she said, shrugging awkwardly and then patting her sides with her arms straight and stiff. "Guess this is it. . . ."

We all stood stock-still, unable to move, or maybe *unwilling*, because it would mean that this moment would actually have to move forward. Maybe, if we stayed like this, if we just breathed in and out and didn't say a word, we could linger long enough for Janice to change her mind.

But Janice wasn't about to let that happen. She walked toward the car.

"Are you sure you have to—?" Grandma started.

Janice interrupted. "You're acting like this is a big deal. I'll be back in a *few days*." The reassurance was for Simon, but Janice didn't look at him or at Grandma and me while she said it.

"See you soon!" Simon chirped, slipping from my side to give his mom a bear hug. "Have a safe trip!"

"I will," she said thickly, pressing her face into his hair. "See you soon."

Grandma moved forward when Simon ran off to chase one of the barn cats, and she caught Janice's arm in a grip that left the skin peeking out white between her fingers. She whispered something to Janice that sounded like "You are stronger than this."

"No, I'm not," Janice replied just loud enough for me to hear. Then she said clearly, with a confidence that I couldn't quite believe, "Thank you so much for your hospitality, Nellie. When . . . when I come back, we'll have to work out something more . . . permanent."

I watched my grandma nod almost imperceptibly; then she enveloped Janice in a hug so tender it made my heart twist. "Come back, Janice."

Janice gave a hollow little laugh and pulled away. "I will."

Grandma backed away because there was nothing else she could do.

When I stepped forward, I wasn't sure what I intended to do. There were no words forming on my tongue. There was no argument that I longed to convey. I was only aware of a need to touch my mother, to let her know in some small way that she had not entirely failed. I could sense an echo of grace somewhere just out of earshot; I wanted Janice to hear it.

I had hated her so much. I had resented her for leaving, blamed her for so many things that were broken and wrong, held her accountable to a list of crimes that could bury the world beneath an immovable mountain of guilt. And while I may have even been justified in my assessment of her utter lack of worth as a mother, while the world around me might agree with my childish accusations, I found that I didn't feel that way anymore. Something was different. As I stood on the driveway and surveyed the woman who called herself my mother, I didn't burn with anger or wish her ill. I didn't feel vindicated in her hasty departure.

Somehow I regretted it.

It didn't feel right.

Janice blinked furiously as I approached her, as if she knew that each tear would be counted as evidence that her little trip was more than a weeklong adventure. "Julia, I—"

I stopped her. "I didn't get to say anything the last time you left. I won't let that happen again."

She looked horrorstruck, as if I had pulled a knife on her and was edging ever closer.

"No, *no*," I tried to clarify quickly. I put my hands out in front of me in supplication, in surrender. "I'm not *mad*. I just . . . actually . . . I think I forgive you." The statement surprised me, but even as I probed it carefully, wondering what darkened corner of my soul it had come from, I knew that it was true.

Her face blanched. "No, you don't," she whispered. "You shouldn't."

"I think it started to happen when you told me that Ben has been calling you," I said, almost more to myself than her. I played back my feelings, retreated to the day on the beach when Janice told us about Simon and the reaching ache of his chosen name. Something had changed then. Something had begun to make sense. Janice *was* like me in some ways, and I had realized it that day. We were both waiting for something, straining our ears to hear that echo of something *more*. That thing that would make us whole. She thought it was Ben or maybe that she would hear it if she could only escape the guilt of all of her missteps.

Janice was shaking her head at me.

"I didn't exactly understand it then," I continued. "I still don't, but I was so illogically jealous when I heard that you were talking with him again. I thought that you'd go back to him. And . . ." I paused, testing what I was going to say before I let it pass my lips, wondering if it was really true. It was. "And I didn't want you to leave."

A part of me wanted to close the last few feet of space between us, to wrap my arms around Janice so she would know I meant what I said. But I didn't quite dare. "I think we could be okay," I murmured instead.

"We are okay," Janice said, making her voice bright, though she looked ready to crumble at my feet. "I just have to go away for a little while."

"You don't have to go," I coaxed, though I knew my words fell on deaf ears. Janice couldn't hear the indistinct whisper of grace: the breeze through the fields, the birds above us, unaware of our four little points of life, but singing, singing, singing.

Janice was nodding and nodding, bobbing her head as if she would never stop. "Yes, I do. I have to go."

I didn't know what else to say. I didn't know what compulsion burned in her soul, making her believe that she needed Ben or didn't deserve us. Maybe she thought that this was her penance, the debt she owed for making so many mistakes—mistakes that left her unwilling or unable to forgive herself. But though I wanted to tell her what to do, I suddenly knew that I couldn't change her mind. There was nothing I could do or say to force her to accept that she was looking in all the wrong places.

I put my arms out for her then, and Janice bowed into my embrace, curled awkwardly around the tummy that held her grandchild. It was a clumsy hug, inelegant, graceless, not at all the tender reunion that I had secretly hoped it would be one day.

Janice gave my cheek a fast kiss and patted my belly. "We'll see you soon," she said resolutely, and I believed her less because she looked me straight in the eye. "You give that baby a good name."

"I will," I promised.

But something in the finality of what Janice said had given her a little shock. "I mean, I'll be back soon. I'll meet the baby soon."

"It's a boy," I told her. I wanted her to know.

The smile that sprang to Janice's lips was real, if only for a moment. Then she visibly gathered herself, gave her keys a hearty jingle, and turned determinedly toward the car.

I whispered so that only she could hear, "You can come back."

Janice didn't turn around.

She was in the car, sunglasses resolutely hiding her eyes and one arm slung over the seat so she could turn her head to back out of the driveway, when I remembered. I didn't even notice that I had taken a step back, a step away from her, until the tiny black pearl around my neck thumped lightly against my chest. I had put it on for supper the night we were supposed to patch things up, and though I had raised my hands many times to remove it, I never did.

The pearl hid in the hollow between my collarbones and became a part of the landscape of my skin. But it was a token that Janice had offered before everything changed; it was for a different life, a different ending. I had to give it back.

I took a few jogging steps toward her car, unclasping the chain with fumbling fingers as I went. "Janice!" I called. "Janice, wait!"

Her eyes were impossible to read behind the windshield and the opaque glasses, but her lips were slack and wary, a limp banner beneath a breathless sky. I could tell that Janice didn't want to stop; she didn't want to wait another second lest she lose her nerve and find herself unable to follow through with the plan she had so haphazardly thrown together. But she stepped on her brakes anyway. She waited for me.

"Here," I said, holding out the necklace so that it dangled from my hand like some wilted flower, its petals plucked and scattered. Janice's window was closed; I didn't say any more. What else was there to say?

The window slowly hummed down, and Janice replied above the lowering glass, "Keep it. I gave it to you."

"It was never meant for me," I heard myself mutter. I thrust it at her again. The pearl swung over the now-hidden glass, back and forth, back and forth, a pendulum between my world and hers. "Ben will wonder where it is."

"Ben?" Janice sounded surprised. "Julia, I didn't get that necklace from Ben. I got it from your father. He gave it to me when you were born."

Suddenly the arc of the necklace seemed precarious. I put my other hand beneath it and caught it in my palm, a cool slither of tangled chain that rested like a still pool in my hand. "Dad?" I whispered. "Dad gave it to you?"

Janice curled her lips together, and I could see her eyebrows bow above the plastic, tortoiseshell rim of her sunglasses. "It was never meant for *me*."

I backed away, the pearl a perfect seed trapped beneath my fingers. It was the catalyst for a shiver that trembled like a rush of water over my skin. I closed my eyes and shook my head to clear it. I said, "Thank you."

Janice didn't say, *You're welcome.*

We watched her go, Simon cradling a kitten that had disappeared over a month ago and was now nearly wild from lack of human contact. "Ouch!" he yelped when the cat scratched him and leaped away. But he was already chasing her down, and Grandma smiled sadly in spite of herself, taking a step toward me and pulling my head onto her shoulder.

"What happened?" she asked. I could hear from her voice that she was crying.

"Ben has been calling her," I said.

"Who's Ben?"

I almost said, *Simon's father*, but somehow that didn't seem to quite get at it. After a moment I replied, "I think that Janice thinks Ben is what she's looking for."

"Is he?" Grandma asked.

I didn't even have to think about that one. "No. He's not."

"What is she looking for?"

"The same thing I'm looking for," I answered. When Grandma

drew away to look at me, I had started to cry. "Did you know that she wanted me to give my baby up for adoption?"

Grandma shook her head. "Are you?"

"No," I said carefully, rolling the word over on my tongue, trying it out. "No. It's what she thinks she should have done. But I'm not her. I'm going to do everything in my power to be an amazing mother to my baby. I think it's what *I* should do."

"And is that what Janice is looking for? what you're looking for?" Grandma's teeth clenched around the question, and an uncharacteristic intensity flared behind her eyes. "For a chance to make things right? to make amends?"

I looked out over her shoulder to the field of corn that lined our gravel driveway. The plants were tall and endless, sweeping up the sloping hill and flowing off into the distance, proud and flourishing and full of the promise of harvest. It happened every year. They grew; they died, then waited for spring and marched on to autumn, producing fruit that benefited them nothing, fruit that was meant as an offering, a gift.

So much of my life had been spent taking and taking and taking. Thinking it was all about me, believing that everything came down to *me* and how I felt, what I wanted. Even in my grasping attempts to know God, I did exactly that: I grasped. I sought. Sometimes I waited. But I never opened myself, spread my soul wide as an offering so He could come and capture me. I never let Him run strong fingers through my soil, watering it with His grace so my fruit could grow and grow above the weeds that threatened to choke it out.

For once, with the dust from my mother's car still settling on the road, I realized that I wasn't interested in looking anymore. I had hunted peace like it was prey to be snared. I had tracked it down like Janice was doing now, figuring that if only I could secure everything around me just so, align my wants and needs while balancing my desires, I would finally figure out the formula that would make me happy. But it wasn't Michael or peace with Janice or sharing the truth with Simon or making a decision about my baby. It wasn't even a combination of all those things that I longed for.

"What are you looking for, Julia?" Grandma asked again, softer this time. Maybe she feared the answer. Maybe she believed that I was finally close. Closer than I had ever been.

"I don't know," I said, but my voice was not hopeless, and in the wake of my spoken words I carved through something deep inside. My soul whispered a prayer.

It was like being undone, cut loose from everything that tied me down and sealed me against everything I could be. It was like finally being opened to the crushing weight of some indescribable significance pressing itself upon my soul, filling in the gaps. Leaving a mark. Leaving an imprint with a hand so heavy, so full and sweet, I almost cried out, but not in pain. In joy.

Because it was enough.

well

"WE NEED A PROJECT," Grandma said with a certain satisfied sense of finality.

It was August 7, my due date, and though we had gone for a drive down a bumpy gravel road, though I had stomped vigorously up and down the stairs half a dozen times in succession, and though I *almost* dug the ancient bottle of castor oil out of the very back of Grandma's medicine cabinet, I was not in labor. The baby did not seem eager to arrive on time.

"What kind of project?" Simon asked, looking up from his coloring book page with a curious twist in his lips. He had a way of screwing up his face when he was really hoping for something. It was involuntary, the same unconscious tightening of muscles that happened while lifting a heavy object, but somehow it seemed to help. When Simon pulled that face, it was hard not to try to shift the weight of the world to get him what he wanted.

Grandma put her hands on his cheeks and rubbed. Simon giggled and purred while she wiggled him around. His voice came out bumpy and uneven, like a motorboat bouncing over a succession of waves. "Wh-at . . . ki-nd . . . of . . . pro-ject?" he asked again, letting his voice box jumble and morph the words.

"A *fun* project," Grandma assured us. "The kind of project that requires the help of a big, strong, hardworking boy. . . ."

Simon raised his hand. "I can help!"

"That's exactly what I was hoping for." Grandma grinned.

"What do you want to do?" I asked, trying not to sound too skeptical, though the thought of a project when the baby was due any day seemed a little daunting. True, I had finally given in and started my maternity leave the day before, and I no longer had to go to work, but weren't these days supposed to be filled with relaxation? preparation maybe?

Apparently Grandma had other ideas. "Come on," she said, pulling Simon to his feet. She marched us both outside. The sun was high in the very middle of the sky, and it cut a sharp angle across the roof of the porch, slicing the shadows in half, separating dark and light. Grandma let the screen door slam merrily shut and walked to the edge of the porch, her toes white in the sun and her feet blanketed by shade. A breeze plucked at the untucked hem of her linen shirt.

"I want to do this," Grandma said when Simon and I had come to stand on either side of her.

We looked around, studying the driveway, the little patch of flower garden beside the cracking sidewalk. Simon craned his neck and surveyed a few of the old outbuildings, obviously searching for some apparent task, some palpable place to set our hands to work. I scrutinized everything too, though I wasn't looking for a project as much as I was looking for something to do to make us forget that Janice hadn't called. I was sure Grandma's line of reasoning corresponded with mine.

"I want to do *this*," Grandma said once more, breaking into our hesitation. This time she began to tap her feet.

I looked down. Not because I understood, but because her toes were asking me to. As I looked, a fleck of peeling white paint pulled loose from the rutted wood and curled itself up the side of Grandma's foot. "You want to paint the porch," I said dully.

Grandma clapped. "Bingo!"

It was hard not to sigh as I surveyed the job before us. The porch was ten feet wide at least, and it ran almost the length of the entire house. It featured a wide staircase and an ornate railing on three sides, with the fourth side ending against the outside wall of the living room. The railing alone would take hours to paint, never mind the fact that we would have to power wash and probably sand the wood first, then prime it, put two coats of paint on it. . . .

"We can't paint the porch, Grandma," I muttered.

"Yes, we can!" Simon shouted.

"Yes, we can," Grandma agreed. "Julia, honey, it's the first week of August. We'll take the rest of the summer if we have to. We'll go slow, do it right. It'll be fun."

"I'm not supposed to paint," I reminded her, pointing at my belly.

"That's why you're the supervisor." She smiled. "And then later when the baby is born, we'll pull the cradle in the mudroom and let him sleep while we work. You can peek in through the screen door a dozen times a minute if you want to."

"And we can have it done by the time Mom comes home!" Simon cheered. He dashed past Grandma and wrapped himself around my tummy, resting his chin on a bump that I imagined to be one of the baby's knees. "She'll be so surprised. It will be great."

I cupped his face in my hands and peered at Grandma over his head.

"He needs this," she mouthed. Then she pointed from herself to me and back again. "*We* need this."

There was nothing more to say. "Okay," I consented, though it seemed to contradict good sense. "We'll paint the porch."

There was an almost tangible excitement when we hopped in the car and headed for the hardware store. I quickly realized that Grandma had been thinking about this for quite some time, and she had already borrowed a power washer from Mr. Walker and checked into the kind of paint we would need.

"Did you know they sell barn paint in five-gallon buckets?" she asked as we pulled into the parking lot of Terpstra's Hardware. "I asked the nice boy working the register what we should use, and he figured that would be our best bet."

"Mm-hmm," I murmured, raising my eyebrows at her as if I questioned her sanity just the tiniest bit.

Grandma laughed and gave my arm a friendly slap. "You wait and see. This is a good idea. Have a little faith," she quipped lightly.

"It's a good idea," Simon parroted, unbuckling his seat belt before we had come to a complete stop and hopping out of his booster seat. He was halfway to the front door of the store before Grandma had switched the engine off.

We bought two huge buckets of white barn paint, a handful of new brushes, a couple of packets of coarse sandpaper, and a rectangular tin can of turpentine so it wouldn't be impossible to get the paint off our skin.

"You know, she shouldn't paint," the lady behind the counter warned us when we brought our purchases to the front. She poked a ballpoint pen accusingly in the air and surveyed me over the tops of her glasses as if she had caught me in the act of plotting to do something dangerous.

"No, she shouldn't," a voice behind me agreed.

I turned to see Michael propping an enormous mass of molded steel against his hip. It looked so heavy and awkward that I didn't even really register that Michael was standing before me. "What in the world is that?" I cried.

"Exhaust manifold," Michael said wryly. "My brother is rebuilding his combine." Then, looking past me, he addressed the surly woman at the counter. "Hey, this thing didn't come with gaskets."

"They never do," she replied, looking bored and somewhat put out. "You have to order those separately."

Michael's eyes got wide, and he looked for a moment like he was going to let her have it. But then he shrugged, hefted the manifold over her stained countertop, and let it drop with a thud.

"Watch it!" she said.

But Michael was already turning to me. "How are you doing?" he asked, a smile reaching from his lips clear to the upturned corners of his playful eyes.

"Good," I said automatically. Then, feeling Grandma and Simon beside me, I started to introduce them.

Grandma had already met Michael, and she reached past me with a grin. "Hi, Michael," she greeted him warmly. "It's nice to see you."

"Nice to see you, too, Mrs. DeSmit." Then, remembering, Michael ducked his head sheepishly. "I mean, Nellie." He shook her hand inside both of his own as she smiled at him. "And who's this?" When he looked at Simon, I could see recognition flash across his face. "We've met before," he answered himself. "I just can't remember your name."

"This is Simon," I cut in quickly. "He's my brother." I put my hand on Simon's shoulder and smiled encouragingly at him.

Michael shot me an unreadable look, but then he tilted his head as if to say, *No matter* and held out his hand for Simon to slap him a high five. "Nice to meet you, buddy."

"We're going to paint the porch," Simon offered, sounding very grown-up, very important. He was watching my handsome coworker with barely concealed reverence; it seemed Michael had an admirer.

"You are?" Michael asked. "I hope Julia's not helping you."

"She's the supervisor," Simon assured him.

Michael looked between Grandma and Simon and then gave me an appraising look. "Is this your crew?"

"Yup." I nodded, affecting a lazy drawl. "They're a mite slow, but a hardworking bunch."

I watched as Michael's eyebrows formed a stern line across his forehead. "You know," he said deliberately, "I don't think your crew is quite big enough."

"We're going to take our time," Grandma told him. "We don't care if it takes us the rest of the summer; right, Simon?"

"Right," he agreed.

"Well . . . ," Michael began, and I could see a scheme forming behind his eyes. "If your foreman will have me, why don't I join the crew for the rest of the day? Are you working on it today?"

"We're starting," Grandma said.

"And we'll be fine," I interrupted. I didn't want to impose on Michael's kindheartedness. Nor did I think it was wise to start forming deeper connections with someone who was going to leave in only a few weeks. Our little wayward trio was well versed in the particulars of leaving. We needed to focus a little on the essence of what it meant to *stay*. And just the skimming thought of Janice—of her sudden disappearance and lack of contact for days that seemed to drag on a little longer with each hour that we sadly tacked on— made my stomach clench. *Bad idea*, I thought. *Better to not let things get complicated.*

But Michael cut a convincing profile. He casually waved his hand in dismissal at the tractor manifold waiting for him on the counter. "I had plans for the afternoon, but not anymore. We can't do anything without the gaskets." Then he mimed a painting motion, making exaggerated flicks at the top and bottom of each stroke. "Besides, I like painting. And I've seen your porch, Julia—this is no small job. Admit it. You need me." His crooked grin broke into a crescent of self-satisfaction that was charming rather than conceited.

"We could use him," Grandma said, nodding at me optimistically, like she was the grandchild and she was vying persuasively for my tightfisted approval.

"We need big, strong, hardworking boys to help," Simon coaxed, and by the adoring way that he was looking at Michael, I thought it probably wouldn't be such a bad thing for Simon to spend some time with a man. In fact, it would be a good thing, a great thing. Absolutely necessary. I made a mental note to seek out more male companionship for Simon. Maybe Mr. Walker or one of his boys. Or maybe Michael, whenever he was home from college—he was already grinning at Simon with a mischievous glint in his eye. They were a matched pair.

"Fine," I said, though it was hardly my place to accept or reject Michael's generous offer. But I added, "Are you sure you want to do this? You really don't have to."

"I know I don't have to. I want to. Sounds like fun."

We paid for our purchases and parted with Michael, making plans to meet him at the porch in an hour. He had to stop at his brother's farm and change clothes, and we had a few more errands to run.

When Michael showed up right on time an hour later, Grandma, Simon, and I had already stripped the porch of all furniture, decorations, and knickknacks. We had made a little pile of stuff beside the garage, and we were scattered across the porch steps, peeling paint with our fingers and wondering how much we should try to get off before painting over the wreckage. Everyone else had changed into grubby clothes, and even though I couldn't really help, I too was wearing an old, paint-splattered T-shirt.

Grandma had set aside a reclining lawn chair for me, propping up an old egg crate beside it with a jug of lemonade and four plastic cups. It was positioned in the shade, and it looked enormously comfortable and inviting with plump gingham cushions and an oversize pillow. As soon as Michael came, he ushered me into it, insisting that the supervisor had to do nothing but relax and boss everyone else around. And though it felt strange to be pampered and fussed over, it was also fun to sink into the lounger and watch the action unfold.

"It's good wood," Michael said, examining a particularly bare board. "But we can't paint over the top of this."

"I thought that might be the case," Grandma admitted with a sigh. "I borrowed a power washer from our neighbor, but I guess I should have done that first before we dragged you all the way out here."

"Are you kidding?" Michael laughed. "Power washing is better than painting! Right, Simon?"

"Yeah!" Simon yelled, though I doubted he knew what he was talking about.

"Join Julia in the shade," Michael told Grandma. "The boys will take care of this." He struck a comical, muscleman pose and flexed for Simon.

Grandma was chuckling when she pulled up a lawn chair beside me. "Simon just loves him, doesn't he? It's fun to watch them interact."

"I know," I said softly. "That's something we're going to have to think about now that . . . now that Janice is gone. Simon needs men in his life."

"We all do," Grandma murmured, watching Michael and Simon wrestle with the hose that connected the wand to the generator. Then she caught herself and whipped her head around to smile at me. "Don't read anything into that," she said, patting my arm with a laugh.

"I didn't," I reassured her.

Grandma hummed a few notes of a tune I didn't recognize. When she turned back to the porch and the boys, I studied her out of the corner of my eye. She seemed content somehow, settled and peaceful in a way that I hadn't seen in her for longer than I could remember. There was a distinct air of satisfaction, of serenity in her manner, and it touched me so much, it clutched at something small and happy inside of me so urgently, that I reached out my arm and took her hand.

I thought that maybe the gesture would surprise her, but Grandma didn't even look at me. With a half smile playing at her lips, she continued to hum her tune. And then with a movement of careful intention, she brought my hand to her cheek and held it there. She closed her eyes.

We sat in silence for a moment, and I could feel the soft exhalation of Grandma's breath on the back of my hand. "She shouldn't have left," I said.

Grandma didn't respond.

"I think we could have worked things out," I pressed carefully.

"Are you angry?" Grandma asked.

I pondered her question. "No," I said finally. "I feel sorry for her."

"Me too."

We were quiet for a long time because, although there was much that could be said, most of our musings would be speculation only or, worse, raw hope. I figured I could come close to guessing at the myriad reasons Janice had left: guilt, inadequacy, fear, a desire for *more*. . . . And, probably most convincingly, the belief that Ben could meet the agonizing, indefinable need that gouged deep fissures in the earth of Janice's soul.

But while I thought I could look back and decipher why, I found it unbearable to look ahead and speculate about what would happen next. Would Janice come back? Would she send for Simon? Would she bring Ben into our lives? There simply wasn't a perfect scenario no matter how I worked and reworked it in my mind. I couldn't even claim to know what would be best for Simon, what would be best for me.

Even though it was impossible to imagine how we would make this work, how we would bring Simon into our family and help him to understand that in her own broken, unfathomable way Janice loved him very much, I did know that the months, maybe years ahead would be hard ones. When Janice left me, I called her Janice. When she left Simon, he called her Mom. It took her ten years to come back to me. I didn't know how long it would take her to come back to Simon.

Maybe this time the split had been permanent.

But these were things I couldn't say out loud, even as I knew Grandma was carefully contemplating the exact same thoughts. Instead I murmured, "Do you think she'll come back?"

Grandma pursed her lips sadly, but she didn't answer me. And then, with a heavy sigh and an almost dramatic flourish, she squeezed the back of my hand and, still clasping my fingers, lowered it to swing in the air between our lawn chairs. She looked me full in the face and smiled. "We—all of us, even Simon—are strong. We'll make it no matter what. We get to rebuild." Grandma's eyes sparkled. "We get to be new."

I believed every word.

As if on cue, Simon's laughter rang out from the porch. Grandma and I looked up in time to see Michael squeeze the trigger on the long wand of the power washer and release a jet of cleansing water. We clapped and cheered.

Stripping off the old paint turned out to be a deafening affair, replete with stinging droplets of water that Grandma and I could feel even at twenty feet away and debris that spun off the porch in a profusion of minihurricanes. Michael helped Simon hold the wand once or twice, but most of the time the dark-haired boy danced behind his new hero, protected by Michael's frame, his mouth open in a shout that was drowned out by the sound of the earsplitting machine.

It was over before too long, and the second Michael switched off the power washer, the air was filled with the happy noise of Simon's hoots and Grandma's and my laughter. The grass all around us was covered with the confetti of grayish white porch paint, as if someone had cried "Surprise!" and opened a trapdoor in the sky. The front porch itself was glistening and wet, the wood mostly bare, but waiting somehow and pretty, almost eager for change.

"That was fun!" Simon yelped, dancing around the porch. "Let's do it again!"

"I think we're done, buddy," Michael said, wiping his eyes on the sleeve of his T-shirt. "But it was fun. Thanks for your help."

"Do we get to paint now?"

Michael dropped the power washer on the sidewalk and led Simon over to where Grandma and I were sitting in the shade. He flopped on the grass, on the millions of flecks of paint, and Simon threw himself down beside him. "Sorry, Simon, but we can't paint right away. The wood is wet now from all that water."

"But we're supposed to *paint* the porch," Simon complained, his voice taking on an uncharacteristic singsong quality.

"How about if I come back tomorrow and we start painting then," Michael offered, casting a raised eyebrow in the direction of Grandma and me. "Would that be okay?" he asked, addressing us directly. "I have to work until noon, but I can come after that."

Grandma consulted me with her eyes. I shrugged. She consented. "If you want to, Michael, we certainly wouldn't turn down your help."

I considered giving Michael an out again, but then I loosened up and smiled at him. He wouldn't have offered if he didn't want to do it.

"Can we *look* at the paint?" Simon asked, desperate to get started on the real project.

"Why not?" Grandma pushed herself out of her chair and went to haul the bucket of paint back to our spot in the shade.

Michael hopped off the ground and beat her to it, taking the bucket in one hand and giving Grandma the screwdriver with the other so she'd have something to carry too.

"I'm not that old," she reprimanded him, wagging the tool at Michael in mock disappointment.

"Oh, I know. Just being a gentleman."

Michael and Grandma pried off the plastic tabs on the paint cover and then gently eased the top off. Long strands of white paint drew lines between the lid and the clean pool of paint below, and a soft, distinct scent filled the air. Simon sighed in approval. Even I had to admit that the porch would look very different swathed in all that shining white. It would make the whole house look different.

"It's *lovely*," Simon said.

I hid a smile behind my hand.

"It's white," Grandma said, pretending to blink at the brightness of it.

But it wasn't too bright for Simon. As we watched, the glossy bucket of milky liquid lured him, and he reached out a tentative hand and touched the very tip of his index finger to the smooth surface of the paint. He pulled away immediately, almost shocked at what he had done, and gaped at the white on his finger. Casting around, he looked for somewhere to wipe it off. My leg was the closest thing. Something in his mind clicked. With a glimmer of trouble in his eye, Simon beamed at me and carefully, *carefully* placed his finger on my skin. There was an impish little hum, a tremble in his voice, and then he drew his finger from my ankle to my knee.

"What do you think you're doing?" I howled, but I couldn't disguise the laughter in my voice.

It spurred Simon on and he stuck his finger in the paint again. This time he went for my face.

"Oh no, no, no you don't!" I shrieked. But I only curled up deeper into the chair and let Simon approach me with a slow, deliberate step.

"Get her!" Grandma urged him.

I shot her a look of pretend horror and struggled feebly while Simon pinned my forehead back with one hand. Then he dragged his finger triumphantly across my cheek with the other. "Looks awesome," he said, backing up to survey his handiwork. He doubled over in a fit of giggles.

And it wasn't enough to stop there. Simon went back for more. "Come on, Michael, help me!"

Michael wavered for a moment, but Simon grabbed Michael's thick wrist and pulled his arm over the bucket of paint. "Come on!" the little boy cajoled.

Tossing a cheerful wink at me, Michael dipped a finger in the paint and walked on his knees to join Simon beside me.

"Make me beautiful." I closed my eyes and laid my head back, listening to Simon laugh as he touched my other cheek with his cool finger.

On the opposite side, Michael took a deep breath. I felt him reach for me. "War paint," he whispered, using his finger to dot a line of circles along my hairline.

Not anymore, I thought.

Hemmed between the heavens above and the earth below, I felt that in this moment, with the sun filtering through the leaves in a glancing touch of blessing, all was well beneath the endless sky. Not perfect. Not exactly the way it should be. But *well*.

humbled

DANIEL PETER DESMIT was born on August 13, shortly after ten o'clock in the morning.

I woke up a few hours before sunrise with contractions that were nothing like the ones I had experienced before, and I knew with an uncanny sense of peace, of acceptance: *This is it.* I stole down the stairs when they were five minutes apart and found Grandma waiting for me at the kitchen table. Her Bible was spread out before her, and there were two glasses of water on the long slats of oak. She sipped out of one and offered the other to me.

"What are you doing up?" I asked incredulously.

"I had a feeling about tonight." Grandma smiled. And then she rose from her seat to help me into a chair as a contraction nearly sent me to my knees. "Did you know that I was six days overdue with your dad?"

"And the date today is . . . ," I panted after the peak of the contraction had leveled off.

"The thirteenth. You are six days overdue."

I narrowed my eyes at my grandmother. "That's superstitious."

She laughed. "No, it's not. It's providential."

Though I wanted to talk, though I felt that there was an endless abyss of things that I needed to plumb, to say, I found that everything had turned inside. It was a solitary feeling but not sad. I felt like the world around me had paused in its rotation, checked itself for this brief moment in time so that everything could pull back, make room for me, for the baby. It was matchless and rare, something to be treasured: I was alone in this fold of eternity with my baby and the One who had knit him within.

When I laid my head on my arms and closed my eyes, Grandma simply ran her fingers lightly over my back. She read to me from the book in front of her, and while I didn't hear and didn't understand, her voice was poetry. It was life.

We waited until six o'clock to call Mrs. Walker, and by that time I was so lost inside myself, so anxious to get to the hospital that I wasn't even afraid of childbirth anymore.

"It's happening!" Mrs. Walker shrieked when she bounded through the door moments later. Then she bobbed her head as if someone had smacked it from behind. "Oops! Sorry! Hope I didn't wake up Simon."

"I'm awake," Simon called from the hallway, still rubbing his eyes. His hair was plastered against both sides of his head and sticking up on the crown like a Mohawk. Blinking and yawning, he gazed from Grandma to Mrs. Walker to me, obviously bemused at the three of us bedraggled-looking women in his kitchen. His stare lingered on me. I was standing hunched over the kitchen table, my hands flat against the smooth surface and a grim smile plastered to my face. Finally it hit him. "You're going to have the baby!" he yelled. "I'm going to be a big brother!"

"Something like that," I wheezed as another contraction began to crest over me.

Grandma and Mrs. Walker hustled me out the door moments later.

"Don't worry about us," Mrs. Walker reassured. "Simon and I will have a great day together." She gently eased my car door closed as if shutting it too hard would harm me in some way. Crossing to Grandma's open window, Mrs. Walker exclaimed a little louder than necessary, "Promise me you'll call as soon as the baby is born."

"I promise," Grandma said quickly; then she threw the car in reverse and sped all the way to the hospital. "I'm not nervous," she explained as I eyed her speedometer. It was nearing sixty-five, an unheard of velocity for my docile grandmother. "I'm just excited."

But the note of anxiety that rang in the car was nothing more than a distant echo when I was settled into one of the prettily apportioned delivery rooms. After a quick exam, the nurse determined that I was close but not yet ready, and that settling in for a few hours of labor was the best thing I could do. They hooked me up to monitors and started an IV just in case, and when the room was finally quiet and relatively still but for the rustle of a long ribbon of paper slowly unwinding as it recorded my contractions, Grandma reached over the low rail of my bed and grabbed both of my hands in her own. Her fingers were strong, calm.

"You are going to be fine," she said.

"Yeah," I whispered slowly. "I think I am."

"You are going to make a great mother."

"I'm going to try."

"Your dad would be so proud of you."

"He would?" I choked.

"*I* am so proud of you." Her eyes were clear and bright and happy as she said it. There was not even a trace of a tear or any lingering tang of the bittersweet nature of our lives up until this point. Instead, there was hope burning there. A hope that was far more certainty, more expectation, than a simple, improbable wish.

"Thank you," I said, because there was nothing else to say. Of course I could tell her "I love you," but she already knew that. It was written all over my face and seeping through my fingers as I held on to her with all of my strength. I had said those words to her every day of my life. But had I ever really thanked her for everything that mattered? Grandma had heard my appreciation for the little things, but did she know that the debt of gratitude I owed her was more than I could ever repay? "*Thank you,*" I said again, willing her to understand what I meant by it.

"Julia," she whispered back, "thank *you.*"

Grandma was an exceptional birth coach, and she never stopped murmuring to me through the contractions, the pushing, the inevitable fear. She rubbed my back and talked me out of panic. She pushed away the little hairs that clung to my neck.

We labored together for over three hours, and when Daniel was only minutes from the world, Grandma kissed my head and laughed. "This is it!" she cheered. "He's almost here!"

And then she began to cry.

After Dr. Morales had cut the umbilical cord, he reached up and gently, gently laid my baby boy on my chest. The nurses hadn't weighed or measured him yet—he was only seconds new—and when I felt the weight of him over my heart, something raw and holy passed over me. I gasped. I struggled for air. Almost involuntarily I put my hands over him, and his little body was so soft and fragile as to be a dream hidden in my palms.

"Daniel Peter," I breathed.

I knew him. This child was mine, a part of me, and yet somehow wholly *other*. We were intertwined, woven together, but only because He had chosen to braid the strands of our lives. I realized even as I pressed Daniel to me that his presence in my arms was an unexpected gift. Something that I could never claim to deserve. Something that would cause me to spend the rest of my life trying to be worthy of what I had been given.

I was humbled.

I was laid low. Spent as a sacrifice burning beneath His glory.

But in the depths blew the sacred wind of freedom, of letting go. I drank it in joyful mouthfuls, swallowing my tears and letting it fill me. It was beautiful. Because I was finally ready. Ready for the imprint of grace like His signature beneath my skin. Ready for all there was to come, knowing that the light only shone bright because of the shadows around it. Ready. Ready and open, willing to receive the immensity of heaven spread wide as a blessing and unfurling above me.

discussion questions

1. At the end of *After the Leaves Fall*, Julia's faith in God seemed to be maturing. Where is she at the beginning of this story? Has your faith journey ever mimicked hers?

2. Nellie warns Julia about the danger of holding on to a bitter root on p. 126. Have you ever been in a situation like Julia's where you needed to forgive someone? What effect did it have on your life?

3. Why do you think Janice behaves the way she does throughout the novel? What is motivating her? Is it the same need that is motivating Julia?

4. On p. 231, Nellie says to Julia: "You're not nearly as lost as you sometimes think you are." Do you think that's true? What did Nellie mean by that?

5. Nellie tells Julia on p. 234 that seeds planted among thorns don't necessarily *die* but are *choked*. What are some of the "thorns" in your life that threaten to choke out God's grace?

6. On p. 293, Julia calls Janice and herself a "group of Simons." What does she mean by that? What does she mean when she observes that they are "not enough, not enough, not enough"?

7. Why do you think Julia was finally able to forgive Janice?

8. How has Julia changed by the end of this story? What was the biggest catalyst for that change?

9. Do you think Julia makes the right decision regarding her future at the end of the story? Why or why not?

10. What was your favorite metaphor, line, or scene from the story? Why?

About the Author

NICOLE BAART was born and raised in a small town in Iowa. After lifeguarding, waitressing, working in a retail store, and even being a ranch hand on a dairy farm, she changed her major four times in college before finally settling on degrees in English, Spanish, English as a second language, and secondary education. She taught and developed curriculum in three different school districts over the course of seven years.

Teaching and living in Vancouver, British Columbia, cultivated a deep love in Nicole for both education and the culturally inexplicable use of the word *eh*. She became a Canadian citizen for the sole purpose of earning the right to use the quirky utterance.

Nicole wrote and published her first complete novel, *After the Leaves Fall*, while taking a break from teaching to be a full-time mom. *Summer Snow* is the sequel. She is also the author of hundreds of poems, dozens of short stories, a handful of articles, and various unfinished novels.

The mother of two young sons and the wife of a pastor, Nicole writes when she can: in bed, in the shower, as she is making supper, and occasionally sitting down at her computer. As the adoptive mother of an Ethiopian-born son, she is passionate about global issues and works to promote awareness of topics such as world hunger, poverty, AIDS, and the plight of widows and orphans. Nicole and her family live in Iowa.

For anyone who's ever wanted to

start over...